ALL THROUGH THE NIGHT

"It's quite simple, Mr Ellington. When you find Fowler, just ask where we can find the truth." With these words, private detective JT Ellington embarks on a seemingly simple case of tracking down a local GP with a dubious reputation and retrieving a set of stolen documents from him. For Ellington, however, things are rarely straightforward. Dr Fowler is hiding a terrible secret — and when he is gunned down outside a Bristol pub, his dying words send JT in pursuit of a truth more disturbing and deadly than he could possibly have imagined.

ALL THROUGH THE NIGHT

M. P. WRIGHT

ISIS
LARGE
PRINT

First published in Great Britain 2016
by
Black & White Publishing Ltd.

First Isis Edition
published 2017
by arrangement with
Black & White Publishing Ltd.

A catalogue record for this book is available
from the British Library.

ISBN 978-1-78541-356-8 (hb)
ISBN 978-1-78541-362-9 (pb)

Published by
F. A. Thorpe (Publishing)
Anstey, Leicestershire

Set by Words & Graphics Ltd.
Anstey, Leicestershire
Printed and bound in Great Britain by
T. J. International Ltd., Padstow, Cornwall

This book is printed on acid-free paper

Dedicated to my parents, Ann and Pat,
and to my literary agent, Philip Patterson.

Prologue

Thursday, 12 May 1966

The Douglas C-124 aircraft rose and fell in the air as it butted and fought its way through heavy rain, strong winds and gut-churning turbulence. Its four Pratt & Whitney engines roared in unison as it flew out some two hundred miles off the coast of mainland Scotland towards Keflavik airfield, on the western tip of Iceland. The plane had been in the air for just over two hours since taking off from the United States Strategic Air Command base at RAF Fairford, in the heart of Gloucestershire. In the cockpit, Captain Gene Westlake glanced quickly at his wristwatch, which read 5.45 a.m. He smiled to himself, pleased that they were still making good time despite the appalling weather conditions. He looked out of the small window on his left-hand side and saw below him the angry, swelling white tips of the North Atlantic beating against the craggy outcrop of the final edges of the Faroe Islands' rugged coastline. There were five other crew members on board the "Old Shaky", as the C-124 was fondly known by all those who flew in or worked on her. This was strictly an all-American crew of the Military Air

1

Transport Service and had made the same long journey back to Dover airfield in Delaware State, USA, more times than they cared to remember.

Sat next to Westlake in the cockpit was his co-pilot, First Lieutenant Dan Knudson and, to their rear, Navigator Ed Barry. Below them in the vastness of the transport hold were loadmasters Carl Brett, Bobby Romaire and Mac Kepner. Once a week they flew the huge aircraft with its cargo of military freight. On a flight out to Britain it could be anything from confidential documentation, armaments and uniforms to newly spruced-up Willys jeeps and troop-carrying lorries. On a run to the US, the cargo could be servicemen and -women, tours of duty complete, all cheerfully homeward bound after months away and packed in like sardines alongside countless sacks of mail bound for armed forces and to news-anxious parents and sweethearts back in the States. Same crew, normal trip, thought Gene Westlake, only today, what was in the cargo hold of his craft made him nervous.

It wasn't unusual to have military police officers on board an aircraft bound for the US. You would normally find them in pairs escorting a soldier, sailor or airman who had committed a serious crime abroad and who would more often than not be tried in the UK before being returned back to a martial penitentiary to serve out their custodial sentence. But military police officers sergeants Paxton and Jardine were not taking the four-thousand-mile flight simply to guard over a criminal miscreant. This was a more personal, delicate enterprise. They sat expressionless beyond the closed door of the cockpit on the upper level of the Douglas aircraft, neither of them perturbed by the way the plane shook as it was buffeted by the squally storm. The seasoned, battle-hardened soldiers, white and in their mid forties, were both originally from different armpit, backwater, shithole towns in the Deep South, Mississippians and staunchly proud of it. Both men were confident that their latest mission would run smoothly, like the previous nine other operations had; a little bad weather wouldn't change the task at hand. There was no going back. Such was the serious nature of their undertaking.

Under their supervision was a consignment that was both precious and unique and of considerable monetary value, not only to the two policemen but also to the five other crew members on board. With nine "special" deliveries complete, they knew the stakes, the risks involved. They had all been keen to go, enjoyed the pay-offs, but one man had got cold feet and asked for this to be his last illicit exercise.

Twenty-four hours previously Bobby Romaire had sat in the mess room after evening chow down and told his fellow crew he wanted no further part in their business, that he'd had his fill and was looking to get transferred to a different unit. He assured the other guys that he wasn't a squealer, that their secret was safe with him. But Romaire's colleagues got spooked and couldn't allow him to walk away that easily. Gene Westlake knew what had to be done and told the rest of his crew to be cool, to leave it to him.

On Wednesday evening Westlake made a couple of telephone calls and informed the military police officers Paxton and Jardine of Romaire's decision to walk.

"Just fly the damn package back stateside, like we done all those times before, you understand? Now, you leave Airman Romaire to me," Paxton had said icily before the line went dead. Gene Westlake put down the phone at his desk, then told himself that the conversation had never happened.

Loadmaster Bobby Romaire stood on the bottom deck at the rear of the cargo hold, staring blankly down at a five-foot-square wooden crate. The crate was held securely by thick black webbing straps that looped through into large metal D-rings that were riveted into the walls and floor of the aircraft. Drilled into the panels of the crate were eight silver-dollar-sized holes, and printed on each side of the large box in big black capital letters were the words "MILITARY POLICE DOG IN TRANSIT TO BE LOADED AND UNLOADED BY MPC STAFF ONLY".

Inside, sleeping after being sedated, was a large three-year-old male German Shepherd. Romaire knelt on one knee at the side of the crate and put his ear to the wooden panel, then covered his other in an attempt to muffle out the thunderous hum of the engines. He thought he could pick out the steady, heavy breathing of the big, drugged-up dog as it slept.

The airman put his face flat against the panel of the crate and called out. The side of his mouth grazed the wood as he spoke.

"Hey . . . you hear me in there? Now you just hold tight, don't you be scared none. It's gonna be all right, I'm gonna have you outta there as soon as this here Old Shaky hits the ground. You'll be safe, I promise you that." Bobby Romaire again pushed his ear as hard as he could against the crate and as he did felt his scalp being grabbed tightly. His head was snatched back and violently slammed into the side of the wooden container. Struggling to remain conscious and unable to cry out, he felt only the briefest touch of cold metal on the nape of his neck as the flat hilt of a stiletto knife made contact with his clammy skin. The needle-like blade rapidly shot up and injected itself underneath the occipital bone and into the soft tissue of his brain. Bobby Romaire felt nothing else as he fell back onto the deck of the cargo hold. He thought he heard the faint voice of a child in his head softly speak the word "Truth" as his life spiralled uncontrollably away from him. Gold shards of light flickered briefly in front of his eyes as a cold darkness took hold of him and pulled a last sharp breath away from his now limp body.

Sergeant Paxton stood over Bobby Romaire's corpse, the dead man's lifeless eyes staring back up at him. The thin stiletto blade in Paxton's right hand made a sweeping sound as it swiftly returned itself into the black lacquered handle. Paxton opened his olive-green tunic and carefully clipped the knife back into a small leather cradle on his belt, then turned around and watched as his colleague walked slowly along the length of the vast hold to join him. As Nathan Jardine grew closer he threw his thumb back over his shoulder towards the front of the plane, then bellowed out to Paxton over the deafening sound of the engines.

"Westlake's starting to take this heap down a couple of thousand feet, says he'll flash the droplight that's over the floor chute, then we can lug this fucker's carcass into the drink."

Paxton smiled back at Jardine. The two men bent down, took hold of Bobby Romaire's body and heaved it over towards the emergency exit situated in the hull of the plane, then waited until the red overhead light began to glow on and off. Jardine bent down and turned the first of three metal handles, then used all his strength to pull back the chute door to reveal the dark emptiness below them. The inside of the plane was filled with the piercing scream of the wind from outside mixed with the growling rumble of the four giant propellers.

Paxton lifted Romaire's body up by the scruff of his lapels, pulling it towards the edge of the door chute, then stood with his legs over either side of it, dropped the cadaver's head and shoulders out of the hatch, and let the dead man's weight drag the rest of his bulk out. Both men watched as it tumbled out into the blackness over the North Atlantic. Paxton stood away from the gaping hole in the floor and brushed the palms of his hands across the other as if to congratulate himself on a job well done before helping Sergeant Jardine to close the door and secure it once again. Neither man spoke as they stood staring at each other. They took a moment to smooth down their tunics with the backs of their hands and straighten the knots on their ties before returning back to their seats behind the cockpit.

As both men strode away from the hold, Jack Paxton stopped in his tracks and quickly turned on his polished boot heels, staring suspiciously at the crate. He tapped at the bronze braid strip on the trouser leg of his dress uniform, his glare burning into the inside of the container. He took a step towards it, then halted again, realising that there really was no need to return to it. After all the contents were still safe and he knew that what was inside had no way of escaping. He'd come back to the caged creature and feed it later. Paxton flashed a fleeting grin at the wooden chest, shaking his head at it knowingly before rejoining his colleague.

From inside the crate, secretly partitioned off from the doped police dog, the watery eyes of a small child stared out. A little girl, no more than seven, peered through one of the drilled air holes at the two men as they walked away. The girl timidly expelled a slow rasp of air from her lungs. She had been holding her breath for what seemed like forever and had stifled her sobs by biting into the back of her hand as, petrified, she had watched the slaughter of the "good" man who had promised her that things would be all right. He'd told her that he would make sure she was safe, that no harm would come to her. But that promise was now broken, snatched away by the monster with the pointed knife. The little girl remembered the piercing, cruel gaze of the killer: he was the same person who had come to her room in the middle of the night and taken her away from the only family she'd ever known. She'd been

7

placed on the back seat of a car, given sweets and told to eat them. She had done as she was told, then fallen asleep. She'd woken inside the crate. The man with the pointed knife had told her not to make a sound, that if she cried out he would release the big dog from behind the partition and the animal would tear her to pieces. She'd done as he said and not uttered a sound. Terrified and still dressed in her flannelette pyjamas, a series of coarse wool blankets had been wrapped around her for warmth. She'd remained silent and sat in a pool of her own cold urine for what seemed like forever. The girl began to cry again as she watched the two men disappear from her view. Then, rubbing away the wetness of the tears from her cheeks with her tiny hands, she slowly sank back into the shadowy, bleak recess of her captivity, curling up into a ball and closing her eyes tightly in the hope that it would shut out the horrific images now etched so deeply into her memory.

CHAPTER
ONE

A boxing gym has a particular smell and sound: the dull scent of old sweat that has seeped into talc-embedded leather, skipping ropes beating against mats or wood, the smack of gloves on bags and pads. This is a male bastion, a timeless place, and not for the faint-hearted. If you spend time around a boxing joint, don't be surprised to find blood and spit splattered over its walls or hear the splintering echo of teeth being knocked out and shot across the bleached-down floors like dice on a crap table. They are not places for idle chit-chat or exchanging pleasantries; they are occupied by the kind of men who say little while trading heavy blows and uppercuts, sparring with each other in a manner that would put a grizzly bear on its back. My cousin Vic's gym was no different.

In the spring of 1966, after much cajoling from my cousin, I had agreed to move into the shabby offices above the gym and start up an enquiry agency. The gymnasium's previous owner, Cut Man Perry, had left in a hurry when Vic had strong-armed him into handing the place over after the tubby reprobate had gotten himself mixed up in a nasty world of vice and killing and had found he'd bitten off more than he could chew. Rather than face the music, Cut Man signed the place over to Vic, then did a moonlight flit and hightailed his sweaty ass on to a rust-bucket cargo ship from the Bristol port dockside back to Jamaica with what was left of his possessions slung over his shoulder in a tatty canvas bag.

Never one to let the grass grow under his feet, Vic had taken over the run-down old gym and pretty soon business was booming. I'd stupidly got caught up in some of Cut Man's mayhem after taking on a job searching for a missing young woman. I ended up with my back against the wall, going toe to toe with a group of heavies that would've liked to see me dead in a ditch, while the local law wanted to pin me for murders I'd had no hand in and send me to the gallows. After the dust had settled Vic presented me with what he called a golden opportunity: he offered me Cut Man's office and thought it a good idea I use the skills I'd picked up as a police officer back home on Barbados and start up as a private investigator. Only the investigator title after my name was a touch too fly for me, so I settled for the more sedate-sounding "enquiry agent" instead. I started small-time and that's how it's stayed: small-time. My work comes in dribs and drabs and I've got no complaints about that. Mostly I find myself dealing with tales of simple human misery, snap-and-shut divorce cases, the occasional missing person, credit checks for a local loan company, nothing heavy.

And that's the real world of an enquiry agent. Not much excitement, plenty of cold nights watching doors and bedroom lights, very little pay, and lots of bitterness and upset to go round. When I was not trudging through the streets of Bristol trying to earn a crust, you'd normally find me hanging out with Vic at the gym among its familiar sights, smells and sounds.

It was just before midday and I was sat at my desk with my head in my hands nursing the kind of hangover that makes you feel like the sides of your temples are being pinched by a pair of hammerhead carpenter's pincers. I'd spent the night before drinking the better part of a bottle and a half of rum with Vic at one of our regular watering holes, the Speed Bird club on Grosvenor Road, and before chucking-out time I'd fallen asleep on one of the cushioned snug benches. Unable to wake me, Vic had left me where I lay and had covered me up in my overcoat. On the table beside me he had hooked my black felt fedora hat over the neck of an empty Mount Gay rum bottle, which I had downed before flaking out. I was woken up at 6.30a.m. by the bellowing of the club's cleaner, Winnie Carlisle, who'd dropped her mop bucket next to my head, reeking of detergent, to hammer the foot of the bench, telling me in no uncertain terms to get my "lazy, no-good ass up!" I'd done as I was told, grabbed my hat and coat and wandered dozily across the dimly lit dance floor of the Speed Bird, out of its double front doors and up the basement steps into the early-morning sunshine and walked the short distance back to my office.

After arriving back at the gym I'd made myself a strong cup of black coffee and decided to catch a couple more hours' sleep before starting my day. I kicked off my shoes and slumped into my high-back study chair, slung my feet up on the desktop and fell fast asleep.

It was just after 10.30 a.m. by the time I roused and my head now felt like it had been kicked in by a mule. I went into the kit room next door to my office and opened up the small refrigerator that Vic kept in there. I stuck my hand into the freezer box and pulled out one of the trays filled with ice cubes, then walked down to the gym's shower room, pulled off my shirt and dropped it onto the bench beside me. I walked over to one of the sinks, stuck in a plug, cracked the ice into it and filled it with cold water up to its brim, then sank my head in and left it there until I felt the chilly water begin to burn the skin on my scalp. I dried myself off with my shirt and went back down the corridor to my office. I waved to a couple of the guys who were working on one of the bags in the gym; they acknowledged my presence with guttural grunts and short nods of their square, muscular heads and went back to their training.

There was no sign of my wayward cousin in the building, but that wasn't a surprise: Vic rarely dragged his ass out of bed before midday unless it involved money or a hot woman. He had, in the last few months, expanded his business empire and had bankrolled a new hairdressing salon in St Pauls, picked up a cheap three-storey tenement building in Montpelier, which he rented out, and had taken on a silent partnership with the latest owner of the Speed Bird club, Ruben Walker, a swarthy Trinidadian who as far as I could see liked

12

sailing pretty close to the wind around all things that were illegal.

Both were using the Speed Bird as their legitimate commercial front. It offered up to the outside world and, more importantly, the local law an image of two successful, entrepreneurial men doing well for themselves. In truth, behind their kosher enterprises lay unlawful trading ventures and black marketeering on a massive scale.

Once back inside my office I opened up the bottom drawer of a grey-metal, four-tier filing cabinet, reached in and pulled out the spare shirt that I kept in there. I put it on, then made myself another cup of black coffee and ate a couple of aspirin. I tried to ignore the nausea that was gripping at my guts as I sat back at my desk and struggled to type up an invoice for an insurance company I'd undertaken some work for the week before. A sharp pain throbbed inside my head each time I hit a key on the battered navy-blue Empire typewriter that I'd inherited from Cut Man.

When I finished I tore out the bill from the old machine and unenthusiastically dropped it onto the desk, then sat back in my chair with my eyes closed and began to massage either side of my forehead with the tips of my fingers.

It was the hypnotic tapping sound of a woman's high-heeled shoes on the wooden floorboards in the corridor outside that finally made me haul my head out of my hands. The footsteps drew closer and came to a halt outside my office. A heavy clout at my door came moments later and whoever was doing the knocking came on in without waiting to be invited.

Stood in front of me was a severe but not unattractive white woman, about fifty-five years old and elegantly turned out in a white-polka-dotted, canary-yellow cotton dress and figure-hugging light-cream cardigan. A small black-wool pillbox hat was carefully perched onto the back of her head and pinned into her tightly curled blonde hair. In her right hand, clutched at the side of her ample chest, was a small white-leather handbag that she was gripping onto for dear life, as if she was worried that I was about to snatch the damn thing from her grasp and hightail it down the hall. She eyed me up and down warily, then slowly walked towards my desk and towered over me in the patent-leather black heels that had noisily announced her arrival a few moments ago. The heady, potent scent of Tweed perfume hit me as I looked up at her.

"Are you the man who calls himself Ellington, the one who has his name pinned up on the brass plaque outside of this . . . establishment?"

"Yeah, the very same. What can I do for you?" I asked suspiciously. Despite advertising my services to the world outside, I was still wary of strangers asking for me, especially mean-looking white women. Still fighting the harsh hangover that gripped at my fuzzy head, I opened and shut my eyes in quick succession, trying to bring myself into the land of the living, then briskly rubbed my face with the palms of my hands before looking back up at the woman.

14

"My name is Ida Stephens. I'd like to discuss a business proposition with you, Mr Ellington; it's a delicate matter that requires a degree of sensitivity. You see, the organisation I represent have been recently placed in a rather difficult situation and now find themselves with a degree of unwelcome trouble on their hands."

"Trouble, you say? Well trouble's my bidness, that's a fact. So, how can I help you, Ida?" From the off, addressing the woman by her Christian name was a bad mistake; I saw her visibly baulk with shock, then glare back at me for having the impertinence to be so informal. Aware that I had offended the woman, I tried to look away, but the steely Mrs Stephens caught my eye and stared back at me indignantly. Like a school mistress about to scold a pupil, she shook her head slowly from side to side contemptuously, considering my ill manners before speaking again.

"I was informed that you were adept at handling . . . sensitive matters. I hope that I have not been misinformed, Mr Ellington." She spat the words out at me, the disapproval at the way I had addressed her etched all over her sour face. I reluctantly back-pedalled and turned on the charm in the hope of finding a little good grace from her. It appeared from her dour expression that "good grace" was not part of her repertoire.

"I'm sorry, Mrs Stephens. Here, please take a seat." I got up, walked around my desk and pulled out a chair, then held out the palm of my hand for her to sit. Once seated, she roamed a critical eye around the room, her mouth crinkling at the edges as she caught sight of the faded maroon-tinged flock wallpaper and shadeless light bulb hanging from the dusty ceiling. While inspecting my office she rhythmically tapped both index fingers at the edges of her handbag. The unkempt look clearly didn't meet Mrs Stephens' standards.

She was still obviously weighing up whether to disclose her "delicate" business to me. I'd already decided that I didn't care one way or another if she did or not. I'd smelt trouble the moment she'd walked in, but truth was, I was in no position to be turning work away. A job was a job and I needed the cash, whether I liked those paying for my services or not. I returned to my seat, dropped heavily into the chair and caught the stern expression on Mrs Stephens' face. I quickly opened up the centre drawer underneath my desk and took out a thin-lined jotter pad, then rummaged around the junk inside searching for a pencil, finally finding a stub. I snapped the drawer shut, turned over a fresh page on my pad, then stared back across the polished wood desktop towards my new client, trying not to let her see how much I already disliked her. I shot her a cheeky smile before finally speaking again. "OK, Mrs Stephens, why don't you tell me 'bout this spot o' trouble of yours?"

For a moment Ida Stephens looked back down at the bag in her lap before raising her head to reply to my question. When she spoke her voice wavered slightly, as if something was holding back the words she wanted to say. She hesitated for a while longer, then cleared her throat a couple of times and continued.

"Do you know of the Walter Wilkins orphanage in Bishopston, Mr Ellington?"

"No . . . can't say that I do." I shook my head slowly as I scribbled down the name at the top of the page on my pad. Mrs Stephens waited for me to look back up at her before continuing.

"I'm one of the administrators at the orphanage. I was originally a senior nurse in the infirmary block; I've been working there now for over fifteen years. Well . . . It has been brought to my attention that a number of unusual thefts have occurred at Walter Wilkins over the past few days and —" Ida Stephens broke off from relaying the details of her story in mid sentence. I watched as she carefully considered her words before continuing. "The stolen property has no monetary value and the person that has stolen the items in question is well known to us."

"So, if you know who the thief is, why haven't you already gone to the police?" I watched as Ida Stephens awkwardly fidgeted in her seat. She nipped at the hem of her dress with her slim fingers and drew the material further down her leg before answering my question.

"As I said to you earlier, this is all very delicate . . . Some tact will be required in regards to any enquiries undertaken. My colleagues and I at Walter Wilkins would prefer not to involve the police at this juncture; we'd prefer someone to investigate the matter without having to bring it to the local constabulary's attention."

"Is that so, Mrs Stephens? You know, that's funny, cos I've heard that one befo'." I sat back in my chair looked down at my lap and shook my head gently from

17

side to side, smilingly to myself, recalling unwelcome memories.

"I beg your pardon?" Ida Stephens' back straightened as she barked at me.

I looked back up at my client, her face a sullen picture of disdain. "Sorry, Mrs Stephens, I was thinking out loud there. Look, I'm kinda interested to know why you chose me to go looking for your thief?"

"Because the thief . . ." Her cheeks flushed as she gulped to find the right words. "Because, Mr Ellington, the thief in question is of the coloured persuasion."

Unable to stop myself, I began to laugh out loud. Ida Stephens impatiently continued to stare at me as I wiped a tear from my left eye with the flat of my palm.

"What's so amusing, Mr Ellington? Do you find theft from a charity amusing?"

"No, Mrs Stephens . . . I don't find any theft amusing; it's you thinking you need another black man to find a brother that's stolen from you that's kinda tickled me. So, tell me, what's the name o' this 'coloured persuasion' crook you looking for?"

"Fowler, Dr Theodore Fowler. He's a small, unpleasant little man, originally from Jamaica I believe, around sixty-five years old. He resides at number 4 Ashley Hill in the Montpelier district, not too far from here. However, my sources tell me he's not been at his rather shabby little home for the last week. His whereabouts are at the moment unknown; however, I'm reliably informed that he rarely strays far from his domicile and can often be found in the local drinking houses in the area. It appears he has a rather

18

clandestine nature and it has come to our attention during these past few days, while making our own investigations, that the man has a reputation as an . . ."

Ida Stephens swallowed hard, as if unable to get the words she wanted to say out. She cleared her throat before speaking again. "That he has a reputation as an illegal abortionist. Do you know of him?"

"Mrs Stephens, it may come as a surprise to you to find out that just because I'm black don't mean I know every black face in Bristol, whether they be abortionist, crook or parish priest. I ain't ever heard of the man. What's he stolen from you that has brought you to my gate door and not the local police's?"

"Death certificates."

"Say what?"

"Death certificates, Mr Ellington. Dr Fowler has stolen from our archives a number of death certificates for children who sadly passed away while in our care." Stephens continued to shuffle in her seat, clearly unsettled by the subject matter. I pressed her a little more, happy to watch her squirm at the impudence of my questioning.

"Why would the man want to lift death certificates of children from you? I don't understand."

"Dr Fowler was employed by us as an informal consultant. He had been in dispute with our administration board in respect to a number of clinical services he had performed on our behalf and for which he felt he had not been correctly salaried. These were services which we had assured him had been previously settled in full. The doctor disputed this and continued to press for further payment. We refused, and during our final discussions on the matter an argument ensued between the doctor and one of our senior board members. Dr Fowler became abusive and aggressive towards my colleague. He was asked to leave the building and not return. He refused and had to be removed by two male orderlies. It was a rather embarrassing affair, upsetting for all concerned. Shortly after, while undertaking an end-of-month audit, it was found that a number of the aforementioned death certificates were missing. It was felt that Dr Fowler could have been the only person to take them."

"And how'd you know that, Mrs Stephens?"

"Well, because Dr Fowler authenticated the stolen certificates in question and he was in dispute with us over those very same certificates: he misguidedly believed that he was entitled to further financial recompense after he'd been employed to concur with our house physician on the exact nature of the deaths."

"And the exact nature of the deaths of these children was what, Mrs Stephens?"

"Many of the children who come to us are already in failing health: some are simply malnourished and have been poorly cared for previously; others have more damaging conditions, and it was those children who passed away. Mr Ellington, sadly a number of children were taken with bronchial asthma earlier this year. Each of the deceased had a predisposition to contracting severe chest infections, pleurisy and the like; two already had weakened respiratory conditions. It was all very tragic."

Ida Stephens' tone had become less aggressive. A more sombre woman now sat in front of me, her face less severe after she had recounted the facts to me. The telling of her sorrowful story had softened her hard edges a little. I remained silent and allowed her a moment to regain a little of the volatile spirit she'd previously shown. It didn't take long for it to return. When she finally spoke again her tone contained all the venom of a woman about to berate a drunken spouse late home from an evening's heavy drinking at the pub.

"Regrettably, Dr Fowler is a drunkard, Mr Ellington. It is the corrupting nature of his severe alcoholism that has deluded him into believing that he is owed money and which drove him to steal from us that which he has no right to possess."

"And what is it you'd like me to do exactly, Mrs Stephens?"

"It's quite simple. We'd like to employ you to locate Dr Fowler, then have him return the documents that he has in his possession. We're prepared to pay you a generous fee to undertake this enquiry, and to make it easier for you to obtain the certificates in question, we're prepared to offer the doctor five hundred pounds for their safe return."

I tried not to show my surprise. Talking large sums of money had Ida Stephens raising her head and sniffing disapprovingly at the stale air in my office. She drew in her cheeks, then blew out a jet of air. I caught a whiff of her menthol-tinged breath as it crossed over my desk. It sounded like easy work, a week at most. I leaned back in my chair, still unsure of whether to take it on.

Usually when I told myself something was going to be easy, it rarely turned out to be.

"Five hundred pounds . . . That's a lot of dough, Mrs Stephens. You must want those papers back pretty badly."

"More importantly, Mr Ellington, Walter Wilkins does not want a scandal. If the press should ever get hold of this, they'd have a field day. The reputation of the orphanage, all its good work, maintained for more than half a century, would be in tatters. We cannot let that happen . . . We won't let it happen. Now, do you think you can find the doctor for me?"

"That all depends on where this Dr Fowler has gone to ground. Finding a man who doesn't wanna be found ain't easy, Mrs Stephens. It'll take me a little time to do some digging, see what I can come up with."

"Time is what we don't have a great deal of, Mr Ellington. We need those certificates back, and quickly. I'm prepared to pay you handsomely for their safe return. So, tell me, what is your daily rate?" The mention of money had tightened Stephens' face up again. It wasn't a pleasant picture.

"Three pounds a day plus expenses." I watched as Ida Stephens opened her polished handbag and took out a long white envelope. She gingerly placed it onto my desk, then slid it across towards me. She squeezed together the silver clasps on top of her bag, closing it shut firmly, then looked at me.

"We'll give you five pounds a day, plus your expenses, and there'll be a bonus of a further one hundred pounds if you successfully locate Dr Fowler and retrieve the certificates swiftly on our behalf. And I'll require a receipt for the money I've just given you."

I picked up the envelope and opened it. Mrs Stephens had come well prepared. I thumbed the wad of cash inside: five hundred to pay off the elusive doctor and a further fifty pounds for myself. Very generous indeed. I then lifted out a small cream business card and read the black italic lettering printed on it:

Ida Stephens
Administrator
The Walter Wilkins Orphanage
142 Cotham Road
Cotham, Bristol
Telephone: Bristol 7511

I scribbled out a receipt for her and watched as she took it and put it carefully in her handbag. Before I had a chance to say anything else, Ida Stephens stood up from her seat and began walking towards the door. She stopped abruptly and turned swiftly on her heels to face me.

"There's one more thing, Mr Ellington . . . Once you have found the doctor and retrieved what is ours, I would like you to ask him a simple question."

"And what would that be, Mrs Stephens?"

"Ask him where we can find the truth, Mr Ellington. Tell him that if he divulges the exact whereabouts of its location then we will pay him a further one thousand pounds cash and give an assurance that there'll be no police involvement, with nothing more said on the matter. Do you understand?"

"A thousand pounds? What exactly am I getting into here, Mrs Stephens?" This simple theft job was taking on some expensive weight. Confused, I took hold of the arms of my chair and was about to stand up to question her further. She took a step towards me, outstretched her right arm and raised a slender finger, which she gently shook in front of her as if to calm herself. She smiled at me before speaking again, and this time her timbre was hushed and precise.

"It's quite simple, Mr Ellington. When you find Fowler, just ask where we can find the truth. Good day to you."

Without replying, I watched as she marched out of my office and listened as her stiletto heels hypnotically struck the wooden floor in the passageway until she was gone.

The beguiling scent of Ida Stephens' perfume lingered in my office for the next few hours like an unwelcome spectre haunting a frail soul. My headache continued to pound away savagely in my skull. I slouched back in my chair wondering what kind of mess I was about to get myself into again. I picked up the white envelope containing the money and tapped it tensely on the top of my desk a couple of times before opening up the drawer beside me and dropping it in. I needed a stiff drink: the hair of the dog might just clear my head. I got out of my seat, walked over to the coat stand and put on my lightweight Aquascutum beige overcoat and black felt trilby.

Before leaving I looked over to the far wall at the attractive naked woman on my Pirelli calendar. Below her I read the day's date. It was Tuesday, 21 June 1966 . . . my forty-fourth birthday.

CHAPTER
TWO

After leaving my office I returned to my digs on Gwyn Street. The place looked good, thanks to some redecoration by my well-meaning uncle Gabe and aunt Pearl, and to some quality knocked-off furniture provided by my cousin Vic. Despite their good intentions to make the place more welcoming, I couldn't shake off the painful memories locked within its walls. Less than eighteen months previously my bedroom had been the scene of two tragic suicides. The deaths of Stella Hopkins and her surrogate father, Earl Linney, had shaken me to my core. Uncle Gabe had urged me to seek other accommodation or to move in with them; I stubbornly resisted and stayed put. Although I'd never seen anything remotely eerie after their deaths, there was something within me that felt their presence in ways I could not explain, and I was somehow strangely content to reside with the veiled duppies who I believed still inhabited my humble dwelling.

I took a shave and a bath, and splashed a little Bay Rum through my hair and across my face. Then I changed into a fresh, pale-blue cotton shirt and a pair of Levi's jeans, pulled on my best brown Oxford brogues, slipped my arms into my favourite brown tweed jacket and strapped on my battered Timex wristwatch. I grabbed my keys and wallet from off the mantlepiece in my sitting room and walked down the hallway and out onto the landing of my upper-floor rooms. It was just after one thirty when I made my way downstairs towards the front door. As I flipped the latch to let myself out, a familiar voice stopped me in my tracks.

"Happy Birthday, Joseph."

I turned around to face my elderly neighbour, Mrs Pearce, who lived in the flat below me. She stood looking up at me, smiling. Her slight frame and small stature hid what was a formidable temper and determined spirit. She had managed to dent my usually impenetrable armour of self-reserve, which usually kept outsiders at bay, and during the last year we had become firm friends. She lifted her slender arm to produce a small, daintily wrapped gift. She waved it at me to take it from her.

"It's not much, but I thought it might come in handy at some point." She took a step backwards, put her hands on her hips and looked me up and down carefully. "You're looking rather well turned out: off to celebrate, are you?"

"Nah, Mrs P, I'm just meeting my cousin Vic for a quiet drink at the Star and Garter pub." I watched as my aged neighbour shook her head slowly in disappointment.

"Why oh why do you have to spend all your spare time with that good-for-nothing delinquent cousin of yours? From what I hear Victor's constantly up to no good, you know that, don't you? I'm surprised at you, Joseph, I really am. A man like you, of good standing, who used to be a police officer, associating with a tearaway like him. You need your head examining." She scolded me with a mouth turned down at the edges, as if she had just sucked on a lemon.

"He's no saint, but he's family, Mrs P, you know that."

"Yes, and Abel probably said something similar about Cain, and we all know how that ended, don't we! Joseph, family or not, you ought to be a little more careful in who you choose to associate with, you really should."

I leant forward and took a hold of the slight shoulders of my frail comrade, then drew her close to me. Bending down towards her head, I whispered into her tiny ear. "Vic says exactly the same ting 'bout you, Mrs P. Thanks for the gift; you really shouldn't have, you know." As I let go I gave a gentle kiss on her cheek, winked, then turned quickly and darted out of my front door before she had time to reprimand me some more.

The Star and Garter pub in the heart of St Pauls was a regular stop-off for me whenever I was in need of liquid refreshment. As I walked along Ashley Road with my trilby perched on the back of my head and my jacket hooked over my right shoulder, I could feel the welcoming warm rays of the summer sun. It was hardly the intense tropical heat of a Barbadian day, but for me anything was better than the bitter winters that had blighted the shores of Great Britain each year since I'd

28

arrived. I turned onto Brook Road and happily wandered the last few yards towards the Star's front door. When I reached it I stood outside for a moment and put my jacket back on, unfolding my shirt collar over the neck and straightening my trilby in front of my face, shading my eyes, just the way I like it.

I opened the ornate stained-glass door, walked in then headed across the room. Inside it was fairly quiet, with only a handful of drinkers sat in different parts of the pub, nursing their half-drunk ale and reading various daily newspapers. Nobody lifted their heads out of their rags to see who had walked in, and as I strolled towards the empty bar I could hear the Test match cricket playing on the radio. I stood for a moment then gave the brass top of the bar a couple of hard knocks to let the landlord know I wanted a drink.

"Who the bleedin' hell's that?"

The familiar Somerset twang of Eric Coles, the Star and Garter's crabby owner, bellowed out at me from the cellar. I listened as he cursed to himself while climbing the steep steps out of his darkened crypt towards where I was waiting. When he finally reached the top, his glowing, crimson face was not best pleased to see me.

"Sod me . . . You, bloody Martin Luther King! Can't you see I'm busy? Whaddya want?"

"Pint o' mild'd be nice please, Eric, if you don't mind?" The Star's landlord slung the dirty cloth he'd been using onto his bar, then turned to pick up a jug-handled glass pint pot from the shelf behind him and began to fill it slowly from the hand pull. I put my hand in the back pocket of my Levi's and pulled out some coins. I picked at the money then placed it on the polished brass top. Eric drew the last few drops carefully into the glass, grunted some obscenity under his breath then slid the ale over towards me. He picked up the money and counted it carefully.

"Here, you bloody idiot, you've given me too much. Can't you bleedin' count?"

"Yeah, I can count . . . I'm paying for one for my cousin Vic too; he'll be in any minute." I beamed a toothy grin back at the crotchety innkeeper to wind him up, but it was clear from the grim look on his face that the mere mention of Vic's name had put him in an even worse mood.

"Oh no, not that thug. I told you, he ain't welcome in here. Not after last time." Eric picked up his moth-eaten duster and started nervously polishing his already gleaming work surface.

"Come on, Eric, you know what went down last week wasn't Vic's fault. It was those greasy bikers that started all the ruckus."

"Went down! Bleedin' went down? I'll tell you what went down: three of my best tables and a chair, that's what went down. Down the sodding tip! That's where they ended up once your loopy bloody cousin had thrown four bikers across 'em! Smashed 'em to bits he did. It was like the bloody OK Corral in 'ere last Wednesday night. Well, I ain't havin' it. He can bloody well sod off if he thinks he's walking back through those doors again. My poor missus was picking wood and glass up out of that Wilton carpet for days."

"To be fair, he did pay you for the damage, which was more than any of those bikers did."

"And whose bloody fault was that? Not one of 'em could've put their hands in their bleedin' pockets after that great big ape relation of yours had finished with 'em, the poor buggers. Two were carried out on stretchers. My customers come in 'ere for a quiet drink, not a bloody re-enactment of the Battle of Rorke's Drift!"

I knew that Eric's bark was far worse than his bite. True, Vic and Eric were never going to be best buddies, but there was a mutual respect both quietly held for each other. Vic admired Eric's straight-talking and Eric liked the money that Vic regularly parted with across his bar. Both understood the status quo that had been silently created. I was right to remind Eric that Vic had paid up a fair wad of cash that night for the smashed-up fixtures and fittings. Eric accepted Vic's cash and took it as his apology. But then he could do no other: Eric feared Vic, too, and he was right to do so.

I went and sat at a small circular table in the Star's back room, a place fondly known as the snug. I took a heavy draught of my pint, sinking half of it in a couple of swift gulps, then sat my glass down in front of me. I remembered Mrs Pearce's gift and reached into my jacket pocket to retrieve it. It was wrapped in white tissue paper, which I ripped off to reveal a small navy-blue box. I looked at it for a moment, smiled to myself then opened it up. Inside was a small Puma pocketknife. I lifted it out and weighed it in the palm of my hand: it was light, no more than four and a half ounces, and its polished stag-antler handle had been beautifully turned. I pulled out the three-inch blade and carefully ran my thumb across its razor-sharp edge. I closed up the knife and returned it to its box then placed it into the inside pocket of my jacket. I was pleasantly surprised by the present that my kindly neighbour had given me: the old woman never ceased to astonish and bewilder in equal measure.

It was just after 2.15p.m. by the time Vic sauntered through the door and strolled up to Eric's bar. I heard him shout out after the landlord; there was real horseplay in the tone of his voice. Eric, who had disappeared back down into his cellar, clearly didn't hear Vic call out to him. I reached for my drink, took a swallow, then put my head down and waited for things to erupt as my wayward cousin bellowed out across the bar.

"Hey Eric baby, git ya honky ass from outta that pit and git me a pint o' that warm piss water you usually reserve for ya best customers!"

From the depths of the basement Eric yelled back, "I'll give you piss water, you cheeky young bleeder. That's best Courage Mild that is!"

Eric, the sweat pouring off his bald head and brow, lifted himself out of the cellar trapdoor and stood in front of Vic, fuming. "I'll have you know I've won prizes for my beer!"

"Yeah, prizes fo' what, best latrine cleaner? I've seen you using it to pour down those scabby shithouses o' yours instead of having to rod 'em out when they're jammed up to the rim. You ain't fooling me, brother."

Vic was laughing out loud, really getting into the swing of things, enjoying his time teasing the old boy.

"I ain't your bleedin' brother!"

"Well, that's mighty strange, Eric old son, cos a lotta folks bin telling me how much we looks alike!"

Eric picked up a beer glass, muttering obscenities to himself, then yanked on the bar's hand pull, dispensing warm alcohol into the vessel. Vic looked on, readying himself for more childish banter. On the radio an announcer began to relay the latest results from the one-day Test match from Lord's cricket ground. Fuel for the fire for Vic.

"You hearin' this, Eric, the West Indies are wiping the floor with you honkies a'gin. I don't know why they is even botherin' ta stick those boxes down their scabby Y-fronts; we're knockin' them stumps over quicker than they can git their lily-white asses outta the changing room!"

"'Ere Sammy Davis Jr, here's your pint o' mild, care of your bloody kin back there." Eric dropped the pint glass onto the bar. He wisely chose to ignore Vic's jibes and went about his business.

"Thanks, brother Eric, that's cool. You know it's JT's birthday today, don't ya? We were expectin' a cake." Vic clapped his huge hands together, took a hefty swig of his mild then put his hand into his coat pocket and brought out his silver hip flask, unscrewed the cap and poured a heavy slug of rum into the pint glass. Eric stood, mouth wide open in disbelief as he watched, and then began to shake his head, tutting to himself at my cousin's questionable behaviour. Vic caught Eric's disdainful look and frowned back at him.

"What? You tink I'm gonna drink this shit without me puttin' someting decent in it? Ain't no way, brother, no way!" Vic howled out with laughter then strode away from the bar to come and join me in the snug.

I watched my cousin swagger towards me. Rather than walk, Vic seemed to glide effortlessly across the floor, his powerful frame not hindering the grace with which he moved. He was dressed, not unsurprisingly, almost totally in black, the collar of his leather jacket pulled up close around his muscular neck and face. He never wore a hat and his tight, curly hair cut close to his scalp glistened with coconut oil. When he sat down next to me the warm scent of the patchouli oil that he was wearing wafted around the room. He smiled at me mischievously, reminding me of the little boy who I used to get up to no good with back home on the dusty Barbadian streets of St Philip parish.

"Hey JT, my man . . . Happy birthday, brother." He raised his glass to toast me and I lifted my pint; our glasses touched, making the familiar chinking sound. Vic sunk the rest of his beer and slammed the pot onto the table then yelled out across the backroom towards the bar, "Hey Eric, we got us a celebration going down, bring us a couple more pints o' that award-winner drain cleaner you got back there." Vic chuckled to himself then turned back towards me. "So, cous, what's happening, you got anyting special lined up for your big day?"

"No, nuttin' special . . . I've got a job lined up."

"Job? You got a job lined up? Shit . . . JT, you should have yo'self some birthday woman lined up, talking like a fool 'bout a job!" Vic huffed indignantly to himself as Eric brought over two more pints of beer, placing them on the table in front of us.

"That'll be two shillings ten." Eric picked up Vic's empty glass as he waited to get paid, looked over at me, forced a smile and nodded. "Happy fucking birthday."

Vic pulled out a bundle of cash from the inside pocket of his coat and handed Eric a five-pound note.

"Ain't you got anything a bit smaller than that?"

"Nah . . . You have one yo'self, Eric brother, then you stick my change behind the bar for later. Like I said, we've got some celebrating to do." Vic beamed up at Eric, raising his eyebrows at speed a couple of times.

"Well, you just make sure you keep your bloody celebrating to yourselves, I don't want another bleedin' punch-up in here just cos you two are full of ale. You hear me, the pair of you?"

"Yeah, yeah . . . We hear ya, ya miserable old goat." Vic stuck two fingers up at Eric's broad back as he wandered back to the bar, whinging to himself. I finished off what was left of my first pint then took a sip out of the one that Vic had just bought for me. My cousin leant back in his chair, his beer in hand, watching me knowingly.

"So, what's this job you got lined up then?"

"You know a Theodore Fowler lives round these parts?"

"You mean Theo the flusher? Shit, JT, everybody knows old Doc Fowler."

"I don't."

Vic blew out a breath and then sucked air back through the tiny gap in between his gleaming white upper incisors, making a faint whistling sound as he did.

"That's cos you got your head up your ass most o' the time. Fine detective you make. Look, any woman got themselves knocked up and don't want no pickney hanging off their titties in eight months' time, they gonna be calling on Theo Fowler, that's for damn sure. Why you looking for that old bastard anyways?"

I took another mouthful of my ale then brought Vic up to speed, giving him all the relevant information before finishing my account with Ida Stephens' unusual request for me to ask Dr Fowler where the truth was.

"You gotta be kidding me, right? Only trute Theo Fowler's gonna be able to tell you is where to git a half bottle o' scotch cheap and how to stuff a crocheting hook up a cock-rat's snatch. That fool wouldn't know the trute if it was hung on the back o' his ass! Man's permanently wasted. How the hell he even finds a bitch's nuk nuk with his shaky ole hands is beyond me, I tell ya straight."

"Can you find him for me, set up a meet?"

"I can try . . . Best way for you to git to him is to git yo'self a woman. Make up some shit 'bout her being in the family way."

"Don't s'pose you know someone?"

"I know a piece o' skirt that'll help you out if you're prepared to drop a few notes into her purse. Name's Rita Lee. Oh she's real sweet, knows the streets and

Doc Fowler too. We use Rita an' he won't git spooked. Hell, she's been to him so often she gets special rates. I'll git a couple o' my guys to sniff 'bout, see where he's been gittin' loaded. Man's never far from a shebeen. Give me a day or two. Don't you worry; we'll find the flusher for ya." Vic leant forward towards me and nodded towards my glass. "Come on, brother, drink up, time fo' more o' Eric's piss water."

I drained the remainder of my beer and put my glass down in front of me.

"No thanks, Vic, I gotta go." I stood up, straightened my jacket and put my trilby on. Vic, baffled, looked up at me seriously from his chair.

"Go? Where the hell you gotta go that's so important on your birthday, you gotta leave me drinkin' on my own in this crap hole?"

"I need to visit an ole friend. I'm gonna buy some flowers, take a walk up to Brunswick cemetery and pay a visit to Carnell Harris's grave." Without farewell, I put my hand on my cousin's shoulder and squeezed it tightly before heading out of the pub. As I left, Vic called after me from his seat.

"That ain't no place for you to be, brother. You need to be staying away from that old boneyard, do you no good grieving for the dead up there, you hear me, JT?"

I kept my head down and walked, Vic's kindly words of warning repeating in my head as a cold cloak of sorrow wrapped itself around my body and ushered me cruelly out into the empty street.

CHAPTER
THREE

After a fitful night's sleep, filled with bad dreams, I was woken early on the Wednesday morning by the sound of chattering birdsong from outside in the street. My pounding head still ached from the day before and had fused with a bad mood that was probably going to be set in with me for the day. My determination to go to the cemetery and lay flowers on Carnell Harris's grave had left me feeling blue and in need of hard liquor. With Vic's earlier words of warning about visiting the dead ringing grimly in my ears, I'd walked out of the churchyard and into an off-licence, picked up a bottle of rum and gone back at my office; there I'd sat alone with an air of bleakness about me and begun to drink myself into a stupor.

It had been a stiflingly warm night, and at around seven o'clock I'd returned to my digs on Gwyn Street, flung the living room sash windows wide open to let in what little breeze there was, then sank into my armchair with a further quart bottle of Mount Gay rum, and finished it off. The booze had done little to purge the blues from me and by the time I'd taken myself off to bed it was late. Staring up into the darkness, angry, drunk and with my belly empty but for the large quantity of dark spirits sloshing around inside it, I lay awake for what had seemed like an age before eventually closing my eyes. I had a head full of dark thoughts still rattling around inside that continued to invade my restless slumber.

I turned over to look at the brass alarm clock on my bedside table: it was just after 6 a.m. Still dog-tired, I crawled out of bed and wearily sat on the edge of the mattress, staring into space, and waited while the last remnants of the nightmares which had plagued me throughout the night finally withdrew back into their darkened recesses. I stared down at the floor and noticed that I was still wearing my socks. I stood up and walked across the bedroom and took a look at myself in the large mirror that was attached to the outside of my wardrobe door. What stared back at me wasn't a pretty picture. I stripped out of the creased shirt, trousers and underwear I'd slept in and made my way into the bathroom, where I wrapped a towel round my waist then opened up the airing cupboard and switched on the immersion heater to get some hot water going in the boiler so I could take a bath.

In the living room the sash windows were still wide open and a gentle wind was blowing cool air through into the hall. I went into my kitchen, stood by the sink and filled the kettle with water, then put it onto the hob of my gas cooker and lit the front ring with a match. I reached over for a large glass that was sat on the draining board, turned on the cold water again and stuck it underneath the fast-running tap. The water ran a sandy brown, so I left it running on full until it choked and spluttered then ran clear. I knocked the cold liquid back then refilled the glass a second time, draining its contents before my thirst was quenched. I leant across the kitchen table, where my Roberts radio was, turned it on and was greeted by the voice of a well-spoken BBC announcer on the light programme breakfast special. After the kettle had boiled I made myself a cup of black coffee and sat and listened to the morning's news as the painful legacy of the previous night's heavy drinking continued to hammer on inside my head.

It was after seven by the time I'd finished my third cup of coffee and had run a bath for myself. I lay in the hot water, soaking my aching limbs, and slowly the hammer in my head began to subside. As I shaved, I stopped briefly to listen to the smooth tones of a new song, Percy Sledge's "When a Man Loves a Woman", which was playing on the transistor out in the kitchen. I got out of the tub, dried myself then brushed my teeth and took a long hard look at myself in the bathroom mirror, scowling at my sorry reflection. The small half-inch scar on my left brow, a memento from a childhood accident, caught my eye, and for the briefest of moments my mind recalled happy times back home on the island of Barbados. Those times were now long gone and I shook off any past thoughts by pouring a small amount of Imperial Leather aftershave into the palm of my hand then splashed it around my face, making me gasp as the cologne stung at my now smooth skin.

I walked slowly back into my bedroom, still feeling like death warmed up, and slowly changed into fresh underwear and a white cotton shirt then pulled on the trousers of my lightweight charcoal single-breasted suit. I slid my feet into my brogues, and as I began to tie the laces, my stomach began to rumble. Breakfast was normally my favourite meal of the day, and my churning guts told me that I'd struggle to make it through the morning let alone the rest of day without some kind of food inside me. I grabbed the small Puma knife Mrs Pearce had given me for my birthday from the top of the chest of drawers and put it into my hip pocket, strapped my old watch around my left wrist then picked up my wallet and retractable pencil and dropped them into the breast pocket of my jacket before pulling it on.

I felt light-headed and unsteady on my feet as I picked up my trilby and overcoat from the stand in the hall and, like a condemned man whose gait is hampered by heavy leg irons, walked listlessly out of my digs.

I stood for a moment on my front doorstep. Looking up at the almost cloudless blue sky, I took in a couple deep breaths of fresh air and squinted as the early morning sun hit my eyes. I quickly fitted my trilby onto my head, pulling the brim down low over the front of my face, cutting out the glare. An unnerving sense of foreboding nagged at my being as I wearily trod down the granite steps towards the pavement. I headed down Gwyn Street, thinking about the large wad of cash in my desk drawer back at the gym, how to find Dr

Fowler, and Ida Stephens' enigmatic request for me to seek out the whereabouts of "the truth" for her.

Her words echoed around and around in my head, over and over again in my brain. "It's quite simple, Mr Ellington . . . When you find Fowler just ask where we can find the truth." As I walked the length of the road, the summer sunshine painted out my shadow onto the concrete slabs in front of me and I watched as the sunbeams dragged my darkened silhouette out into the gutter. I stopped and stared down at the dark stone trench that ran along the length of the road, my mind carrying itself towards places I had no right returning to, back to my forgotten life in Barbados as a police officer. An unwelcome recall crept out of my psyche as if it had just crawled up from the sewers below to taunt me. It threw out at me the unwelcome, hidden memories I had so carefully kept suppressed, black memories that I wanted to remain undisturbed: the crime syndicate I had once fought and fallen foul of, the corruption and betrayal I had uncovered within my own squad, and the murders of both my wife, Ellie, and daughter, Amelia.

I felt the early warmth of a June morning suddenly become a blazing heat at my back: the tortured screams of those I loved calling out from a blistering furnace for me to come to them, their scorched hands reaching towards my ankles to pull me into their searing hell. I tore myself away from the side of the road, the sweat running down my face. I wiped away the perspiration with my shaking hand then continued walking, yet the cries of the dead clung on inside me, their pleading

42

resonating with my footsteps as I paced away from a fiery underworld I never wanted to revisit.

The Black Cat café on the corner of Wilde Street in the heart of St Pauls was not exactly true to its name, being the last place that a man like me could expect to get a warm welcome. Not that I was after one: I never went for the hospitality or for company; I went in there because it served good food and it was cheap. The Black Cat was one of those joints that "decent" people stayed well clear off. It was mostly frequented by what I came to know as grafters, hard-working types: builders, chippies, carpet fitters, factory workers on their way home from the night shift, postmen having a crafty breakfast cuppa before finishing their rounds, delivery drivers filling their faces before starting the day's slog. And crooks. How I fitted in as one of the café's regular customers wasn't something I thought a great deal about. I turned up most mornings, sat at the same table in a corner, ordered my meal, tucked into it then left. Few engaged me in conversation; no one was interested in what I did for a living and most sitting inside the place ignored my very existence. All except one: its owner, Donald "Muff" Walker.

Known as "Mr Muff" to everyone who knew him, he'd picked up his nickname years before from the fellow merchant seamen he had served with during World War II. It was given to him on account of the comical old cap complete with swing-down earmuffs that he wore on his head during the perilous, freezing Atlantic sea crossings he'd made. Muff was the kind of guy I could never get a handle on. He was all looks and smiles when you walked through his gate door, came over like your best friend, offering up his warmest welcome, then called you a dirty coon no sooner than he'd taken your money and your back was turned. Early on, I'd come to the conclusion that Donald Walker was not a man to be trusted, and my friends in the black community considered him to be a sly, tight-fisted and racist chump. For as long as I'd been taking my custom into the Black Cat, Muff had always offered up the same greeting to me; today was gonna be no different to any of the others that had gone before it.

"How you doin', John John?" Muff cocked his head and winked at me as I approached his bleached-out Formica counter. He was leant against the worktop, arms outstretched in front of him, his faded blue naval tattoos proudly on show as I made my way towards him.

"I'm swell, Mr Muff, yo'self?" I shot him a smile then looked up at the printed menu behind the old duffer and read what was on offer.

"Can't complain, John John, can't complain. Now what'll you be having?" He slapped the palms of his hands together then picked up a small lined pad from the top of the cash register, took a pencil from behind the back of his ear, licked the lead tip and prepared to take my order.

"I'll take a couple o' rashers o' bacon, a fried egg and two slices o' toast." I watched as he wrote, his handwriting more a scrawl than legible print.

"And to drink?" He fired his enquiry at me in a manner that was more a command than a question.

"A cup of your special coffee would go down a treat, Mr Muff."

"That'll be two and six." He didn't even stop to look up from his notepad to stick his hand out in front of me.

I took out my wallet, picked out the necessary coins and handed him my money. He carefully counted through what I had given to him in the palm of his hand with the tip of his index finger, double-checking I had not cheated him, before turning and ringing the amount up in the till. The drawer shot open and Muff dropped the coins inside then slammed the cash register shut. He yelled out my order towards the kitchen then picked up a copy of the *Daily Mirror* from off a stool behind him, opened it up in front of me and started to read.

As all the corner seats were taken, I went and found myself a table over by the front window of the café and looked out across the street at the people coming and going. While I realised that the colour of my skin always caused Donald Walker a great deal of displeasure, taking my money on a regular basis did not. If I wanted to eat out in a local café then Muff's was the only place and his unpleasant behaviour was something I had to put up with. He was happy just as long as I paid up and didn't sit next to any of his other customers while they stuffed their faces with his food. Although I did not like the man, I knew how to play the game with the bigot: I generally kept my conversations with him short and sweet. Whatever I may have thought about his attitude towards me, the fool had one good thing going for him and that was stood out back in his kitchen making my breakfast.

Elsie Walker, Muff's wife, could sure cook up a mean plateful of food. In no time she'd rustled up my order, and I watched as she walked carefully across from her kitchen towards me with my meal in one hand and my coffee in the other. I smiled at her as she approached my table and placed my breakfast in front of me. She turned to check if her husband was still reading his paper then bent down towards my ear to whisper to me.

"Growing lad like you needs more than two rashers of bacon and a miserly egg to set him up for the day. Here, get that lot down ya." I looked down at the mountain of food she had prepared for me: along with the extra bacon and egg there were sausages, mushrooms and grilled tomatoes. It was a generous gesture from a kind-hearted woman and one that I was grateful to receive, throbbing hangover or not. As Elsie walked back to her kitchen I glanced over towards Donald Walker, who was peering suspiciously back at me from behind his morning paper. I nodded back at him in gratitude then picked up my knife and fork and began to tuck in to my huge breakfast. The old fool stuck his nose back into his rag, none the wiser that his old lady had taken a shine to me and had been feeding me up with princely amounts of his food for the best part of a year. I sat back in my chair, gulped down a mouthful of coffee and looked back out into the street. It was going to be another hot day for sure. I returned to my hearty breakfast and smiled to myself, realising that my little victory over the Black Cat's stingy proprietor had lightened my frame of mind and, for the first time in a while, I felt strangely good with the world.

It was just after three in the afternoon when the telephone on my desk rang. I picked up the receiver and before I had the chance to speak was greeted by my cousin Vic's cheerful, booming voice.

"JT, it's your lucky day, brother. Ole flush-it Fowler gone an' took the bait!" Vic, clearly pleased with himself, began to laugh loudly down the phone. I pulled the receiver away from my ear as he guffawed into it, only daring to return it to my head after he'd finally stopped.

"You saying you found the doc already?"

"Course I did, fool. I said I'd put one o' my boys on to it for you, didn't I? You know Levi Caesar?"

"The pimp?"

"Yeah, that the brother. You know Levi, he could find pussy in a convent. Hittin' on that raggedy-assed ole drunk for ya wasn't gonna vex Levi none. He sniffed him out real sharp. Levi had words with your missin' medic, told him how one of his girls needed the good doc's bedside manner, if you git my drift. When Levi tole Fowler it was Rita Lee needed his services, urgent like, he was on the case like a fly round a horse's ass. Just like I tole ya, Doc Fowler has a soft spot for the woman, so he wasn't too shifty when Levi asked if he'd mind going to work an' stickin' his hand up Rita's moo moo fo' a fee. I'm hookin' you up with the two of 'em

47

later tonight; you know the King's Head pub on Victoria Street?"

"Yeah, you talkin' 'bout the place out by that bombed-out old church?"

"That's the one, it's anutha one o' those rough-assed honky joints. You should fit in real nice. Anyways, to keep the doc on side and not git him all spooked up, our cock-rat's gonna meet him in a public place. They'll be sitting doing their bidness in the King's Head at eight tonight. I've kept Rita sweet with a little up-front bread; you just slip her another five notes for her trouble when you git there and she'll be cool."

"Five pounds, Jesus, that's damn steep for a night out an' an hour's work."

"Hey Dick Barton, don't you be gittin' all cheap on me. Just pay the bitch her five sheets and let her walk. All you gotta do is pinch the doc and git outta him what you is lookin' fo', it's as simple as that."

"How the hell am I gonna know what they look like?"

"Son of a bitch . . . You want me to come down there an' point the fuckas out to you? It ain't gonna be that much o' a problem. Shit, you lookin' for a clapped-out ole whore an' a washed-up elderly nigga sitting in a back room full o' honkies. How goddamn hard is it gonna be to pick 'em out o' the crowd?"

"OK, you made your point, but if I find myself sitting in some dive for the night and come away with nuttin' more than a sob story from a hooker and five pounds poorer, Levi Caesar is gonna have to go into hiding, never mind Doc Fowler."

"Quit bitchin' on, will ya? It's like I said, Fowler needs a steady stream o' cash coming in so his drinks cabinet don't dry up. He ain't gonna let you down if he tinks there's easy money to be made. Now you're the detective: go detect. I ain't gonna be holding yo' hand every time you be facing a brick wall; you is a big boy now, JT, ain't like we's eight years old no more." My cousin chuckled down the line at me, goading me a little more. I didn't bite.

"Well, thanks for coming up with the goods. I owe you one."

"Yeah, don't I know it. Hey, just so you know, I'm gonna be outta town for a few days, on a spot o' bidness."

"Yeah? Where you goin'?"

"London."

"London! What the hell you goin' all the way up to London for?"

"Like I said, brother, I got me some bidness in the big city. I'm gonna be expanding my commercial interests, that's all."

"Commercial interests? What the hell you talkin' 'bout?"

"I'm talkin' 'bout football, JT."

"Football! You ain't thinking o' putting money into a football team, are you?"

"Hell no! Do I look stupid enough to be putting my dough into some honky football team? Shit, who'd you think I am, some kinda blacked-up Alf Ramsey? In case you didn't already know, next month we got ourselves the World Cup hittin' these shores. Everybody and

49

anybody who can so much as kick a hogskin ball round a yard is gonna be haulin' their asses up to the smoke for those games. The city's gonna be heaving to the seams with chumps wantin' to watch a game, kick back with a cold beer and spend their hard-earned cash. I intend to git myself a piece o' that action."

"Yeah . . . and how you plan on doing that?"

"What you tink, fool? I'm gonna be doin' what I always be doin' when there's money to be made. Gittin' out on the streets with my supply-an'-demand enterprises. By the time the World Cup arrives on my gate door I'm gonna be supplyin' booze and bootlegged game tickets to any sap that's willin' to buy 'em from me and my boys. I'm lookin' to make myself a small fortune."

The line had gone dead before I had time to wish my cousin well. I dropped the receiver back into its cradle then slid open my desk drawer and pulled out the envelope containing the money that Ida Stephens had left. I tipped the contents out onto the desktop in front of me and fished through the bank notes for the swanky-looking business card with Stephens' contact details printed on it. I picked it out, reread the details then leant across my desk and pulled the telephone towards me and dialled the four-digit number to the Walter Wilkins orphanage. A faint dialling tone purred back at me as I sat waiting for a reply. I pushed the receiver closer to my ear and readied myself to break the good news to the stern administrator, unaware that the call I was about to make would reap terrible consequences for me in the coming days.

CHAPTER
FOUR

My phone call to Ida Stephens was both brief and succinct. Surprisingly, the formidable overseer had expressed little excitement at the good news that I'd located her missing doctor and set up a meeting with him for later that evening. She'd listened quietly as I'd relayed all the facts and explained what was going to go down at the King's Head pub. If there had been little fire in her belly in hearing of my success in establishing the whereabouts of Fowler, there sure was plenty of heat coming off her tongue as she delivered her parting sermon to me.

"I don't have to remind you how sensitive this situation is, Mr Ellington. Just retrieve what belongs to us, pay the man and make sure that you come away with all the relevant particulars in regards to the truth. Am I making myself clear?"

"Yeah, I understand —"

"Good. I expect to hear from you in due course, Mr Ellington." The line went dead and I was left with the sound of static crackling in my ear. I slumped back into my chair and swallowed hard. My hand tightened around the receiver of the telephone, infuriated by the manner in which I'd just been spoken to. I stared down at my desk and looked at the white envelope containing the wad of cash Stephens had left with me. My instincts told me that something really stank about both the job and Ida Stephens. I asked myself how much crap could I take from people who talked to me like dirt, but with nothing in the bank and plenty of bills to pay, I sure as hell could do with their dough. As I sat thinking about the rights and the wrongs of my decision to see the job through, I nervously recalled how the last person who'd employed me to find someone for them had also had a nasty habit of cutting short their phone conversations with me . . . and they'd ended up dead.

It was just after 7.30p.m.: I drove the short distance out of St Pauls into Bristol and parked my car up on Church Lane, just around the corner from the King's Head pub. I pulled the key out of the ignition of my 1963 Mark One Ford Cortina, which had been previously owned by my late friend Carnell Harris, and switched on the car's radio and turned the dial slowly until I found a station playing something worth listening to.

I tapped my fingers on top of the dashboard in time to the beat of the Chiffons' "Sweet-Talking Guy" as I gazed through the windshield at the sun slowly beginning to drop out of the evening sky. As it fell behind the buildings in front of me, dusk quickly encroached across the city streets, giving the night heavens a beguiling reddish tinge, which, for some unexplainable reason, started to set the hairs on the back of my neck rising up as if responding to an unseen threat. I checked the time on my wristwatch: 7.45 p.m. I was tired of sitting alone in the fading light, worrying about the whys and wherefores of a job I never really wanted to undertake, and my suspicions of its dubious nature. All I knew was that the die was now cast and I felt that I was once again about to enter into the mouth of the wolf, my better judgement no longer an ally to my usually cautious sense of self-preservation. I grabbed hold of my overcoat and hat from the passenger seat and took myself off towards the back entrance of the pub.

The King's Head was one of those old drinking dens that felt like you were travelling back in time. It was infamous for being frequented by every kind of criminal lowlife known to the city. Local thieves, fences, cat burglars, pimps, whores, pickpockets, every bent and lawless stripe known to man at some point wandered through its battered oak doors and drank in the gaslit shadows of the simple long, narrow, one-room bar. Those who wished to undertake some form of nefarious criminal activity within the hushed walls of the public house and out of view from prying eyes often took advantage of the curiously named "Tramcar Bar", a snug shaped like a Victorian tramcar with just a narrow passage running alongside it that gave access to a small private area in which to conduct one's illicit business. Vic had been no fool: he'd carefully chosen the venue for Dr Fowler and Rita Lee to hook up, making sure both their presences would arouse little or no suspicion. A black dude in a predominantly all whites' boozer generally caused someone or other to kick up a fuss about it, but this joint was different. Here in the King's Head, black crooks were welcome too.

I wandered in through the inner rear door with its "Bar" gold-etched glass panel. The place was dead, with the exception of two old boys who were soused up to their eyeballs and a woman in her late twenties who was sat at one of the small square tables nursing what looked like a lime and soda in both hands. The woman peeped up at me from her drink as I walked past and, as if recognising who I might be, offered up a brief and uneasy smile. I didn't return the gesture and made my way towards the Formica-topped bar to get myself a drink. I ordered a large rum, paid and made my way back to where the young woman was sitting.

I stood at the entrance of the snug for a moment and watched as she sipped at her pale drink. With her legs crossed, she fidgeted in her seat as she looked over at me, her eyes darting back and forth anxiously in their sockets like a scared animal caught in the headlights of a fast-moving vehicle. She was dressed in a matching denim jacket and miniskirt and a bright-pink low-cut blouse displayed the top half of her skinny-looking breasts and deep cleavage. As I walked towards her the stink of cheap perfume hit me. I shot her a smile before speaking in an attempt to calm her nerves.

"It's OK, don't worry, I ain't the police. You Rita Lee?"

"All right, me luvver? Yeah, I'm Rita, and you gotta be Mr Ellington."

I nodded at her. "That's me. I didn't mean to scare you."

"Hark at ee, you scare me? I ain't scared, me, not of you or no coppers. In my game there ain't no point in being scared. An' besides, I never met a spade who'd be calling himself no copper."

I sat down on the stool opposite the cocksure streetwalker and took a nip of my rum. Rita Lee was talking up a good fight at me, but frightened eyes never lie: this girl was scared.

I leant forward and spoke quietly. "Look, we ain't got much time. My cousin Vic tells me you know this Dr Fowler pretty well. That right?"

"Yeah, me an' the doc, we goes back a way. He's done his bit when I've needed a quack. What you wan' him for?"

"All you need to know is that I need to speak to the man." I looked over my shoulder quickly then put my hand into the inside pocket of my jacket and took out a folded-up five-pound note and shot my hand under the table for Rita to take it from me. I felt her fingers briefly touch mine as she snatched the cash then stashed it out of sight. "All you gotta do is git the man to sit down with you, give him some bull 'bout you being in the family way, and by the time you done that, I'll be back in here and you can be on your way: it's as simple as that. You clear on what needs to be done?"

Rita Lee shot me a suspicious look. "You ain't gunna hurt the poor old bugger or nothing, are ya? I mean, he ain't never done me no harm —"

I butted in, aware that precious time was ticking away. "I ain't here to hurt him, I promise you. Now when the doc turns up, you don't even look at me when

I come over to join you, just git up and walk on outta here. You understand me?"

"Yeah, I got it: you come in, I piss off . . ."

I nodded back at Rita, picked up my drink and raised my glass then lifted myself out of my seat and began to walk away. As I did, the call girl called after me.

"Here, Mr Ellington."

I stopped in my tracks and turned around to face her.

"Word on the street is you do this kinda thing a lot. You really one o' those private eyes, like in the films?"

"Nah . . . I ain't no detective. I'm just a guy whose bin paid to snoop around some."

"Snooping around, you say? I suppose somebody's gotta do it, but sounds like a real shitty way to make a living if you ask me, Mr Ellington."

"I wasn't asking."

I walked away, thinking to myself that Rita had some nerve commenting on how I made my living, especially coming from a woman in her shifty line of work.

I found a doorway to stand in across the road from the King's Head and waited patiently in the shadows for Fowler to turn up. I didn't have to wait long. It was just before eight o'clock when I first caught sight of the wary-looking elderly black guy standing under the orange glow of a street lamp. I watched as he carefully checked behind and in front of him before entering the pub. Since I'd left, not a soul had gone in or out, so it was odds on that the brother who'd just walked into the place was the man I was after. I strolled across the street, took a look inside the window of the alehouse and watched as the old boy stood at the bar and ordered himself a drink. He knocked back a double scotch then quickly bought himself another. After he'd walked away towards the snug, I waited a moment then took myself back in the place, bought myself a pint of mild and supped at my pint for a few more minutes before joining Rita and her old medical acquaintance in the smaller room at the rear of the building. As I leant against the door jamb, Rita looked up at me and I motioned with my head that it was time for her to leave. Without a word, she did as she was told: got up then walked out, staring at her feet and with the five pounds I'd given her earlier burning a hole in her pocket.

I made my way over to join the old man and sat down on the bench seat next to him. He stank of stale booze and smoked-out cigars. The dark jowls of his heavily lined face were unshaven, his eyes bloodshot and watering. He looked like a washed-up corpse and gave off an unpleasant air of a man used to being around death. I gave him the onceover, then stared hard right into his face: one of those long, knowing looks I'd perfected while strong-arming a suspect when I'd been a cop back home on Bim.

"Is your name Fowler, Dr Theodore Fowler?"

"What's it to you who I am?" The old man went to get up. I grabbed hold of his elbow and dragged his ass back into his seat. I could feel him shaking through his overcoat. I kept hold of his arm to let him know I meant business.

"I'll only ask one more time befo' I start gittin' pissed at you." I burnt into him harder with my stare. "Is your name Fowler?"

"Yes . . . I'm Fowler," he stammered. "Who the hell are you?"

"Good, now we're gittin' somewhere. My name's Ellington."

"Well, what do you want with me, Mr Ellington? I'm a busy man; I don't have time for any foolish games."

"Oh, I ain't playin' no game here, doc, and from that knocked-fo'-six look on ya face I think you know why I'm here."

"I haven't the faintest idea what you are going on about, man. Let go of me or I'll have the landlord call the police."

"Go ahead. I'll even dial 'em for you myself. In an hour's time you'll be sunning yo'self in the pokey."

"Pokey? What are you talking about?"

"Theft's what I'm talkin' 'bout. A pile o' paperwork that didn't belong to you. Confidential stuff that the people you used to work for want back, and damn sharp too."

"Theft? Paperwork? I don't know what you are insinuating. This is all highly irregular." The quack looked down at his scotch, desperate to take a drink. I took hold of the bottom of the glass and slid it across the table out of his reach.

"Cut the 'innocent me' crap, will ya, doc, I'm here on behalf o' your previous employer to retrieve a bundle o' medical records: death certificates that for

58

some godforsaken reason you decided you wanted fo' yo'self."

The doc leaned towards me, suddenly getting bolshie. "Look, I never took a damn thing from out of that place. You've been sent on a bloody fool's errand. Is this some sort of joke?" Theodore Fowler was pushing his luck with me. I applied a little more pressure to his puny elbow and, as I did, realised I'd already broken my word to Rita Lee about not harming the old fellow.

"Do I look to you like I'm joking to you, doc? Now you pin back those well-educated, drunken old ears o' yours an' listen up, cos this is how it's gonna roll tonight. I've been retained to find both your thieving butt and to retrieve those death certificates you stole from the orphanage. Now from where I'm sitting I've completed half o' the task by locating your miserable hide; all I need is fo' you to cough up those documents and I can be outta ya hair forever."

"Didn't you hear what I said? I don't have any documents belonging to the orphanage." Fowler was getting shirty and I was getting hot under the collar.

"All I've heard from you up to now is a crock o' shit. You got more do-do coming outta your scruffy black mout' than a farmyard muck spreader. Look, we can do this the easy way or the hard way. Personally, I'd prefer it if you took the laid-back route."

I saw the quack's face soften a little, so I let up on the pressure on his arm a little and leant across the table and drew his glass of whisky back towards him.

He gingerly picked up his drink then gulped back the remainder in three short mouthfuls.

"What exactly do you want from me, Mr Ellington?" Fowler's shoulders slumped; defeated resignation appeared to take over him as he looked down into his empty glass.

"Just like I said: the death certificates are what I'm here for. Once I git 'em, there'll be no comeback on you, and to sweeten the deal I'm to offer you a heap o' money for their safe return."

"Money . . . How much money?"

"How's five hundred sheets sound to you?"

"Sounds like a lot. Whatever I'm accused of taking, they must want it back rather badly."

"That's just what I thought, doc, so what's it to be: you gonna play straight with me or am I gonna have to break your arm to get what I want outta you?"

"Five hundred, you say?" The old man was starting to see sense.

"On the button. Got it stashed in my inside pocket, right here." I partially pulled out the envelope and let Fowler see the edge of the cash. "Look, doc, I ain't here to roll ya. You give me what I want and you walk away, free as a bird."

"And if I get you what you're looking for, neither you nor Walter Wilkins will involve the police?"

"Nobody gonna be the wiser. We're talking serious money here, doc. That could buy you a lotta scotch, brother."

"I'm not interested in buying alcohol, Mr Ellington. The money could be useful to me, though."

60

I watched Fowler's face as he began to weigh up the pros and cons. "So, have we got us a deal?"

"Perhaps . . . If I could obtain what you are looking for, how do I know I can trust you?"

I took the envelope out of my inside pocket and quickly slung it onto Fowler's lap. "Here, that's how you know you can trust me. You hang on to it while we go get what I want. Go on, take it, skim your fingers through those notes and make sure it's all there, brother. I ain't here to stiff you. But I warn you, you think 'bout runnin' out on me with that dough, I'll break your legs from under ya feet befo' you have time to cook up a sweat. You understand me?"

"I understand, Mr Ellington. It looks like we have an understanding."

"Good. Now there's one more ting befo' we sign this off."

Fowler looked up at me as he was stuffing the envelope into his coat pocket." "Yes . . . What is it?"

"Tell me where I can find the truth."

CHAPTER
FIVE

"Truth . . . What damn truth?"

For a man with a complexion of pure jet, Dr Theodore Fowler's face had just turned a nasty pale colour right in front of me. My strange question had clearly knocked any healthy pigmentation right outta the old doc's bombed-out features. He sat staring back at me with an icy, panicked look of shock on his time-worn face. I watched as he licked at his dried-out lips then anxiously rubbed at them with the tips of his fingers. He looked down and covetously eyed up the drink that was sitting in front of me. His eyes darted back up to briefly look at me then shot back to my half-finished pint of mild.

"Go ahead, brother. You look like you need this more than I do." I leant forward and pushed the beer across the table towards him, his trembling hands instantly reaching out to snatch up the jug. He knocked the contents back in one swift chug then nervously returned his gaze back to me.

"So, come on, doc, tell me."

"Tell you what? What is it you want from me, Mr Ellington?" Fowler pleaded.

"Just like I said . . . the truth."

62

"You're not making any sense, man. Look, I told you that I'd get you the certificates, I thought we had a deal."

"We do, don't worry, that deal's still sweet, but befo' we get down to that, your old employer wanted me to ask you the truth question. She was very specific in the way I should ask you."

The doc looked cautiously around the room, and then whispered. "Who's 'she'?"

"Woman by the name o' Stephens, Ida Stephens. You know who I'm talkin' 'bout?

The doctor's breathing became heavier, his posture sunk, and his body dropped forward from out of his seat. He had the kind of pained look on his face that comes over a man when he needs more hooch.

"Yes . . . Yes, I know her."

"I'm gonna ask you again, just like Ida Stephens told me to ask you. Where can she find the truth?"

"The truth? That bitch is insane. I don't know what it is that she expects me to tell you."

"Do I have to squeeze this shit outta you? Doc, I can tell you're stalling me, man. Now quit while you can. The sooner you git out with it and tell me what I need to know, the sooner we both can git outta here, go pick up those papers and you can get on and drink your ass into oblivion."

"Please . . . Enough of this madness. I don't know what truth Ida Stephens is talking about, really I don't. Now, if you want the certificates I suggest we make a move." Fowler lifted himself up unsteadily out of his seat. I was about to heave him back when he dropped down next to me with a thud, looking like he'd just seen a ghost.

"Now what the hell's the matter with you? Jesus, doc, if you weren't such an old fart, I swear I'd clip up across the back o' ya nut fo' jerkin' me around like you doin'."

Fowler cowered at my side, looking like something had just gone and tore the very life force out of his soul. "Dear God above . . . We're both dead."

"Dead? What crap you talkin' 'bout now, man?"

"I'm talking about the devil incarnate, Mr Ellington, right here with us, standing at the bar in the very next room." The doc sank down even further and for a moment I thought he was about to go hide under the table. I grabbed his collar and pulled him up.

"Fowler, what the hell you on? You bin drinkin' too much o' your own surgical spirits, brother. Listen to what you sayin'. It don't make no sense. Now come on, what's this 'truth' that Ida Stephens needs to hear from you?"

"We need to leave now."

"Doc, we ain't going anywhere till we're finished."

"We will be finished, Mr Ellington, if you don't listen to what I'm saying. We have to go. We only have a few minutes. He won't be on his own, he never is."

"Say what? Who won't be on his own?"

"Paxton, his name is Paxton."

"And this man is the devil you just bin ramblin' on 'bout, yeah?"

"Yes . . . Look, Mr Ellington, I beg you, just get me out of here now, please. I'll tell you everything you need

64

to know once we're safe, but we must leave this very minute."

I stared at Fowler suspiciously for a moment. The fear in his eyes was as real as I'd seen in any man. Damning myself under my breath as I did, I slowly rose up out of my seat and caught sight of a muscular-looking guy standing with his back to me at the bar. I looked back down at the doc, angrily pointing my finger into his already terrified face.

"Man, I swear if I find out you bin jerkin' my chain 'bout all this, you gonna wish the devil was hangin' off your back instead o' havin' me in ya face again. Now, come on, shift your bony ass off that pew and follow me."

I held onto Doc Fowler's coat sleeve and dragged him behind me out of the snug towards the rear entrance of the pub. As I did, I snatched a fleeting glance towards a big white guy at the bar, who was now slowly heading towards us, his right hand moving towards the inside of his leather jacket. I yanked at the old man's arm to speed him up.

"We've been made . . . This way." I tightened my grip on Fowler's arm as we hurried down the small corridor and through the glass-etched door onto Church Lane. I kept moving along the dimly lit pavement and turned the corner out into the open road.

"Where are you taking me?" Fowler rasped at me breathlessly.

"Now ain't the time to be asking dumb questions, just get a sprint on, will ya? It looks like the devil on our coat-tail's packing some firepower. You got some real choice friends, doc."

Fowler dug his heels in, bringing me to a standstill in the street like some pig-headed mule that'd had enough of its toil. "He's no friend of mine. What did I tell you? It's the devil, he's come for me."

"Shut your mout', old man, and move it, or so help me I'll leave your sorry butt to Lucifer back there." I bullied him along, grabbing him by his collar and heaving him in front of me towards where I'd parked my car. I took the key out of my jacket pocket as we approached the Cortina, jabbed it quickly into the lock and got both my and the rear passenger door open for the sluggish doctor to get in. I looked back into the shadows towards Temple Church and in the distance could see the figure of a large man running towards us in the twilight with both arms stretched out in front of him, his hands appearing to be clasped together in prayer.

I grabbed hold of Fowler by the shoulder of his coat and pushed him towards the back seat, and as I did I saw in the encroaching blackness the briefest muzzle flash erupt into the dimness and heard the telltale *phut, phut* sound of a silenced pistol recoiling softly in my ears. I heard Fowler scream out in agony as I jumped into the Cortina and frantically stuffed the key into the ignition, turning it clockwise and pumping my foot down onto the accelerator pedal, knocking some gas into the engine. As it roared into life, I quickly looked into my rear-view mirror and could just pick out the white face of the fast-moving gunman, who was now only a few yards away, off the rear bumper. I saw him take aim as I stuck the car into reverse and hammered full-pelt backwards at him. The boot of my car made contact with something hefty. I slammed on the brakes and shifted the gear lever into first then sped forward out of the secluded back road into Victoria Street. I put my foot down and started to head east out of the city. I looked back into my mirror to see if I was being followed but could see nothing coming up behind me. Nor could I see Doc Fowler.

"Fowler, you OK back there?" I kept staring into the mirror, trying to pick him out in the pitch-black. "Fowler, speak to me, brother, you OK?" It was a relief when I finally saw the doctor's head come into view as he strained to pick himself up from the footwell in the back seat.

"The devil has his claws in me, Mr Ellington." Fowler coughed heavily and I felt his warm spittle hit the back of my neck.

"Quit the gospel sermon will ya, doc? Start talkin' sense instead o' that mumbo jumbo you been selling me fo' the last half-hour. Now, tell me, who was the cat firing at us with the cannon back there?"

I watched in surprise as Fowler leant forward in his seat and reached over towards me, plastering the side of his right hand down across my cheek. My face felt wet as he slumped back in his seat. I wiped my cheek and jaw with my hand and, as I did, the smell of uncooked liver wafted up my nostrils.

"What the fuck is that you smearin' all over me?"

"I'm afraid it's my blood, Mr Ellington."

"Your blood? You cut yo'self or someting?"

Fowler's breathing was more laboured. I switched on the interior light so I could get a better look at him.

"One of Paxton's bullets found its mark."

"Aw shit, doc! You better not be bleedin' over that leatherwork back there." I took my foot off the gas, slowing down and looking for a place to pull over.

"No! Don't stop . . . Just do as I say . . . Get us out of the city, head out towards Hillfields. Do you know Speedwell?"

"Yeah, I know it." I put my foot back down on the accelerator and did as Fowler asked.

The doc spoke in a low, calm voice. "Now, listen to me, Mr Ellington . . . Don't interrupt . . . We don't have much time. You need to make your way over to the swimming baths on Whitefield Road. When you get there, you'll need these keys." Fowler hauled a large ring of keys out of his pocket. "I'm leaving them on the back seat for you here, along with the envelope of money you gave me earlier."

"Hey, man, that's your money. It's like I said, I don't welch on a dea —"

Fowler cut into what I was saying, coughing savagely. "I told you, shut up and listen . . . Where I'm going, I ain't gonna be needing money, son . . . When you reach the baths, climb over the wall and take the service entrance at the back of the place. These keys will get you in. You need to follow the stairs down into boiler rooms underneath the pool. Just keep going until you reach a storeroom right at the back. The tiny skeleton key will open it up; inside, you need to search carefully

68

because I've hidden the certificates that you want well. You'll find what you are looking for inside there, and when you do, Mr Ellington, you'll understand. Some real cruel people want what I've hidden and there'll be more men like Paxton coming to get it. Do you understand?"

"Yeah, I think so. Look, man, I need to git you to a hospital now. I'll go pick up the damn certificates later, let's git you sorted —"

"No, it's too late for me, just do as I say ... Speedwell baths, now. Can't this thing go any faster, damn you?"

I pushed my foot down on the accelerator and watched as the dial on the speedometer raced up past sixty-five miles an hour then turned my head quickly to check on the doc. As I did, he spoke to me, his voice faint and quavering.

"When you see Ida Stephens again, tell her I said that I'll see her in hell."

I turned to get my eyes back on the road, and as I did I heard the blistering scream of the wind tear through the interior of the car as the rear door was flung wide open. I hit the brakes: the piercing sound of rubber screaming to a halt on the tarmac filled my ears. I watched in the rear-view mirror as the flailing, frail body of Theodore Fowler was violently thrown down the middle of the road behind me, his ragged, battered corpse finally coming to a bone-shattering halt in the gutter on the other side of the street.

CHAPTER
SIX

I got outta my car and ran across the road to where Doc Fowler was lying. Under the orange glow of a street lamp, I stood and stared down at the shattered remains of the old man, which were huddled up against the kerbside. He was a real mess. His battered face was covered in sticky blood, which poured out of a massive wound from above his right temple. Both of his frail arms had been dragged back behind him with the force of the impact. The cloth from his left trouser leg had been torn completely off at the knee and the shinbone below it had split and was poking out of the calf muscle at a right angle. I crouched down and got close to the doc's head, my ear close against his mouth, in the hope he might still be breathing. All I could hear was a deathly silence. I raised my head and put two fingers under Fowler's chin to check for a pulse, but the only thing I could feel was the warmth of more fresh blood, which was now seeping into a pool in front of where I was knelt.

I lifted myself up off the tarmac and scoured the length of the road for a telephone box so I could call for an ambulance, but there was none to be seen. My heart felt like it was pounding out of my chest. My jumbled brain struggled to think through the carnage I had just witnessed. As I desperately tried to fathom out what to do next, Doc Fowler's prophetic words sprang back into my head, words that he had spoken just before he had thrown himself out into the street: *Where I'm going, I ain't gonna be needing money, son.* I looked at my watch: it was just after nine fifteen. The roads were empty of cars and not a soul was out on the streets. I gazed back down at the body at my feet. Fowler's earlier words rang out at me again: *Some real cruel people want what I've hidden and there'll be more men like Paxton coming to get it. Do you understand?* The sound from my car exhaust chugging away brought me back to my senses. I looked across the road towards the reddish glare of the rear brake lights and followed the hazy beam a few yards back up the road. I could just pick out the faint outline of something lying on the darkened asphalt. It was one of Theodore Fowler's shoes, which had been ripped off as he was thrown from the vehicle and was now in the middle of the road. I walked across and picked it up then returned to where the doctor lay, bent down and placed the scuffed old shoe back onto his cold foot.

With an indescribable feeling of malevolence clinging to my insides, I returned to my car, retrieved the envelope containing Fowler's money and the set of keys he'd given to me, and tossed them both onto the passenger seat before I got in. As I drove away I stared straight ahead of me, not returning my eyes to the rear-view mirror to again witness the horrific scene I was leaving behind me, fearful that I would glimpse the vile aura of some demonic entity as it wrenched Fowler's screaming soul down into a fiery underworld for all eternity.

The sign read Poplar Road as I pulled into the dimly lit side street next to Speedwell swimming baths. I took a torch out of the glovebox, stuck the envelope full of cash into my inside pocket, picked up the keys from off the seat next to me then got out of the car and walked round to the boot. I opened it up and took out a tyre iron and looped it through the belt of my trousers. The air was still and humid, the clear night sky moonless and star-filled as I made my way back on to Whitefield Road and walked the short distance to the baths. I headed to the rear of the building until I found the wall Fowler had told me about. I clambered over and switched on my torch, scanning the shaft of light in the dark in front of me until I could pick out the doorway I was looking for. I fished for the keys in my coat pocket and shone the flashlight on them until I found the skeleton key.

Getting into the place wasn't a problem; in fact, everything up to now had been a walk in the park, and that had me on edge. I closed the door behind me quietly and let my eyes adjust to the darkened surroundings of the strange and silent building. The heady aroma of chlorine from the pool water hit me as I edged my way further inside. I used the torch's thin stream to scan the walls and floor. Even if I found a block of switches to fire up the overhead lighting, I knew that doing so could arouse suspicion from passers-by outside and I couldn't risk getting hauled in by the police for breaking and entering after the kind of night I'd had. The idea of explaining to the old bill why I was wandering around the corridors of a swimming pool during the hours of darkness with a pocket full o' cash and my hands covered in the blood of a dead man I'd left back on a Bristol roadside hardly filled me with joy. I'd have to find the entrance to the boiler room the best I could in the dark.

I continued along the unlit passageway until I came to a staircase. I shot the torchlight along the remainder of each side of the corridor but couldn't pick out any other stairs, so I guessed this was the one Fowler had said I should take to reach the storeroom. I put the palm of my left hand out onto the warm wall; my fingers splayed out and ran it up and down until I felt a wooden handrail. I grasped hold of it then shone my flashlight at my feet to pick out the first set of steps in front of me. I carefully made my way down into the belly of the building, and as I went further into the unknown, the air around me became clammier. I counted each step as I descended into the depths: twenty-four over three flights of stairs. I finally reached flat ground again and moved the beam of my light around me. I picked out a door in the blackness and carefully headed the four odd feet from the foot of the stairs towards it. I found a handle midway down, turned it and opened up the door; as I did, the full force of the overwhelmingly steamy heat from the boiler room hit me.

Inside, I felt around on the wall at my right-hand side and found a bank of light switches. I quickly knocked each one of them on and had to quickly snap my eyes shut from the intense glare for a moment. I squinted until my sight adjusted and I was able to see straight again. The sweltering room was lit with the severe brightness of the seven or eight high-wattage bulbs which were hanging from a series of shortened roses on the low ceiling above me. The pungent chemical hum of the water-purifying solution had travelled down the stairwell and wafted its unpleasant, choking fragrance around me. I took a look around me: the room was a good forty feet long and there were six large boilers gently warming up the pool above me — not only were they kicking out a hell of a lot of heat but they made a hefty racket too. Heavy pipework ran up the walls, and above my head each tank hissed and belched compressed hot air and gurgled noisily as if they were about to erupt at their seams with jets of boiling water.

I continued to walk towards the end wall in search of the storeroom where Fowler had told me he'd hidden the certificates. When I reached the end of the underground chamber all I found was a row of green-painted industrial metal shelving. It was around eight feet long, and apart from a few boxes of tools and a couple of stacks of grubby, yellow-edged copies of the *Bristol Evening Post* on its midsection, all the shelves were surprisingly empty. The wall behind was masked by a sheet-metal back that was pot-riveted to the rear of the shelves' long frame. I stood at its end and switched on my torch again to see if it was attached to the brickwork. It wasn't.

I grabbed at the frame, dragged it away from the wall and shone the torch in. I held the beam on the midsection of the wall, my light picking out a small wood-panelled door, perhaps no more than two or three feet wide by five high. I yanked at the frame again, pulling it further across the floor, then got on my haunches and shuffled along to the doorway. Halfway up its right-hand side was a looped iron handle. A large brass padlock was fitted above it, holding it firmly shut. I pulled out Fowler's loop of keys from my coat pocket and searched through them, trying each one for size in the padlock until it finally released. Rather than pull out towards me, the door opened inwards. I clicked my torch back on again then gingerly pushed open the door and shone the light in.

The stink was the first thing that hit me; the rancid odour of stale urine that filled the place made me gag. To my surprise, the room was already dimly lit from the floor up by a series of candles, each one at different stages of burning. Wax had spread out and hardened on the red-brick floor.

I crawled in and tried to take in what I was seeing. This was no storeroom for damn sure. It had the eerie feel of a mausoleum and was certainly the right kind of place for Doc Fowler to be keeping his darkest secrets in. It was cramped, damp and unbearably hot; I felt like I was in a rabbit's warren. At its best it was no more than eight feet high by ten wide, and looked like it ran another fifteen feet towards its back wall, which I could barely make out in all the gloominess.

Across the centre of the tiny chamber stood what looked like a decorator's table, which had been covered with a long length of hessian cloth that reached down to the floor, obscuring anything that might be behind it. On my hands and knees, with my torch gripped in my right hand, I made my way towards the end of the table. As I grew closer I heard the scuttering sound of a rat as it retreated into the darkness. I shone the torch out towards the rear of the room and could see laid on the ground a small, beat-up mattress. At the foot of it was a crumpled mess of tatty sheets. I crawled over to the makeshift bed, checking up and down the sides of the walls with the torch's beam. At the top of the mattress lay a ragged pillow. I felt at its indented centre with the flat of my left hand: it was still warm.

As I squatted on my haunches, trying to fathom out what the hell was going on, I heard a faint rustling sound coming from behind me. I turned and shot the flashlight's fading beam along the length of the cloth-covered table and began to quietly move closer towards it, listening carefully for the noise again. I took hold of the edge of the hessian covering and yanked it sideways away from me. I swiftly ran my light inside the small recess but could see nothing. I was about to return my attention to the bed behind me when my rapid strafing of the dusky air caught the flickering of something white in the furthest inner nook of the table, close to its back leg. I desperately tried to make out what it could be that I'd briefly caught sight of. I inched in closer, stuck my head under the table and pointed my light into the darkness.

Staring back at me were the unblinking, petrified eyes of a child, a little girl no more than eight or nine years of age. She continued to glare back at me as I fell back on my ass in shock. The girl had drawn her legs up tight towards her chest, her delicate arms wrapped around them as if she was shielding herself from some kind of unspeakable evil. Her head was tucked on top of her scuffed knees, and her matted hair fell around her shoulders, partially covering her face. I ran the beam of my torch along the length of her motionless body and finally allowed the beam to settle at her feet. I moved slowly towards her, and as I did, the girl edged further back away from me, making the table above us judder noisily. I pulled back away from the scared little thing and held the flat of my hand against my chest, as if to offer up an assurance that I meant her no harm.

I was astonished by what I was looking at: a kid, filthy and alone, down here in the dark. Why the hell would Fowler want to stash a child away in these terrible conditions? None of it made any sense. I knew there was no way I was going to walk away and leave her to rot in what was nothing more than an over-heated prison cell, I just didn't know how I was going to go about getting her to trust me. My mouth was dry, and when I tried to speak, the words I wanted to say caught in my throat. The two of us sat there in silence for a moment, and when I finally spoke my voice felt as if it belonged to another person.

"Hey there, how you doin'? I ain't gonna hurt you none. I'm here to help you. Do you know a man, he got my skin colour, calls himself Dr Fowler?"

I shone the beam of the torch up towards the child's face but not directly into it. I watched as she fearfully stared back at me. I smiled and gently repeated my question back at her.

"Do you know who I mean? Dr Theodore Fowler?"

The child continued to stare directly at me, and then she nodded her head ever so slightly, never taking her eyes off me for a moment.

"Well, that's good, cos Dr Fowler, he asked me to come an' get you. Take you to a place where you are gonna be safe . . ."

The girl continued to glare at me, unsure of my intentions, perhaps weighing up in her head if I was a bogeyman in the same way that Fowler might have been. I cleared my throat before speaking again.

"Look, I know you're real scared of me, but I give you my word that I'm not here to frighten or do you any harm, child. I'm one of the good guys . . . I promise." I put my hand out towards her by way of a friendly greeting. "My name's Joseph . . . but my friends call me JT. Tell me, little ting, what's your name?"

The girl remained silent. I lowered my head towards the floor and closed my eyes as I tried to think what to do next. I could hear the child's heavy breathing ringing through my ears as a tangible sense of her distress filled the small room. A strong feeling of inexpressible and irrational shame came over me, and in my head I thought I could hear the voice of my own deceased daughter, Amelia, calling out to me. As I opened my eyes to face the girl again, the hushed

78

whisper of five short, simple words sang back at me from out of the darkness.

"Truth . . . My name is Truth."

CHAPTER
SEVEN

The sweat was pouring from my scalp and ran in thick droplets down my face and neck, soaking into the collar of my shirt as I sat in the flickering candlelight with the girl called Truth in her sweltering and oppressive dungeon. As my eyes became more accustomed to the dark surroundings I began to see the telltale signs of just how the young child had been surviving down there in the dark. I ran the beam of my torch around the area behind me, picking out some of the things that Fowler had left the little girl with. Close to the top of the mattress a large Dewar's whisky jug that was half filled with lukewarm water. A rusted-up Jacob's cracker tin filled to the brim with arrowroot biscuits, some unopened tins of Heinz lentil soup and Fray Bentos corned beef were stacked against the back wall along with a half-dozen bags of Smith's crisps and a brown bag filled with what looked like apples.

At the foot of her rough-and-ready bed were some old folded-up woollen blankets. A dirty light-green plastic plate and bowl sat on top of them and a solitary spoon poked out from the centre of the tired-looking dish. Beside the blankets was a box of matches and some fresh candles and a large metal blue-and-white

Johnson's first-aid kit. I opened it up and found it filled with plasters, bandages, ointments and a small Eveready torch. Tucked underneath the medical supplies was a folded brown envelope. I lifted it out and quickly leafed through the contents. Inside were a dozen or so death certificates and some passport-sized black-and-white photographs. I closed up the tin, stuffed the envelope into my inside jacket pocket then continued with my recce around the place.

On the left-hand side of the room I caught sight of a crude toilet that had been hastily set up for the youngster. The large galvanised bucket was sat in a murky corner of the basement cell and reeked of the putrid stench of piss and shit. A single roll of lavatory paper sat in the dust and dirt at the base of the bucket.

As I was nosing through the kid's paltry belongings, Truth remained silent. I grabbed a couple of the candles and the box of matches and lit the two wicks then dripped five or six drops of wax onto the floor in front of me and sealed the candles to the floor, to give us a little more light. I turned back to face my reluctant young host and smiled at her.

"You got yo'self quite a collection o' stuff back there. Did Dr Fowler bring all these tings here for you?"

Truth nodded slowly a couple of times.

"Well, it looks to me like you got yo'self a real cool den going on down here. Did Dr Fowler bring you here, sweetheart?"

Another slow nod.

"And does anybody else ever come down here to see you, other than Dr Fowler?"

This time I got a slow shake of her little head.

"Why'd Dr Fowler bring you down here, Truth?"

Nothing this time. No nod or shake of the head in reply. I tried a different tack.

"Can you tell me where you lived befo' you came here with Dr Fowler? Where's your mother and father, Truth?" I looked down at the dancing flame of the candle in front of my feet then glanced back quickly at the girl, who was watching the taper hypnotically quiver and curl. When Truth spoke again, it caught me by surprise.

"Theo . . . I called him Theo, not Dr Fowler . . . Where is Theo?"

"He's real busy tonight, lookin' after somebody who's awful sick. He asked me to come down and check in on you, see if you were doing OK," I lied. "Tell me, was Theo your family doctor?"

Another shake of her head, only this time more determined. "Theo was my new friend."

"Your friend . . . Why would a friend want you to stay down here, all alone in the dark?"

"To stay safe." Her retort was as quick as it was surprising.

"Safe? Safe from what?"

"From the bad men. The ones who come in the night to take us away."

"Take you away from where, Truth?"

"From the home."

"Your home? Why would bad men want to come to take you from your home, little one?"

82

"No, not from my home . . . I haven't got a home. I'm from the Walter Wilkins."

"The orphanage? You lived at the Walter Wilkins orphanage?"

"I did, but I don't any more . . . I live here now."

"And Theo brought you here to keep you safe from those bad men you been tellin' me 'bout, did he?"

Silence again, just another slow nod of passive validation.

"Truth, Dr Fowler . . . I mean Theo, he's asked me to tell you that he wants you to come with me, back to a nicer place, one that's gonna be a lot better than it is down here right now."

The little girl shot further back into her hideaway and began to get agitated.

"No! I ain't going nowhere with you. He said there's a special time I'm going to be leaving. I'm stopping here and waiting for him."

"Honey, you can't stay here no more. It ain't safe for you. Theo, he told me so, told me to tell you that now is the special time. He said you had to come with me so I could keep you safe from those bad men that have got you so scared. He didn't want you hiding down here no more."

"Go away . . . You're a fibber! Theo never told me about you. He said it was our secret den. No one else was to know."

"Maybe he just forgot to tell you 'bout me. Old people do that, they forget. Listen, if I ain't telling you the truth 'bout Theo wantin' you to come with me now, then how'd you think I knew where to come lookin' for you, hey? It was because Theo told me exactly where to find you, that's why."

I held out my arm towards her, my hand palm up, reaching into the dark. I kept my huge mitt hanging in mid-air there for what seemed like an eternity, and when her tiny fingers finally clasped hold of the tips of my own, I could feel the rest of her little body shaking. I slowly drew her closer from underneath the table, and as I did she stopped in her tracks and spoke to me again, her voice broken and wavering in the soft light.

"Joseph . . . You're not one of those bad men, are you?"

"No . . . No, Truth, I ain't."

I felt the child's hand instinctively squeeze my own as she moved towards me. I'd never been more grateful for the darkness that surrounded us, my tears thankfully obscured by a welcome veil of shade and shadows.

CHAPTER
EIGHT

I carried the frightened little girl out of her makeshift hideaway from underneath the swimming baths and back to my car. Inside, I found a small pool of Fowler's blood that had run onto the upholstery. I quickly mopped it up with a rag then drove out of Speedwell back to St Pauls with Truth wrapped up in a blanket on the back seat. Unsurprisingly, she'd looked scared stiff as I'd navigated my way carefully back along the roads in an attempt to keep out of the suspicious sights of parked-up panda cars or patrolling bobbies on their late-night beats. By the time I'd reached what I considered to be the safety of my home turf, it was just after eleven thirty. I parked my car at the rear of a row of tenement houses next to a couple of secluded garages on Backfields Lane. I opened the rear door of the car and scooped up Truth in my arms from the back seat. I pulled the blanket up over her head and smiled down at her as she stared into my face.

"Where are we going, Joseph?" she asked quietly.

"To a place you're gonna be safe at, that's where. I'm gonna git you some fine food in that belly o' yours, a hot bath and a warm, clean bed for you to sleep in. It's a place you're gonna be safe."

I carried Truth the short distance into Brunswick Street and headed for the end red-brick basement flat that Carnell Harris' widow, Loretta, rented. I looked at her curtained windows to see if she would still be up. There were no lights on; it didn't look good. I took a deep breath, kicked open the waist-high crimson gate with the toe of my shoe then walked up to the front door and rapped on the glass panel in the centre of it. I gave it a while then knocked again but got no answer. By now the child was getting heavy in my arms, and I impatiently hammered at Loretta's door again, only this time a lot louder than previously. A single unshaded bulb lit up the darkened hallway and I saw the pissed-off outline of my none-too-pleased friend approaching. I swallowed hard and waited for the verbal onslaught to begin as I listened to her aggressively unlock the door.

"Who's that knockin' at my fuckin' gate do' at this time o' night? Muthafucka, you better have fuckin' good reasons to be gittin' me outta my bed . . ."

Loretta tore the door wide open, her tongue ready to erupt with a further assault of foul-mouthed obscenities.

"Joseph! What the hell you playin' at, fool, disturbin' me while I'm tryin' to git some damn sleep? I swear, if you've gone an' woke up Carnell Jr, I'm gonna rip your spine outta your ass, you hear me? Damn near took me the best part of t'ree hours to git that little bastard to go down earlier. The last ting I need tonight is that pickney's mout' hanging off one o' my titties till the fuckin' cock starts crowing."

Loretta cut herself off mid rant and stared at the bundle I was holding in my arms.

"What in Christ's name have you got stashed under that dirty old rag?"

I pulled the blanket away from Truth's face for my friend to see what was underneath and began my apologies. "Loretta, I'm real sorry 'bout this —"

"Oh shit . . . Don't you gimme any o' your 'sorry' shit, Joseph, just git you ass in off the street. What the hell you got some honky kid with you for?"

"It's a long story . . ."

"Ain't it always with you, Joseph?"

"Look, I need a place to stay for the night."

"What the hell's wrong with your joint? Take her back there." My friend took a step back, her hand on her hips, eyeing me up and slowly shaking her head disapprovingly.

"I would if I could . . . but it ain't the best place fo' me to be tonight. Trust me. I've gone got myself into some nasty trouble."

"Again! You know, trouble, it follows you round like you is hitched to it, fool."

Loretta stared me down, gave a deep sigh then cursed under her breath. She looked back at the child in my arms then laughed to herself and pointed at the blanket with her slender finger.

"That poor ting looks scared half to death, what the hell you bin doing to git her in that state? Shit . . . You best bring her on down into my sittin' room."

I followed Loretta into the front room. She switched on the light and I laid Truth onto the settee. I knelt down next to her and slipped a cushion under the little girl's head and smiled. I glanced across the room over to the framed photograph of my late friend Carnell that was sat on the mantle above the fireplace, then turned back to his widow, who was waiting for some kind of explanation as to why I'd got her out of her bed at such an ungodly hour.

"Loretta, this here is Truth."

"Trute? What damn kinda crazy-assed name is Trute?"

"Shhh! Will you go easy?"

I turned back to Truth and tucked the blanket tight around the back of her body. "Now, you just rest back there for a minute. Aunt Loretta and me, we're just going into the kitchen. You want some hot cocoa?" The little one nodded back at me. "OK, cocoa it is. We'll be back in just a minute."

I got up, took hold of Loretta's hand and led her out of her sitting room. When we got into the hallway, she snatched her hand out of mine and jabbed her crimson manicured digit into my face.

"Who the fuck you callin' Aunt Loretta? Do I look like some coloured jazzed-up version o' Beatrix Potter to you, hey? Aunt Loretta my ass. JT, you is full o' shit, you know that, don't you? Now, move your ugly butt outta my way if you wants me to make that fuckin' cocoa for ya."

I walked on ahead of her, flicked on the light switch next to the kitchen door then let Loretta seethe on by me as I stood with my back to the pantry door. I watched as she filled the kettle with fresh water at the sink then lit the front hob on the gas cooker and put the pot on the flaming blue ring. She leant over to the kitchen cupboard at the side of the sink and pulled out a small ceramic mug and two glasses then aggressively dropped them on the blue Formica-topped kitchen table. I pulled out a chair from under it and sat down as Loretta walked behind me back to the pantry. When she returned she had a jar of Bournvita in one hand and a bottle of Mount Gay rum in the other.

"You best pour each o' us a shot of that hooch. Sure looks like you need it."

She sat down next to me while I filled our glasses. I pushed the thimble of rum over to Loretta and raised my glass to her before knocking back the dark spirit in one gulp. I poured myself a refill then sank back in my chair, rubbing out a pain in my left temple with the tips of my fingers while my friend stared at me with a troubled look on her face.

"So come on, let's hear it, what kinda trouble you gone an' got yo'self into this time?"

"The worst kind, baby. The kinda trouble that has me with my back against the wall. You know a doctor by the name o' Theodore Fowler?"

Loretta tilted her head back and gave a wry grin. "You talkin' 'bout Theo the flusher? Cos I do, any woman round here who's got herself knocked up and don't want what she's got in her guts knows 'bout ole man Fowler. What you wantin' that ole fucker for anyways? If you thinking o' giving him a call to git rid o' that pickney you got crashed out on my sofa back there, I'd say you gone and left it 'bout eight years too late."

"Well, there ain't no way he's gonna be taking any phone calls after tonight."

"Why, what's wrong with the man?" Loretta was mildly intrigued.

"He's dead, that's what's wrong with him. Fool, t'rew himself outta the back o' the Cortina as I was racin' on my way to Speedwell."

"Dead! Oh that's sweet, Joseph, just sweet. There, you just got yo'self another damn stiff that you can rack up for your collection."

"Will you just git off your high horse and let me finish?"

"Let you finish?" Loretta snapped back at me. "What in the name o' God were you doin' with that scabby ole quack on the back seat o' your motor?" I tried to speak but was quickly interrupted by my friend's angry interrogation. "What the hell have you gone an' got mixed up in now, Mr Detective? You bin pokin' your nose round in other people's shady bidness again? Come on, I'm all ears, tell me. Why'd Fowler decide to sling his greasy ass out into the road? Didn't like the way you drive? What, the prick was struck dumb or someting? Couldn't be bothered to ax you to slam on the fuckin' breaks so he could just git outta the car?"

I snapped back, "If you'd just shut ya damn mout' fo' one minute, I can explain everything."

Loretta, instead of firing back at me, looked dumbstruck at the way I'd just yelled at her. I got my friend to drink up her rum then I poured each of us another measure into our thimble glasses. While she stayed silent and drank her booze, I enlightened her on all the facts about how Ida Stephens, administrator of the Walter Wilkins, had visited me at my office and how she had retained me with a wad of cash to locate Fowler and the death certificates, then I told her about Vic's involvement and finally the shooting of the doc outside the King's Head pub earlier that evening.

"Why'd anybody wanna take a potshot at Fowler? He was just some drunken GP with a reputation for sinkin' his hand down the drawers o' whores. You really tink whoever it was shot him did it cos he'd snatched some poor child from outta that orphanage? They seems like pretty desperate measures to me."

"I don't know what to think, Loretta."

"You don't know . . . Then what the hell do you know, JT? What 'bout this bitch Stephens axin' you to find that girl Trute you got back there, surely that's got someting to do with all this mayhem?"

"It could be, but Stephens didn't ask me to find her. All she wanted me to ask Fowler was where she could find the truth, not to go lookin' fo' no girl. Look, she was prepared to pay me a heap o' dough. Why should I give a crap what she wanted me to ask him? I thought it was just some crazy riddle and paid no mind to it. I had no idea it was gonna turn out to be the name o' some kid."

"The name o' some white kid, Joseph. And for a black man round these parts that really does spell trouble. Looks to me like you gone an' got the word 'patsy' stamped on that damn fool forehead o' yours.

91

You bin lined up to do some honky's dirty work and now they want you to take the fall for all the shit you just gone an' trod round the streets this past twelve hours. You ain't gonna wanna hear this, JT, but you needs to go to the police."

"Oh no . . . No way, Loretta. I ain't having no bidness with the law until I know what the hell is going on here. Just look what happened the last time I walked into a police station. They had my ass in a jail cell quicker than shit t'ru a goose . . . It ain't happening to me again, that's damn straight."

On the stove the kettle began to boil. Loretta took a another sip of her rum, picked up the Bournvita jar then got up to go and make the hot drink. I listened as Loretta carefully poured hot water into the mug then spooned in the chocolatey powder and stirred it. She dropped the spoon onto the metal draining board then rested the steaming drink on the table in front of me.

"Thanks, Loretta, you're a diamond." I took hold of Loretta's hand and kissed the back of it. As I did, I felt her arm go stiff and she slowly drew away from me.

"We got ourselves a sleepy visitor looking for her cocoa, Joseph."

I turned in my seat and found Truth standing in her bare feet in the kitchen doorway. It was the first time I'd seen her standing fully upright. She wore a pair of blue denim dungarees and a filthy white T-shirt. She was around four feet tall, her skin pale and creamy. Her true complexion could barely be seen through all the dirt that was encrusted upon her face, arms and legs. Her long blonde hair was matted and hung across her slender shoulders. She stared back at me with the deepest blue eyes I'd ever seen. I opened up my arms and gestured for her to come over to me.

"Hey there, Truth . . . I'm sorry, little one. Me and Aunt Loretta, we just been chewing the fat some. Here's that hot chocolate we promised you." I pulled up one of the kitchen chairs and tapped at the seat for her to come and sit next to me. Truth slowly wandered over and sat down. I picked up the mug and offered it to her. "Here, be careful now, it's hot." Truth took the mug of cocoa in both hands and slurped her first mouthful noisily.

Loretta looked at me gravely. "I'm gonna go run that child a hot bath, git her cleaned up. You make sure she drinks that cocoa, you hear me." As she walked out of the kitchen, leaving me with my new ward, she called back to me. "I hope that bastard Fowler rots in hell!"

It was the second time that evening that I'd envisaged the mysterious doctor languishing in the fiery netherworld my good friend had just condemned him to. Although I said nothing in reply to her damning remark, something inside told me that she was wrong and that Theodore Fowler's soul did not deserve to be doomed to Hades for his sins and earthly indiscretions.

CHAPTER
NINE

It was just after ten the next morning when I caught my first glimpse of the Walter Wilkins orphanage. I was in a foul mood and looking for answers from the children's home administrator, Ida Stephens. Past experience had taught me not to be hanging about on the end of some damn phone if you wanted the truth. The questions I wanted to ask Stephens were the kind that required me to get a look into her eyes when she gave up the answers. I drove through the ornate black wrought-iron gates and up the gravel drive towards a grey building with darkened windows that no one in their right mind could have considered calling a warm and welcoming home for children. I parked the Cortina up outside of the main doors and briefly peered out of the passenger-side window at the foreboding and austere entrance before getting out and walking up the stone steps to yank on the doorbell pull. As I reached for the cord, a bitter-looking middle-aged white woman dressed in a blue nurse's uniform with white piping on its collar and cuffs opened up and stared down her nose suspiciously at me.

"Yes, can I help you?" She spat the question out at me with a crusty air of inconvenience in her voice.

"I'm here to speak to Ida Stephens." I deliberately forgot my manners. I could tell from the off that any pleases and thank yous on my part weren't going to ingratiate me to this old goat.

"Do you have a prior appointment with Mrs Stephens, Mister . . . ?"

"Ellington, Joseph Ellington . . . and no, I don't have any prior appointment."

"Well, Mr Ellington." The ogre in blue stared at me with disdain before continuing with her speech. "Mrs Stephens is a very busy woman; it's normal practice to arrange an appointment with a member of our directorial body before attending the orphanage. I don't know what you're selling but Mrs Stephens won't be buying anything from you. We don't take in doorstep callers, I'm afraid." She went to slam the door in my face, but I stuck my foot out hard at its base, preventing her from closing up, and barged on in past her.

"Good, cos I ain't selling anyting."

The look on the tyrant gatekeeper's face was a mixture of incredulity and disgust. I kept on walking right past her into the whitewashed, clinical-looking lobby. A large oak-banistered staircase stood square in the centre of the foyer. I took a look around: something was mighty wrong with the place. There were no interior doors I could see, no pictures on the walls, and for a place that was supposed to be filled to the brim with unwanted kids, there was not a child's voice to be heard. I'd been in the place less than twenty seconds and it was already giving me the creeps. The ogre was soon on my tail and grabbed at my elbow to try and prevent me from walking towards the stairs.

"Where do you think you're going? How dare you. You just can't come swanning in as you please, this is a private establishment. I'm calling the police."

I stopped and looked her square in the eye. "Lady, you go ahead an' make the call. You're the second fool to say the same ting to me in the last twenty-four hours: they ended up dead in a gutter. Now, while you're on the phone to the law, tell me where I can find your boss Stephens?"

"You can find me here, Mr Ellington." The administrator's brittle voice cut through the air like a knife with a curse dripping off its edge. She glared down at me with a face like thunder, her thin arms leaning against the wooden balustrade like a prizefighter about to push himself back out into the ring. "I thought I told you to telephone me when you had news of your progress. What's the meaning of this ill-mannered intrusion?"

"What I gotta say to you ain't fo' no phone call. I need to speak to you face to face and in private."

Stephens looked across towards the ogre, who was still clinging on to my arm for dear life, and her voice softened a little as she motioned with her hand for her to let go. "It's all right, I'll deal with this, Sister McNeil. Would you please bring Mr Ellington up and show him to my office."

I was led up the stairs in silence and shown into a high-ceilinged office. Ida Stephens stood with her back towards us, looking out of a large bay window; she turned her head briefly as a cursory acknowledgement that we'd arrived then nodded over to Sister McNeil to leave us. The ogre turned swiftly on her heels like a Nazi storm trooper and then marched out, closing the door behind me. The administrator stayed put, not turning to address me when she barked her next question at me.

"So, you've forced your way in here. Now, what is it you have to tell me in person?" Stephens was blunt and to the point with me; I saw no reason to address her any differently.

"That wild-goose chase you sent me on, searching for your Dr Fowler, has stirred up a whole hornets' nest o' trouble. I'm here to settle up with you. Get some damage limitation behind me."

I watched as she remained motionless, as if glued to the spot. She stayed like that as she chipped in her next blunt enquiry to me.

"By trouble . . . do you mean that you've been unable to locate the doctor?"

"Oh no, I found him all right. That was the easy bit. I met him in a local public house last night. When he turned up he had the shakes like he was possessed and managed to knock back a glass o' whisky and sink back my half-pint o' mild befo' he coughed up a load of gibberish 'bout being a dead man."

"Like I said to you previously, Mr Ellington, Fowler is a charlatan; nothing he says should be trusted. You said you've come to settle up. Did the doctor tell you of the whereabouts of the stolen death certificates. Were you able to retrieve them?"

"Oh sure, I got your precious certificates." I walked across to Stephens' desk and threw the brown envelope containing the documents I had found at Speedwell baths down onto the green baize top.

That got her attention. She turned to face me, walked back to her place of power, pulled out her chair and sat down. She didn't ask me to take a seat. She was happy for me to stand in front of her like her subordinate. I went along with her game; it wasn't like I hadn't played it before. Stephens withdrew the paperwork from the envelope and leafed through each certificate carefully.

"Your man Fowler may not have been trustworthy, but he was right 'bout one ting."

Stephens looked up at me from behind her desk.

"And what was that?"

"Well, he was sure as hell right 'bout being a dead man. In the time it took me to get him to part with those papers, he'd managed to sink another half bottle of scotch then chucked himself outta the back of my car while I was driving him back to his digs. He never made it to the other side o' the street befo' he'd become a stiff."

"Dear God . . . Did you say he actually threw himself out of your motor vehicle? What did I tell you? The man was unhinged. Did you call the police?"

"I did not. I slammed on my brakes and ran straight over to the doc, but, like I said, he was already dead. I saw no reason to get myself tangled up with the law. Me and the police, we don't always see eye to eye, Mrs Stephens, if you get my drift."

"Yes, of course ... How unfortunate, such a nasty business. I fully understand that you must protect yourself in a situation like this. You were right, a real hornets' nest of trouble. In retrospect it was very wise of you not to contact the authorities, Mr Ellington, very wise indeed."

Stephens' reaction to the doctor's violent end was far too controlled. It was an icy response that set the hairs on the back of my neck up on end, because something told me that the sly old woman already knew Fowler was dead. Everything I'd just said to Ida Stephens had been a load of bull apart from the way Fowler had bought it and how I'd run to his aid. Now I was sure of a couple of things: Stephens knew more about Doc Fowler's death than she was letting on, and when her back was against the wall she was a bigger liar than I was. Finally looking into her cold grey eyes told me as much.

The administrator began to quiz me a little more. "Tell me ... was there anything else with these certificates?"

"No ... nuttin' else, just what you're holding there." The lie rolled off my tongue, but it was no doubt privately dismissed as such by my inquisitor. I was tired of playing our game of show and tell. I'd found out what I'd need to know; it was time for Ida Stephens to show her hand. Shit or get off the pot.

"Are you sure? There's nothing else that needed to be returned to me today? What about the five hundred pounds I gave you to get Fowler to release these over to us?" Stephens slapped the death certificates down onto the desk. "I don't see the cash being returned to us. I'm sure the doctor had no further use for it after his untimely passing."

"It's funny you should say that. Fowler was of the same mind. Let's just say he bequeathed the dough to me befo' he died. And like I just said, you got in your hands there all the man had to offer me."

"And he bequeathed nothing else to you?

"No . . . Not a ting. Were you expecting someting else, Mrs Stephens?" She nodded her head calmly. I watched as she thoughtfully mulled over my answer

"What about the truth, Mr Ellington? You know I was insistent that you question the good doctor on that important matter. Could he enlighten you on my request?"

"Y'know, that was the funny ting: the more I asked, the more Fowler denied he knew what you were talking 'bout. He looked real bamboozled when I asked him 'bout the truth and that's a fact."

"Oh, I bet he did, Mr Ellington." Stephens flashed a grin across at me. It was the first time she had smiled and showed her teeth: it wasn't a pretty sight. As a kid fishing off the shores close to home, I'd often looked down into the crystal-clear waters as I reeled in my catch to see the jaws of blacktip reef sharks tearing at the fish on the end of my hook. The administrator's two-faced beam reminded me of those snapping beasts.

"As far as I'm concerned, you got what you paid me to retrieve. I'm gonna distance myself from you and this mess if you don't mind. Illegal abortionists going crazy and throwing themselves outta speedin' motors

100

tends to get me spooked, if you get my drift. Fowler being found in the gutter full o' booze is gonna look like a hit-and-run to the police when they start nosin' around, and that's fine by me, I'm outta it. There's nobody to tie me to him taking his own life like he did. It was late at night and the streets were empty; as far as I'm concerned I was never there. Now, if it's all the same with you, Mrs Stephens, I'll be on my way."

I turned to leave but was stopped dead in my tracks by the snapping of the shark at the backs of my legs.

"But we're not finished, Mr Ellington. You saw Dr Fowler get himself killed, and whether you like it or not you are involved. If the police do come here to Walter Wilkins and question me about his death, I'm duty-bound to disclose your involvement in investigating the matter of tracing him on our behalf. And of course there'll be the issue of the missing money we entrusted to you. Again, I'd simply have to reveal that we'd been unable to account for its disappearance and that you had been responsible for its safekeeping. You see, that little hornets' nest of trouble could reach out and sting you, don't you think? So, tell me, are you absolutely sure that there was no mention of the truth to you by Dr Fowler?"

I looked upwards and sniffed loudly into the air a couple of times. "You smell that, Mrs Stephens?"

The administrator glared back at me with a bemused expression on her face. "Smell what, Mr Ellington?"

"Smell all that bullshit that's coming off o' your hide as you're giving me your 'squealing to the police' act.

101

Whatever truth you're looking for was lost with that dead man back in that gutter."

I made my way across Stephens' expensive office carpet towards the door and she shouted after me, her tone streaked with spite. I froze on the spot for a moment as her malice sunk itself deep into my hind.

"Oh, Ellington, don't take me for an idiot. I think you know exactly what I'm looking for." Stephens moved from behind her desk. "I have a strong notion that you are in possession of what I'm talking about, and I'll tell you this for nothing: only a fool would think they could keep it from us. I'll give you twelve hours to return what belongs to us. Do you hear me?"

I kept on walking, but this time it was my turn to respond to a question with my back turned to the enquirer.

"Oh, I hear you, lady . . . and it sounds to me like a lotta hot air. You keep on yelling. It may scare the poor young tings you got locked up in this place, but it ain't scaring me none, woman."

"Mr Tanner!" Ida Stephens bellowed out the name as I was closing her office door behind me. Moving speedily across the landing towards me was a bald-headed, heavy-set, brutal-looking excuse for a man. He was dressed head to foot in a white ward orderly's uniform. His biceps strained out of his short-sleeved top and I could see the collar of his mandarin tunic biting into his thick, muscular neck with each determined step that he took towards me. Mr Tanner looked more like a jailer than a nurse. This was a confrontation I couldn't walk away from, but rather than keep walking towards the oncoming freight train of a thug I squared myself up to his bulk as he rapidly closed in on me.

Behind me, I felt Ida Stephens' unwelcome presence standing gloating like a Roman empress about to become the willing spectator at some kind of vicious gladiatorial games. I dug my right hand deep into the bottom of my coat pocket, took hold of the bunch of keys that Doc Fowler had given to me the night before, and gripped them tightly in the centre of my closed hand then quickly withdrew it and let my hand fall loosely at my side. I slipped my left leg back behind me a little and dropped myself down lower, putting my body weight onto my right leg and at the same time tucking my chin into my chest, tightening my frame, tensing myself for the inevitable collision.

Tanner struck first, his fist raised in the air to rain down a heavy strike across my jaw. At the same time, I buffeted my shoulder towards his solar plexus, and as he came in to hammer me, I smashed my own fist as hard as I could up between his opened legs. The massive orderly screamed out, instinctively grabbing at his testicles with both hands, then fell hard on to his knees. As he hit the deck, I gripped at the back to his tight-fitting collar and smashed his face repeatedly against the wooden balustrade before short-arm punching him across his right temple.

The skin at the edge of Tanner's eye socket split open with the force of my blow, sending a thick spurt of the man's blood flying through the air, plastering itself in a lengthy streak across the anaemic-looking landing

103

wall. I watched as the big man fell at my feet with a heavy thud. I struggled to rein in my temper and took a couple of steps back from the downed heavy. I breathed deeply, the sweat pouring from my brow and every muscle in my body tensing. I looked up at the shocked face of Ida Stephens, who had backed herself into her own office doorway, cowering from my rage.

"You need to get yo'self a better class o' hired help if you're thinkin' of comin' on heavy with me, Mrs Stephens. Your man down there, he ain't up to the job."

I winked at the administrator then walked slowly across the landing and began to make my way down the stairs. As I opened up the front door to leave, Ida Stephens hollered down to me from the top of the staircase.

"Nothing's changed, Ellington. I want the Truth . . . The clock's still ticking. Twelve hours and not a second more. If what I want is not back here with me by 11 p.m. then it won't be the hired help I send to get it from you, I promise you that."

Her threat pierced through me like a hot poker through ice as I walked out of the door and made my way back to the car and the steely malice of Stephens' chilling warning echoed in my ears as I drove back to St Pauls.

CHAPTER
TEN

As I headed back towards Loretta's place, all I could think of was the little girl, Truth, and what I had to do to keep her out of the rathole I'd just left. Ida Stephens' nasty threats had secreted themselves into some hidden pocket of my brain for now, but I knew her words of intimidation would drag themselves back into my consciousness as the twelve-hour deadline approached. My late mama often used to tell me that talk was cheap. My mama's advice might have been right, but my gut instinct told me that Stephens had friends in low places and that she was a woman of her word and I'd be a fool to take her mouthy strong-arming too lightly.

I had more questions than answers. Why would a seemingly respectable administrator of an orphanage use threats of violence and go to such extreme lengths to have this child returned to her? Was I just a smaller player in a game whose rules I was yet to figure out? Ida Stephens clearly thought she'd get herself a dumb-ass ex-cop to do her dirty work in a part of town she could step foot in. She'd known from the start that by sending a patsy like me looking for the doc armed with a pocketful of cash she'd either get the results she sought or her money back. Well, Stephens had lucked

105

out on the result she'd hoped for and I still had her cash in my pocket. Loretta had been right when she said that I was drawn towards trouble: Fowler was dead and I was hiding a mystery child who probably held the key to some kind of dark secret. I'd promised myself after Stella Hopkins' and Earl Linney's deaths that I'd never put myself in a place where an outsider had such power over me. But my own hubris and a need to pay off a few bills had shattered any chance of keeping that vow intact. As I berated myself, I recalled the biblical proverb that said as a dog returns to his vomit, so a fool repeats his folly . . . And my folly had been twofold: my foolish zeal in falling again into the employ of strangers whose motivations I had not questioned sufficiently beforehand, and accepting the thirty pieces of silver to do their clandestine bidding.

Outside, the sky was cloudless, and the brightness of the sun poured through the windscreen of the Cortina and lit up the normally dull grey roads and pavements. I looked at my wristwatch: it was just after eleven thirty and I could feel that the temperature was stoking itself up to be another real hot day. My body was tense and I ached after my brawl with Mr Tanner. I stretched myself back in my seat as I drove and could feel my shirt sticking to my back with sweat. I caught the funky hum of body odour coming off my hide and realised that I'd spent the better part of the last twenty-four hours in the same clothes. I wound down the window so that I could get myself some fresh air and decided I'd best stop off at my digs to clean up and change before returning to Loretta and Truth.

106

My upstairs flat on Gwyn Street consisted of four rooms, each so small that you couldn't have found the room to swing a cat around any one of them. In the winter, with snow three inches on the ground and with thick ice stuck to the insides of the panes of glass in the windows, you froze. In the height of summer, it was like living in a greenhouse. Inside, the place was stifling and smelt fusty and airless. I walked into the sitting room and then my bedroom and flung up the sash windows then propped open the front door with the wooden coat stand to let some cooler air through. I went into the bathroom and fired up the immersion heater so I could get myself some hot water to scrub some of the stink off me. I went back into my bedroom, stripped and slung my clothes down by the door, then pulled a white cotton short-sleeved shirt and a fresh pair of grey-check single-pleated trousers off their hangers and hung them on the back of a chair by my bedside. I felt at the rough stubble on my cheeks and chin with my hand and decided to take a shave while I ran a bath.

In the bathroom I took my cut-throat razor from out of the medicine cabinet, uncurled the blade and dunked it into the hot water in the sink. I lathered up the soap in my shaving bowl, slopped the suds across my jowls with the badger-hair brush and went about the business of removing the two-day-old beard from my face. I washed off the remaining soap and looked at myself in the mirror but in truth paid very little attention to the reflection staring back at me. I stuck my head out of the bathroom door and looked at the kitchen wall clock. My head was again preoccupied

107

with Ida Stephens and her twelve-hour deadline for me to return Truth to her. With time running out fast, I knew that I had to get myself one step ahead of whatever game Stephens was playing. Thing was, I just didn't know how to go about staying out in front of her.

I'd let the bath fill up with as much hot water as possible before turning on the cold tap to bring it to a bearable temperature to bathe. I got in and stretched out, letting the warmth of the water cosset my tired limbs. My body began to finally relax; the sound of water dripping from the taps lulled my weary eyes as they became heavy. I felt my lids flicker a couple of times before they shut out the daylight and sleep welcomed me to its darkened sanctuary.

Respite from my worries was short-lived. The intense shock of feeling my head being shoved deep down into the bath and my nose and mouth filling with water while I was held firmly underneath was a pretty effective way of bringing me back into the waking world. I grasped blindly at the edge of the bath with my soaking hand to try and pull myself up, and frantically lashed out with my legs as the pressure on my scalp and forehead increased to keep me down. I gulped in another mouthful of water as I struggled to free myself, clawing with my fingernails at the wrist and arm of whoever was holding me under. As I continued to wrestle, I felt the pressure of the hand release and grab at my right earlobe, yanking me quickly and painfully to the water's surface.

I gasped air backed into my lungs as I hacked and retched. I rubbed at my face with the palm of my hand, squeezing at my eyes with my fingertips, trying to get them to focus on my surroundings again. My throat and stomach stung from the warm water I'd ingested. I attempted to lift myself up out of the tub but was pushed back down on my ass.

"Hello, Joseph . . . Bit late in the day for a soak, ain't it, son?"

I opened up my eyes to see the unwelcome face of Detective Inspector Bill Fletcher staring back at me. He was sat on the edge of the toilet seat, his shirtsleeves neatly folded above his elbows as he rested his outstretched arms on the lightweight mohair jacket lying on his knees. He rubbed at the short, military-style moustache above his top lip with the tips of his thumb and forefinger. He smiled at me then motioned towards the hallway with his head.

"You need to keep your bleedin' front door shut, mate. Who knows what kind of undesirables you could get swanning in here while you're trying to take your daily ablutions. Your good neighbour Mrs Pearce downstairs let us in off the street. Most impressed with my constable's warrant card she was — not too impressed with the police visiting you, though, not from the look on her face anyhow." He nodded with his thick head again, making me look behind me to my left. "You remember Detective Constable Beaumont don't you, Joseph? Sorry, he's looking a bit pissed off: it's on account of him getting his jacket sleeve all wet while he was giving your hair a good wash."

I looked up at Beaumont, who was leant against the door frame staring back at me, his face like thunder, the

109

right arm of his coat soaked and dripping water down onto the bathroom lino. I turned back to his boss perched on my khazi and snapped at him like a rabid dog.

"What in Christ's name's goin' on, Fletcher? That goon o' yours half near drowned me. Why you comin' into my place uninvited? Roustin' me like you doin'."

"Rousting, rousting? I ain't rousting anybody, Joseph. I'm just here making a friendly house call, here to see an old friend . . . Word is you're doing all right, old son. Private detective, I hear: that's a first in these parts. What's the going rate to hire you for the day then?"

"What the fuck's it to do with you how much I earn? Git the hell outta my bathroom, the pair o' ya."

"Easy now, Joseph, I'm only asking . . . I'd like to think I've got your welfare at heart. Besides which, I'm nosey."

"Last ting I need is you taking an interest in my personal life. Why don't you and Tess Trueheart there haul it down to the docks and find yo'self some real criminals to play with."

"Well, it's funny you should mention criminals, Joseph, because your name's gone and come up on another of my very short lists of miscreants. Come right to the top of it, in fact."

"Oh yeah? Don't tell me . . . you're here to pin the Kennedy assassination on me. Well you're shit out o' luck. I was in the pub when it all went down and I got an alibi as tight as the crack between Beaumont's ass cheeks." I flashed a grin up at the detective constable

110

next to me. I watched as Beaumont raised the flat of his hand to strike me, but Fletcher quickly pulled the reins on his subordinate.

"All right, less of the smart alec stuff from you, Joseph. I don't want Beaumont bruising his lily whites on you, especially after he's already gone and got himself drenched sorting your locks out. Now, what do you know about a man called Fowler, Dr Theodore Fowler?"

"Nuttin'. Now who's telling you I know the man?"

"Word on the street. Let's say I have it on good account that you were seen drinking in the King's Head pub with him last night."

"Bullshit . . . Whoever's told you that crock needs to git their facts straight. I was hanging it up with my friend Loretta Harris last night; she lives on Brunswick Street. We were sat playing crib and drinking rum in her back kitchen till way past one o'clock this morning. I didn't go in no pub with no doctor and that's a fact."

"Well, that's all I'm here for, Joseph: the facts, simple as that. This Fowler fella was found this morning with his head caved in and a gunshot wound to his guts. He was sprawled out in the gutter on Forest Road. Apparently the poor bastard looked like he'd been just dropped out of the back of an aeroplane without a parachute . . . a right bloody mess, if you'll pardon the pun." DI Fletcher smiled at me again then rested his back on the cistern. He gestured towards Beaumont with the back of his hand. "My colleague here's been doing a little digging on the deceased."

Beaumont crouched down on his haunches to face me as I sat in the cooling bath water.

"This wog doctor, Fowler, we hear he was a little bit shady. Apparently had a thing going on the side as an illegal abortionist. Known to every scrubber from here to Portishead, he was. By all accounts he liked his scotch too: big boozer, I've been told. The jungle drums are saying he couldn't keep himself upright let alone run a GP's practice any more. I hear he had a bit of a fall from grace after the death of his wife: nasty shock, took to the demon drink. Shame, I heard he was a pillar of the community back in the late '50s: big with the local church, kids' charity work, trusted figure he was, even did a spell as a school swimming instructor for a time." Beaumont stopped his chatter for a moment and eyed me up knowingly.

I knew Beaumont was trying to gauge some sort of reaction from what he had just told me, weighing me up. I stared back at him blankly, giving nothing away. Riled by my lack of reaction to being browbeaten, the detective constable continued with his sermon. I watched Beaumont as he rose up from the floor beside me to stand over me with an intimidatory air. He stuffed both hands into his trouser pockets and rattled on.

"So like Detective Inspector Fletcher told you a minute ago, the deceased turned up lying face down in a drain, stiff as a board, looking like he'd gone twelve rounds with Sugar Ray Robinson and with a hole in his belly the size of a golf ball. I think you had something to do with Fowler's death."

112

"Yeah . . . is that so? Well, you just keep on thinking that thought, Beaumont. If you're lucky, in 'bout six months' time you might get another one come along to keep it company." I watched as the detective constable's face became crimson. He balled both fists in an attempt to contain his rage and glared over towards DI Fletcher, who quickly came to his aid by taking up from where his minion had faltered.

"Look, Joseph, Fowler's body was found at around five this morning by a milkman starting his round. The poor bleeder got the shock of his life as he was about to start delivering his first gold tops of the day. Then your name cropped up less than an hour ago when my desk sergeant got a phone call with a tip-off. This caller tells the sarge that he saw a commotion near the King's Head pub on Victoria Street last night, says they saw two coloured blokes getting into a car and speeding off. Now, even though they admitted that the light was fading, the caller was sure that one of the two men was an old geezer and the other, and these were their exact words, Joseph, 'was that coon who was in the *Bristol Evening Post* last year after finding that mute bird'. You got any ideas who he could be talking about?"

I kept schtum and looked at Fletcher then dumbly shook my head in reply to his enquiry. The pair of them had been more than happy to push my buttons in the hope of getting me to rise to their accusations; it was time for me to start pushing theirs. The detective inspector leant forward and then, shaking his head, stood up next to Beaumont. Darkness fell over me as both their huge frames blocked out the shafts of sunlight that had previously been illuminating my bathroom. I was sat, naked in my bath, waist-deep in lukewarm water with two coppers standing over me and thinking to myself, "How can this day get any worse?", but of course days like the one I was having generally tended to go downhill fast.

Fletcher looked at his assistant, laughed to himself then swung his leg back and kicked out at the bath panel with the toe of his boot before bending down towards me, getting into my face with his own.

"Stop taking me for a twat, Ellington: you been sticking that big black conk of yours where it don't belong and I think you're messing about in other people's troubles again. Now, cough it up, how are you mixed up in all this crap?"

"I ain't mixed up in shit. Whoever's been spinnin' you that pile o' junk 'bout me being at some pub last night is just spoutin' hot air. I told you where I was and you can check it out for yourselves. Somebody's bin pullin' on your dick for a laugh, Inspector, cos I know what I'm telling you is straight down the line."

My mouthing off to his boss got Beaumont back on his high horse. He shot his arm out towards my head and took hold of my ear again, bending it back and squeezing it tight between his fingers.

"Listen, Sambo, you wouldn't know straight if it stuck its head out of that shithouse of yours and bit you on the arse. Stop pissing us about and start telling us what we want to hear." The DC let go of my ear then pushed me backwards. My head cracked against the

114

wall behind me, sending a surge of pain through my skull.

"You just wanna hear me admit to someting I ain't had no part in. Well, brother, you gonna be waiting a damn long time befo' I do that. You really think the word o' some faceless grass that's been on the blower to your sergeant can fit me up for killin' this Fowler fella? Well, you on a hidin' to nuttin' with that one. You need to git back out there and prove what you bin accusin' me of rather than just standin' over me while I'm in the tub starin' down at my dick."

Red-faced with anger, Fletcher pushed DC Beaumont back out into the hallway and followed him out, then turned and stood in the doorway of the bathroom and pointed his stubby finger down at me. "You think you've got a smart mouth on you, Ellington, don't you? I think you're a man who's got himself neck-deep in the shit again and no amount of your sharp talk is gonna help you. I'll check that cooked-up alibi of yours and then we'll have another chat. I'm going to be keeping a real beady eye on you, my son." Fletcher walked away back down my hall as silently as he'd entered. I yelled after him as he beat his hushed retreat.

"That's fine by me, brother, I ain't bothered what you git up to just as long as your beady eye ain't watching me in my bathroom no more. You wanna hand me a towel befo' you leave?" I heard the coat stand topple to the floor outside then the front door of my digs was slammed so hard that I swear I felt the walls around me shake.

CHAPTER
ELEVEN

Two straight shots of Mount Gay rum settled my nerves as I sat at Loretta Harris's kitchen table before recounting my earlier encounter with Bristol's boys in blue. Truth was in the sitting room playing with Carnell Jr, who was strapped into his high chair. I could hear him giggling back at the little girl as she made silly noises in front of him. Loretta had let the child sleep in and it was after eleven before she had wandered downstairs and had asked my friend where "Joseph" was. They were her first words since the harrowing events the night before. Loretta had made a fuss of the child, fed her breakfast, washed her, brushed her hair and dressed her in a blue cotton summer dress and decked her feet out in a pair of white ankle socks and sturdy-looking black patent-leather shoes.

While I'd been paying a visit to Ida Stephens at the Walter Wilkins and having my brush with the law, Loretta had seen fit to call in an old friend of hers, Prudence MacDonald. Everybody in St Pauls knew Pru Mac. Most people simply referred to her as "Cutpurse Pru" on account of her ability to walk into a store and pick up a handful of goods then walk out again without anyone seeing her do it. She was an accomplished shoplifter with magically light fingers who stole to order on occasions and had a reputation for being able to get you anything you desired, quick and for a price. Loretta had made a sizable list of clothes she needed for Truth, and Pru had gone out and got them for her there and then. The stolen clothing was sat stacked in a neat pile on the worktop by the draining board. I shook my head in amazement at the amount Cutpurse Pru had managed to pilfer and in such a short space of time.

"You can sit starin' an' shakin' your head at those new duds all you want, JT, it ain't gonna make 'em anyting other than what they are, brother, and that's hot gear . . . Git used to it. That pickney back there needed kittin' out quick; poor child was standin' in rags. I didn't tink you were gonna spring it down to Lewis department store any time soon an' git the stuff fo' her, so I sorted it. You owe me the better part o' ten pounds for that lot."

"Ten pounds, for a heap o' nicked kid's clothing? You gotta be kiddin' me." I rubbed frantically at my eyes with the flats my hands, my face flushed. I poured myself another nip of rum to help me get over the shock. Loretta snatched the liquor off me, stuck the stopper back into the top and held the bottle against her chest then began to rant at me.

"I ain't kidding you shit, Joseph. Just stick your mealy-assed fuckin' hand in your wallet and pay up. Those sneakers that child's got on her feet didn't just walk outta Clark's damn shop window by themselves, you know. It took skill to thieve those shoes and them there clothes. I took to tinkin' you wouldn't much care

117

to be seen shopping 'bout town with some honky pickney, so I got Pru to come up with the goods for you, and that, brother, that just cost you money whether you like it or not." Loretta held out the palm of her hand in front of me.

I reached into my inside pocket of my jacket, pulled out the envelope that Theodore Fowler had given me and drew out two crisp five-pound notes. Loretta looked down at the envelope in my hand and the hefty wad of cash inside it. Her mouth was wide open in disbelief and the veins on her temples began to rise at the same time as her temper did.

"Oh you . . . Muthafucka . . . And there you are gripin' at me at havin' to hand over ten miserly pounds to put clothes on that poor child's back when you got half o' the Bank o' England stashed in your coat pocket. I'm strugglin' every day to make ends meet here. Damn well ought to be ashamed o' yo'self, Joseph."

I stuffed my hand back in the envelope and pulled out another fifty pounds and laid it out on the table in front of me.

"Fifty sheets . . . Is that it, you cheap bastard? I got my own pickney out there in need o' new clothes. Fifty ain't gonna cut it, brother. You think I'm gonna let Cutpurse Pru go get my child's gear? Shit no . . . No child o' mine's wearing knocked-off duds. I pay my way. Now don't you tink 'bout stiffin' me again. Hand over another twenty and do right by me."

I grunted to myself then pulled out another two tens from the envelope and placed them next to the five I'd already dished out.

"There, that's more like it. Thank you kindly." Loretta dropped the bottle of rum back on the table in front of me and snatched up the dough. "Put a damn smile on that sour-assed face o' yours. Here, you can take the rest o' that hooch into the sittin' room and have a good cry while I make those kids someting to eat."

As I got up and headed out, Loretta called back to me as she took out a white loaf from the bread bin.

"Thanks, JT."

I turned to face her and smiled. "For what? You don't need to thank me fo' handin' over no money, Loretta. You were right, it's the least I can do to help you out some." I went to walk back into the sitting room to join Truth and Carnell Jr but Mrs Harris' parting words stopped me in my tracks.

"I ain't thankin' for the money, fool, its fo' lettin' me bellow at you like I'd got old Carnell sittin' back there on his fat ass in front o' me . . . I miss my man, JT, I surely do miss him."

I watched in silence as she began to cry, her shoulders rising and falling to the rhythm of her quiet sobs. The tears that fell from her eyes gathered in tiny pools in front of her. I went to walk back towards her and take my friend in my arms. I wanted to absorb all of the pain and grief she felt, but my feet refused to move and my legs weighed heavy on me as if lead had been tied to each ankle. So there I remained, rooted to the spot as Loretta helplessly wept. The unseen presence of her late husband, Carnell, stood beside me,

119

his spirit as incapable of offering her solace for the heartache she felt as I was.

About twenty minutes later Loretta returned to her sitting room as if her earlier outpouring of sorrow had never happened. She'd carried in with her a tray laden down with individual plates of cheese and onion sandwiches, as well as crisps, biscuits and glasses of ice-cold lemonade. She smiled as she lifted Carnell Jr out of his high chair and sat with him on her lap while she fed him. Truth sat at my feet on the floor, tucking into her sandwich. I watched as she munched away at every mouthful, chewing the food over and over, her little fingers tucking the crumbs that sat on the edges of her lips back into her mouth so as not to waste a morsel. Apart from asking where I was, she had not uttered another solitary word all day.

After we'd all eaten, Loretta got up and cleared away the dishes then returned with a box of toys and a cream-coloured baby blanket tucked under her arm. On the far side of the room she cleared a space on the floor and laid out the blanket then took her son back out of his high chair and sat him in the centre of it, surrounding the child with the toys. As she knelt next to her boy, she called over to Truth.

"Why don't you come over here and mind my boy for me for a while? See if you can git him to play nice with you. Me and Joseph, we just gonna have ourselves a chat over on the couch."

Truth did as she was asked and joined Carnell on the blanket. Loretta stroked the top of the little girl's head and smiled sweetly at her before getting up and walking across the room to her bright-red Dansette record player. She switched it on then rifled through a selection of LPs in the rack below until she found Sam Cooke's *Ain't That Good News* album. She pulled the black vinyl out of its sleeve and placed it on the turntable, dropped the stylus on to the revolving disc then came to join me on the sofa as "A Change Is Gonna Come" began to play.

"So what now?" She spoke in a hushed tone. There was a look on Loretta's face that I was rarely privy to seeing: she was scared.

"I ain't sure . . . but she's a kid. I'll be damned if I'm sendin' her back to that bitch Ida Stephens. Everyting 'bout that old hag and the place she works in stinks to high heaven. I need to find out why a man like Fowler hid her away, why we were chased and why the hell he would kill himself first rather than give her whereabouts away to the heavy who shot him."

Loretta sat listening to me, slowly shaking her head from side to side.

"Don't you ever learn, JT, you ain't the police no more, ain't gonna do you no good gittin' involved in other people's shit. Hell, you got no bidness keepin' that child like you tinkin' o' doing, but you know that."

I held her gaze for a moment and she shook her head.

"Makes no difference what I say. You gonna go your own way, no matter how much I yatter on. So you need to start gittin' yo'self right with some kinda plan, either that or you gonna have to face the music right here in St Pauls. You know, the law, they already got your cards marked for the doc's death. I suppose it ain't gonna be too long befo' they come sniffin' round here."

"They may come knockin' later today. I told 'em that I was playing crib with you last night in your back kitchen. Said I got myself legless on your Mount Gay rum then crashed on this here sofa for the rest of the night until you chucked me out earlier this morning."

Loretta glared back at me. "Great, so now I've gotta lie my ass off to the Babylon just so you can keep your hide outta a prison cell. You got some nerve, you know that, Ellington?" She laughed to herself then leant across, tapped her hand on my knee and grinned. "You still really know how to put a girl in a jam, don't ya? Lord knows, only your Ellie, bless her, could keep you under the thumb and outta trouble. You know that, don't ya?"

"Oh yeah . . . She . . . Ellie had a way o' keeping me in check, that was for sure." I laughed as I thought about my late wife and how she could cut me down to size whenever I got too big for my boots or was heading into a mess of my own making. "Loretta, whatever I do, it's gotta be the right thing. I didn't expect I'd end up with a kid on my hands when I took this job on. These are the cards I been dealt, I just gotta play 'em out. Main ting is, that child down there needs to be safe."

"Well, it sure as hell ain't safe for you or her to be hangin' 'bout in these parts, if you ask me. You need to git the two of you some distance between whoever wants to put the pair o' you in harm's way. I know that this Stephens bitch is sure to send more o' her thugs, like the one you went head to head with earlier this

122

morning. You need to pack a bag and hightail it out o' Bristol for a while, at least till you can make some sense o' what's going on."

"You talkin' 'bout me going on the run with a nine-year-old little girl in tow? You gotta be outta your mind."

Loretta shot me a glare. "Who said anyting 'bout runnin', fool? What I'm talkin' 'bout is keeping a low profile and goin' to ground. That ain't runnin'."

"Runnin' or goin' to ground, it all sounds like the same ting to me. I'm havin' to scram with my tail between my legs while either the cops cook up some trumped-up charges 'bout me killin' an old man and kidnappin' a white kid or Ida's mob take a potshot. Shit, they catch me and they might as well both lynch me up from the nearest casuarina tree."

"Stop being so damn overdramatic and listen to me. I know a place the two of you can be safe. You can lay low with my uncle Benjamin: him and his wife run a garage 'bout seventy miles from here, place on the coast, called Porlock. It's quiet and it's outta the way. You can lay low there for a few days until you got your head together on what needs to be done next. At least down there you ain't gonna be lookin' over your back constantly, worryin' 'bout gittin' pinched."

"I don't know, Loretta, I don't feel good 'bout puttin' on people when I got this amount o' heat on me. It don't seem right, puttin' your folk out at my expense."

"Will you shut your hole and wise up? My uncle Benny, he's more crooked than a ram's horns. Won't be the first time somebody on the run from the police has holed up at his place. Shit, the house is a regular meeting ground for poachers and thieves. You'll be right at home. I'll tell him straight why you gonna be knockin' on his gate door. He ain't gonna turn a brother away, specially one who was as good a friend to my Carnell as you were. Besides, when you git down there, just slip him a couple o' those crinkly tenners you got stashed in your pocket. That'll keep him real sweet."

I thought about what Loretta was saying for a moment, weighing up the good and bad in her idea. I didn't like the idea of having to travel with a child I barely knew hanging on to my coat-tails, especially if I was gonna get myself into a jam at some point. But beggars can't be choosers, so I took the only deal that was laid out on the table.

"OK, but only if it ain't gonna be a problem for your kin."

"Ain't gonna be no problem. Now shift your butt. You go back to your digs and pack a bag. Don't be hangin' around none, you hear me. Then when you're sorted, you drive round to that lock-up on Brook Lane, the one Vic owns. While you're away, I'll try an' git word to him, let him know you got your back against the wall with the coppers and probably a lot worse too. I'll meet you with the pickney by those garage doors at t'ree thirty." I looked over towards Truth, who was pushing a toy car up and down the length of baby blanket to keep Carnell Jr amused.

My head was full of doubts and if I was honest I was more than a little scared to be travelling away from the only place I felt truly safe. Leaving for the Somerset wilds didn't fill me with joy, but I knew I couldn't hang about in Bristol for much longer, not unless I wanted to spend the next few weeks or longer in Bridewell nick at Her Majesty's pleasure. I thought about the last time I'd ventured away from the city, to a village called Cricket Malherbie. There I'd encountered cruelty and death in a way that I'd never imagined. I'd promised myself I'd never be touched by such evils again. Something told me that I was about to break that promise to myself and I felt sick to the pit of my stomach. I stared out across the room for a moment, in a world of my own pessimistic thoughts. Loretta jabbed at my arm with her finger and snapped at me again.

"Hey fool, I told you, you need to put a light to your ass and git yo'self movin'. What the hell you daydreamin' 'bout anyhow?"

"I was just thinking 'bout Vic ... I really coulda done with him here right now."

"Yeah, well, he ain't here. Far as you're concerned, for now all you got to rely on is your wits and a fresh set o' wheels that I got stashed up in that hidey-hole that belongs to that no-good cousin o' yours.

"Wheels, what damn wheels are you going on 'bout?" Loretta had lost me.

"It don't matter now, but brother, one day you gonna thank me for what I got stashed away for you. JT, if tings git rough on the road I'd be tinkin' 'bout packin' that service pistol you got stored outta sight in that

125

pokey old dosshouse you call a home. It may come in a lot handier than them ragged-assed wits o' yours."

Sometimes the truth hurts, especially when it's spoken by someone you care about. I stood up, took Loretta's face into the palms of my hands, drew her towards me and gently kissed her on the forehead. I walked out of her home knowing how blessed I was to have her as a friend and headed back to my digs to pack that bag and blow the dust off my old Smith & Wesson revolver.

CHAPTER
TWELVE

It was just after four in the afternoon by the time I pulled up outside the row of garages at the back of Brook Lane. I knew Vic owned all four of the red-brick lock-ups but I didn't know what he kept in them, nor did I want to. Loretta was already waiting for me; she stood with one hand holding Truth's and the other rocking a Victorian-style pram that I could hear baby Carnell bawling out of. I was late and she had a mean impatience. I smiled at her through the glass of my windshield and in return she mouthed a string of obscenities back at me. When I got out of my car, her vulgar language became audible.

"Where the fuck you bin to, Joseph? I told you to be 'ere at t'ree thirty, not damn four o'clock. You had me waiting here standing in all this heat, sweatin' my tits off, and I got this little bastard drivin' me half mad while he's screamin' his lungs out for the rest o' the world to hear. Git your sorry ass over here and gimme a hand with this pickney while I git this gate door open."

Loretta swung the pram towards me. I took the handle then held my hand out for Truth to take it. She hesitated for a moment, then grasped at my fingers and came to stand nervously by my side while Loretta knelt at the foot of the garage door in front of us. She stuck a key into a large brass padlock and released it from a metal ring then slung open the two wood-panel doors. Inside was a vehicle that had been covered with a large tarpaulin. She walked into the garage and grabbed at the corner of the sheet.

"Wait till you two git a load o' this little beauty."

Loretta stood back and beamed at me, then pulled at the tarp. It made a swishing sound as it glided over the paintwork of the vehicle and fell to the ground. Underneath was a flash 1962 Mini Cooper with buffed-up chrome and pristine, dark racing-green paintwork.

"Hell, Loretta, did Vic buy this or win it in a goddamn bet? It's hardly what you'd call inconspicuous."

Loretta stood back and beamed at me. "Incon-what? Just shut ya overeducated shit, JT. This is a class set o' wheels. Ain't she a dazzler? This honey ain't Vic's; my Carnell won her in a craps game six weeks befo' he passed away. Said he was gonna teach me to drive it. Damn fool knew I had no interest in gittin' behind a wheel. I told him to git rid of it, but he never got the chance. Vic's bin storin' it fo' me until I found a buyer. I just ain't had the heart to deal with it. The way I see it, the law is gonna be looking out for that shitbox Cortina you crawl 'bout in. May as well store your motor in this here lock-up while you're gone. I'll give it a clean up inside when you leave, make sure there ain't any o' old Doc Fowler's blood on the upholstery. You

128

can take this little runabout down to the seaside. Far as I know, the fuel tank's filled with gas. Vic says it's running like a dream. Just try an' bring it back without any dents in it."

"Thanks, Loretta." I took her elbow, pulled her towards me and gave her a kiss on the cheek.

"Git off o' me, you fool, don't be doing that kinda ting in front o' the pickneys. Here, you gonna need these." Loretta reached in her handbag and pulled out a set of keys, a small Somerset county road map and a folded-up sheet of lined paper. She handed them over without looking at me. "That note has my uncle Benny's address on it. He and his wife run a garage just outside of Porlock village, down by the fishing port. It's the only gas station for miles around; you won't miss it. There's Pru Mac's phone number written down on there too; she's the only person I know has a telephone. You can get a message to me there. Don't worry, Pru won't tell a soul 'bout our bidness. I'll pay a visit to your aunt Pearl and uncle Gabe later, let 'em know I seen you and not to worry. I'll say that you'll be out o' town for a while on a job. Now, get in this motor and bring it out so we can git that other pile o' rust inside outta sight."

I drove out of Bristol towards Portishead then headed west down the quiet A38 coast road. Carnell's Mini may have had some poke under the engine and held the road like a dream, but the interior of the car was as cramped as hell. I'd pushed the driver's seat back as far as it would go just so I could get myself into the damn thing. My legs were tucked tight up under the steering wheel and it felt more like I was sat in a go-cart than a real motor. Truth was sat directly behind me on the back seat; I looked into the rear-view mirror and watched her as she stared out of the side window, her tiny face sombre and expressionless as we journeyed through open countryside closer towards the Somerset coastline. We'd been driving for over an hour and her continuing silence made me feel uneasy. I needed to break the quiet that was overwhelming me.

"Hey, Truth, you wanna hear some music?" Truth looked over at me but didn't speak. "How 'bout we fire up this transistor, see what station we can find?"

I continued to glance through the mirror at my hushed passenger and caught her briefly nod her head to my question. I reached out my hand towards the walnut dashboard for the radio and clicked it on then fiddled with the tuning dial until I found a station playing some music. Otis Redding's "My Girl" burst out of the speakers and I cranked up the volume a little.

"Yeah, this is what I mean . . . You know this one, Truth? Oh, this a real fine tune, fo' sure."

I tapped my fingers against the steering wheel as I drove, occasionally checking back on the little girl, who had returned to gazing blankly through the window. I still had no idea what she had been through or what was going through her scared little head. The late afternoon sun warmed the inside of the car and I found myself feeling a little less apprehensive about our situation. Perhaps it was catching sight of the ocean every now and then, reminding me of back home on Bim, that had lifted my spirits.

We drove along narrow, winding rural roads for another twenty minutes, the music from the wireless fading in and out, keeping us company. At just after six o'clock, and with no road signs visible, I pulled the Mini onto a grass verge as we came into a sleepy hamlet called Allerford to read my map. I followed the route I was travelling on with the tip of my finger and guessed we had just over two miles until we reached Porlock. I turned off the radio then wound down my driver's side window fully to let the fresh sea air roll through into the car. The sound of gulls hovering overhead seemed to be welcoming our arrival to a new home, and as I drove the short distance into the little fishing port, the sight of the birds gliding effortlessly in the peaceful evening sunlight took my breath away.

The road that led us down into Porlock was surrounded by the barren, wild moorland of Exmoor. I eventually found a road sign informing me that we were a half-mile away, and took a left into a lane that led into the village. The slender roadway had been carved through a steeply wooded valley and was lined either side by a row of large overhanging chestnut trees. Their lush dark-green canopy blocked out the late sunlight and slowly thinned out, giving way to a steep-sided hedgerow of hawthorn. As I drove into the heart of the fishing port, I reached across to the passenger seat and picked up the piece of paper that Loretta had written her relations' address on. I pulled up on the narrow gravel road that masqueraded as the village high street and read what my friend had scrawled onto the lined paper notelet.

JT, you looking for Goodman's Garage. Go past a row of thatched cottages, a corner shop then the local pub. The place ain't no bigger than a postage stamp so it ain't gonna be rocket science you finding where you need to be. Once you see the church in front of you, drive straight for it, cos Uncle Benny's place is right opposite. Look after that pickney now and be safe. Love Loretta x

Loretta's directions to her family's place, although crude, were spot on; I kept on driving along the quiet street and it wasn't long before I could see the short spire of the village church ahead of me. As I neared the village green opposite the church, I could see a large red and yellow Shell sign hanging from a white post at the side of a small, grey stone cottage. I pulled into the garage forecourt opposite the yellow petrol-pump livery and switched off the ignition on the Mini. I leant back in my seat and stretched before turning my head to check on Truth.

"How you doin', Truth?" She looked at me blankly for a moment then returned to staring back out of the passenger window. "This is where Aunt Loretta's folks live. I'm just gonna see who's 'bout, let 'em know we've arrived. I won't be a minute, OK?"

Truth stared back at me briefly and shot me another of her sharp nods before gazing back out into space.

I got out and wandered across to a small red-slated building that stood at the rear of the forecourt. Two large glass windows sat either side of a green-painted wood-panelled door. I walked in and the tinkling of a small bell above my head chimed my arrival. Inside smelt of linseed oil and newly hung purple mothballs. Stacked up on shelves were a multitude of different products, ranging from spark plugs to shampoo. A henna-haired old black woman not a day older than one of Scott Joplin's widows sat behind a counter at the top of the little shop; laid out on the table in front of her were what looked like tarot cards. I nodded across to her and smiled. She returned the gesture by staying stony-faced and eyeing me up like I was just about to rob the place.

"Is Mr Goodman around?"

"He's out back." The old witch barked her reply to me in a distinctive Barbadian accent then turned over one of her cards, peered down at it and looked back up at me suspiciously. "Been working on a motor."

"You mind if I go and look for him?"

"Do as you please . . . Make no difference to me."

"Thanks." I lifted my hand in gratitude but the old woman ignored me, seemingly lost in a dark divinatory spell of her own making.

I found a big man I thought was Loretta's uncle Benny in a workshop directly behind the store, just as the spooky old woman said I would. He was lying on his back on a creeper seat underneath the engine of a Hillman Imp that had been driven up on a set of ramps. I tapped on a glass window panel then called down to him.

"I'm looking for Benjamin Goodman, he 'bout?"

"Why, you owe him money?" the man yelled before shooting out from underneath the motor on the wheeled creeper seat and glaring up at me. The guy was as black as pitch and must have weighed in at two hundred and fifty pounds of solid muscle. "Only folk round here calls me Benjamin are them that are in debit or that nasty fuckin' Bajan witch I got sitting out on my front porch. You must be Ellington."

"Yeah, my friends call me JT." I walked across and shot my hand out."

"They do, do they . . . Mine call me Benny." The big man lifted himself off the ground and stood in front of me, weighing me up before taking my hand firmly in his own and shaking it. "Good to meet you, JT, we bin expectin' you. Loretta called, told us you needed a place to hang ya head, said someting 'bout you having a pickney in tow with you?" Benny grabbed an oily rag from off his workbench and wiped the dirt from his palms and fingers then threw it back.

"Yeah . . . I got her with me in the car. Her name is Truth."

"Trute? That's a helluva strange name for a pickney." Benjamin laughed and shook his head. "Well, let's go git the little mite out. Take you both in to meet the wife. I take it you already bin introduced to Madame Pisspot in the shop?"

134

"If you mean the old woman reading the tarot cards out front, then yeah, we already met. She's different, I'll give you that."

"Different, oh she's different all right. Crazy as a shithouse rat, that what she is, gives me the damn creeps. The old bastard's my mother-in-law, name's Cecile. Silly fucker's the bane o' my life, her an' that mangy black cat o' hers. Still, you'll be glad to know she's good with kids. I keeps her out front like that cos she stops the flies from settlin' on the sweets on the counter." Benny winked at me then let out a big belly laugh and slapped me hard in the centre of my back, making every bone feel like it was rattling under my skin.

We walked back up to the Mini. I opened up the passenger side door to let Truth out. She peered out of the window and looked up at Benny's massive frame, her eyes widening to take his bulk in. Benny bent down at the glass, offered a massive grin and waved his huge fingers at her.

"You like dogs, missy? Cos I gotta hound that's gonna love you fo' sure. Come on, git yo'self outta the back o' there and come take a look at the mutt I got back at the house with JT and me."

Truth looked at Benny, puzzled, then whispered through the window to him, "JT, who's JT?" They were the first words I'd heard the child utter since the night I'd met her.

Benny looked baffled. He stared back down at Truth and shot his thumb out at my face. "Well, this guy here tells me he's JT, honey."

"No . . . That's Joseph, not JT."

"Ah . . . Joseph, you mean you use his Sunday name, do ya? Then I tell you what we'll do. From now on everybody gonna call him Joseph, that way old Benny here won't be gittin' himself all confused. I ain't too hot wid names at the best o' times, me. Now let's git you out the back o' this four-wheel rotisserie befo' you cook inside o' there in this heat." Benny looked over at me and laughed. "These some snazzy wheels you got yo'self here, Joseph. Kinda small, though, for a tall guy like you, ain't it, brother?"

"It's on loan from your niece, Loretta. Carnell won it for her in a dice game."

"Well, that don't surprise me none. Shit, that fool could gamble . . . and cheat! Stupid as a mule and as loyal as a hound on heat was old Carnell. Damn, I miss that boy."

Benny turned back to Truth, who was still hesitating to get out of the back seat of the Mini. He curled an enormous index finger at her and beamed a big toothy grin.

"Now, Trute, did I tell you the name o' that mutt o' mine? I call him Claude. You can't miss him, smells like a skunk. He's as big as a house and gentle as a lamb, so you don't need to worry none 'bout him. Just don't try an' steal his chow, cos that dog, well, he sure does love his food. Let's go inside o' home, git ourselves some lemonade, hey?"

Truth nodded her head in agreement. Benny stuck his hand out to her and she timidly took hold of his fingers. She stood next to the big man, looking up into the sky to try and see whether his huge frame reached up into the clouds or not. Benny cupped his hand to his mouth and bellowed across the garage forecourt.

"Claude, hey Claude, come on boy, we got ourselves a couple o' visitors."

Claude came bounding out of the back of the cottage that stood at the side of Benny's garage. Truth let out a scream and drew herself close to my leg as a huge grey Irish wolfhound, a good two and a half feet tall, hurtled towards us. It came to a clambering halt, sat obediently at Benny's feet and waited for his master's next instructions. The dog's ears pricked up when the big man spoke to it.

"Claude, this here's Trute and her friend Joseph; they gonna be stoppin' wid us fo' a while. So you need to be a gentleman. That means no lickin' anybody to death or pissin' on any o' these good folks' shoes, you hear?" Benny laughed to himself then turned to me, grinning. "You don't want Claude here takin' a leak on your brogues; he got himself a fondness for it. Best you take your shoes up to bed wid you at night. Now let's go find that wife o' mine, git us a drink."

I grabbed our bags and followed Benny, Truth and Claude across the forecourt and into the rear garden of our host's home. I stood at a creaky wooden white-painted gate and admired the ivy and yellow-rose-clad thatched cottage. Benny jabbed at the back door with his toe and called in after his wife.

"Estelle . . . Estelle, where the hell you at, girl?"

An as-yet-faceless Estelle hollered back at her husband, "Mind that language o' yours, Benny. Cussin'

137

after me like that ain't gonna git you far." Estelle appeared at her kitchen door and smiled down at Truth then called me into her home with a waving gesture.

"This must be Trute and Mr Ellington?"

Benny quickly butted in, correcting his wife; he motioned backwards with his head towards me. "Boy here has to be called Joseph, Estelle. He tells me his friends calls him JT, but Trute here, she don't approve o' people callin' him that. Don't wanna be upsettin' our new house guest now, do we?"

"No, we don't want any upset, that's fo' sure. Joseph it is then." Estelle put out her hand towards me and smiled. "Good evening, Joseph, pleased to meet you. Come on inside now, make yo'self at home."

I left our bags by the door and followed Benny and Truth into the kitchen. Estelle ushered us in and stood with her back against a wooden worktop. She was a large-bosomed, heavy-set Bajan woman with light Creole skin and hazel eyes that seemed to twinkle back at you when she spoke. Her brown hair was streaked with grey flecks and it was tied above her head in a neat bun. She looked over at her husband; her once friendly and warming face had turned to thunder when she caught sight of Claude. "Benny, git that mangy dog outta my kitchen befo' I kick it out, you hear me?"

Benny immediately turned to his faithful wolfhound and pointed his finger into the next room. "Claude, you go take yo' ass onto that bed o' yours, boy." The dog did as it was told and slunk off.

Estelle pulled out a couple of chairs from underneath the dining table "Here, you two, come and have a seat,

138

I'll get us someting to drink. Benny, get those bags off o' the porch and take 'em upstairs."

The big man, as obedient as the dog he owned, did as he was told and went to collect our luggage. I watched as he dipped his head so as not to hit it on the low, black-beamed ceiling.

When Benny returned with our bags he motioned with his head towards the kitchen cupboard. "Estelle, git me a couple o' bottles o' light ale outta that there larder for me and the boy. Joseph, I'll be back in a minute, you and Trute make yo'self at home."

I sat down and looked at Truth, who was gazing all around the kitchen, her eyes seemingly unable to take everything in. A tall oak Welsh dresser, its shelves filled with ceramic mugs and glasswear, sat next to a huge white stone sink. The steam from the hot water inside the sink rose up and fogged up the windows above it with thick condensation. Copper pans, sieves, wooden spoons and practically every other kind of utensil hung from hooks from the ceiling, and a large black range stood on the back wall of the kitchen. The cooking aromas coming from inside the oven made me feel like I was twelve years old and sitting at my mother's kitchen table back home again.

Estelle fetched two bottles of beer from the larder, lifted the caps off with a bottle opener and brought them and a couple of glass pint pots over on a tray. She sat the drinks in front of me then filled two cups with lemonade from a jug and placed one of the beakers in front of Truth.

139

"Here you go, Trute, you must be parched in this heat, child. Go on now, drink up."

Truth looked at me as if I needed to give her permission to drink. I nodded over to her that it was OK to go ahead, and she began to drink, slurping noisily at the lemonade. I was about to thank Estelle for the drinks when Benny came back into the room, his booming voice make everybody jump in surprise.

"Is that beer on the table, Estelle? Good girl, damn yes it is. I tell you, Joseph, my mout' is as dry as a nun's doodah."

"Benny, what did I tell you 'bout cussin' like that, we have a child in the house."

"Aw, damn it, Estelle. 'Doodah' ain't no cuss word. Shit . . . I coulda said c —"

Estelle leant across the table and snapped at her husband. "One more foul word out you and you don't git fed tonight . . . You hear me?"

"Oh, I hear you straight. No more o' them bad words, fo' sure. Not outta my mout'." Benny picked up a bottle of beer and handed it over to me. "Here, git this down you, boy, you looks like you in need of a drink." Benny grabbed a glass and pushed it towards me then filled his pint pot with ale and sank half of it in a couple of swift gulps. "Hey, Estelle, someting smells real fine. What we got on the menu tonight, honey? I could eat a horse." Benny winked at Truth and chuckled to himself.

Estelle, her back to us, stood at the sink filling up the kettle. "We got pork chops and potatoes and greens. Everything you just love fillin' your face with."

140

Benny slammed his hands together. "That's what I like to hear. Pork chops, oh I love pork chops. They got plenty o' fat on 'em, Estelle? Cos you know I like my chops with plenty o' fat on 'em."

"They got enough fat on 'em to keep your greedy gut more than happy. Now less o' your mout' and go show Trute where the bathroom is, let her wash her hands befo' supper."

Benny sank the rest of his pint and wiped the froth from his mouth with the back of his hand then looked across at me. "Come on, Joseph, git that down ya. We'll have a couple more when Trute and me git back." He raised himself out of his chair and tapped the table with his huge knuckles. "Come on, Trute, let's me, you and Claude go find that bathroom and wash our paws, shall we."

Truth cautiously got up and followed Benny. As they walked down the hall Benny called back to his wife. "Estelle, speaking o' plenty o' fat, is yo' momma gonna be joining us for supper tonight?"

Before Estelle could bite back at her husband, Benny had begun to roar with laughter, drowning out any berating of him that she could muster. It was only as he was climbing the stairs and had quietened down that I heard the very faint sound of a giggle coming from Truth. I took a hearty swig of my cold beer, smiled to myself and felt my body relax for the first time in days. I slumped back into my chair and closed my eyes, finally allowing myself to bask for a moment in the warming sensations of a safe and happy home, aware that the feelings of joyfulness I felt at that moment could be all too fleeting.

CHAPTER
THIRTEEN

It had been a long time since I had last sat with a family in good company at a dining table. Back in St Pauls I normally found myself eating either in some backstreet café or alone in my digs. I'd forgotten what it was like to be together as a family. Sure, I had my own kin in Aunt Pearl, Uncle Gabe and Vic, and I went over to their place often enough to get my fill of some good home cooking, but this felt different. Truth was sat between Benny and me, and I watched her as she noisily chowed down on her second plateful of pork chops and mashed potatoes, eagerly shovelling in mouthfuls of Estelle's fine food, which she kept washing down with lemonade. Estelle sat with her mother, Cecile, on the opposite side of the table. Old Cecile had barely spoken to any of us but made more noise stuffing her face than Truth. She only seemed to come up for air every now and then to cast a dark, wary eye over towards her son-in-law.

It felt strange having the little girl sitting next to me eating dinner, and something about the child brought flashes of past happy mealtimes I'd once shared with my own child and her mother. Once, those feelings would have made me leave the room, or even the house, but this time the feeling was not so painful. As everybody was finishing up I continued to stare across at Truth, lost in how uncanny the similarities were between her and my own late daughter, Amelia. It was only when I felt Benny jabbing at my arm that I broke out of my melancholic reverie.

"Hey there, you look like you drifted a million miles away, brother. You OK there?" Benny gave me a concerned look as he leant over and topped up my glass with more beer.

"Yeah, I'm fine, Benny, sorry man . . . Just tired. It's bin a long old day." I took a swallow of my beer and caught Estelle shoot a quick smile at me from across the table then looked across at Truth.

"How 'bout Momma and I take Trute out to feed the chickens befo' the sun goes down? You boys take your beer into the sitting room and get better acquainted."

Estelle and Cecile got up from the table, and Estelle gestured for Truth to follow her and the old girl. Truth pushed her chair back and, without saying a word, went and joined Benny's wife.

"When we get back from our chores with the hens, I'll run a warm bath for this young lady. Get her settled for bedtime. From the look o' this child's eyes, it ain't just you who's had a long day, Joseph."

Benny got up and kissed Estelle on the cheek, and watched as his wife, Cecile and Truth walked down to the bottom of the garden to where the chicken coop was. He picked his pint pot off the table, went into the larder and returned with two more bottles of light ale then looked down at me. Benny motioned with his

144

head for me to come and join him in the next room. I got up to follow him and, as I did, he turned quick as a whip, stuck his elbow into my ribs and winked at me.

"You see how that soundless old bitch Cecile was trying to rattle up one o' her hexes from across the table at me. It's all in her eyes, I tell ya. That woman never wanted me to hook up with her daughter, thinks I'm no good for Estelle. Shit, we bin married for twenty-five years, you'd think the miserable sow would gimme a break. She got herself a voodoo doll in her room looks the spittin' image o' me. Pins stuck all over the fuckin' ting. Ain't any wonder my ass stings so damn much." Benny chuckled to himself. "Come on, sleepyhead, let's do as my good lady says." Benny chinked two beer bottles together. "We'll crack a couple more o' these open, then you can tell me why you and that cute little pickney out there have travelled down from Bristol in such a goddamn rush and ended up knockin' on my gate door like you have."

Benny and Estelle's sitting room was small but comfortable. I walked across the flagged stone floor, which was partially covered by a threadbare Persian rug at the foot of the fireplace, and joined my host, who was already sat in one of two upholstered armchairs sat opposite the unlit hearth. A large single standard lamp sat in one corner and threw a feeble blanket of dim light across the room. The walls were decorated with gaudy flocked wallpaper and above the mantlepiece hung a bleak-looking painting of a sailing ship out at sea being battered by high waves. Benny handed me one of the opened bottles of beer then began to refill

145

his own glass with ale. He took a long swig before resting the glass in his hand on the arm of his chair.

"So, you a Bim boy then, Joseph. Where'bouts on Barbados you spring from?"

"Place called Six Cross Roads out in St Philip Parish."

Benny nodded his head as I spoke, formulating his next question for me in his head.

"Loretta said you used to be a policeman back there. That right?"

"Yeah, that's right, I was a sergeant on the force."

Benny looked across at me suspiciously for a moment then hit me with another pointed question.

"And what you do now in St Pauls?"

"Well, the sign outside the place I work says enquiry agent . . . but most o' the time all that means is me stickin' my snout into other folks' bidness and gittin' myself into trouble of one kind or another." I shook my head slowly and laughed to myself then realised that Benny's eyes were burning into me.

"My niece gone and told me 'bout the kinda trouble your work gets you in, Joseph, an' I ain't likin' what I heard. I'm just tryin' to weigh up if me and Estelle wanna git involved in any of your mess. More importantly, I needs to know why you got that white child out there hangin' on your coat-tails and if she's gonna bring me some kind o' misfortune too. Loretta said you and Carnell were good friends, said you were a good man. That may be so, but I ain't got to my age trustin' the word o' good men; I need to see 'em

146

spreadin' some o' that goodness 'bout befo' I trust 'em. You git my drift?"

I nodded my head in agreement. Benny sat back in his chair and took another mouthful of beer.

"So, Joseph, why don't you chuck a bit more o' that ale down your neck then start tellin' me, just like my Estelle says . . . the whole story."

During the next half-hour, and for the second time in as many days, I narrated my bizarre tale of death and deceit to a charitable soul who would have been wise to have thrown me out on my ear and shunned my very existence. But luckily for me that wasn't going to be the case. That night my chronicling of a cruel and unusual subject matter was heard by stranger whose actions after the telling made him a friend. That's the thing about decent folk and the one thing that never fails to surprise me, no matter how much disarray and hardship you bring into their lives, they still remain true to what they believe in and keep doing whatever they can for you. Benny Goodman was that kind of guy and I was grateful to him for his kindness.

We sat in silence for a moment. It was just after eight thirty and the sun had started to set low outside. What was left of the fading evening light began to shroud the sitting room in an eerie gloom that the standard lamp behind us was failing to cut through. I could hear Estelle's voice outside as she, Cecile and Truth returned from the garden. Benny leant across from his chair and rested his hand on my arm.

"You leave me to speak with the wife 'bout what you've bin tellin' me. She'll be fine once she knows the

147

score. But be sure o' one ting, Joseph. Any o' these men you say may be lookin' for you or that poor child come sniffin' 'bout here and they step one foot in my home or try and bring harm to me or my family . . . I gonna take 'em out at the neck. You hear me?"

I stared into Benny's dark, unblinking eyes as he spoke, and the fearful and intimidatory look on his face left me in no doubt that the big man would be true to his word.

After she cleaned and put away our supper dishes, Estelle boiled up some water in three big saucepans on the stove while Truth sat on Cecile's knee at the kitchen table. I had no doubt that this old woman of few words was more than just the mean-spirited hag that Benny said she was. Cecile had the elderly poise and knowing aura of the kind of woman who back home we called a traituer. Traituers were a powerful kind of faith healer with one foot in the here and now and the other in the spirit world. Women like that gave me the creeps, but Truth had clearly taken to her. Cecile sat with her back to me, rocking the little girl in her lap and singing a Caribbean folk song, "Lang Time Gal Mi Neva See You". Truth was captivated by the lilting tones of Cecile's deep Jamaican accent as if she was almost hypnotised by the mystical tone in the elderly woman's voice.

I heard Benny curse to himself outside and watched as he carried a big galvanised tin bath in from one of the sheds in his garden. He dropped the metal tub onto the kitchen floor and began to cuss again.

"Damn, I swear that bastard bath gits heavier every time I hump it in from outta the yard!"

Estelle glared a look of disgust at her foul-mouthed husband.

"What I tell you earlier 'bout using profanity in this house? We have a child and my momma in our home. I won't hear no more of it, Benny, you understand me?"

"Profanity my ass. Your momma got a dirtier mout' on her than a steamboat navvy."

Benny went on venting his wrath, only this time focusing it towards his slyly grinning mother-in-law, who was sitting across the room from him. Benny jibed at the old girl some more.

"I feel like Samson with his hair chopped off. Cecile, you bin messin' wid my mojo, you old witch? I can tell when you ain't up to no good. You git that look on your face, like the one you got on you now . . . I know you bin cookin' some o' that nasty root medicine shit in your room again. Damn house smells like yo' cat's ass after you bin boilin' up them plants o' yours. You keep ya damn voodoo shit outta my home, you hear?"

Cecile didn't say a word; she just kept on singing to herself and the child, occasionally moving Truth back and forth on her scrawny knees. Benny looked at me and winked. There was tomfoolery in his voice and mischief etched across his face as he said to his long-suffering wife, "Estelle, honey, tell yo' momma this is 1966. We is living in Somerset, this ain't no African shack she's dossin' down in. People in the village, they gonna start to talk. Get me a bad reputation."

149

"You already got yo'self a bad reputation, fool." She pushed Benny to one side with her shoulder then poured a boiling pan of water into the galvanised bath. The scalding water spat back at Benny, splashing his feet and trousers as his wife emptied the rest of the pot out. The look of shock on Benny's face was a picture to behold.

"Estelle, what they hell you tryin' to do to me, woman, gimme third-degree burns? You damn well nearly had me shrivelled up, pulling a fool stunt like that."

Estelle glared back at her disgruntled other half then stuck her finger in his face. "Shrivelled up, ain't no chance on earth that water, hot or cold, could seep into that oily ole hide o' yours. When Trute's finished taking a bath, you can sling your dirty butt into it. Git some of that grease that's stuck under those filthy fingernails o' yours cleaned out. Perhaps while you're in there you could try scrubbin' that foul mout' o' yours out with soap too."

Benny, now berated within an inch of his life by his wife, sat down on a chair at the kitchen table and looked at me with hangdog eyes. He shrugged his shoulders as if to say, "I know when I'm beat." He slumped back into his seat like a sullen schoolboy and shut his eyes. He mumbled to himself, "I ain't got no dirty butt, Estelle," then began to laugh.

Cecile and Truth, clearly amused by Benny's comment and by Estelle's victory in getting her grubby spouse to take a bath later, stared at him from across the steam-filled room like gleeful jurors gazing at a

150

guilty felon in the dock. As Estelle picked up another pan and continued to fill the rest of the tub with blistering water, she began to laugh along with her good-humoured husband whose initial quiet chuckles had now become a full belly roar. The continuing laughter echoed around the old cottage, and the palpable sense of warmth and love that the Goodmans exhibited filled their home in a way that was hard to describe. I too had often experienced such special times with my own loved ones, but those tender reminiscences now seemed like distant memories that perhaps belonged to another man. Being with such a fine family at a special moment as this was a joyous thing to behold, and I envied the happiness and contentment that they shared with each other.

Truth and I had been given the spare room, which was located upstairs at the furthest end of the old cottage. The room was warm but well aired and a small bedside lamp on a table next to the headboard offered a comforting hum of soft light. Benny had already laid down a single mattress at the foot of the bed that I'd be sleeping on. Estelle had kindly covered the mattress in soft white cotton sheets and a pretty patterned quilt for Truth.

Truth, scrubbed till she shone and smelling of lavender bath salts, snuggled underneath the quilt and lay looking up at me, a quizzical expression on her little face.

"Where's Theo? I want Theo, Joseph."

The child didn't take her eyes off me and waited for an answer. I knelt down by where her head was

151

bolstered by two huge duck-down pillows, thinking of what I could tell her. I'd already spoken of Dr Fowler's death once this evening; I wasn't up to going over the story again. I didn't want to lie, but now, staring down into the child's questioning eyes, a lie was all I had to give.

"You remember back at the baths I said Theo was unwell." Truth nodded her head at me. "Well, even though he wanted to, he was just too sick to make a trip like the one we're on. That's why he gave me the job."

Truth looked away; her gaze became pointed towards the white skirting boards on the other side of the bedroom. I was about to get up and say goodnight to her when she spoke to me again in a hushed tone.

"Theo's dead, isn't he, Joseph? I know the bad men got him, didn't they?"

I felt the hairs on both my arms and my neck stand on end as Truth's question shot through me. My mouth dried and I struggled to find any words to reply.

Truth continued to stare across at the far wall. "Are the bad men going to kill us, Joseph?" She drew her hand from underneath the quilt and reached out for my own.

I took her tiny hand in mine then gently stroked the top of her forehead with the other. "I ain't gonna let nobody hurt either o' us, you understand me? You got my word on that, little one. Now, you shut those eyes o' yours and git yo'self some sleep. We got us a fun day to have tomorrow."

I rested my back against the side of the single bed, still holding Truth's hand, and watched as she slowly

152

fell into a dead sleep. I tucked her arm back underneath the quilt and walked out of the bedroom, closing the door behind me quietly. As I began to walk down the landing, Cecile came out of her room and called after me.

"Mr Ellington, do you have a moment fo' me?" I could hear the rasp of her breath as she spoke.

I hesitated then turned around to face the old woman and began to walk back towards her. "Of course, Miss Cecile, what can I do for you?"

"Ain't nuttin' you can do for me, son. More someting I need to tell you."

"Yeah, what's that?" I was starting to get spooked again.

"You need to know you got more than one little girl on this journey o' yours."

I felt my throat tighten and I took a step back from the old traituer.

"This other child, she by your side even though you can't see her. She always bin by your side, even when you thought you was on your own. Child that spoke to me, she on the other side. She don't ever sleep, she just watches over you. She told me to let you know that it ain't safe round these parts and that you gotta keep movin'. Said that when they come for you with their guns, they'll come in the night, and you was to pay mind to that." Cecile backed into her room, and as she began to close her door she spoke to me again, only this time her voice seemed distant, as if it was not coming from out of her own mouth. "Pay heed to what you bin told, Mr Ellington. Remember . . . they'll come for you in the night." The door snapped shut and I heard a key turn in the lock.

The air around me suddenly smelt of ash and burnt hair. Rooted to the spot with fear, I stared down at my hands: they shook at my sides as if I'd been struck down with a maligning palsy. My heart pounded hard and fast as if it was about to split out of my chest and fall at my feet. The image of its frantic beating as it lay on the floor in a pool of my own blood still visible in my mind, I closed my eyes to try and shut out the horror of a waking nightmare I had no control over. The self-imposed darkness did little to ease my anguish.

CHAPTER
FOURTEEN

The gentle rays of warming sunlight crept through the gap between the curtains and caressed the side of my cheek, rescuing me from the nightmarish world I had inhabited in my sleep. I turned onto my back, staring up at the yellowing Artex ceiling for answers, then took in a couple of deep breaths as I tried to mentally shake the gory images from my troubled sleep out of my head. The sheets around me, soaked with sweat, were the only outward physical proof of my trials; the clammy wetness of the fabric clung to my naked skin. Inside, my head throbbed. The bad dream had left me feeling hollow and washed out.

The brass alarm clock on the bedside table said nine fifteen. I yanked the bedding away then swung myself out onto the edge of the bed and looked down at the empty mattress beside me. I stumbled across the room to where I'd hung my trousers over the back of a chair and pulled them on, then slipped my vest over my chest and walked barefoot downstairs and into the kitchen. Estelle was standing over the sink with the cold tap running, slicing the green caps and stems off some of the reddest fresh strawberries I'd ever seen. As I walked over towards where she was stood, my shadow passed across the wall in front of her and Estelle turned and jumped in surprise, holding her hand to her chest.

"I'm sorry, Estelle. I didn't mean to make you leap outta your skin like that." I held up my arms, the palms of my hands splayed out in front of me by way of a further, unspoken apology.

"Joseph! You scared me half to death creeping up on me. Are you OK? You're looking kinda peaky, didn't you sleep too well?"

"No . . . I slept fine, thanks. I think I have the leftovers of a bad dream still rattling around in my head. I get 'em sometimes. They make me feel kinda cranky first ting, that's all."

"Bad dreams, hey? You know that's Mother Nature's way o' telling you to lighten up, young man? Benny told me 'bout your troubles. Ain't nuttin' like worry to unsettle your sleep. Perhaps you and Trute can find yourselves a small measure o' peace these next few days while you stoppin' here with us. I say there ain't nuttin' like the sea air to restore the body and spirit."

I looked out of the open kitchen door into the garden. "Where's Truth, Estelle?"

"Oh, she's down in the meadow with Momma Cecile, feedin' the goats. The two of 'em seem to be gittin' on like a house on fire."

I flinched at Estelle's mention of the old woman and her choice of words. I struggled to push a smile into my mouth as she continued to talk excitedly about her mother and the child.

"Trute ate herself a full cooked breakfast of eggs and bacon, she wolfed it down like she hadn't been fed fo' a

156

month. She and Momma took themselves off to explore for a while." Estelle, a concerned look on her face, looked me up and down as I stood barefoot on her kitchen floor. "Speakin' of a cooked breakfast, it looks like you could do with feeding up. That's the way to git you started in a better frame o' mind. We can't be having you mopin' around just cos o' some bad dreams."

She turned to the stove and placed a large black skillet onto the hob. Then, with a cloth wrapped around her hand, she lifted up a boiling pan of hot water and poured some of it into an enamel wash bowl that was sat on the draining board, and then filled the remaining water into a matching jug. "Here, while I cook you up someting to eat, you take this out into the yard and freshen yo'self up. There's a small mirror, cut-throat razor and some soap and towels laid out for you in your room. You need anyting else, just holler out."

I felt a whole lot better after I'd washed and shaved. I tipped the dirty shaving water down into a drain in the yard. As I watched the bowl empty I got the feeling that any lingering remnants of the nightmare I'd endured as I slept were now flushing themselves away into the sewers below me. I changed into a fresh pair of khaki lightweight trousers and a pale-blue short-sleeved shirt and went back downstairs to the kitchen, where Estelle was dishing up two fried eggs from a iron spatula onto a plate to go with the mound of bacon and grilled tomatoes she'd cooked for me.

"Here you go, come on, sit yo'self down and git this eaten. Benny said to tell you to go on down to him when you're finished up here; you'll find him up to his neck in motor oil down at the garage."

She smiled at me as I sat down to eat. In front of me was a teapot, its spout steaming, and a rack full of hot toast. I felt Estelle rest her hand on my shoulder.

"Befo' you fall into bad habits with my husband for the rest o' the day, bring those clothes you an' Trute bin wearin'. I'll git 'em washed and hung out to dry, ain't no point in wasting all that sun we got shinin' down on us, is there?"

I began to tuck into my hearty breakfast, my hitherto uneasy state of mind comforted with every glorious mouthful I consumed.

I found Benny in his garage, just as Estelle had said I would, only he wasn't working underneath a car. He was sitting behind a large wooden workbench with a long length of green baize felt that had been laid across the rough timber surface. Sat on top of the felt were a half-dozen pistols of different calibre and a double-barrelled 12-gauge shotgun, each of which was in various stages of being broken down and cleaned.

At Benny's feet lay Claude. The wolfhound shot up off the floor and growled as I walked towards his owner but quietened down as soon as he recognised who I was and that I was no threat to his master. Alerted by his faithful hound's grumbling, Benny looked up from behind a pair of brass wire-framed spectacles that were perched at the end of his bulbous nose and grinned at me as he ran a bore brush through the barrel of a blue-hued Colt 45.

"Hey there, Joseph, how you doin', brother?"

"I'm fine, thanks, Benny. You thinkin' o' startin' a war or someting?"

The big man laughed at me as he began to reassemble the gun in front of me.

"Nah. I already had my war, son; in fact, I brought this here shooter back home from some crap hole out in the Far East: 1952 I tink it was, Korea. I went out there on the *Empire Fowey* in the summer o' '50: travelled in style too, the *Fowey* was an ocean liner. I was a corporal in the Royal Electrical and Mechanical Engineers. I won this damn ting playin' poker with a bunch o' drunk Yanks. I'd got the better hand, fo' sure. When it came to seein' what I was holdin', the owner o' this handgun had little else to play with. It was either this here hunk o' metal or the dumb bastard's front plate, and I didn't have much use fo' no second-hand dentures." Benny laughed to himself then laid down the pistol next to a small pot that was filled with springs and screws and tiny mechanisms, all of which were soaking in paraffin. Benny looked down at his collection of firearms and nodded towards them with his head.

"You own one o' these tings, Joseph?"

"Yeah, I got me a Smith & Wesson .38. It was my service revolver; I got it wrapped in an oiled rag in my bag up in the bedroom."

"You got shells fo' it?"

I nodded my head slowly before replying. "Well, the ting ain't no good without 'em."

"Well, ain't that the damn trute." Benny picked up the shotgun from the bench and opened up the breech,

159

inserted a couple of double-ought buckshot shells into both barrels then snapped it shut. "You keep that water pistol o' yours close by, son. If what you said last night 'bout those fellas who killed that old man, Doc Fowler, is right, then it's probably wise to assume that sooner or later they're gonna come lookin' fo' the two of you round here. Let's just be sure we're ready fo' 'em when they do, hey."

Later that morning Benny had me pull Loretta's Mini Cooper into one of the larger garage buildings at the rear of the petrol station. He stood by two large double doors while I backed the car in, closing them as soon as I'd cut the engine off. Inside on a metal trolley were a spray gun and some large tins of red vehicle paint. Benny pulled on a pair of dirty overalls then picked up a roll of masking tape and some old newspapers and dropped them on the bonnet of the car. He rested himself against the side of the door panel as he pushed a screwdriver into the gap around the lid of the paint tin and began to prise it open.

"Best we give this nasty jalopy of my niece's a new paint job. May as well be covering your tracks while we can. When it's time fo' you to move on, I got a motor that neither the police nor anybody else is gonna be lookin' for you to be drivin' 'bout in. Here, come take a look next door, I gotta little surprise fo' you."

I followed Benny towards the back of the garage and through an adjoining door that led into a dark, smaller lock-up. His huge frame stopped dead and flicked on the light switch on the side of the wall then grabbed

160

hold of my arm, drawing me close towards him. He put his arm around my shoulder and stuck his other out in front of him, like a circus ringmaster, to proudly introduce me to his "little surprise". In the middle of the outbuilding stood a hulking great military-style jeep that resembled a tank more than it ever did a car. Benny dragged me over towards the monstrosity and started showing me around it like he was trying to sell the damn thing to me.

"This, Joseph, is an ex-army Series II short wheel based Land Rover. Take a good look, cos you don't git much finer than this on four wheels." Benny clapped his hands together, sending a ringing sound around the lock-up, then began to walk around the sizable automobile to show it off. "OK, it comes in one colour, an' that's shitty green. It's got itself a 2.25-litre petrol engine and a four-speed manual transmission. On a full tank o' gas this ting can git you from the shithouse to the swamps without you even having to change down into second gear, and it's gonna be a damn sight more agreeable for gittin' 'bout in than that midget mobile you dragged yo' sorry ass all the way down from St Pauls in. Tell me you ain't impressed, son?"

I tried not to let my lack of enthusiasm for the ugly Land Rover dent Benny's keenness in his motorised pride and joy. Life has taught me that there are times when underestimating a man's passion for what he holds dear can be an imprudent thing to do. Now was one of those times.

Later that afternoon, just after lunch, Benny drove the Land Rover out of his lock-up, parked it up on the forecourt then came and stood next to me as I was watching Truth play out in the garden. It was good to see the little girl out in the fresh air having fun. I smiled to myself as she laughed while chasing Claude the dog between our drying clothes hanging on the line. But in reality my mind was troubled by worry. Was the heavy burden of my promise to protect the child from forces whose strength and numbers I was as yet unable to calculate really beyond my capabilities? To all intents and purposes I'd taken off out of St Pauls knowing the trouble I'd be getting myself into without a back-up plan or any thought of the consequences of my actions. All I knew for sure was that I had to keep Truth safe at any cost.

Benny put his hand on my shoulder, bringing me back from my private world of dark thoughts. He dangled the keys of the Land Rover in front of me.

"Here, rather than moping 'bout here with a face like a wet weekend, why don't you take that pickney out for a drive. Go git yourselves an ice cream an' a change o' scenery. It'll do the pair o' you good."

I looked up at Benny and he rattled the keys in the air then pushed them into my hand. His eyes bore into my own, his lined face contemplative and edgy.

"Loretta, she told me 'bout your late wife back home, son. I'm sorry fo' your loss, I really am. It's a hard ting to have to endure, losing what you love, specially a child. Estelle and me, well, we lost t'ree to miscarriage. Fair broke her heart each time the Lord saw fit to tear her unborn offspring outta her belly like

162

he did. No rhyme or reason to it, Joseph. It's just the Lord's way, but it didn't lessen the heartache any. Now, from what I can see, that child there, Trute, she's seen more than her fair share o' heartache herself. That kid probably only ever seen a handful o' smiling grown-up faces in her tiny life. Ain't no good gonna come o' you starin' into space lookin' like you got the blues when she's around. You need to git a beam runnin' across that good-lookin' mug o' yours, even if you don't feel the smile inside of you, brother."

Benny nodded his head to himself as he thought about the wise words he'd just spoken then turned and began to walk back towards his home. I watched him kicking off his boots as he stood at the kitchen door, and without turning around he called back to me before going inside.

"My old man, he used to say to me, 'Bein' a parent, it's the hardest damn job in the world. Full o' worry and wonder in equal measure. But once you a father, you always a father.' Perhaps it's time fo' you to start bein' like a father again fo' a while, Joseph. You got enough worry in your life fo' sure. But you never know, maybe that child Trute's gonna bring you some o' that wonder that's bin missin' from outta yo' world fo' so long."

With the sun blazing high above us in the afternoon sky, Truth and I made the short two-mile drive from Benny and Estelle's home, rattling along the Worthy toll road down to the small fishing village of Porlock Weir. I parked the cumbersome Land Rover in a dead-end,

163

narrow road next to a row of ivy-clad, grey slate Gibraltar cottages. I got out and helped Truth from the passenger seat and then we made our way across the main street towards the tiny quayside. The air was warm on our faces as we stood admiring the view in the harbour. The fragrant scent of fuchsias and jasmine growing in the hedgerow behind us clashed with the strong aroma of discarded fish and ozone that drifted up from the jetty below. Overhead, the herring gulls weaved and bobbed, voicing shrill calls to each other as they darted about for leftover scraps on the dockside. Truth, her eyes drawn towards the mysteriously altering colours of the sea, put her head to one side as she stared out across the Bristol Channel at the small white-tipped waves and listened as they rolled gently back and forth onto the shingle beach.

I watched as the little girl curiously gazed along the shoreline, fascinated by her new surroundings; there was a look of enthrallment that had become etched on her face and a faint smile broke at each corner of her mouth as she watched a large fishing boat come into view out on the headland. It was only then that I realised Truth had never seen the sea before. I knelt down beside her and took hold of her petite hand in my own oversized mitt. She shot me a quick enquiring glance of uncertainty then looked down at my fingers wrapped around her own before returning to gaze back out across the harbour towards the ocean.

"You wanna go take a closer look?" I pointed out across the beach towards the sea. Truth nodded slowly without looking at me, absorbed by the new landscape in front of her.

We made our way hand in hand along the harbour wall until we reached a series of steep granite steps that led down to the stony beach. This wasn't the fine golden sand I remembered from back home; in fact, this wasn't like any beach I'd ever encountered before. The large pebbles felt uncomfortable to walk on and I was grateful to reach the shoreline, where the shingle was small and less painful underfoot. As we continued to wander along the flinty strand, gentle waves rose and fell at the water's edge, just missing our feet. I looked back at the foreboding, steeply wooded slopes that rose up behind us, and which led back to the high moors beyond.

Truth and I walked for over half an hour without speaking a single word to each other, both of us happy to exist in our own little silent worlds. Despite the day's glorious weather, I felt that the expansive and barren shoreline gave off a bleak aura of remoteness and decay that seemed to want to seep inside of me and put me oddly on edge. I suddenly felt empty to the pit of my stomach and a shiver ran through me that put goosebumps on my arms. I shuddered as I looked out across the channel at a small group of dark clouds that hung ominously across the Welsh coastline, and I wondered what kind of misfortunes and heartbreaks this stretch of ancient landscape had witnessed over the years.

Truth was still enthralled at watching the waves ebb and flow at our feet. She occasionally offered up a quiet

165

giggle or gasped as the water just missed the tops of her shoes and rolled back out to sea again. As we continued to trek across the beach towards a rocky outcrop ahead of us, I remembered something that Benny had told me earlier in the afternoon. I called back to Truth, who was still dodging the waves.

"Hey, Truth, did you know that this part of Somerset was once crawling with smugglers and pirates?"

Truth stopped and dragged on my arm for me to halt too. The expression on her face was confused; her small nose was scrunched up and her eyes squinted in the sunlight as she looked up at me.

"What's a smuggler, Joseph?"

"It's like a thief, you know, someone who takes someting that doesn't belong to them. Smugglers used to steal anything they could get their hands on. On this stretch of the coast, if a big ship got into trouble out at sea and sank, its cargo could get washed up on the beach. If it did, that's when the smugglers would arrive. They'd come and take whatever was around, mainly at night, so they didn't get caught."

Truth nodded again as she pondered on my answer for a moment then kicked at the pebbles with the toe of her shoe. I looked back up the beach towards the village in the distance then turned on my heels and gently spun Truth round to face me.

"Hey, how 'bout you and me, we head back towards the quayside and try and find some place to git you an ice cream. That sound good to you?"

The mere mention of the word "ice cream" lit up her little face so much she darted out in front of me,

166

pulling at my arm to hurry me along. Truth's sheer excitement at the mention of such a rare treat lifted my spirits too and I found myself suddenly smiling.

I found a newsagent opposite the harbour that sold ice creams. I bought Truth a large vanilla cone with a chunk of chocolate sticking out the top of it, which she lapped at as we walked along the High Street back towards the Land Rover. I laughed to myself as I watched Truth biting into the cold dessert, her face and chin covered in a thin layer of milky white cream. As we reached the car, she took hold of my hand and yanked on my arm.

"Joseph." The child hesitated for a moment and twisted on the heel of her shoe as she thought about what she was going to ask me. "Joseph, do you think smugglers take children?" Truth bit into her ice cream again then looked back towards the seafront.

"What makes you think smugglers would take children, Truth?" I unlocked the car, opened up the rear door and helped the little girl to get in. She turned to face me, her eyes glazed over with a watery film.

"That's what Theo said was going to happen to me if I didn't stay put and out of sight in my hiding place back at the swimming baths."

I took my handkerchief out of my pocket and wiped the ice cream from her mouth and dabbed the burgeoning tears from her eyes. "Tell me, what did Theo say, Truth?"

"Theo told me that it wasn't safe for me to stay at the orphanage any more. That one day the bad men would come and smuggle me away. He said they'd

167

come and take me away in the night. Theo said the bad men always came and took the children in the night."

CHAPTER
FIFTEEN

I sat alone with my head back in a deckchair outside of Benny and Estelle's to work out my next move. I watched the white flicker of lightning in the distance as it broke out of the darkening skies around me. The air was humid and smelt of damp moss and the fragrant honeysuckle that climbed up and along the back wall of the cottage. I slowly sipped at the glass of rum that Estelle had brought out to me earlier while Truth's chilling words about the mysterious bad men who took the children in the night rolled uneasily around in my head. There were so many unanswered questions about the child. So much that just simply didn't weigh up. Christ, I didn't even know Truth's surname. Getting the girl to talk was like pulling hen's teeth; whatever secrets were locked away inside of her weren't going to be let go easily. I realised that I had to go easy on the child if I was to successfully coax out of her exactly what had been going on back at the orphanage. What had made Truth so special to Ida Stephens? Whatever it was, the administrator had been prepared to either pay handsomely or use some hefty force to get her back.

Across the meadow out in front of me, a rolling rumbling of thunder echoed as the last of the evening's light began to fade. I sank back in the deckchair and downed the remainder of my rum in a single gulp then cursed myself under my breath at what a fool I'd been earlier in the day. Taking the little girl down to the beach had been a mistake. I'd not thought things through before taking her out, I'd not considered what kind of jeopardy I'd be putting the two of us in. After all, I was trying to keep Truth out of harm's way. What if we'd perhaps been spotted by one of the locals or, worse still, a keen young copper on his rural beat? We'd stuck out like a sore thumb. A middle-aged black man hand in hand with a young white kid was hardly something you saw every day. Thankfully the harbour village had been both remote and quiet. With the exception of the elderly shopkeeper I'd bought the ice cream from for Truth, the child and I had luckily seen no one else.

I felt a sharp chill run through me and looked at my wristwatch; it was just after eight thirty. Estelle had bathed Truth earlier for me and I'd tucked her up on the mattress at the bottom of my bed and told her I'd go check on her in half an hour. That was forty-five minutes ago. I hauled myself up out of the chair to go see if she'd fallen asleep just as the telephone began to ring loudly. I felt my guts tense then churn as I began to walk back inside the house, an unwelcome response to hearing the trill call of the phone, and perhaps a forewarning that the caller did not have good news to convey.

I found Benny standing in the cramped hallway as he silently listened to the voice on the other end of the

170

phone. His normally jovial face had become contorted with deep frowning lines, his eyes filled with anger. I watched his expression become increasingly more enraged as the nameless caller continued to communicate with the big man. Finally Benny took the phone away from his ear and held the receiver up in front of my face, his huge hand shaking with temper.

"It's a friend o' Loretta's, name's Prudence MacDonald. You know her, Joseph?"

"Cutpurse Pru? Yeah, I know her."

"Well, you need to hear what this woman got to say." Benny handed the phone over to me then leaned himself against the hall wall, staring down at his feet and balling his fists together. I slowly held the phone to my ear and listened to the repetitive pips as coins were frantically pushed into the money slot of a call box before Pru could speak again.

"Pru, can you hear me? What's going on?"

"Ellington, that you?" The cagey shoplifter bellowed at me from down the other end of the telephone.

"Yeah, course it's me, ya old fool. Who the hell you think it was gonna be? Where's Loretta at?"

"Don't be callin' me no fool, you bastard. You gone an' caused a shit pile o' trouble back here, you hear me? I'll tell you where Loretta's at: she in the hospital, and in a real bad state too."

"What you talkin' 'bout, hospital? What the hell's she doing in hospital, Pru?"

"She in there cos she took herself a beatin' on account o' your sorry ass. The police paid her a visit last night, came axing questions 'bout you an' some white pickney they said you gone an' snatched from some home. They wanted to know where you might o' taken off to. Loretta said there was two of 'em, said one was the old bastard that had been giving you grief last year and that the other was a nasty-looking shit with a chip on his shoulder."

"Police? That'd be Fletcher and Beaumont from Bridewell station. You saying the two o' them beat up on Loretta?" I couldn't believe what I was hearing.

"No, not that pair o' fuckers, they slung their pissy hooks after Loretta fobbed 'em off by tellin' 'em you got yo'self drunk and was crashed out on her sofa after the two o' you had bin playing cards. Said she hadn't set eyes on you since you walked outta her gate door night befo' last. The law came back 'bout two or more hours ago. Only this time I tink it was the younger pig you just mentioned and he was with some other guy that Loretta said was givin' her the creeps no sooner than she set eyes on him. Said he was cruel-looking an' spoke like a Yank, she said he was more like GI Joe on his day off than a copper. The Yank slapped her around some when she told 'em to piss off. Then they beat on her like she was a dog. Broke a couple o' her ribs and knocked her face 'bout. The bastards threatened to take Carnell Jr away from her unless she told 'em where you were."

"How'd you found out she'd been hurt, Pru?"

"Loretta crawled out her back door and called out to her neighbour; when they seen her covered in blood, sprawled out in the yard, they called an amb'lance and then got their pickney to come get me. I'm in a call box

172

outside o' the infirmary. She told me I had to git in touch with you as soon as I could. She said to tell her uncle Benny that he had bent law comin' to stay across the road at the Ship Inn, said he'd know what to do. She told me to tell you that she was sorry 'bout dropping you in it and that you was to git yo'self as far away from wherever you are as quick as you can, you hear me?"

"Yeah, I hear you, Pru. Where's Carnell Jr now?"

"He's back at my place. I got my eldest child, Marianne, lookin' after him. He'll be fine with me and my kin till Loretta git herself back on her feet."

"Is she gonna be OK? How is Loretta, Pru?"

Another series of pips sounded, interrupting the call just as Pru was about to reply to the most important question I needed to ask her. The line went dead. I stood rooted to the spot and listened as the static humming noise on the end of the line rang through my ears, coursing its way into my soul to meet my burgeoning shame head on.

Benny moved towards me. The expression on his face was engorged with anger, his eyes moistened by a thin film of tears that he was suppressing. He took the receiver out of my hand and gently eased me backwards by my elbow towards the open hallway door so that he could use the telephone. I could feel Estelle's nervous presence as she stood quietly behind me. We both watched as her husband dialled a number on the phone then waited for it to be answered. The big man's face looked a little less savage when a welcome voice answered his call.

173

"Lazarus? Lazarus, man, it's real good to hear your voice. It's me . . . Benny, Benny Goodman . . . Yeah, I know, it's bin a long time, fo' sure. Look, I ain't gonna beat 'bout the bush with you. I need ya help. You know that favour you always said I could call on you anytime fo'? Well, I need to cash it in tonight if that's all right with you, brother." Benny suddenly cupped his hand around the mouthpiece, his voice turning to a low whisper as he continued his conversation. When he finished the call, he stared back at me and jabbed one of his stubby fingers towards the stairs.

"Joseph, listen to me: we ain't got ourselves a lot o' time here. You go git your shit packed and we need to git on the road now."

Benny hurriedly began to make his way back through the house towards the kitchen door. Confused, I called after him.

"On the road? On the road to where, Benny?"

Benny turned back and snapped at me. "Don't you worry 'bout where you headin', son, just you do as I say. Go grab your stuff while Estelle here gits Trute up outta her bed. We're leaving in the next ten minutes."

Estelle had gone ahead of me to wake up a sleepy Truth. She was just starting to dress her when I came into the bedroom to collect our belongings. I quickly pushed all our clothing into our case while Estelle tied the laces of Truth's shoes then pulled a large grey woollen blanket around the child's slender shoulders. Estelle sat the little girl on the edge of my bed and ran her fingers through the child's long blonde locks.

"When you leave here, you just take good care o' this child or you'll have me to answer to, Joseph, you hearin' me? I don't doubt that you and Benny can take care o' yourselves, no matter what happens, but this little ting, she needs to feel safe and looked after. For now, all she's got is you." Estelle laid her hand on my arm and smiled at me. "I'm gonna go pack Benny a bag with some overnight stuff. You better get the two of you on downstairs, he'll be waiting for you. One ting gets Benny's hackles up more than anyting else is bein' kept waitin'."

I quickly zipped up the case then leant across the bed and slyly slid my hand underneath the pillow to retrieve my Smith & Wesson revolver. With my back to Truth, I snapped open the .38 and checked that it was as I'd left it. Happy that the five shells were still in the cylinder, I carefully closed it then set the hammer onto the empty chamber. I clicked on the safety then hooked the gun into my trouser band and covered it with my jacket, its heavy bulk weighing awkwardly against my stomach for a moment. I turned back to Truth and smiled at her before bending down and lifting her up off the bed. She looked at me, her eyes stared into my own, the bewildered expression on her sleepy face mirroring my own sense of uncertainty. She put her face close to my ear and spoke in a trembling and hushed tone, and her whispered enquiry with all its prophetic knowing sent a shiver down my back.

"They're coming, aren't they, Joseph? The men are coming."

175

"Ain't nobody coming for us, Truth. We're just going on a night-time trip with Uncle Benny. He says he's got a surprise lined up for us."

I tucked the top of Truth's head under my chin and drew her in tight to my chest then bent down and picked up our case. As I carried the child downstairs a heavy roll of thunder growled from the sky and the first splatter of raindrops began to hit the front door of the cottage.

Benny already had his Land Rover pulled up by the garden gates, the engine running and the rear door of the bulky motor slung open. He and Estelle stood embracing each other in the kitchen. Benny looked at me and made a backward motion with his head towards the vehicle outside.

"Go put Trute in the car, Joseph, git her settled fo' our ride, yeah?" he said.

Estelle smiled tenderly at the two of us as I carried Truth past them and out to the car. I hurried across the garden as the rain, coming down fast, bounced off my head and the back of my jacket. A bolt of lightning lit up the sky, and as I sat Truth on the back seat, the little girl grabbed at the sleeve of my coat and pulled me towards her. I saw her mouth begin to tremble and her wet eyes looked into mine with the realisation that she believed I could not help her, that no one could. Truth knew I had lied to her about the men. She knew that we were running and that the men she feared were close. At that moment the expression on the little girl's face told me that the world she had been born into was a far more terrible one than I could have ever imagined.

176

Truth's tiny fingers held onto mine for a moment. I leaned into the car and gently touched her cheek with the back of my hand then smiled at her. She forced a smile back then looked over my shoulder back out into the rain. Another roll of thunder grumbled above us as I turned to see what she was looking at. Standing in the downpour behind me was Momma Cecile. She held out her arm to me and opened up the palm of her hand. I wiped the rain off my face, attempted to focus my eyes in the fading light and tried to make out what she had in her hand: it looked like a piece of jewellery.

"Here, take it, man." Cecile pushed her frail hand into my face. I took the small leather cord from her and looked at it. A small silver sixpence with a hole drilled through its centre had been threaded onto it. I looked back at the old woman and began to thank her, but she impatiently waved her hand at me, interrupting my gesture of gratitude.

"We ain't no time fo' that. You tie that round the child's ankle now. It'll keep the juju away from her." I did as Cecile told me and stuck my head into the back of the Land Rover to tie the cord around Truth's ankle. As I did, I felt the old woman's hand touch my back and her body move closer to my own. She held her face against my arm and began to talk in the same way she had on the upstairs landing the night before. Rather than being spoken, her words seemed to sing inside of me.

"That girl's got ghosts hangin' on her spirit, mister, bin there since that pickney took her first gasp o' air. They bin cursin' her kin too fo' as long as they bin walkin' on the earth. Listen to what I be tellin' you now. Be strong, brother. When you gotta be travellin' wid that child in the days to come, then do yo' journeying through the night. The night-time can be yo' ally as well as yo' enemy, remember that. If you afraid o' the dark, the dark it'll know it and it'll bring you down like a pack o' hounds after rich meat. Yo' let the night be yo' companion. Yo' trust it, Mr Ellington."

When I turned back to face the old woman, she had gone. The damp air around me smelt of sulphur and the rain. A sharp gust of wind blew a spray of lukewarm rainwater against my face and chest. I wiped at my face with my fingers as another crack of lightning flashed above my head. A deluge of water began to fall from out the blackening sky. I looked down at the ground where Momma Cecile had been standing moments earlier. It was still dry.

CHAPTER
SIXTEEN

I watched Benny through the rain-spattered passenger window of the Land Rover while Truth sat in the back. He stood at his kitchen door talking to Estelle then drew his wife towards him and held her in his big arms, kissing her on the forehead before turning on his heels and running through the downpour to join us in the car.

It was just after nine fifteen and pitch dark as we set out. What started as heavy rainfall was now developing into a real nasty storm. Huge hailstones bounced off the bonnet and roof of the car as Benny drove out of Porlock village. The wind buffeted the side of the big vehicle as we headed out into open countryside, and rain, hail and loose leaves whipped in a frenzy at the windscreen as the rubber wipers struggled to clear what was being thrown at them. We drove in silence for about three miles before Benny glanced in his rear-view mirror and called over to Truth.

"Hey there, baby doll, don't you be worryin' ya pretty head 'bout all this blowin' an' howlin' you be hearin' outside. This ain't nuttin'. Just Mother Nature having herself a tantrum, that's all. Befo' you know it, sun gonna be up and shining. Now, why don't you to lie yo'self down on that back seat. You pull that warm blanket Aunt Estelle gone an' gave you up round yo' face, and shut yo' eyes, git yo'self some rest. Me and Joseph here, we gonna get you outta this here nasty little squall real soon, honey."

Benny wiped at the inside of the steamed-up windscreen with the palm of his hand then wound down his side window a couple of inches to let in a little air. Tiny drops of rainwater flew through the gap, hitting the big man in the face. Benny cursed under his breath and wound the window up again. He nodded his head out in front of him and laughed to himself.

"This turning out to be a muthafucka o' a storm fo' sure, Joseph. We gonna be driving across some pretty wild country fo' 'bout an hour an' a half or more. Keep an eye on that pickney back there, make sure she don't bounce off that seat if we start pitching up against some potholes in the road."

I looked over at Truth, who had done as Benny had told her and snuggled herself up underneath the blanket. Quiet and curled up into a ball, the little kid truly amazed me. No matter what seemed to be thrown at her, she took it square on. She might not say a lot, but the girl had strength of character way beyond her years. I glanced back at Benny, who was staring out of the windscreen, a look of heavy concentration on his face.

"What did Loretta mean when she told Pru to let you know that there was bent law coming to stop at the Ship Inn?"

180

Benny nodded his head slyly then smiled to himself. "Joseph, whoever the hell it is that's lookin' for you and Trute, they think you gonna be holed up at the Ship Inn on Porlock High Street. That's gonna be the first place they look after Loretta told 'em you'd be there. She and Carnell loved to drink in the Ship when they came down to visit me and Estelle. Loretta isn't stupid, son, she knows not to send strife to my home and she knows the Ship well enough to realise the place is like a den o' thieves, only it's got rooms for 'em to bed down in. Hell, I do all my under-the-counter bidness in there. Before we left I made a call to Sid the landlord, told him anybody come snoopin' 'bout, askin' if a black guy and a little white girl had been stoppin' in the place, that he was to say yes and tell 'em that the two o' you had moved on earlier today. I told Sid to tell 'em where you were headin' to."

"And where was that?"

Benny had me confused.

"Same place we goin' now." Benny smiled back at me and winked.

"You're sending 'em after us?" I couldn't believe what I was hearing.

"Sure I am . . . Listen, son, befo' you explode, there's method in my madness, just you wait an' see."

"Where we goin', Benny?"

"Little place called Priddy, 'bout sixty miles from here. I got an old war buddy, name o' Laszlo Dolan, we go back a long way. Served with him in Korea. Tough bastard too. The boys in our regiment used to call him Lazarus on account that no matter what shit he ended up in, he always came outta it without a scratch. Me and Lazarus, I tell you, we seen our fair share o' death out there, enough to get me tinkin' that the only way I would be going home was in a body bag or, worse still, I'd be buried out there in the cold ground. But Dolan, he didn't have no truck with death: bullets whizzed past him, an' fear, well, it seemed never to enter into him. I soon got to believin' what the other guys did, that he was just like his biblical namesake: he was a man who, if fancy took him, could rise up from the dead."

"An' this Dolan knows what kinda trouble I'm in?"

"Damn, Joseph, Lazarus known trouble all his life. I told him we was probably drivin' outta one shitstorm into another and that I didn't like bringin' trouble to his gate door. Far as Lazarus sees it, he feels he owes me. Once I called that favour in from him earlier, the die was cast, in his eyes. It don't matter none to him if the fight's personal or not. It's a simple matter o' honour and integrity to Dolan. I tell ya, God broke the mould when he done made Lazarus."

"What does Dolan owe you, Benny?" The big man cleared his throat then shuffled irritably in his driving seat.

"That don't matter none. All that matters is we get that child and you outta harm's way."

"And you'd do that fo' a stranger like me? Shit, this ain't your fight, man."

"No, no it ain't . . . But from the moment you two walked into my home, you made it my fight. Like I gone told you yesterday, ain't nobody gonna hurt my family without me havin' someting to say 'bout it.

Whoever gone an' beat up on Loretta is comin' for you and that child. They ain't settin' foot in my world, turnin' it upside down and tinkin' they gonna walk away from it scot free. Man messes wid my kin, son, he gonna find out soon enough that fuckin' around wid me an' those I care 'bout ain't a wise move. From what you told me, it sounds like you got men bringing a war to you, boy; I'm just levelling up the battlefield befo' they git to us, that's all. Now, tell me 'bout those two bastard coppers who set 'bout my Loretta."

"Well, I only know o' one o' them that would be capable o' doing harm to a woman, like they did to Loretta. A young detective constable called Beaumont. He's got himself a mean streak as wide as the stripe on a raccoon's tail. Now, his boss's name is Fletcher, a white, military type. I had a run-in with both of 'em last year. Fletcher seems like an OK fella. He's old school, a bit by-the-book; he ain't the type to go knockin' a woman 'bout or to give the orders for somebody else to do it, I'm pretty certain of it. We're lookin' for an American. Loretta told Cutpurse Pru that the other fellow that beat up on her had a Yankee accent and that he was real mean-lookin'. I reckon his name might be Paxton. Doc Fowler befo' he died said that the man who'd shot him's name was Paxton: he called him the devil. Now, I never did see his face, let alone hear him speak. Whether he was an American I couldn't tell you, but one ting's fo' sure . . . I ain't never heard o' no Yank hangin' 'bout in St Pauls befo'."

"Well whoever this Paxton or Johnny-Joe is, fo' some reason he's sure eager in getting his hands on little

Truth back there. Why'd you tink some American dude would be so desperate to seek her out like he is?"

"Hell if I know . . . The child's a mystery. Shit, I'd be surprised if she's spoken fifty words to me since I found her. I know as much 'bout Truth as you do. The woman who got me involved in all this mess, Ida Stephens, I know she'd a given her eye teeth to have got the kid back. That place Truth was stayin', the Walter Wilkins orphanage, that joint made my flesh crawl, Benny. Place was like a morgue. I didn't hear the voice o' one damn child the whole time I was there. There was a whole cesspool o' badness in there, I could feel it. There was no way I was sendin' that child back there, no way."

I rubbed at the top of my head with the flat of my hand, my frustration at not being able to fathom what was going on all too evident. Nevertheless, the big man kept pushing with his questions.

"None o' it makes a bit o' sense, Joseph. What's that kid have that's so damn special to that broad Stephens and the Yank? Why would this Paxton tink nuttin' o' beatin' Loretta 'bout to find the child's whereabouts, an' that Dr Fowler be crazy enough to t'row himself outta the back o' your car to keep the pair of 'em from findin' her?"

"Beats me, Benny. What I do know is befo' Fowler killed himself he told me that there'd be some real cruel people wanted what he had hidden, that I'd understand once I saw what he'd been keepin' stashed away. He warned me that there'd be more men like Paxton lookin' to find what turned out to be that little girl

184

there." I looked over my shoulder at our young companion. She was fast asleep.

We continued to drive along minor roads until we reached a signpost for a place called Wheddon Cross; from there on we started on our bleak journey across Exmoor. The wind was still howling outside and heavy rain continued to pelt out of the sky, making it difficult for Benny to see where he was going. He pulled up at a fork in the road and hung a left onto a thin dirt track that led back out on to a more established stretch of highway. Around us it was pitch-black and the headlights of the Land Rover struggled through the deluge to pick out the tarmac road in front of us. Benny dropped into second gear and slowed the car right down as a torrent of water hit the windscreen. The noise of the rain as it hit the roof was deafening. Benny braked suddenly then looked across to me and laughed.

"At the rate we're goin' this fuckin' storm is gonna kill us befo' any other son o' a bitch gets a chance to do us any harm. You climb over into the back, hook your arm round Trute. From here on, this toll road is full o' potholes. It's gonna get a bit hairy, best you keep an eye on her, don't see no reason fo' the child to be wakin' up alone back there and gettin' scared."

It was a real squeeze, but I finally managed to haul myself into the back of the Land Rover and settle next to Truth. Benny looked back at the two of us and smiled to himself as the little girl tossed and turned for a moment, then kicked her legs out across my lap. I covered her back up with the woollen blanket, and as I did the coldness of the sixpence attached to the leather cord tied around Truth's ankle grazed against my wrist. I looked out of the window into the black void around us and shivered as I remembered what Momma Cecile had said to me earlier: "If you afraid o' the dark, the dark it'll know it."

Benny called over to me, breaking the spell of the old traituer's foretelling words.

"You ready to rock 'n' roll back there, brother?"

"Yeah, I'm ready."

"Good, you try an' git yo'self some shut-eye with the pickney. Next time I stop this here jeep we'll be at the Hunters Lodge inn. If we gotta face ourselves some hostility in the next day or so, there ain't no better place than Lazarus's lodge fo' us to be standin' our ground in."

Benny stretched in his seat then took off the handbrake and put his foot slowly down onto the accelerator as we drove off into the dead of night. I remember closing my eyes and my head rocking from side to side as the Land Rover drove over divots and holes in the road. I felt the comforting warmth of Truth's body against my own as the memory of my daughter Amelia crept into my unconscious. The whisper of her gentle voice calling me to sleep was never more welcome nor more heartbreaking.

CHAPTER
SEVENTEEN

I woke with a jolt to the sound of the car's handbrake being pulled on and heavy rainfall still ringing in my ears. I yawned then looked across at Truth, who was still fast asleep next to me. Rubbing at my eyes with the tips of my fingers, I sat myself up and stretched my arms out at the side of me. The faint interior light of the Land Rover had been switched on and was illuminating Benny, who was staring at the two of us. He was leant across the back of his seat, resting his chin in the palm of his huge hand with a grin on his face and mischief in his eyes.

"'Bout time you raised ya head. You pair o' sleepin' beauties sure missed one helluva storm. Wind damn near blew us offa the road at one point."

"We here, Benny?" I broke out yawning again as I asked my question.

"Well, I ain't stopped for no piss break. Course we here, fool." Benny shook his head to himself, opened up his door then turned back to me. "I'll come round and get Trute, carry her in. You get your bags outta the back. Leave mine in there, Joseph."

I did as I was asked. We were parked up directly outside of the Hunters Lodge inn. A large single bulb lit up the peeling sign that hung outside of a dilapidated grey pebbledash building. Benny came round to the passenger side door, opened it up then wrapped the big blanket underneath Truth before hooking his arms under the child's tiny body and lifting her off the back seat. Benny nudged the rear door to with the side of his hip. He looked back at me then motioned towards the pub with his head. "Come on, let's git outta this damn rain."

I followed Benny onto a low porch that ran along the length of the front of the pub. Two large bay windows sat either side of a mahogany-veneer front door. I could see a series of candles flickering inside, shining meagrely through the Marmite-brown windows out into the darkness around us. I stood in front of Benny for a moment then turned the brass knob on the door and opened it for him to walk in with Truth. We stepped into a dimly lit saloon bar: the place was empty and stank of stale cigarette smoke and spilt beer. At our feet were bare boards and on the far wall a large, welcoming open fire burnt in the hearth. At the bar, veiled in the shadows, stood a large white guy, his bulky silhouette just visible, aided by the flame from the tapered wick of a low-burning candle that sat underneath the bottles of optics behind the dimpled brass-topped bar. The man drew himself out of the darkness and spoke, his voice deep and rich with a West Country accent.

"So, you managed you get yourself across them moors did thee . . . Thought that storm out there mighta beat you, Benny." The big man, ignoring me, walked out from behind the bar and stood in front of Benny, staring at him coldly, poker-faced. Benny, clutching a sleeping Truth at his chest, took a step forward and glowered back unblinkingly. The two men stood in silence, eyeing each other up suspiciously for a moment as if they were squaring for a fight. Benny finally broke the hushed air and spoke.

"When did a bit o' rain ever stop me from findin' my way to this run-down rat-'ole o' yours? How you doin', Lazarus?" Benny winked at the hulking giant, who burst out laughing.

"Benny Goodman . . . you old bastard, you. It's good to see you, old son. That a dead body you lugging around with you there?"

"Lazarus, this here's Trute." Benny pulled the blanket carefully down a little to reveal the child's angelic sleeping face.

"Jesus, Benny . . . I knew you said you were bringing guests, but I didn't think one of 'em would still be needin' her mother's tit."

"Kid's beat. You got somewhere I can lay her down? She may look like a cherub, but shit, she weighs in like a side o' beef."

"Sure, Benny, bring her through the back. I got a couple of spare rooms upstairs. Beds are all made up." The big man looked me up and down enquiringly then stared back to Benny and nodded his head towards me. Lazarus shot me a suspicious look. "Well, who's this then?"

"Sorry, Lazarus, this here's a good friend o' mine, Joseph Tremaine Ellington. Joseph, meet the landlord

189

of the Hunters Lodge and my old buddy, Laszlo Dolan."

Lazarus took a couple of steps towards me and stuck out his sizable hand in greeting. I took hold of the man's big paw: his grip was firm and powerful. He pumped at my arm, making it feel like it was about to be torn out of its socket.

"Pleased to meet you, Joseph. Call me Lazarus, son. Here, let me take those bags from you. You just sit your arse down by the fire and get yourself warm. Benny and me, we'll be back in a minute."

Lazarus took the bags from me. Benny followed him behind the bar with Truth and the three of them disappeared behind a curtain. I took off my coat, hung it over the back of a chair and went across to the snug and sat on a small wooden seat that was facing the open fire.

I warmed my hands in front of the flames for a moment then sat back in my seat and listened to the rain beat against the glass of the small multi-paned windows. Despite having slept for over an hour, I still felt shattered. I wearily looked up at a large teak Napoleon-hat-shaped clock on the mantel: it was just after eleven thirty. I yawned and rubbed at my eyes again in an attempt to try and shake out the fatigue that was enveloping every part of me. I stared down into the hot embers and watched as white-hot pieces of wood crackled then spat themselves out of the flames onto the wood floor, their fiery glow dying at my feet, leaving black singe marks on the panelling.

I closed my eyes and listened to the gentle ticking of the clock. In the background I could hear the muffled sounds of Lazarus and Benny laughing. Their merriment became louder as the two of them returned through the bar and came over to join me in the snug. Benny was carrying a wooden board laden with food in one hand and three plates in the other. He placed the food and plates down on a small circular table then carried the table over to where I was sitting.

"Trute, she tucked up in a comfy little bed. You git the one next to hers. It's kinda pokey, but shit, any port in a storm, hey brother?"

I looked down at the mountain of food that Benny had brought over.

"Lazarus thought we could do with some supper. Man, he sure likes to put on a fine spread for his guests, yes sir!"

On the board were three ivory-handled butter knives, which were lined up neatly by a pile of two-inch-thick slices of bread, six sausage rolls, a pork pie and a half-round of cheese. Next to the cheese, slices of thick-cut ham had been fanned out on a pretty but chipped porcelain plate. Pickled onions, a large pot of mustard and a dish of butter finished off the hearty spread. From the bar, Lazarus called over to me.

"Here, Joseph, come and choose your poison, son."

Lethargically I hauled myself out of my seat, walked over and found Lazarus standing in front of a row of seven wooden barrels racked up against the side wall. He held a dimpled-glass pint pot in his right hand and

191

waved his other hand across the front of the barrels by way of an introduction.

"We got four ales and three scrumpys: you take your pick, they're all good."

"Scrumpy? What the hell's scrumpy?"

Benny laughed out loud at my ignorance.

"It's rough cider, son. It's made o' fermented apples, strong as a fucker it is too. Couple of pints o' that stuff and you'll be on your back and out for the count until sun-up. Have a hangover on you like somebody hittin' the inside o' your head with a jackhammer."

"Fermented apples? And you drink that stuff?"

"Well, we don't rub it on our pricks, you bloody idiot. Course we drink it! You fancy tryin' a pint?"

Somehow I wasn't convinced by Lazarus's home brew and pointed to one of the other barrels at the far end of the row. "You got any stout?"

Lazarus broke out into a big smile and dropped the pint pot on the table next to the barrels. "Ah, we got ourselves a dark drinker, 'ave we? Here, come an' get yourself one of these."

I followed the big man and leant against the bar and watched as he bent down to a low shelf and picked off a small bottle with a dark crimson label on its side. Lazarus blew off the dust from around the bottle's neck then slammed it on to the brass-topped bar.

"Here, try this: Courage Imperial Russian stout." Lazarus shook his head to himself as he took a bottle opener from off a hook and uncapped the metal top from the bottle and began to pour it into a half-pint beer glass. "Christ, you turn your nose up at scrumpy, you want your head seeing to. You like stout? Well, this fucking stuff is donkey's years old. It's like black battery acid. It'll put hairs on your chest and strip the lining outta your guts. You're welcome to it. I've had a dozen bottles of the bloody stuff collecting dust at the back o' here for over two years. Help yourself to it, cos no other bugger's daft enough to drink it." Lazarus laughed to himself again and went back to one of the scrumpy barrels, turned the brass tap at its base and began to pour the fermented apple drink into his pint pot. I lifted the half-pint glass to my lips and took a swig of the strong, aged stout: it tasted of brown sugar, chocolate and dark fruits. It was my kind of beer. I took another swig and waited for Lazarus to finish filling his glass, then raised my own to thank him.

"Cheers." I sank another mouthful of stout.

"Cheers to you, son . . . So my mate Benny tells me that you an' the little one upstairs are a pair o' runaways with trouble on your tail, that right?"

I leant my back against the bar and thought to myself for a moment before answering the big man's question. "Well, that sure sounds 'bout right. Although what kinda trouble we're in, I ain't too sure of yet. All I know at the minute is that I'm indebted to Benny and now you for keepin' us one step ahead of whoever wants to do that child and me harm."

"Well, Benny never was a man to walk away from a fight, especially when family or friends were involved. He says his niece has been hurt because o' the trouble you have yourself mixed up in, says that the little girl and you are in some deep water. I know Benny; he wouldn't have come seeking me out in a storm without a good reason. Benny, he can stand his own ground in a punch-up, I've seen him do it countless times. He must think that the people after your hide really mean business."

"Benny may well be right. I don't think, whoever these guys are, that they're small-time operators, Lazarus. They're well connected, tough and seem pretty determined to get what they want."

"And what do you think they're after, Joseph?"

"As far as I can work out, they just want Truth." I took another draught of my bitter, dark beer and stared back at Lazarus.

"That child upstairs? What's so important about the kid?"

"I don't know, but I intend to find out, even if it's the last ting I do."

The hefty landlord stared down at the ground and dragged his foot rhythmically across the wood floor while he thought to himself for a moment. He looked back at me with a wry smirk on his face and cleared his throat before speaking. "Well, if these boyos are as tough as you say they are, that may well be the case." Lazarus rested his elbow against the rack of barrels and looked at me curiously. "Benny says that you're some kinda detective, that right?"

"I prefer enquiry agent, sounds less Dick Barton. It's a job, but it barely pays the rent."

"That a worthwhile job then?"

"Worthwhile? I don't know 'bout that. In my line o' work I'm asked to find people who are missin; I may recover valuable property that's disappeared. I give people a hand if they're being swindled, and sometimes, if I'm lucky, I like to think I put tings right when it's all gone wrong. I don't always succeed, but when I do . . . Yes, I think you could call my job worthwhile."

"Well, sounds like a dirty little job to me."

"It's a dirty little world, Lazarus."

Lazarus smiled and slowly nodded his head to himself. He looked across to Benny, who was greedily tucking into his supper. He then walked back behind the bar and picked up another bottle of stout and the opener, then slapped me on the side of my arm and handed them to me. He nodded towards Benny.

"Come on, son, let's go and get you something to eat before that big-gutted bleeder eats me outta house and home. We'll worry about your problems in the morning."

Lazarus walked off in front of me to join his friend. I watched them for a moment as they raised their glasses to toast each other then settled back to eat the supper. I thought of Vic and where my cousin might be tonight. I thought how much I missed him now that my back was against the wall and what I wouldn't give to have him here by my side tonight. I thought how I should never have taken Ida Stephens' money and her stupid job on, and I wished that I'd never listened to Theodore Fowler and walked down into the basement of those swimming baths and found the child Truth huddled up in the dark. Most of all, I wished I didn't feel so damn scared.

I walked over and sat down next to Lazarus and Benny, my appetite lost. I uncapped the bottle of dark ale and poured it into my glass then took a long draught. Shame overcame my hesitant thoughts as feelings of grim fear dragged at my belly. The laughter of my two companions was lost to me as I entered a private and opaque domain deep within my mind, an unforgivable place where my bleak spirits would lure me down into a murky world of my own making, its cruel grip pulling at my battered consciousness like a demon tearing at the broken will of a lost soul.

CHAPTER
EIGHTEEN

It was the smell of bacon frying that woke me from my usual unwelcome night-time reverie. Bad dreams had plagued me through what little sleep I'd managed to get. I'd finally dragged myself off to bed at around one thirty, leaving Benny and Lazarus to tell old war stories and drink themselves into a merry stupor. My head was throbbing, the early sign of an unwelcome hangover brought on by the six bottles of strong Imperial Russian stout that I'd sunk during the small hours of the morning.

I looked over at Truth's bed: the blankets had been pulled back and she was nowhere to be seen. I snatched my wristwatch from off the bedside cabinet and peered at the face; it was just after eight thirty. I kicked the sheets off me and sat up with my legs hanging off the edge of the mattress and immediately felt woozy. I squinted around the dull-looking room while I acclimatised myself to the steady, painful thumping going off in my skull. I could hear the sound of rain gently bouncing off the bedroom window. I leant forward and grabbed hold of the edge of one of the curtains and drew it back then stared out blankly at the grey skies and drizzle that greeted me. I finally mustered the will to get myself up then slowly walked to the foot of the bed and picked up my shirt and trousers from where I'd dropped them before turning in for the night. Feeling like death warmed up, I sluggishly got myself dressed then slipped on my shoes and at a snail's pace made my way downstairs.

I found Benny and Truth in the kitchen, sat at a large wooden dining table; both of them were watching Lazarus, who was standing over the stove at the other end of the room spooning hot oil over the yellow yolks of six large hen's eggs that were spitting and crackling inside a huge iron skillet. Benny turned and looked at me and began to slowly shake his head.

"Hey, Trute, will you just look at the state o' this . . . If it ain't Uncle Remus. Good to see you finally managed to drag yo'self outta yo' pit, Joseph," Benny gently nudged at Truth's belly with his big elbow and winked at her. Truth began to giggle. "You know, you is lookin' rougher than a badger's ass'ole. You need to keep off the stout, brother." Benny clapped his hands together and burst out laughing.

Lazarus nodded at me by way of a morning welcome and pointed to a dining chair with the greasy end of his spoon.

"Dear oh dear, looks like you best take a seat before you fall down, old son. I told you that damn ale was bloody strong; you'd've been safer on the scrumpy."

Benny pounded the flat of his hand on the top of the table and the two men roared with laughter again. I felt the inside of my head pounding away as I dropped down in the seat next to Truth. I rubbed at my scalp with my fingers then smiled gingerly at her.

Truth stared up at me, scrunched up her nose then began copying what she had just seen Benny doing and began to shake her head from side to side in disapproval at the sorry state I'd gotten myself in. She looked me up and down with a sneer on her face then began to laugh, joining the two big men in their rowdy amusement at my pathetic and fragile condition.

My hangover certainly didn't stop me from eating the hearty breakfast that Lazarus had prepared for us all. I wolfed down a plateful of bacon and eggs accompanied by grilled mushrooms, tomatoes and thickly sliced toast. I washed it all down with three mugs of freshly brewed black coffee and at least a pint and a half of cold water. Truth attentively kept getting up from her seat and refilling my empty glass from the tap at the kitchen sink. Every time she returned to the table, I thanked her for her thoughtfulness. Truth simply smiled at me as she placed the glass of water in front of me and then, without uttering a word, continued to eat her breakfast.

I realised that Truth was still very wary of me. Hell, why shouldn't she be distrusting of a stranger after all she had been through? Getting Truth to trust me wasn't going to be easy, but there was so much more I needed to find out about her. So many pieces of the child's sad little life remained an enigma. I was finding it tricky to think of a way to get her to open up and confide exactly what had gone on back at the orphanage, what secrets she held within her and why a group of men were prepared to kill to get her back.

As I finished off my coffee, I thought back to how I had seen the little girl making quiet conversation with both Benny and Estelle. Truth had seemed less tense in their company, and in the brief time we had been stopping in their home, the child had struck up a blossoming relationship with Benny's spooky mother-in-law, Momma Cecile. True, Truth had spoken to me briefly down at the beach in Porlock, but she'd given up very little information and what she had told me simply revolved around the nameless men that she feared so very much, the men who came in the night to steal children.

After breakfast I took myself up to the tiny bathroom, washed and shaved, then changed into a fresh shirt. On top of a dresser by one of the beds stood a tin of perfumed talcum powder and a small bottle of Old Spice aftershave lotion. I pulled out the small stopper from the white bottle of men's cologne and rubbed some of the fragrant liquid around my jaw and chin, smarting as the alcohol stung at my freshly shaven jowls and neck. Welcome rays of sunshine now poured through the tiny windowpanes into the bedroom and had begun to warm the place up a little, lifting my flagging spirits a touch.

As I was hurriedly running my fingerstips through the dense curls of my knotted-up hair, I heard a faint tapping sound from outside in the hall. I took a look out of the bedroom door and found Truth sat on the top step of the stairs staring into space, the fingers of

200

her petite right hand drumming on the wall beside her. I picked up my hat and coat from off the chair and walked out to join her, just as Benny bellowed up the stairs to me.

"Hey, Joseph, you all spruced up and back in the land of the living yet?" Benny was chuckling to himself as I leant over the banister and peered down at him. He smiled mischievously back up at the two of us.

"Yeah, just 'bout." I pulled on my coat, fitted my hat onto my head and looked back down at the big man.

"'Bout time too. You know, the pair of you look like a couple of waifs and strays that are 'bout to get up to no good. Git yourselves down here. Lazarus thought you and Trute might like to take a look 'bout now we've got ourselves some finer weather out there. We're in some mighty pretty countryside. Do the two of you good to get out in the fresh air for a time, what you say?"

Benny held out his arm to Truth and called her to him by wagging three of his stubby fingers back and forth; in his other hand was the little girl's coat. Truth looked cautiously down at Benny's huge open hand for a moment then back up at me. I smiled at her and she returned her gaze to Benny.

"Sounds like a good idea, Benny."

Truth slowly rose from the top step and began walking down the stairs. I followed behind and waited while Benny knelt down and helped Truth to put her coat on.

"OK, come on little lady, let's go find ourselves Lazarus. He tells me they got themselves some real special animals that live in these parts: horses, lambs, big-horned cattle — you ever seen big-horned cattle, Trute?" Benny boomed enthusiastically as the child began to slip her arms into her coat.

Truth, her eyes excited and wide as saucers, quickly shook her head as Benny looked up and winked at me while he gently pulled the collar of the coat around the back of Truth's neck. He raised himself back to his feet and turned and swiftly made his way through the pub towards the front door. He turned briefly and hollered back after us. "Well then, what you waiting for, Christmas? Let's get the two of you out in those wide-open spaces. You and Joseph here have got some explorin' to do."

Truth and I followed Benny out and around the side of the big public house into the gardens at the rear of the property. In the near distance we could hear the sound of some kind of machinery.

We found Lazarus in one of his large outbuildings. He was dressed in a woollen World War II khaki army shirt and dark-green overalls, and was stood over an electric grinder, sharpening the edges of a blackened Fairbairn-Sykes commando knife. Sparks flew around his face and chest as he glided the metal blade across the fast-moving wheel. Benny called out to Lazarus over the din, the landlord turning quickly when he heard his friend's booming voice over the noise of the grinder. Lazarus flicked a black switch at the side of the machine, shutting it off, then slid his thumb carefully along the now razor-sharp knife-edge, nodding his head in approval at his own work before turning and staring down at Truth, the fierce-looking weapon held at his side. He bent down towards the child, his sweaty arms at his side, the blade-point towards Truth.

"So, I hear you'd like to see some of our local beasts?"

Truth took a step back and stared back at Lazarus, a fearful look on her face at hearing the knife-wielding giant's talk of beasts.

Benny looked down at Truth, scrunched up his nose and shook his head frantically to let the child know there was nothing to worry about then snapped back at his old friend, jabbing his finger towards the commando dagger in Lazarus' hand. "Put that damn cutter away, Lazarus, you a fool sometimes, you know that? You got the child scared witless befo' she even set foot in a field. She's probably tinking she's 'bout to take a look at the Loch Ness monster, you yakkin' on 'bout beasts. This pickney ain't bin any further than the edge of the River Severn on a day trip. She's a damn city kid, probably never even seen a cow befo'."

Berated, Lazarus realised his lack of sensitivity and laid the knife on the bench next to him, covering it with an oily rag. He put the flat of his hand to his mouth by way of some kind of juvenile apology to Truth. He then attempted to dig himself out of trouble with Benny by softening up the poor child some more.

"I'm sorry, young 'un. Benny here's right. We just got ourselves some farmyard animals, that's all. There ain't anything for you to go fretting about round here, you're as safe as houses, promise." Lazarus shot Truth a contrite smile then quickly grabbed his old leather army jerkin from off a peg on the back of the door. He stuck his muscled arms into the cut-off sleeve of his worn military tunic and began to march off across the yard. "Come on, you pair, let's start this here tour o' the place."

As Truth and I began to follow after Lazarus, Benny gently took hold of my arm and held me back for a moment, then got close to me and whispered into my ear.

"I'm gonna give Estelle a call, let her know we're OK, see if she's heard how Loretta's doing or has any more news on that trouble you got after your tail."

"OK, you send that wife o' yours my best wishes. We'll see you in a while."

I was about to thank the big man for all he was doing for me and young Truth, but before I could utter another word he'd turned away from me and was starting to walk back towards the pub, the sun at his back, his hulking frame casting a huge shadow in front of him as he strode off to make his telephone call.

I caught up with Lazarus and Truth just as they were about to climb over a wooden stile into a pasture carpeted with a mass of yellow buttercups. Lazarus helped Truth over the stile and the two of us climbed over and joined her. After last night's storm, the wet grass under our feet squelched as we trod across it. I watched as my silent young companion walked a few feet ahead of us: oblivious of the sodden ground underneath her, she gazed cheerfully out at the picturesque open expanse of countryside and the golden blossom that sprang up all around her. Lazarus had also noticed how Truth was lost in the pretty surroundings; he spoke as we continued to walk, the timbre in his voice much softer, making him sound more like a learned Sunday school teacher than rough publican.

"You really think that child 'as never seen countryside like this or livestock before, Joseph?"

I shrugged my shoulders. "It's hard to tell. From the look on her face at the minute, I'd say not."

Lazarus smiled to himself then stopped in his tracks, watching Truth as she stared out across the hilly terrain in the distance. I stood at the big man's side, the warmth of the sun caressing my neck and shoulders. Lazarus turned to me, a look of bemusement on his face.

"She sure doesn't have much to say for herself, does she? Doesn't that come across as being a little strange to you?"

I took my handkerchief out of my trouser pocket, tipped my hat back on my head and wiped the perspiration from my brow. "Lazarus, someting in my guts tells me that child has only ever known strange. I can't say exactly, but I get the feeling Truth's silence is the only way she can keep whatever's putting the fear o' God into her at bay."

Lazarus slowly shook his head to himself. "Don't seem right, does it? A young girl like that being smothered in so much darkness."

I shrugged my shoulders again as I stared out across the pasture and felt a small measure of the child's despair begin to creep into my being. "Who knows, Lazarus, who knows? Perhaps the darkness has been a better friend to her than we can ever know. Maybe the cold light of day isn't a companion that Truth wants to keep."

I began to walk on, leaving Lazarus standing, deep in thought. I called back to him after I'd taken a couple of paces. "Take it from me, brother: where I come from they say a fallen angel ain't never far from your side. I think the same is true for that child in front of us there. Her demons, they come out to haunt her in the daylight just the same as they do in the blackness of night."

The three of us continued to walk for a good while longer. I tagged behind a few paces while Lazarus introduced Truth to various breeds of cattle and sheep that lazily grazed as we strolled from field to field. It was good to see the youngster begin to relax a little. Both Benny and Lazarus had been able to gain a little of Truth's confidence. I, on the other hand, felt as if I was drawing her closer to the devils she feared rather than being able to offer up any solace to her.

It was just after midday by the time we started to make our way back towards the pub. The sun was high up in the sky, the air hot and thick with the heady perfume from the foxgloves and dog-rose blossom that ran alongside the bramble hedgerows. Butterflies fluttered around our heads and summer birdsong trilled and quavered around us, reminding me of my once idyllic existence back home on Barbados. I felt content in the moment, and the worries and fears that had been gnawing away in the pit of my stomach had thankfully abated for now. Truth, her coat tied by the arms around her waist, was knelt picking dandelions and daisies. She'd barely uttered a word again since we'd been out but had occasionally broke out into a smile when she'd seen something that amused her and appeared to have relaxed a little. I got the feeling that, like me, she had found a brief measure of contentment while being enchanted by the picturesque countryside. As we climbed back over the stile, Lazarus raised his arm in front of him and pointed towards a wooded area at the rear of the pub.

"You come and take a look at this; I've got something that may interest the pair of you."

Truth and I followed Lazarus onto a dust path that ran across the last meadow. We made our way underneath a dense canopy of oak trees and continued to walk further into the shaded coppice, which sat only a few feet away from the landlord's outbuildings. Some twenty yards in, Lazarus abruptly stopped in his tracks and pointed down towards a small dip between the trees. Sat amongst the moss and lush green grass was a low, square stone structure with a four-foot wooden fence and gate around it.

"Is that a well of some kind, Lazarus?" I asked.

Truth took a few brave steps closer and peered gingerly over the fence then stared back at the publican.

Lazarus chuckled to himself then beamed down at Truth, who was now eagerly hanging on the big man's next words. "That ain't a well, Joseph old son, that's one big old cave down there."

"A cave, down there? You're kidding me, right?" I moved closer to get a better look and stood next to Truth, the two of us intrigued.

"I ain't kidding you. Here, come and take a look." Lazarus opened up the gate then bent down next to the stone edging and began to brush away at the dirt and leaves with his big hands to reveal a small wooden hatch that was held shut by two large black bolts. A large metal looped handle sat in the centre of the previously hidden door. Lazarus drew back the two iron bolts and hauled the hatch open. As Truth and I peered in to get a better look, Lazarus stuck his hand into his jerkin pocket and took out a packet of Park Drive cigarettes and a box of matches. He casually stuck one of the filterless cigarettes between his lips, struck a match and lit it, taking a deep drag before throwing the burning match into the pitch-black forest-floor doorway.

"That down there is part of the Mendip cave system. They run underground for miles around us, they do. There are vast caverns and chambers right beneath where we're standing now. Labyrinthine, they are; dangerous too." Lazarus stabbed his index finger towards the darkened cave entrance. "You go down there, you had better know how the hell to get out, that's for sure. That one down there's called Hunter's Hole: takes you right out towards Cheddar Gorge, it does."

"And you've been down there?"

"Yeah, course I have." Lazarus pulled on his cigarette again then blew out a thick trail of smoke, making Truth cough. "That's a sixteen-foot drop down to the cave floor. I fixed a series of wooden ladders to the wall so I could get to the bottom. Hunter's Hole ain't like most of the caves round here: dry as a bone, it is, no stream running through it. Makes it a little different."

"Different, how come?" I got the feeling that Lazarus was a master of the tall tale, but I was happy to go along with a story that was being so imaginatively recounted. Lazarus had another hefty pull of his cigarette and continued.

"Well, people round these parts say that Joseph of Arimathea used to travel to the village, that he was here to trade in precious metals. On one occasion he was supposed to have brought a young child with him: his nephew, by all accounts. That child was Jesus of Nazareth, so word has it. Story goes that the two of 'em used that cave down there as a place to bed down. A place Joseph could keep his precious metal from thieves and vagabonds. I don't know how true it is, but I can think of bloody better places to rest my head for the night, that's for sure. Still, it's a useful thing to have so close at hand; let's just say I sometimes keep my ill-gotten gains down there." Lazarus winked at Truth and then dropped the hatch cover back down. He snapped the two bolts back into their hoops then re-covered the doorway with the dirt and leaves and got to his feet. "Let's go find Benny, shall we, have ourselves a nice spot of lunch. You like roast-chicken sandwiches, Truth?"

Truth nodded her head enthusiastically.

"Good, roast chicken it is then." Lazarus shut the gate behind him and we began to stroll back through the coppice towards the Hunters Lodge inn. As we broke back out into the warm sunlight, I felt Truth pull at the sleeve of my jacket with her hand. I turned to see what the matter was and found the little girl standing behind me, her arm outstretched, the posy of dandelions and daisies she'd picked earlier held out towards me.

"For me?" I asked. Truth just stared back and jabbed the flowers insistently at my hand. I reached down, took the tiny bouquet from her and stood for a moment, admiring how she'd carefully interlinked the flowers together. It was a fine job. When I looked up to thank her, Truth had already begun to make her way back inside the pub with Lazarus.

As I followed on after them both, I thought I could just make out the gentle laughter of a little girl at play in the meadow behind me. Something in the pit of my stomach told me not to turn and see who was out there in that field, so I just kept on walking. As I reached the doorway of the old inn, a gentle breeze whirled up around me and I could have sworn I heard the sweet, hushed voice of my own departed child, Amelia, call out "Daddy" to me. I closed my eyes as the warm air wafted around me and caressed my face. I held on to the posy in my palm a little tighter. The fragile stems felt like the delicate fingers of my little girl's hand cradled in my own.

CHAPTER
NINETEEN

I had the jitters as I stepped back into the Hunters Lodge inn. Since childhood I'd had a habit of holding on to old ghosts. My mamma called them duppies, inexplicable manifestations that dogged both my waking days and nocturnal slumber. These unbidden lost souls would on occasion return, crossing into the threshold of my own unguarded mind, making me feel ill at ease in my own skin and my surroundings, which was perhaps why I'd picked up on the edgy atmosphere inside the pub as soon as my feet hit the doormat.

Lazarus had told me that the pub didn't open for business at lunchtimes. Walking into the empty inn gave me an unwelcome, frosty feeling, like a solitary black cat caught mooching about the place, bringing its bad luck in with it. The aroma of oak-aged beer and stale cigarette smoke couldn't mask the sombre mood of the old tavern. Despite the sun beating down outside, the inside of the pub felt like it had been draped in an eerie, twilight-soaked shroud. What little illumination there was emanated from the two wall-mounted lights that hung on either side of the fireplace. I looked around the taproom; there was no sign of either Lazarus or Truth, which notched up my anxiety a little more. I was about to call out to see where everybody was when I caught sight of Benny standing in the shadows. He was leant against the bar between two hand pulls, his huge mitts resting against the edge of the brass top. The sleeves of his shirt were rolled up high on his outstretched arms, revealing muscles that were taut and unyielding. Behind him a small transistor radio, which was turned down real low, was playing Peggy Lee's "Don't Smoke in Bed". He looked across at me coldly, like he was staring out an opponent in a boxing ring. I put the posy Truth had given to me into my jacket pocket and started walking over. I got the feeling I was about to be hit with bad news and Benny was the man to break it to me.

"Lazarus is out back makin' Trute some lunch; the child gotta eat and we need to talk." Benny reached up to the shelf above his head and took down a couple of small glasses then filled both of them with generous measures of Navy rum from the optic behind him. He turned to face me, gently sliding the filled glass across the bar. "Here, git that firewater down you, son. You gonna need it." Benny put his own glass to his lips then knocked back his shot of hooch in a single gulp, turning for a refill before the warm liquor had the chance to hit his belly.

"Did you call Estelle? She OK?"

"Yeah, she is now, but she wasn't a few hours back."

"Why, what's happened?" I nervously took a sip of my rum, felt it burn as it went down, and waited.

"She was paid a visit by those coppers that are lookin' fo' Trute."

212

"Jesus, not Estelle, they didn't . . ."

Benny quickly held up the palm of his hand in front of my face, silencing me. "It's OK, Estelle's fine, she ain't in harm's way no more. Same goes fo' that witch of a momma of hers." He lowered his hand and took another sip of rum then looked back at me. "Soon as I knew that those mangy cops had put the strong arm on Loretta, got her to talk an' hurt her like they did, it didn't take no fool to guess they'd be headin' outta Bristol and comin' hammerin' at my gate door fo' the cock got the chance to crow."

Benny turned back to the optics behind him and unhooked the bottle of rum from out of its cradle. He walked back out from behind the bar, took a chair from underneath one of the tables and sat down in front of me then sank the remainder of his rum. He poured himself another three fingers' worth into his glass, pulled out the chair next to him then jerked his head at me to join him. "Sit yo' ass down."

I dropped down next to him. Benny put the lip of the bottle to my glass and topped it up with the dark liquor. I bit at the bottom of my lip and shook my head.

"Benny, I'm sorry, man. I never meant for Estelle to get hooked up in all this mess."

"We is all hooked up in this mess, brother, ain't no way o' runnin' from it now. I knew it wouldn't take 'em long to come lookin' fo' the two of you. They drove down an' headed straight fo' the Ship Inn, like they was told to. Found out you and Trute weren't there. Then they muscled in on the landlord, Sid. He tole 'em where you was headin', but that wasn't good enough.

They needed to be sure. So they hurt him: hurt him till he coughed up all he knew. He told 'em 'bout me, where I lived, and that's just where they went next. The cop you was tellin' me 'bout, one by the name o' Beaumont. It sounds like it was him."

"Did they get heavy?"

"Not at first. They kicked off with the 'good citizen' bullshit. You know the kinda ting. Told her if she had any information on yo' whereabouts then she had to cough it up. Said how you were a dangerous man who'd took off with a vulnerable kiddie. When they could see their flim-flam wasn't workin' on her, they got mean: pinned her to the wall by the throat to git her to talk."

"Jesus, Benny. I don't know what to say."

"Ain't nuttin' to say. You can rest assured I'm gonna be having words with that pig. Estelle, she ain't no fool. I tole her if the heat came a knockin' that she was to let 'em play their hand then give up where we was headin' to. That's just what she did. Estelle said there were two guys that gave her the third degree. She said she thought there was a bunch more outside in the car. The one askin' all the questions was a skinny little runt, blond hair, had a face like a whipped ass. The other one was a big-set fella. He just stood givin' Estelle the evil eye. She said he looked real mean, not like your common-or-garden copper."

"That could be the Yank, Paxton, the fella Doc Fowler told me 'bout."

"Could be. We ain't gonna know fo' sure till they git here, are we?" Benny shot me a curt smile before

214

continuing. "Look, I heard you tell Lazarus last night that you thought these guys meant bidness. Well they do, ain't no doubt 'bout it. Now they gonna find out we mean bidness too."

"What you talking 'bout, 'mean bidness'? There ain't no barterin' with these guys, Benny."

"Who said anyting 'bout barterin'?" Benny stretched his legs out in front of him and knocked back the dregs of his rum, refilling his glass afterwards.

"Look, I need to get Truth the hell outta here. Get her somewhere safe."

"Safe? While these bastards are on your tail there ain't gonna be no safe. Not fo' either of you. You gotta make a stand now or they're gonna hunt you down like a pack o' dogs after a fox."

"Hunt us down. This is Britain you talkin' 'bout, Benny, not the Deep South." Even as I was speaking the words I knew how naive I sounded. Benny hauled himself up in his seat, took a mouthful of rum and leant across the table to me.

"Joseph, if you still tinking you're in the green and pleasant land, son, you're wrong. This might not be Montgomery, Alabama, but it might as well be if you're coloured and breaking some damn honky's laws." Benny spat out the words at me then sank another shot of rum. "Come on, you ain't stupid. You tole me you bin up against dirty cops back home an' right here in Blighty. Shit, you were a policeman fo' long enough. You know the way the Babylon work, especially ones like Beaumont and Paxton. They don't give two shits 'bout hurtin' nobody. Man or woman. They're just

215

plain cruel. They bin prepared to kill an ole man, beat up an' scare women, an' go crawling across half o' the West Country to snatch some little girl from you. Now, you got trouble o' the worst kind going down an' runnin' from it ain't gonna fix nuttin'."

Agitated, Benny filled his glass again and tapped at the corner of the table with his index finger as he thought to himself.

"Joseph, I tole you on the way here how I needed to level up the battlefield fo' us. Beaumont and the others are comin' whether you like it or not. We gotta fight on our hands. This here's our battlefield now, right here. We're gonna fight, take those bozos out at the neck."

"Out at the neck? These are policemen you're talkin' 'bout going head to head with here, you gotta be some kinda mad." I frantically rubbed at my eyes with my fingers, not believing what I was hearing, but Lazarus' booming voice behind me sharpened my focus on the matter at hand.

"Benny's mean, Joseph, he ain't mad. The former quality might be a bit more useful to you than the latter, if you get my drift?" Lazarus winked at me as he walked to the bar; he leant over and grabbed himself a glass then joined the two of us at the table. Lazarus stuck his glass out in front of him and pointed at the bottle in Benny's hand with his stubby finger. "Give me a drop of that coon juice, will you?" Benny poured the spirit into Lazarus' tumbler then the two friends burst out laughing at each other. I felt like I was the only one in the room who didn't get the joke.

216

"This is insane, Benny. You're right. I know the way the law works. Good and bad. There's gotta be another way. Not every copper's dirty. I gotta find some of them. Get them to see what's going on, investigate what happened to Fowler and why the orphanage and Beaumont want Truth so badly. Taking these guys on is gonna get us in a shitstorm of trouble."

"And you ain't in a shitstorm o' trouble already? Git real. You bin in trouble from the moment you found that kid. What makes you tink anybody's gonna wanna listen to some nigger makin' noise 'bout the Bristol Police giving him a hard time when they is already investigatin' some black guy who's just got off the boat and is runnin' 'bout the countryside with a stolen child. Pigs'll sling your black ass in the pokey quicker than a goose can shit. You run now, you're dead. So is Trute."

Lazarus chipped in, eager to add his two pennies' worth. "Joseph, old son, Benny's right: you haven't got a cat in hell's chance if you run. Let's just say you bolt for it now, where the hell you going to go? You might be able to put some distance between you and these coppers for a couple of days, but they'll catch up with you in the end, sure as God grew little green apples."

Benny stuck his finger in my face. "You a black man with a little white girl in tow. You tink you ain't gonna stand out from the crowd?"

Both men had rammed home their point. Both of them were right. I was in a real jam and they knew it. Now I was scared to hear how they planned to get me out of the mess I was in.

"So what do you wanna do, Benny?"

217

"I wanna kill the fuckers, that's what I wanna do."

"You can't go round killin' police officers. This ain't the Wild West."

"You got a better idea?" Benny snapped back at me.

"There's gotta be some other way." The thought of having blood on my hands again turned my guts over.

"There ain't, believe me. They gonna be coming for that child real soon. Next few hours, that's all we got. Lazarus and me, we cooked up a way outta this. You just gotta hold your nerve, do as I say."

More violence, more corpses. I'd had my fill of death, but it was becoming clear that death had other plans for me.

Benny topped up our glasses with rum. He savoured his first sip then downed the rest. "Beaumont and the others have gotta be workin' off the books on this. It's a strictly 'nobody needs to know' kinda operation and a stitch-up job for you. They got plenty to hide but ain't bothered how much shit they let fly around keepin' it secret. They're gonna come here with some bargainin' chip to play, probably money, someting to twist your arm with, an incentive to give up the girl. Let 'em play their hand, Joseph. Once they got their cards on the table, you make 'em swallow that you'll go for the deal. Offer 'em Trute fo' a price and get 'em to come back fo' her later."

"That's a pretty slim kinda plan you got going on there, Benny. What makes you think they won't just muscle in an' try to take Truth by force?"

"Oh, I ain't got no doubt that they'll have consider that. It'll be an option; that's why you gotta make 'em tink they got the winnin' hand from the off. Make 'em tink you just a greedy nigger, happy to make himself thirty pieces o' silver fo' that child's hide. Whatever they offer, ask fo' a bit more. Don't go crazy now, just up the ante a little. Get 'em to come back fo' Trute later, preferably after dark. We in the middle o' nowhere here, get 'em to see the benefit of a night-time switch. The rest you gotta make up as you go along. Hey, you're the detective, making stuff up gotta come easy to a fella like you."

Benny and Lazarus chuckled to themselves. I still wasn't convinced. Benny shuffled in closer and elaborated on his plan.

"These boys, they gonna be tinking you have someting up your sleeve, gonna be suspicious that you could be stallin'. That's why you gotta convince 'em otherwise. They ain't gonna want any witnesses to what they got planned. Well, the same goes fo' us. They'll have already thought you'll maybe try and run with the girl, that you'll wanna git to the authorities. They ain't gonna let that happen. They're gonna be leavin' somebody to watch this place, keep a firm eye on what's going on. They ain't stupid; don't treat 'em like it either."

I swallowed hard, trying to get everything Benny had just told me straight in my head. "What 'bout the Yank, Benny, where does he fit in all this?"

"Where the Yank fits into all this? I don't give a fuck where he fits in. He goes the same way as the rest of 'em."

"And by the same way, you mean dead." I couldn't believe I was actually talking about being involved in the cold killing of another human being.

"Well, I ain't gonna slow waltz him outta the joint, cos he gonna be dead."

"And what do you plan to do with these dead cops? You can hardly barrow 'em down to the village cemetery."

"The question you need to be askin' ain't what we gonna do with 'em, it's where they're gonna go."

Lazarus leant across to me and spoke under his breath into my ear. "Hunter's Hole, Joseph."

"Jesus, you mean that damn cave you showed me earlier?"

Lazarus slowly nodded back at me. "Yeah, once they go down there that's the end of it, there ain't nobody ever gonna find them."

I felt my insides turn over. I wanted to be sick, wanted no part in Benny and Lazarus' butchery. I ran my clammy fingers through my palms and looked back at Benny.

"And Truth, what happens to her after all this murder and havoc has taken place?"

I saw Benny gesture with his head for Lazarus to give us a moment alone. Lazarus quietly got up and put his hand on my shoulder. "I'm going to check on Truth, see how she's getting on with that mountain of chicken sandwiches I left her with earlier." The publican left us alone to our conversation, heading for the kitchen, whistling to himself.

Benny waited until Lazarus was out of sight then leant forward and rested his hand on top of mine. When he spoke, it was in a whisper. "Look, son, you remember how I tole you 'bout Estelle an' me, 'bout how we lost them t'ree babies of ours? I tole you the Lord, he took those pickneys fo' we even had chance to hold 'em. Well, I tink the Lord's just seen fit to give us a child to hold and look after, Joseph. Why don't you let me and Estelle give Trute a home. We'd love her like she was our own blood, give her the best she could want. Let me do right by the child: give her to me, son."

I slowly drew my hand from underneath Benny's palm and sat back in my chair. "She ain't mine to give, Benny."

"She ain't anybody's, Joseph, that's the point. She's an orphan. Even if you thought you could make all this madness go away, get her to some place safe, what's gonna happen to her then, when you've left her, where's she gonna end up? You gonna let her go back to some hellhole of an orphanage?"

"That ain't up to me, Benny. It's not my place to be makin' those kinda decisions. I can't just hand Truth over to you cos you wanna give Estelle a kid to love. She ain't my kin, she ain't yours. I just gotta do what's right by the child."

The muscles in Benny's jaw tightened; his eyes were hard and unblinking.

"And you tink sendin' Trute back into care is gonna be right fo' her? You gone an' seen what them folk in that orphanage have done to her. You tellin' me that's right?

"No, it ain't right, but me handin' Truth to you ain't right either. Say you did take her on. Tell me, how you gonna explain to folks that start askin' how Estelle and you have come to be parentin' a little white girl? What you gonna tell 'em, that Santa Claus left her as a Christmas gift at the bottom of your chimney?"

Benny rose out of his seat and walked back over to the bar. When he spoke, he did so with his back to me. His tone scolding, like a parent berating a naughty child.

"Listen to me, I got myself a wedge o' cash stashed away; I got property an' a bidness I can sell. Estelle and I got dual citizenship. We'd take her back home, back to Barbados. Nobody be the wiser. She'd grow up in paradise."

"Barbados ain't paradise, Benny."

"Maybe not, but Bim would be a helluva lot kinder place for her to grow up than what she's bin used to over here. Surely you can see that. What right you got decidin' on what's best fo' Trute? You gonna take her in, be her father? Do the right ting, son, give her me."

It was hearing the big man say the word "give" that stuck in my craw the most. The idea of handing Truth over as if I was trading her at some slave market just didn't sit right with me. Just thinking about it brought me out in a cold sweat. But despite all my objections Benny was right in what he had just said about Bim. Truth would certainly have a better life back on my old home on Barbados. If you had cash you could live out a

222

pretty comfortable existence on the island, but money couldn't buy love. I had little doubt that both Estelle and Benny could provide for the child financially, I believed that with them Truth would want for very little, but would they love her as if she were truly their own? Could they be the parents that Truth needed, that she deserved? Something deep inside me told me that they could. But was my intuition enough? Was handing over Truth to Benny and Estelle based on my gut instinct really the right thing to do? Or was I just looking for an excuse to let others take on a concern I knew deep inside I just couldn't handle? Was I prepared to wash my hands like Pontius Pilate and walk away, telling myself "It ain't my problem any more"?

I scratched at the back of my scalp with the tips of my fingers, my head filled with problems I had no answers for. I dropped my head, my chin touching my chest. I could feel Benny's agitation from where I was sat. I looked down at my hands, opened up my fingers and stretched them. I felt dirty with all the talk of killing I'd just heard. Talking about killing a man was one thing, actually snuffing him out was another, and no amount of hand washing could get the stink of the dead off your skin once the deed was done. I got up without saying another word, my silence telling Benny more than words ever could. I grabbed my jacket and headed back to my room. I needed time to think, to get my head straight and make sense of what was about to go down. Most of all, I needed to get word to Vic about the trouble I was in.

CHAPTER
TWENTY

Getting hold of Vic wasn't going to be easy. I asked Lazarus if I could use his telephone and make a call back to St Pauls. I stood by the staircase in the small hallway at the back of the pub with the phone receiver in one hand. I fished out my little notebook from my inside jacket pocket with my other. I flipped through the pages with my thumb, found the number I needed and dialled. The line on the other end gave a dozen rings or so before somebody finally picked up. The voice answering was both intimidating and strangely comforting in equal measure.

"Wuh you want?" Everton "Redman" Innes' earthy Bajan accent boomed down the phone at me. His tone was impatient, his breathing heavy and laboured after being called away from his punchbag.

"Redman, that you?"

"Yeah, wuh you want wi' me, man?"

"Redman, it's me, JT. How you doin'?"

"Hey JT! I'm good, brother, good. You?"

"I ain't too hot, Redman. Look, I need ya help."

"Help, what's up? If you lookin' fo' cash you axing the wrong fella."

"I ain't looking for a loan; I need to get hold of Vic."

"Vic ain't 'ere, he in London."

"I know he ain't there. Can you get a message to him? It's real important."

"I can try, but you know Vic, he's one shifty Negro to pin down. I know he's stoppin' at some floozie's joint in the East End. He left me a number so I could give him the nod 'bout a special delivery he got comin' later this week." Hearing Redman mention a special delivery gave me a little hope. Vic had illicit booze and knocked-off goods being shipped in from all over the place. My cousin could make a sloth look industrious at the best of times but Vic was never lazy when it came to business. I knew he'd check in to make sure that his cargo was in one piece and ready to roll. If he hadn't heard from Redman that everything was good, he'd call the gym to find out what was going on himself. I just had to pray that Vic would be making the call sooner rather than later.

"OK, Redman. When I get off the phone I need you to call Vic straight away. You got that?"

Redman blew hard down the phone, irritated by my demand. "Yeah, I got it. Look JT, what's all this shit 'bout? Vic ain't gonna like me chasin' his tail like this."

"You let me worry 'bout Vic. When you get hold of him I need you to tell him that JT is in real trouble and that I need him to get his ass back to St Pauls. Tell him I ain't foolin' 'bout and that I'll call you back with word on where he can meet me. You see a pen anywhere round you?"

"Yeah, there's one down here." I heard Redman grunt as he leant across Vic's desk to retrieve the pen.

"OK, take this down." I reeled off the address of the Hunters Lodge inn and the number I was calling from. "If you get a hold of Vic in the next few hours, you tell him what I've said and give him those details. I don't know how much longer I'm gonna be here; tell him as soon as I can get to a phone I'll be calling back. Understand?"

"I got it." Redman blew a jet of air impatiently down the phone at me.

"Thanks, Redman, you're a gent."

"Ain't that the trute. People always be sayin' 'bout how I'm this gent. Somebody needs to be tellin' my woman that's the case next time she badmout'in' me. I'll be seein' ya, JT." I could sense the boxer becoming impatient on the other end of the line and called out to him before he cut me off.

"And Redman, if the police come callin', askin' 'bout me, you tell 'em you ain't seen or heard from me, OK?"

"Fuck the police."

The line went dead. I stood for a moment, alone in the hallway, my hand still gripping the receiver of the telephone, a low burring tone humming away in my ear as I mulled over Redman's defiant last words.

I found Benny sat back on his chair in the bar about to down another shot of rum. When he saw me walking towards him, he smiled and pulled out a stool for me to join him. His serious mood appeared to have receded and he'd returned to being jovial and relaxed, and that put me on edge. It was as if our earlier conversation about Truth had never occurred. He chuckled to himself and poured a small measure of rum into my

226

empty glass. I nodded my head in thanks but left the dark spirit sat in front of me. I'd had my fill of hard liquor for the day. My head was already becoming thick and pained by another unwelcome boozy haze.

Benny nudged me in the side of my ribs, a roguish look on his face. "Estelle and that old hag of a mutha of hers are on their way to my cousin's in Hartland Quay. It's remote, but the wife likes it quiet." Benny chuckled to himself again. "Damn, though, if that poor woman gonna git any peace with that witch naggin' on her ass like she does. Rather her than me, I say."

Benny finished his drink and reached for the bottle just as Lazarus came in from the kitchen with Truth. The publican was carrying a small metal tray, which he placed on the table in front of us. He bent down and lifted a couple of plates containing cold roast chicken, pickled onions and thickly sliced wedges of bread and butter, and handed them over to Benny and I. He then turned back to Truth and pointed his finger across the pub towards one of the window seats.

"You come with me, young 'un. Let's see if we can't find you something to mess about with while the grown-ups eat their lunch and have a natter."

The little girl did as she was told and followed after Lazarus. He sat her down on a cushion on the floor, and she watched as he headed over to a small, copper-edged wooden chest that sat next to the hearth. Lazarus opened up the chest lid and brought out a set of ancient-looking skittle pins and a worm-eaten polished oak ball. He set the pins up on the floor beside Truth and gave her the ball.

"Here, you have a play with these, see how many you can knock down." Truth got up and looked at the ball in her hand for a moment then slung it at the pins, sending them sprawling across the wood floor. Lazarus clapped his hands and burst out cheering then turned to the two of us. "Looks like we've got a skittle champ on our hands here, lads."

Truth, a beaming smile on her face, ran for the ball then began to stand up the pins on the floor again, eager for another go. Lazarus went back to the bar, uncapped a bottle of Corona orange soda, stuck a straw in it and took it over to Truth. "Here, you'll need a drink. It's thirsty work is skittles." Truth took the bottle and stared at it for a moment.

Benny called across the room to the bemused little girl. "It's OK child, it ain't poison you got there. Ain't you ever seen a bottle of pop befo'?"

Truth stared at Benny and then shook her head at him. I watched Lazarus' big shoulders slowly stoop in disbelief when he saw Truth's response to the soda pop. The jovial publican leant down and rubbed the top of Truth's head with his hand and smiled at her. "Go on, try it, it tastes gert lush."

Both Benny and I were bewildered by Lazarus' remark. Truth, scrunching up her nose, was equally puzzled. Lazarus nodded at the bottle then gently nudged Truth with his elbow. "Have a sip, then."

Truth reluctantly stuck the straw into her mouth and began to drink. When she finally released the little plastic tube from her lips the look of joy on her face was a picture. Lazarus, pleased with himself, headed back to join us, calling back to Truth as he did, "See, I told you. Gert lush, that's what that is, bloody gert lush!"

Benny, his chin and lips covered in grease, was sat chomping down on the thick end of a chicken leg when Lazarus sat down next to him. The publican poured the two of them another hefty shot of rum then leant back in his seat, shaking his head to himself, and watched his friend tearing at the rooster flesh with his teeth. "That man loves his food, Joseph. Always been a real hog has Benny."

Benny, hurt by Lazarus' remark, sneered back at him as he continued to munch at the chicken flesh like a wild dog. Lazarus went to top up my already full glass with more rum. I bent forward in my seat and placed my hand over the glass. "No more hooch for me thanks."

Lazarus eyeballed me suspiciously for a moment then shrugged his shoulders and drank the remainder of his rum. He poured another shot for himself and took a sip. I could feel the man's gaze burning into the side of my face as I sat watching Truth playing with the ball and skittles.

"Joseph, far as I'm concerned, this here rum is Dutch courage, and I get the feeling that we're gonna be needing a whole barrel of the stuff before this day is through. Take my advice, old son, have another slug of the firewater. It'll help take the edge off those screaming abdabs you've got clawing at your insides."

Lazarus' foreboding words felt like a death knell ringing through my ears. A bitter taste rose up into my

229

mouth. I swallowed hard but couldn't shift the unpleasant lingering tang. I looked pathetically at the shot of rum sat in front of me, hesitated for a split second then reached down for my glass and knocked back the hooch. I let the harsh spirit run down my throat and ignite low inside my belly then felt a dark wave of shame wash over me. I continued to stare at Truth, deep in thought, unable to shake my lingering sense of self-loathing. I felt alone except for the unwelcome presence of fear sat on one side of me and defeat on the other.

Heavy black rain clouds had begun to gather in the sky and the air had taken on the musky aroma of damp leaves and freshly mown grass. It was just after five thirty that afternoon when the first of two cars pulled up outside of the Hunters Lodge inn. I stood alone looking through the bay window across the bar and watched as two heavyset men got out of a Rover Coupe. Its mud-spattered olive-green paintwork told me that the heavy-looking car had most likely been travelling across the same inhospitable terrain that we had driven across the night before. The two men, both with sharp military-style crew cuts and dressed in short brown leather jackets and denims, stood surveying the pub and the surrounding area for a moment, neither speaking nor appearing to be in any great hurry. They gave off an aura of depravity and malevolence that I could feel in my bones from thirty feet away.

The second motor, a blue Vauxhall Viva, stunk to high heaven as the kind of unmarked police car I was used to seeing patrolling the streets back in St Pauls. The driver's door swung open and Detective Constable Beaumont pulled himself unceremoniously up out of his seat and leant on the arch of the car door frame for a moment before sticking his head back into the motor. I struggled to see but could just make out a fourth individual, another man sitting in the passenger seat, that Beaumont was talking to. If there were more of them inside both vehicles, I sure as hell couldn't pick them out. Beaumont finally withdrew his head from the cab of his car, a grey suit jacket in his left hand. He quickly pulled it on then walked across to the two other men. The three of them spoke briefly then headed towards the pub. I leant my back against the bar and waited.

The sound of the iron door latch being lifted out of its cradle trumpeted their arrival. More bent law. Beaumont entered first, dwarfed by the two bigger guys staying back a few feet either side of him. He stood with his hands behind his back, his sandy hair thinning across his scalp. I would have put his age at about forty-five. A smug smirk stretched across his freckled, pompous-looking face. Surprisingly, it wasn't Beaumont that kicked off the conversation. That pleasure went to one of the thugs stood behind him.

"Joseph Ellington?"

I didn't answer and waited for the man to say more, but he remained silent. He spoke with an American accent, deep and rich, like molasses falling off the back of a spoon. The man's voice was filled with arrogant authority. Just from him saying my name I could tell that I was being addressed by the law. Beaumont turned to the man behind him briefly and shook his head to himself before returning to stare at me and offering up another self-satisfied snigger.

"You'll have to excuse Joseph here, he's the quiet type. Isn't that right, Joseph?"

As expected, I stayed quiet. Beaumont let his arms fall at his side and walked across the room and stood in front of me. He held out his hand. I looked at it. An outstretched policeman's hand normally holds handcuffs or a truncheon and rarely a welcome sense of equality to a black man. Beaumont let his hand hover in mid-air for a few more moments before awkwardly withdrawing it. He turned back to the two men behind him and began his formal introductions, pointing to each of them with the flat of his hand as he did so.

"Joseph, these gentlemen with me are Mr Paxton and Mr Jardine."

Paxton nodded by way of a haughty acknowledgement. Jardine just stared back at me coldly. Both had the kind of grisly look about them that said they were as mean as a couple of hungry wolves. I let them keep on giving me the evil eye and thought now was as good a time as any to open my mouth. I was already sick of hearing Beaumont's whiney, fawning voice spouting at me.

"What is it you want, Beaumont?"

"That's a good question, Joseph . . . good question. Straight to the point, I like that. Truth is, I've got myself a little bit of a problem."

"That right? People got problems the length and breadth of this country. What yours gotta do with me?"

232

Before Beaumont could answer me, Paxton snapped out a brutal retort.

"For a quiet man you got a real smart mouth on you, nigger."

"It's 'bout all I have got."

Paxton grunted under his breath and took a step forward toward me, his right fist clenched. I let my right arm drop to my side and slowly let it rest behind my back. Beaumont, feeling the aggression seeping out of the two men behind him, raised his hand in an attempt to placate their aggrieved dispositions.

"Let's keep this friendly, shall we, Joseph. I'll come to the point. These men have a vested interest in some property you have acquired recently. They've come a long way to negotiate that property's return to its rightful owner. I'm here to mediate the successful transaction of any business we may do this afternoon."

"What the hell you talkin' 'bout, Beaumont?"

"I'm talking about being the man who can improve your lot in life."

"I doubt it."

"Hear me out."

"OK, get talkin' then. But keep your jive to yo'self, try stickin' to plain English. That way I won't have to keep reachin' for the dictionary every time some crap climbs outta your mout'."

I watched Jardine grin to himself at my remark. When he realised that I'd seen him drop his guard briefly, his face turned back to stone and he returned to eyeballing me. Beaumont rattled on with his dime-store spiel.

"It's like I said a moment ago. We know that you are in possession of a certain item that both Mr Paxton and Jardine here are very eager to retrieve. These men are United States lawmen. It goes without saying Bristol Constabulary also wishes to see the item mentioned returned to its rightful owner as swiftly as possible."

"And you're speaking for the Bristol police, are you?"

Beaumont shuffled on his feet, thrown a little by my question. "Yes . . . In a roundabout fashion, I am."

"Detective Inspector Fletcher sent you up here on this fool's errand, has he?"

"I don't think it matters to you who sent me."

"I think it does to Ida Stephens. I think she's the one paying your wages for this job you moonlightin' on, not the police."

Beaumont, red-faced, was pushed aside by Paxton, who took a couple more steps towards me. I felt my body tense as Paxton pointed a thick finger in my face and spat out his words.

"Look, boy. You are in way above your head here. It's time you cleaned the wax outta those black ears of yours, listen to what the man here's telling you. It's time to give it up."

"That right? By give 'it' up, I assume your talkin' 'bout Truth?"

"It don't need a name. You know I'm talking about the bastard that belongs to the Walter Wilkins."

"Oh, it's the Walter Wilkins that wants her back so badly . . . So that's why Ida Stephens is employin' you and your friend back there. You're boltin' across half of

234

Somerset with a double-dealing copper like Beaumont, just so you can get your hands on a runaway child, yeah? Someting stinks, and it ain't Beaumont's feet."

Paxton looked across at Beaumont. "I ain't listening to any more of this nigger's horseshit. Give him the envelope. Let's get this over with."

Beaumont reached into his jacket pocket, pulled out a white envelope and stuck it out in front of him. "If you have any idea of what's good for you, you'll take it." Beaumont took a step forward towards me and shoved the envelope at my chest. "There's eight hundred pounds in there. All you have to do is bring me the girl and that'll be the end of it."

"The end of it, just like that? I take the money and just forget all this, do I?"

"Yeah, it's as simple as that, Joseph." Beaumont flashed another one of his "cat got the cream" grins.

"Simple? How's it simple? What 'bout Doc Fowler? Who's gonna be in the frame for what happened to him?"

Jardine finally broke his own silence and barked at me. "Why'd you give a shit? Nobody's gonna be weeping over some drunken, dead old nigger doctor. The finger ain't gonna be pointing at you if you do the right thing here. Get wise, take the fucking money."

Beaumont made another desperate attempt to get me to take the envelope from him by prodding the thing limply at my chest again. Droplets of sweat were forming on his forehead and temples; his scared eyes, panicky, were darting from side to side. His voice crackled when he spoke to me.

"Joseph, let's be honest here." The stale, unpleasant stench of his body odour hit me as he desperately reached out one more time towards me. "You really have gone and pissed off the wrong people. Do yourself a favour. Take the money and go and get the girl. You can walk away from this clean and eight hundred quid richer. You hear me?"

I looked down at the thick envelope filled with cash, thinking for a moment, then slowly lifted my left arm and pushed it away from my chest with the palm of my hand. Beaumont blew out a jet of air from his mouth in fearful exasperation.

"You can keep your blood money, Beaumont. Go back to the orphanage with the Yankee Doodle Dandy twins here and tell Ida that it's gonna take a lot more than eight hundred pounds to buy either my conscience or my silence. Are you hearing me?"

Beaumont didn't get the chance to reply. Paxton pushed him out of the way and took up the reins. He'd already got his speech for me worked out.

"Nigger, this is how it's gonna play out." His Southern drawl began gnawing out his words, his tone dipped in spite and malice. Paxton held out his arm and looked at his wristwatch. "It's just after five thirty. I'm gonna give you five hours. That's three hundred minutes you got to sit and think about how this is all gonna play out. Plenty of time for you to come to your stupid senses, I'd say. Beaumont here is going to leave the envelope on the bar. That's gonna be our final offer. Take it or leave it. In the meantime, we're gonna sit out front and back, and we're gonna wait. Now, it ain't any good you trying to call the police. We already cut your phone line. Shit, one of them boys out there, I think he went and cut nearly every damn phone line from here back to Bristol. Now, I know you ain't on your own, I know you got another nigger with you and most likely whoever runs this old flop joint too. But it don't make any difference. Think about it: you're in the middle of nowhere here and there ain't nowhere for you and that bastard to run to."

Paxton raised his voice as if preaching to an invisible audience. "There ain't nowhere any of you can go. Give me any trouble and I got British police officers outside ready to keep the lid on all of this. You can rest assured that me and Jardine here, we'll be happy to get on with the dirty work if you don't agree to our terms."

Paxton took another step closer towards me. "And you really need to be agreeing, boy. You got till ten thirty to give me what we want or we'll come in and take it from you by force. I'll leave you and your friends' bodies out front of this shithole for the crows to pick over."

I stared back blankly at Paxton and said nothing.

Beaumont leant forward, put the envelope on the bar and spoke close next to my ear. His voice quivered like a frightened child's. "Ellington, he means it. If these men don't get what they want there's going to be a bloodbath here. Don't be a bleedin' fool, give him the girl."

As Beaumont stood back from me I caught sight of the terrified look on his face as the thin barrel of a

L1A1 self-loading rifle was raised from behind my left shoulder and held up to the three men in front of me.

"You gentleman quite finished?" Benny slowly moved out of the shadows from behind the back of the bar and stood at the open hatch for a moment before stepping out to stand next to me, the muzzle of the rifle now aimed squarely at Paxton's face.

Paxton stood his ground and called back over his shoulder to Jardine. "Shit, that's all we need, some old cotton picker with a shooter."

Jardine laughed to himself then nodded at the rifle in Benny's hands. "Boy, you need to mind how you're going. Somebody gonna get hurt, you start pointing that thing about like it's your flopper." I watched as Benny altered his aim slightly so that the rifle was now pointing directly at Jardine. Benny squeezed on the grip, his finger resting gently on the trigger.

"Boy? You callin' me boy?" Benny took a step forward, making all three men retreat a couple of paces towards the door. "Well, I suppose it's a step up from nigger." Benny slowly brought his aim back towards Paxton's head.

Paxton didn't flinch an inch. "Old man, you must have just heard what I just told your friend here."

"I didn't hear nuttin' but a lot o' hot air comin' outta your ugly-assed mout'."

"That ain't a very friendly thing to be saying."

Benny moved a couple more steps out in front of me, the butt of the weapon tucked firmly into the crook of his huge shoulder, the rifle steady in his hands. He slowly raised his thumb, releasing the rifle's safety

238

catch, his aim still directed at Paxton. Next to the American, Beaumont was beginning to look pale, stinking the place out with his sweaty hide. Heavy beads of perspiration poured down from his balding pate and forehead into his eyes, which were glued on the barrel of the gun in front of him.

"Well, I ain't a very friendly man, especially when some backwater shit-kicker starts callin' me boy."

Paxton forced a laugh through his gritted teeth, shaking his head slowly. He stared back at Benny, his expression poker-faced. "You are making a big mistake, old man, big mistake."

"Bin makin' 'em all my life. I sure as hell don't see no reason to stop now."

"Well, in five hours' time you're gonna be wishing you'd been a little less carefree with the way you shrugged off my threat."

Benny took another step forward and levelled the barrel of his rifle a few inches away from Paxton's right eye. "See, that's my problem. I ain't quakin' in my boots yet, cos all you bin doin' since you walked through that gate door back there is threaten folk. Your talk's as cheap as that honky pig's aftershave." Benny shifted his gaze briefly over towards Beaumont, who looked like he was about to pass out, then quickly shifted the muzzle of the rifle a little closer towards Paxton's face so that the tip of the barrel was just touching his flickering eyelid. "Now, mister policeman, why don't you take your stinky friend Beaumont and laughing boy there back out into the car park and start that waitin' game o' yours, cos if you hang 'bout here any longer, my trigger finger's gonna start to git real jumpy."

Paxton took a step back away from the barrel of the rifle and stared at Benny, a look of pure hatred etched on his face. When the Yank finally spoke there was bloodlust in his voice. "I'll be seeing you boys then."

Jardine took a step forward and grabbed the now terrified Beaumont by the back of his jacket collar, dragging him backwards towards the door, slinging the copper out in front of him. Paxton never took his eyes off the two of us as he slowly backed up across the floor of the pub. He reached the doorway of the alehouse then turned on his heels and walked out, leaving only his bigotry and the evil stench of sweat permeating the room.

Benny stood still and calm, the rifle in his hands unwavering, watching as the three men walked back to join the others sat in the cars parked outside. I walked across to join him and stood at his side then looked down at my blood-drained, clammy right hand. Gripped for dear life in my palm was the taped butt of my Smith & Wesson .38 service revolver. Benny looked at me then down at the gun in my hand before flicking his own weapon's safety catch back on. He slung the rifle across his shoulder and chuckled to himself before heading out back behind the bar, calling after me before he disappeared.

"Was you tinkin' o' firin' that pea-shooter at any time or was you just holdin' on to it to keep your hands warm?"

240

I turned around to answer him, but Benny was already gone.

CHAPTER
TWENTY-ONE

I was in a daze as I walked back through the bar to head towards my room. I needed a moment to get my head together, to think straight about Truth and about what I had to do to protect her. The ten thirty deadline that Paxton had fixed loomed over my thoughts like a vulture hanging over a rotting corpse. It was Lazarus who broke my morbid, trance-like state by calling down to me from the top of the hall stairs. I found him stood on the top step, resting against the side of the banister, chewing on a bright-red apple. His right arm hung lazily at his side: in his hand he held a 9mm Beretta semi-automatic pistol. The bluing of the dark metal on the barrel glistened as it was caught by the thin rays of early evening sunlight that shone through the small window next to him.

The clock on the wall behind Lazarus said it was just after a quarter to six. I climbed the twelve steps, stood next to him and glanced down at the gun resting against his thigh. Anxiety had crept into every fibre of my being; my heart felt like it was about to burst out of my chest, my guts fit to spew. I headed for the bedroom, stuck my head around the door and saw it was empty, then glanced back out along the landing, looking for Truth. I turned back to Lazarus.

"Where is she, Lazarus, where's Truth?"

"Will you calm down, son, the child's fine. Come with me."

I followed Lazarus along the short hallway into his bedroom and watched as he walked across the room towards a large walnut chest of drawers stood on top of a threadbare Persian rug. He took the corner of the antique dresser in his hand and pulled it across the wooden floorboards away from the wall to reveal a small hatch door.

Lazarus knelt down and put the Beretta into the waistband of his trousers then looked over towards me, a big smile etched on his face. He jabbed at the secret trapdoor in the floor with his finger as I walked across the room to join him.

"Priest's hole. It goes into the cellar, then if you need to you can climb down into Hunter's Hole and the caves. Take you out as far as the edges of Cheddar Gorge, it will. Come take a look."

Lazarus hooked two fingers through a brass-looped handle on the hatch door and lifted it up. Stale air drifted up out of the hole into the bedroom as I nervously peered down the steep stone steps into the small candle-lit underground room below us, realising as I did the horror of what I was staring down at.

"Jesus Christ, Truth is down there?"

"Yeah, course she is, it's the safest damn place in the pub for her to be. Why, what's the matter, did I do something wrong?"

243

I rubbed at my mouth with the tips of my fingers, struggling to find the words to explain. "In the name of . . . Look, just stay here a minute, will you, I'll go down there and get her."

Lazarus nodded back at me, a crestfallen look on his face. I dropped to my haunches then shuffled onto my backside, squeezed through the hatch opening and began to make my way down the slim limestone steps into the badly illuminated cellar.

A half-dozen or more candles had been lit and placed in four oval cut-out recesses in the white alabaster-covered walls. I searched around in the half light and found Truth at the furthest end of the underground room, sat on an old red satin cushion between two large oak beer barrels. A large grey woollen blanket had been wrapped over her head and around her shoulders. I stood staring at her for a moment, trying to process in my own head what the poor child must have been going through for the past half-hour, stuck down in yet another hideaway dungeon, alone.

I called out to her, "Hey there, how you doin', little one?" but got no reply. I hunched my body down so as not to hit my head on the low ceiling and made my way across the damp cobbled floor over to where she was sat. Truth looked up at me blankly, her eyes wet with tears. Even in the poor light I could see that she was shaking underneath the blanket. I knelt down in front of her and reached out and took her tiny hand in my own. Her pale little fingers felt frozen in my palm. "I'm sorry, Truth. Lazarus, he didn't know 'bout where you'd been

244

stayin' befo'. He didn't know where Doc Fowler had hid you. He brought you down here thinkin' you'd be safe. It's not his fault, it's mine. I should have explained to him. You sure are one brave little soldier, down here in the dark like this on your own."

"Have those men gone?"

I nodded back at her in the low light. "Yes, they ain't here no more."

"Are they coming back?" she asked softly.

I shook my head and gently squeezed her fingers with my own. "You needn't worry 'bout them comin' back; they ain't gonna hurt you."

Truth slowly nodded her head, thinking to herself, uncertain of the honesty of my words.

"Theo told me those men always come back for the children, Joseph. They're just like the smugglers we talked about down at the beach. Theo said that the children those men went away with went forever."

I watched as she pulled at the sleeve of her top, gripped at the cuff then wiped away the last of the tears that had fallen down her cheeks. The kid was proving to be braver than I was.

"Forever? I don't understand, Truth. What do you mean they went away forever? Do you mean that those children died?"

"No, silly . . . Theo said they went across the sea."

"Across the sea, to where?" Truth had me baffled by what she was telling me.

"He didn't say. He just said the children from Walter Wilkins went across the sea with those bad men and that they never came back."

"Well, there ain't anybody takin' you across no sea, no smugglers, and no bad men. You hear me? I promise you that."

In the flickering candlelight I saw Truth break out into the briefest of smiles. It was the first time since I'd taken her out from underneath the makeshift hidey-hole that Dr Fowler had kept her in that she had properly opened up to me. I still didn't have a clue what was going on and why Paxton and his goons wanted the child so badly, but at least I felt like I was becoming less of a bogeyman to the poor child.

Truth stood up and slowly took a couple of paces towards me. I reached across to her and drew the blanket back around her shoulders, then got to my feet and took Truth's hand again. "Come on, let's get you outta here, get you warmed up, shall we?"

I felt Truth's dainty fingers tighten around my palm as we headed across the darkening cellar and back to the foot of the stone steps. I looked up to see Lazarus staring down at us from the hatch door; he smiled then reached down to help the little girl up. Truth eagerly climbed on ahead of me. I clasped onto her fingers and followed. It felt like I was being guided by a heavenly messenger, away from a wretched inky netherworld and led to shelter, drawn back into the safety of the light.

The sky had gone black at sunset and I could feel a storm brewing itself up into a frenzy way off in the distance, behind the Mendip Hills. The air outside had turned cool, and the first light rain had slowly begun to fall; the branches of the ash trees that were dotted

246

around the car park blew to and fro as the wind began to pick up. I was stood in the bar, leaning against the wall inside one of the bay windows, watching as Paxton and his men sat patiently in their motors outside.

I looked at my wristwatch: it was a few minutes after eight thirty and the encroaching darkness of night-time was beginning to drape its unwelcome mantle, heightening my already grave sense of disquiet.

"You be standin' there fo' much longer, brother, you're gonna start puttin' down roots." Benny marched up past me, grabbed hold of the edges of the thick velvet curtains and drew them across the large window. He then walked across to the two other bays either side of me and closed up the drapes, leaving the room in semi darkness. Benny stuck his hand into his back pocket and pulled out a handful of wax candles and a box of matches, and began to light each one in different parts of the room then walked quietly back across to the pub. We both remained silent until we were joined a few moments later by Lazarus, who came in from behind the bar carrying a World War II olive-green army-issue metal ammo box in one hand and a large black canvas holdall in the other.

"Right, gentleman, let's have a look at what goodies I've got in here, shall we?" Lazarus sat both the ammo box and the holdall on the bar then unzipped the huge bag and began to pull out an array of handguns of various shapes and sizes, along with a number of attachable suppressors and silencers. He laid the pistols out on the circular brass-topped table behind him then reached back into the bag and took out a Sterling submachine gun and a handful of magazines.

"This is for you, Benjamin old son." Lazarus handed over the black-blued SMG and two curved magazines to Benny. Benny looked at the gun, weighing it up in his hands for a short while, then swiftly unfolded the shoulder stock on the machine gun, fed one of the magazines into the receiver and raised it in front of him to check the sighting.

"You'll have no trouble with that, mate," said Lazarus. "Been well looked after, that beauty has." He pointed at the SMG in Benny's hands. "Joseph, with the suppressor fitted on that thing like it is, the only thing you're gonna hear when it's being fired is the bolt reciprocating. It's that quiet. All the guns you see here have silencers. When the mayhem starts later we won't be the ones making the noise, that's for sure."

I looked down at the guns laid out across the table and swallowed hard before speaking. "Neither will Paxton and his men, cos I'm pretty sure they used those damn pistol mufflers when they shot at me and old Doc Fowler."

Benny laughed to himself and looked at me coldly. "That right? Then, Joseph old son, it looks like we're 'bout to have the quietest firefight in history."

CHAPTER
TWENTY-TWO

The first signs of the storm rolled in with the darkening early evening sky at around nine. Lightning crackled out over the far reaches of the Mendip Hills followed by the dull bass rumblings of thunder. The wind had started to pick up and was pelting a steady torrent of rain against the glass of the pub's windows. In the candlelit bar I anxiously sat and listened while Lazarus and Benny went over their meticulous and savage battle plan one more time. They played out their intended defence to protect Truth and the Hunters Lodge inn with military precision, which I found both comforting and disturbing in equal measure. Benny stared across at me, the vicious-looking submachine gun resting on his lap.

"When Paxton an' his goons make their play, they're gonna come in here hard: we gotta be just as nasty when they do. You git yo'self the chance to take any one of 'em out at the neck, you do it, you understand me?"

Reluctantly, I slowly nodded my head back at Benny, agreeing with him. Benny wasn't convinced by my silent accord and decided to ram home his point.

"Joseph, these fuckers, they ain't gonna be foolin' 'bout when they hit us. They mean bidness. They want

249

Trute, but they ain't gittin' her. It's as simple as that. They come at me, I ain't showing one o' those bastards any quarter. Git it in your head and heart that you gonna do the same when the time comes."

The two men had already taken themselves around the building, making it as secure as they could, bolting and barricading each of the doors in the old inn. The few windows upstairs all had their curtains drawn and were blocked up with heavy blankets and old boxes weighed down with thick brasses and other ironwork from the kitchen and cellar. The larger bedroom furniture had been dragged across to the windows to provide further makeshift protection. It was ramshackle for sure and I knew that the make-do fortifications would not withstand a serious assault from Paxton and his men. Benny looked over towards the drawn blinds of the bay windows, thinking to himself, then pointed at the closed drapes with his stubby finger.

"They'll take them windows out first, I'd put money on it. Put us under some real heavy fire fo' sure. Keep us busy an' pinned down while a couple of 'em try an' git in through that back gate door in the kitchen." Benny pointed towards the hallway with his SMG. "Joseph, we'll need you to dig in by the back door, try an' keep 'em at bay while Lazarus and me do the same out front here. I'll tell ya, it ain't gonna be pleasant, brother."

Lazarus nodded his head in agreement and chuckled to himself. "All this mayhem for one little kid. She better be worth it." The publican winked at me then turned his attention back to Benny. "It'll be like the OK

Corral in here, it's a bloody good job this place needed redecorating."

The two men roared with laughter but both fell silent when they saw I was not sharing their blackly humoured joke. Lazarus stared across at me, weighing me up. I tried to my stifle my unease by forcing a meagre smile back at him.

"Joseph, there ain't no shame in being scared. I know I am, be a fool if I wasn't." Lazarus leant forward in his seat and rested the palms of his hands on his lap. "You've been asking yourself why Benny and me are so willing to help you out like we are, yes?"

I nodded my head.

"Look, you were a policeman back home, you must have stood by your mates when the shit hit the fan, yeah?"

"My mates on the force were few and far between, Lazarus."

"OK, but you had to have some men around you that you trusted, men you'd stick your neck out for if things got bad?"

"Maybe. When it got bad there weren't too many I coulda counted on in a scrap, that's fo' sure."

Lazarus smiled to himself. "Well, that ain't the case for me and Benny here. We made promises to each other a long time ago. Made those promises when we was fighting up to our waists in blood and shit in the Kuala Langat swamps. Ain't that right, Benny?"

Benny nodded his head in agreement.

"Hell yes!" Lazarus went on. "For blokes like Benny and me, back then all we had was the army. It taught us

251

to stick together, made us like family. We looked out for each other, cos for most of us that's all we had, one another. War brings out the worst in men, Joseph, but it can bring out the best too. In Malaya, Benny and me, we made a promise to look out for each other, and we always did. No matter how hairy it got, through thick and thin we never broke our word. Let's just say we're keeping our word to one another tonight, for old times' sake. Now, what I need to know is if you're a man that can keep his word too."

"My word, whaddya mean my word?"

"It's simple, Joseph. I know about the conversation you and Benny had earlier, about what's gonna happen to Truth and where she's gonna go after all this mess is over with. I think my man here's been talking sense. I think, deep down, you do too. That little girl upstairs has had no life as far as I can tell, it sounds to me like it's been a pretty miserable existence for her in that orphanage. You can change all that, change it in a heartbeat, and I want your word on it that you will."

I began to speak, but Lazarus interrupted me. "Benny and me, we're gonna get you outta this mess tonight or we're gonna die trying. What I want from you is your word that you'll keep her out of the hands of those animals outside and get young Truth back to Estelle, give the child a chance to find herself a small measure of peace. Perhaps if you do, you'll find yourself a little peace too."

I closed my eyes, dropping my head as I did, my chin resting on my chest. Not knowing what to do for the best, I rubbed agitatedly at my face with the palm of my hand and pinched at the bridge my nose with my thumb and forefinger as I felt a rapid pulse of the blood rushing through the veins in my temples. I ran Lazarus' words around and around in my head, searching for the right answer within me.

The publican spoke again, breaking my troubled train of thought. "We don't have a lot of time here, Joseph, the clock's ticking. Do the right thing by the girl, please. I want your hand and your word on it, old son."

I swallowed hard and opened my eyes to see Lazarus' and Benny's outstretched arms in front of me. I looked down at their open palms and hesitated for a moment before slowly reaching out my own hand, shaking both of them in turn. As I did, I felt as if I was selling my soul to the devil himself.

Lazarus got up and fetched three fresh glasses and a bottle of Johnnie Walker Red Label scotch from behind the bar. He poured a nip in each, handed the tumblers of whisky to Benny and me, then raised his own glass to toast us. "May you be in a heaven an hour before the devil knows you're dead." The three of us knocked back the scotch and Lazarus promptly refilled the glasses and sat down again.

"Now, it's like I was saying to Benny here, earlier. Truth's gonna have to go back down into that priest's hole soon."

I glared over at Lazarus, about to object; Benny leant across and softly placed the flat of his hand on my chest to calm me down. "Hear the man out first, Joseph."

253

"Trust me, we know she's not going to be happy about it, but it's the safest place for her to be. If Paxton and his men get the better of Benny and me, you have to haul your arse up to my room pronto, get yourself into that priest's hole and get Truth and yourself away into Hunter's Hole. At the furthest end of the cellar behind the stack of beer casks you'll find a door that'll lead you down into the cave. It's stone steps for the first thirty feet, then you'll have to clamber down the ridge to the cave floor. That bit's a doddle, but the rest ain't gonna be a barrel of laughs. Just follow the dry riverbed north. It's gonna get tight and uncomfortable and you'll have yourself some hard caving on your hands. You ever been down into a cave system before?"

"What? Gimme a break, will you, Lazarus. Do I look like the kinda fool that's been down a cave recently?"

Benny slapped the table with the palm of his huge mitt, laughing out loud. Lazarus went on. "Well, if things go belly up here, you ain't gonna have a lot of choice. You either stick it out to the end with us and Paxton and his cronies get their hands on Truth, or you get on your belly and crawl your way out to Suncliff Wood with the child."

"Suncliff Wood, how far is that?"

"Just over two miles."

"Two miles, crawling on our bellies to get out? You gotta be kidding."

Lazarus slowly shook his head at me. "Keep your nerve and you'll be fine." The thin words of encouragement fell off Lazarus' tongue with ease. The bleak look in his eyes told me a very different story.

254

Earlier in the evening Lazarus had run a bath for Truth and then made her supper while she bathed. He'd taken a huge sausage sandwich and a bottle of lemonade with two yellow straws sticking out of the top up to her room, along with a box full of coloured pencils and some paper for her to draw on while we were talking downstairs. I left Benny and Lazarus to drink a little more Johnnie Walker and went back to my room and found Truth stretched out on the rug colouring in a picture of a ship that she had drawn on a large piece of paper. I quietly walked across the room and sat on the end of the bed for a moment, watching as the little girl etched away with a blue crayon at the edges of the rolling blue sea.

"That's how I came to Britain, on a ship just like that one," I said.

Truth stopped colouring and looked up at me. "You did? Where'd you come from?"

"Place called Barbados."

"Is that a long way away from here?"

"It's a long way all right, thousands of miles from here."

Truth laid the crayon onto the paper and sat up, crossing her legs, staring at me inquisitively. Her long blonde hair was still damp and she had brushed it tight across her scalp then tied it back with a length of red ribbon that Estelle had given to her. She had carefully dressed herself in a pair of light-blue denim jeans, black plimsolls and a white long-sleeved cotton shirt; a tiny patchwork red ladybird had been embroidered in silk onto the edge of the breast pocket. Truth continued to scrutinise me from where she was sat on the floor. I watched as she carefully traced the outline of the ship she had just drawn with the tip of her finger.

"Who'd you come with?"

"Nobody, I travelled here on my own."

Truth's nosed scrunched up, her eyebrows rising in disbelief at my answer.

"On your own? Why, don't you have any family?"

"Yeah, I did, once upon a time. They're gone now though."

"Gone where?"

Caught off guard by the child's forthright question, a heavy lump rose in my throat as I struggled for a moment to give her an answer. "Well, heaven, I suppose."

"Heaven." Truth looked down at the floor, deep in thought, and then reached down with both hands to the ends of her plimsolls, nervously squeezing at the tips of her toes. She looked back up at me, her face pale and forlorn. When she spoke, her voice was muted and fragile. "Is heaven a real place?"

"Well, I don't see why not." I watched as Truth carefully took in my words.

"Is that where Theo's gone, to heaven?"

I bit at the bottom of my lip as I thought of my own lost family, struggling to reply, choking to utter the words the child needed to hear. "Yeah . . . Theo's there, for sure."

Truth smiled, nodding her head to herself "That's good." The little girl sat thinking a while longer, her need to quiz me not quite over. "So what about you,

Joseph, is that where you'll go one day, to heaven, to be with your family?"

I wished I could have told her yes, that I was certain that the Promised Land would be my final resting place. But I wasn't so sure I'd ever reach the islands of the blessed, not after the ungodly deal I'd just made with Benny and Lazarus. Saint Peter himself would surely banish me from the pearly gates for such a sullied act.

Heavy thunder continued to growl outside, but I barely registered its angry presence, my mind already preoccupied with uneasy thoughts of how I was going to get Truth back down into the priest's hole. It wasn't going to be easy and I was dreading telling her what had to be done.

Lazarus had just gone back down into the underground room and Truth had gone out onto the landing to chat to Benny, who carried with him a lamp, a length of mountaineering rope and a box of candles to hand to his friend down in the priest's hole.

Lazarus lit and positioned the candles in different parts of the hideaway then hung the Eccles miner's lamp from the ceiling, illuminating the place a little more. A few minutes later he climbed back out, dropped the hatch door back down then pointed with his finger over to the chest of drawers by my bed. "I left you a few bits and pieces that may come in handy, did you see 'em?"

"I did notice, thanks, man."

"No problems, just you spend that cash wisely, old son." Lazarus winked at me mischievously as he walked

257

out. On the chest of drawers Lazarus had left me an old wax Highlander haversack. Sat on top of it was a large Eveready camping flashlight, an ex-army compass and the white envelope containing the eight hundred pounds Beaumont had given me earlier. I took a spare set of Truth's clothes from her bag, folded them tightly and put them into the waterproof holdall along with the compass and torch then stuffed the money into the inside pocket of my jacket. I reached behind my back and took out my Smith & Wesson .38 from my waistband and broke open the breech, emptying the six cartridges into the palm of my hand while I checked the action and the fixed open iron sights. I returned the shells back into the cylinder then snapped it shut and weighed the pistol in my palm before hooking it back in my waistband out of sight underneath my jacket. I bent down to my case, opened it up and took out the box of Remington .38 rounds I'd brought with me, emptied a couple of handfuls into my back pocket along with my Puma pocket knife then put the box with the remaining cartridges into the haversack just as Benny and Truth came back into the room. Benny gently rested his hand on Truth's shoulder, his hulking frame dwarfing the little girl as she stood by his side. She looked up at him like a faithful and obedient gun dog.

"Me and Trute, we been having ourselves a little chat. Child knows what she's gotta do, ain't that right, little soldier?" Truth nodded and looked uneasily across to where the priest's hole hatch door was. Benny smiled at her then continued talking, his tone sunny, much lighter than I was used to. "I tole Trute, she ain't gonna be down there on her own fo' long. That you ain't gonna be spittin' distance away from her, ain't that right, Joseph?"

"Yeah, that's right. I'll be real close by, I promise."

Benny may have thought he'd talked Truth around, but I could see in the child's eyes that she was petrified at the thought of having to descend back into the dark hole behind me. I walked over and crouched down in front of her, then reached out and placed my hands on each side of her tiny arms and drew her closer towards me.

"See, I'm gonna be at the foot of those stairs out there." Truth turned around and looked as I pointed my finger out of the bedroom door behind her. "Lazarus, he's gone and made it good and bright down there for you. You're gonna be snug and safe while the grown-ups sort tings out up here. There ain't any need for you to be scared. You got my word on that."

Benny butted in, offering up more well-intentioned words of solace. "See, Trute, I tole you, everyting gonna be fine. Just you remember what I said earlier, 'bout those bangs and crashes you're gonna be hearin'. You just close your eyes and cover up those little ears o' yours. It's gonna be just like that thunder your hearin' outside at the minute, an' I tell ya, it'll be over befo' you know it. You just hang on in there fo' ole Joseph to come get you. OK?"

Truth nodded passively and stared back at me, the tears quickly welling up in the lower lids of her eyes. Her dainty body shook and she began to cry. Flinging herself at me, she clutched frantically onto my neck and shoulders with her trembling arms. I lifted her up and carried her back across to the edge of the bed and sat her down on my knee. I looked over towards Benny, his eyes wet, his hand rubbing nervously at his mouth and jaw, visibly distraught at what he was seeing. I held Truth tight against me, her face tucked into the side of my jacket, her tears soaking my shirt. I cradled her head in my hand as she sobbed uncontrollably. She held on to me so tightly that I could feel her frightened little heart pounding against my chest.

CHAPTER
TWENTY-THREE

In the half light of the priest's hole I watched Truth's eyes search mine as I carried her the short distance across the damp stone floor of the desolate cellar. I could feel her thin body trembling as I set her down on a pile of cushions behind the beer casks at the furthest end of the underground vault. I quickly wrapped a thick eiderdown quilt that I'd brought with me tightly around her back and shoulders. I told myself that I was doing the right thing, that I was protecting the child from the worst kind of evil, men who had no remorse for their woeful deeds and little thought for the human lives they had no doubt callously extinguished in the course of their nefarious duties. Men like Paxton had been hanging off my coat-tails for the better part of half of my life and I was sick of having them trailing in my shadow, tired of the blood-letting and death that followed in their wake. I'd already made a stand against injustice and villainy and paid a heavy price in doing so; now I was making a stand again, taking on a fight I didn't really want, playing hero to a cause I felt was already lost. This time, I told myself, I had less to lose. It was tough talk, but who was I kidding?

Truth, bundled up like an abandoned puppy, stared up at me from behind the small stack of miniature ale barrels. In the dim lamplight her ashen, scared face said more than any words ever could. I crouched down low in front of her, gently brushed her cheek with the back of my hand and smiled at her.

"OK, you remember what Benny and me told you?" Truth nodded her head back at me. "This ain't gonna be for long, right? I'll be back down to get you befo' you know it." As I got to my feet, Truth's little hand shot out from underneath the blanket and grabbed hold of my own. When she spoke, her voice was hushed and shaky.

"And then can we go and get some ice cream with Benny?"

"Yeah, course we can. We'll all go get ice cream, I promise."

Truth let go of my hand and my arm dropped limply at my side as I began to slowly walk away from her, not knowing if I'd be able to keep my simple oath. Considering all the poor child had been through and was still enduring, it wasn't much that she was asking for. My pledge to get her ice cream seemed like such little recompense, but it was all I had to give.

I'd known better than to trust the word of a man like Paxton, let alone the word of a policeman. They say there is honour amongst thieves; the same cannot be said for bent law. It was raining hard outside when I heard the first shot ring out. I was stood in the hall and glanced up at the clock at the top of the stairs when the madness was unleashed; the hands of the clock read 10.15p.m. The first bullet shot from a silenced weapon pierced through the top pane of the bay window in the bar fifteen minutes before our agreed deadline. Their attack upon us had begun. All bets were off; chaos was about to descend; let the slaughter begin. As I drew the .38 from my waistband, every light in the place went out in unison, the power cut, the pub encased in darkness.

Just as Benny had predicted, Paxton and his men took out the two main windows in the bar but it wasn't the clandestine assault as we had expected. As my eyes began to acclimatise to the dark, a series of shotgun blasts to each of the bays blew glass and wood across the pub. Benny, pinned down behind the bar, bellowed back at me to get myself back upstairs to Truth. Adrenaline coursed through my body as I ignored his demand and ran towards the hall door that led out towards Benny and the bar. I raised my revolver just as I reached the entrance and fired off a couple of shots across the pub. Benny raised himself up from behind the bar, the SMG held closely at his hip, and began to strafe the room in front of him with heavy suppressed machine-gunfire. In the corner of my eye I saw the flare of further shotgun fire burst through the front door followed by the *phut, phut* sounds of repeated pistol fire. I aimed out into the pitch-black towards where I thought the gunfire had come from and loosed off another two slugs. In the shadows in front of me I saw the brief burst of bright flame erupt from Benny's

SMG again as he returned fire at his as yet unseen opponents.

Benny, out of ammunition, tucked himself flat against the edge of the wall of the bar, unclipped his empty magazine and quickly snapped in another. I let off two further rounds then stuffed my hand into my jacket pocket and pulled out a handful of bullets. The air smelled heavily of cordite as I broke open my revolver and reloaded the .38, snapping it shut as another rapid volley of muffled gunfire was discharged, cutting through the bottles hanging in the optics at the back of bar, sending alcohol and splintered glass everywhere. From behind me I felt a hand touch my shoulder and quickly drag me backwards out into the hall. "You gotta get up to Truth, move!" At that very same moment, in a burst of further dampened gunfire, I could have sworn I saw Benny, his arms flailing either side of him, thrown back hard against the back wall of the bar.

Desperate to halt my enforced retreat and help my friend, I turned on my heels in anger, raising the .38 revolver. Lazarus, his Beretta held out in front of him, took a firm grip of my arm and was pulling me towards the stairs just as more shots rang out behind us. Over the bombardment of gunfire I barked at the publican, "I think Benny's been hit, we gotta go back for him." But Lazarus paid me no heed. He grabbed hold of the lapels of my jacket and pushed me against the wall at the foot of the stairs.

"Move your arse, man. You keep your word!" Lazarus slung me towards the stairs, pushing at my back, then ran off towards the kitchen door.

264

I heard the boom of a shotgun roar at the rear of the pub. Without thinking, I ran after Lazarus, but it was all too late. As my shoulder clipped the frame of the kitchen door, I briefly heard the clack of metal sliding back on metal. I leaped aside just as another shotgun was fired, exploding a hole the size of a frying pan through the door and hitting Lazarus square in the chest. The buckshot blew splinters of wood, blood, macerated flesh and charred clothing across the kitchen. I was knocked off balance and was on my knees as the next two shots blasted the door clean off its hinges. Outside, I could see a car parked up just a few feet from the door, its engine still running, the beams of its headlights illuminating the inside of the kitchen. I heard two more shells being dropped into the shotgun's magazine then watched as Detective Constable Beaumont made his way cautiously inside and stood over Lazarus' bloodied body, grinning cruelly to himself. He lifted the sawn-off in front of Lazarus' face and pulled both hammers back.

I'd already scrambled to my feet and was leant against the door jamb. I raised my arm, the .38 aimed directly at Beaumont's head. Realising something wasn't right, the policeman slowly lifted his head in the half light and found himself staring down the barrel of my Smith & Wesson snub nose. I saw the animal fear and anger in his face as he stood motionless in the shadows for a moment; I watched his eyes twitch then dart from side to side as the panic began to set in. He saw the vengeful expression on my face just as he attempted to raise the barrels of his shotgun at me, his

265

last thoughts forever his own. I squeezed the trigger and fired. The bullet entered Beaumont's head just below his nose and exited out of the centre of the back of his skull. His limp body hung lifelessly for a second then dropped onto the stone flag floor at Lazarus' still-twitching feet. In front of me, picked out by the wide beam of the car headlamps, were the spattered remains of the dead copper's brains and bone matter, smeared in a crimson and grey arc across the white tiled wall. The nauseating stench reminded me of a stripped-out carcass on an abattoir floor.

More gunfire rang out in the bar behind me. I swung my body around and hugged the side of the hall wall, my arms outstretched in front of me, my grip on the taped handle of the .38 tightening. I took a couple of steps forward in the dark and glanced down one last time at Lazarus' lifeless body stretched out only a few feet away from me, then turned and bolted up the stairs towards the bedroom and the safety of the priest's hole. As I ran, I almost expected that, like his biblical namesake, Lazarus would rise up from the dead and follow on after me. It was a miracle I knew in my heart could never happen.

CHAPTER
TWENTY-FOUR

The air inside the bedroom was hot and still; sweat poured out of me, my pulse raced and my heart felt like it was about to burst out of my chest. I knew I only had a small amount of time; Paxton and his mob would be on to me real quick. I grabbed hold of the haversack, ran across the room and dropped to my knees, then lifted the hatch door to the priest's hole and climbed in.

I quickly closed the door and jammed the bolt into the socket then sped down the narrow stone steps two at a time into the old crypt. The damp cellar was eerily quiet; I stood still at the foot of the stairs for a moment and listened. There didn't seem to be any movement above me. I looked around in the candlelight, my eyes now more accustomed to the absence of light. Particles of dust floated in front of my face, caught by the dim glow from the lamp hanging from the ceiling. I headed across the cellar over to the beer casks and found Truth just as I'd left her, huddled up in a ball, the eiderdown covering her head and body. I lifted the quilt quickly, throwing it against the wall. Truth instantly jolted backwards in fright, cowering in the shadows.

"Hey, hey, it's OK, it's me, Joseph."

Truth edged forward cautiously to get a better look at me. I smiled down at her and she looked back at me blankly, her face pale, etched with fear. I turned around and unhooked the lamp then shone it over Truth's head to reveal the small, cobweb-covered wooden door behind her.

"Come on, we gotta go this way." I squeezed behind the beer casks and put my hand out for Truth to take it. Confused, Truth hesitated and looked at the door then up at me. "Child, believe me, we ain't got no time to be messin' 'bout, we gotta go now. Come on."

Truth got to her knees and grabbed hold of my hand. I pulled her up from the ground then hung the lamp out in front of me to get a better look at the door. Two large rusting iron bolts at the top and bottom of the door held it closed, the pins buried into deep holes in the alabaster-covered wall opposite. I put the lamp at my feet then pushed at the top bolt with my palm. I rolled the metal pin back and forth a few times until it eventually slid back and then bent down to release the bottom one. The second bolt was harder to move, the corroding metal crumbling away in my fingers as I tried to dislodge the pin from the wall. I leant back and repeatedly kicked at the end of the bolt with the heel of my shoe until it finally gave way.

The heavy door creaked at its decaying hinges and began to swing open to reveal the darkened void behind it. The air released from behind the door smelt musty and damp. I picked up the miner's lamp, got to my feet and put the haversack over my shoulder then stood in the doorway to see what was out there. The kerosene

268

lamp picked out the limestone steps cut out into the rock, which led down into the pitch-black of the cave below. I turned to Truth and put my arm out for her to come to me. The little girl hesitated again; she peered out into the dark behind me, reluctant to move.

"Truth, you gotta trust me. It's gonna be all right, we need to go right now."

Truth hung back a moment longer, still in two minds. She turned briefly and looked at the bleak cellar she'd been staying in, then slowly walked towards me. I reached out, swept her up in the crook of my arm, put my back to the door and pushed it to. With Truth clinging for dear life around my neck, I held out the lamp in front of me and began to make my way down the stone steps. The air around us became cool and earthy; I trod down each of the stone steps carefully, unsure of my footing, the moss-covered stairway underneath my soles slippery and unsafe. Around ten or eleven steps down I felt a chilly stillness round me. I swung the miner's lamp in my outstretched arm out into the blackness and caught sight of jagged rocks at my feet. Just as Lazarus had told me, the steps leading down to Hunter's Hole opened up onto a ledge. I held Truth close to my chest and warily stepped down onto the stone shelf then lowered the little girl down beside me.

Again, I swung the lamp back out in front of me. Below where we were standing I could just pick out a series of limestone ledges that looked like they had been cut out from the rock face: each had around a three-foot drop to the next and gradually led down to the cave floor. I could hear what sounded like rainfall above me; I stuck my head out and looked up into the blank chasm but could see nothing. I knew we had to keep moving. We'd be sitting ducks for Paxton and Jardine if we slowed the pace and began to waver. I held the lamp above Truth's face. She peered back at me, her eyes squinting at the light.

"We're gonna head down there. I know you're scared: just you do as I say and stay close to me now, you hear?"

The little girl said nothing and simply nodded her head.

"Here, you look after this for me." I offered her the miner's lamp. She took hold of the handle in her tiny fingers and held it out at arm's length as I got down on my backside. I hung my legs over the edge then carefully eased myself down to the next ledge. I stretched my arms back up to Truth and lifted her down next to me. I got back on my ass and slid myself on to the next ledge, and we kept climbing down into the impenetrable blackness. Finally, I dropped my legs down and felt my feet touch the cave floor. I reached up for Truth one last time, set her down beside me and took her hand in mine.

Loose stones shifted underfoot as I swung around, casting the beam of the kerosene lamp behind me. The sound of water dripping was more prominent now we were on solid ground. The lamplight picked out the glistening spray of rain falling from above us; I followed it back up the walls, which arched perhaps another two hundred feet up towards the surface. The outside

270

entrance to the cave Lazarus had taken us to was in a field at the back of the pub. That had been covered, but could it be where the rainfall was coming from? There was no way that I was going to be able to climb up to there; even without Truth tagging along it would have been nigh impossible to consider it as a possible escape route. I took a couple more tentative steps forward, searching out in front of me with the kerosene lamp for the dry riverbed that I'd been told about. We continued to stumble across the uneven cave floor, walking deeper into the cavern. I was unsure of where I was actually taking us. The glow of the lamp finally picked out what looked like a low opening in the rock face, about twelve feet away from where we were standing. I swung the haversack round in front of me, fumbled around inside and took out the compass and torch. I switched the flashlight on then gave the lamp to Truth.

"Here, you hold on to this and stay here while I find us a way outta this place."

Truth reluctantly took hold of the handle of the lamp from me again and grabbed hold of the tail of my jacket with her hand. "Joseph, please don't —"

I interrupted her plea. "It's OK, honey, I'm just gonna check out where we're going next. I promise I won't be long." I reached down and touched the top of Truth's head with the palm of my hand and rubbed her hair with my fingers. "I'll be back in a couple of minutes." Truth sat down, holding the kerosene lamp out in front of her.

I held the torch over the face of the compass until its magnetic needle hit north. It pointed directly towards the opening in the rock. I made my way over, squatted down and shone the beam of the torch inside then stuck my head in to get a closer look. I scanned the tunnel roof and floor with the light, trying to imagine if it was possible to slide my body into the stony hole. Rainwater trickled down the wall next to me, seeping its way through the rock up above, trying to find its way out, just like I was. I took a deep breath then climbed inside. I got onto my belly and began crawling along the slim passage, edging myself slowly along the shaft. Halfway up, directly in front of me, I could see a cleft in the stone wall; I reached up and grabbed hold of it then dragged myself further along the hole for about another twelve feet until I reached an opening.

I stuck my head out, shining the torch's beam out in front of me. I could make out a very short low-ceilinged passageway that looked as if it led down into what I thought was a larger chamber. I knew Truth and I couldn't stay where we were; we had to keep moving forward and try and find our way out to the woods Lazarus had spoken about. I shuffled back down the limestone tunnel, crawled out of the entrance, got to my knees then raised myself back on to my feet. That's when I heard Truth scream.

I heard the sound of stones being trampled by swift-moving feet and I turned just as something came out of the darkness speeding towards me. It was fast, so fast that I nearly missed seeing both the man and his first blow coming out of nowhere. My body seemed to react on its own, without conscious thought; the torch slipped out of my fingers and fell to my feet. I slid to the right then jerked backwards in a desperate attempt to get away from the assailant.

A blow meant for my head or throat whizzed by in a blur of knuckles and steel. From the corner of my eye, I saw the knife in the man's hand then his other arm raining down towards my face. I ducked down low and lashed out with my right fist, aiming for his gut, but I didn't connect and my hand continued to shoot upwards, smashing into something hard close to his chest. I heard the sound of metal hitting stone just as my attacker clipped the back of my skull with a heavy blow. My left foot slid on the wet rock; I tried to brace the heel of my shoe against the slippery ground just as another body shot, this one to my ribs, sent ripples of pain through my torso. I saw the man's other arm begin an upward trajectory towards my face, the knife only inches away. I dipped and weaved to the side, blocking his hand with my arm, then rose in the air and smashed my forehead down onto the man's face, headbutting him away from me. I heard the knife hit the ground somewhere at our feet and I immediately slammed my foot out towards him in the semi darkness, clipping some part of his body. Then he was gone.

I immediately began to run back towards where Truth was holding the lamp. I took only a couple of paces when a vicious blow glanced off my ribcage, sending a wave of pain through me. I felt my shin hit the leg of the my attacker and the two of us fell to the ground, both sprawled out in either direction across the cave floor. I rolled onto my back, my legs kicking out in front of me, my heels trying to find something to dig into on the wet ground. I panicked and began grappling at the gravel and loose stones underneath the palms of my hands, desperately pushing myself further backwards. I tried to lift myself up as I retreated into the blackness, my hands flailing about as I searched for anything solid to help me to my feet. I began to feel the ground shift and rumble underneath my back as rapidly moving footsteps heading towards me became louder.

In desperation, I twisted my body to my left, and as I did, my fingers hit something metal. I frantically criss-crossed the damp earth around me until my palm felt the familiar grooved grips and guard of a .45 semi-automatic pistol. I grabbed it up in my shaking hand and lurched myself onto my back. I felt a hard rush of air hit my face as the man sprinted out of the pitch-black and screamed towards me. I raised the gun in my outstretched arms and fired. The muzzle flash lit up the murk around me, and for the briefest of moments I saw the shocked and twisted expression on the face of the white man who had been trying to kill me as he was blown backwards across the cave floor. I pulled myself back onto my knees then scrambled to my feet and ran and grabbed the torch that was lying on the ground a few feet away from me.

I looked over towards the lamp glowing behind me and ran back to Truth. I found her pushed up against the rock face, her head buried between her knees, her right arm hooked over the tops of her tightly drawn-in legs, the handle of the kerosene lamp still clasped between her fingers in a vice-like grip.

274

"Hey, little soldier, it's OK, I'm here now." I knelt down in front of her, prised the lamp from out of her pinched fingers and rested it on the ground next to her. Truth looked up at me. I reached out for her hand and gently held onto her tiny fingers, not knowing what to say to her. I turned around and shone the torch back out into the cave behind me, worried that the man I'd just shot was perhaps only winged or that Paxton and the others would be on their way. As I looked back towards Truth, I heard the sound of rocks being knocked against each other and a human voice moaning in the darkness behind me.

"Truth, I need you to be brave for just a little while longer. Can you do that for me?"

Truth shot me an angry glare then reticently nodded her head. "OK, but only for this long." She held out her hand in front of me, making a tiny gap between her thumb and forefinger.

I smiled at her. "That doesn't give me long. I'll be back in a couple of minutes. Just you sit tight."

I walked across the cave towards where I thought the man and I had just fought. I followed a low silt gully that I knew I had crossed when I had returned to Truth and continued to travel along it in parallel with the cave wall on my left-hand side. The Colt .45 was clenched tightly in my right hand, my left holding the torch at head height, pointing down at my feet. In the near distance I heard more groaning. I scanned the gravelly earth in front of me with the flashlight, shining it down onto the ground, the beam bouncing back and forth over the rocky floor of the cave until it finally caught

275

the head and shoulders of my attacker. He was slowly crawling across the ground, his right arm clawing at the dirt in front of him. When my light encircled his head he came to an abrupt halt and rolled himself onto his back to face me; as he did, he clutched at his stomach and screamed out in agony like a wounded dog.

As I moved in closer, he yelped out again and clutched back at his guts with his hand. I shone the torch at his stomach. His hand and jacket were drenched in blood; it spewed from between his fingers and was beginning to seep into the ground by the top of his thigh. I aimed the pistol at the man's head as I closed in on him. The man stopped writhing around and stared up into the beam of the torch, his face etched with pain. He looked like a scared rabbit transfixed by the headlights of an oncoming speeding vehicle. I stood over him and he glared back at me. Blood and spittle flew out of his mouth when he spoke; the twang of his southern American accent reverberated around the cave.

"Look what you done to me, you crazy nigger."

I slowly knelt down next to him, and as I did he tried to edge away from me, pushing at the gravel beneath his feet. "You're damn lucky we're in the dark, cos I was aiming for your head." I rested the Colt underneath the man's chin.

He looked down at the gun, then at me, then turned his head and spat a globule of blood at my feet.

"How many more of you are coming down here?"

"Go fuck yourself, buddy, you'll soon find out."

276

I pulled back the slide of the .45 and chambered a round then stuffed the muzzle into his abdomen, just above the gunshot wound.

"How many, I said!"

The man screamed out in agony as I forced the barrel deeper into his guts. He gasped in mouthfuls of air as he started to speak. "It's just me, man . . . but you . . . you still shit outta luck."

"What you talking 'bout?" I increased the pressure, jamming the pistol harder into the man's stomach. The man bellowed out another deafening scream and spat out more blood.

"Paxton . . . knows where you and the kid are heading for, he knows about where you're heading for down here. He made that old nigger talk. He gave you up when they used a blade on him. If I didn't get you then they're gonna be waiting to take you out as soon as you stick your head outta the dirt."

"Why does Paxton want that child so badly?"

"She's cargo . . ."

"Cargo, what the hell you talkin' 'bout?" I grabbed hold of a handful of the man's matted hair and pulled his head up off the ground then stuffed the gun hard into his belly again. He bawled out, his hands grabbing at the barrel. I pushed harder. He screamed again, his arms falling to the ground either side of him.

"She's somebody's property." The man was becoming breathless, his face pale, about to pass out.

"Property, what you mean she's somebody's property?"

"We just gotta deliver the kid, that's all I know."

"You're insane." I shook my head in disbelief at what I was hearing. I let go of the man's hair and dropped his skull back onto the ground. The man spat out more blood then began to laugh at me like a jackal as I got to my feet. He looked up at me, his eyes crazed with hate and pain.

"Insane? You got no idea, nigger."

I set the hammer back down on the Colt, stuck it into my trouser band and began to walk away from him.

"Hey, where you going, man, you ain't gonna leave me here?"

I said nothing in reply, just kept on walking back towards Truth and the glowing lantern.

"You can't just leave me to die down here!"

"No? Just watch me."

The dying man's screams and pleading echoed through the cave as I slowly disappeared into the darkness.

CHAPTER
TWENTY-FIVE

"Ready?"

Truth quickly shook her head at me and looked down at the hole in the rock face in front of us. "No, I don't want to go in there."

I took hold of her hand and crouched down on the ground in front of her. "Truth, it's the only option we've got. If we don't go through that tunnel we're gonna be stuck down here for good. We either climb up through the tunnel or we stay and wait for more o' those damn men to get here. You really wanna do that?"

Truth shook her head at me again.

I got down on my hands and knees, then onto my elbows, and looked in again. The miner's lamp, now low on kerosene, threw out a small circle of light in front of me. "This is our only way out. Look, I've been through here already. I know you can do it too. I'll be holding your hand, you're gonna be right behind me."

Truth knelt down beside me and peered into the darkness of the tunnel entrance. "Is there no other way we can go, Joseph?"

"None. I wish there was, but there ain't." I pushed the lamp into the tunnel mouth a little further. "It ain't as long or as bad as it looks. Here, take a look."

Truth reluctantly lay down on her belly and stared into the dark passageway. "It doesn't look like a short hole. I'm scared."

"Me too."

Truth looked at me in disbelief. "You're scared?"

"Sure I am. It's a scary thing, climbin' into a hole like that. That's why we gotta be brave for each other. Can you do that for me?"

Truth thought for a moment. "I don't know."

I took her hand in mine. "I know you can do it. When we go in there I want you to close your eyes. I'm gonna have a tight grip on you. You just keep shufflin' your body along with me and push against the rock with your feet, understand?"

Truth gave a short nod of her head, her face filled with anxiety.

"Good. OK, here we go then."

I got onto my stomach, my left arm outstretched, my hand holding the lamp, my other clasped tight onto Truth's wrist, and we slowly began to crawl along the limestone tunnel. At first the going wasn't easy. I wanted to get her out into the next chamber as quickly as I could, but I could feel her holding back, afraid to move further into the blackness. Truth was obviously very frightened.

We slowly shuffled deeper into the tunnel, inch by inch. Any sound we made as we crawled along lingered in the ears, heightening the sense of claustrophobia. My mouth was dry and my voice sounded muffled as I called words of encouragement back to Truth. We edged further into the passageway. I leaned into a cave wall and inched myself sideways a little, pushing the two of us along with my hips and heels, taking my time, constantly aware of the fragility of Truth's body and how tightly I was grasping at her wrist. I stopped for a moment, the top of my head skimming the tunnel ceiling, and shone the lamp at the side of my face then squeezed at Truth's wrist.

"You OK back there?"

Truth coughed loudly. When she spoke, it was almost a whisper. "No . . . I want to get out of here, Joseph."

"It's not much further, keep those eyes shut, we're nearly there." I arched my back away from the wall again and began pushing at the rock with my heels, dragging the two of us forward on my elbow, pushing with my left hip and then my right foot, holding the fading lantern out in front of me, the tunnel growing ever darker around us as we moved forward.

I kept doing that until I felt a cold sensation creep over my face. The tunnel began to widen a little. I pushed at the ground beneath me with my legs until my head finally broke out of the tight passageway into the second chamber. I laid the kerosene lamp on a rock outcrop by my head and pulled myself out up to my waist with my free hand, then dropped onto my buttocks and dragged my legs out, still gripping at Truth's wrist.

I got to my knees and hauled Truth out next to me. We lay against a wall, Truth collapsed at my feet. I looked back into the hole that we'd just crawled through then out into the cavern behind us, having no idea what lay ahead of us. I felt the weight of the earth above me, probably a mile and a half of solid rock, and wondered for a moment if we'd ever find our way out of the damn place. I stared pathetically out at the inky blackness stretched in front of us, my morale crushed by the leaden cave.

I got to my feet and held up the miner's lamp, its light finally dying. It faintly picked out chunks of angular rock in front of us, huge limestone blocks tilted or propped against one another, some with knife-sharp ridges and others flat as altars. Even in the poor light it was an overwhelming landscape to behold. I took hold of Truth's hand and pulled her up onto her feet. She looked beat. Her face, hands and clothing were covered with dust and dirt.

"Come on, little one, let's keep moving."

I shone the lamp at my wrist and looked down at my watch face: it was just after midnight. Up above on the surface it would be as dark as it was down here in the cave, and that would serve us well if we could get out. It would give us the chance to push on unseen in the pitch dark, cover more ground, safely, hopefully away from Paxton, Jardine and their mob. I knew I needed to keep us on the move: if we were to get to some place safe by dawn, then we had to push on, all through the night.

Truth in tow behind me, we climbed down a series of two-foot-high stone ledges onto the floor of the chamber then scrambled up a slope in front of us that led to the next tunnel entrance. I hoped that this was the cave system that would lead us back to the surface. I searched around me but could see no other way out.

This had to be the passageway Lazarus had told me about. I put the kerosene lamp on to the ground, its light about to fade, and took the torch from my haversack, switched it on and shone it into the tunnel.

"This is our way back up, Truth."

The little girl nervously looked into the shaft. "Not another tunnel, Joseph?"

"Yeah, 'fraid so, but it's the tunnel that's gonna get us outta here." The hole in the rock face at the foot of the chamber was no more than four feet high. I pulled the haversack out in front of me then got down on my knees and crawled in. I shone the torch beam back at Truth and reached out my hand to hers. "Come on, we can do it. Me an' you, just like befo'."

Truth grabbed hold of my fingers and climbed on in next to me. We moved on our hands and knees for the first thirty feet or so until the walls of the passageway began to tighten around us. Truth gripped on to my hand for dear life as I pulled her along behind me. Unlike the previous tunnel crawl, where we had slid downwards, this deep trench was cut vertically into the rock. Thousands of years of water had forced out an uneven and dangerous pathway, which I hoped would lead us back up to the surface. The hole became more hazardous as we progressed through it. As I pushed on, pulling Truth after me, small stones and shards of loose earth fell from the ceiling onto our heads and bodies. As we climbed higher through the hole, more rocky obstacles held us back. After about twenty minutes of scrambling over stone and shale, I came to a sharp curve in the passage where the tunnel reached upwards into the darkness. I pulled the two of us up and started to climb again. The stone walls began to draw in closer, tightening around my back and shoulders. I tried to bend my right leg, as if readying for a sprint, but my knee smashed immediately into the wall. It was as if I was in a full-body straightjacket shoved head first into a too-small casing inside solid stone. Truth's left arm was stretched above her, her cold tiny hand clasping at mine, her right arm pinned to her side. Her head was turned to the left, close to the rock face. Like me, the two crevice walls must have been squeezing at her body, the whole length of her back, her rear, her knees, her chest all pinned in tight in the small tunnel. I told her to breathe and to keep her eyes closed. I could just about move my head, lift it slightly to look out in front of me. I shone the torch and saw in the crawlspace an opening to the left. It took another ten minutes to finally squeeze into it.

I was too physically drained to speak. I just keep crawling forward, pulling Truth after me. The little girl cried out as I tugged on her arm too sharply. We both lay sideways against the wall then inched forward on our hands and elbows and continued to belly-squirm down the passage. I gripped hold of Truth's arm even more tightly, until she screamed out in pain. I closed my eyes and breathed, pictured what little air there was around me filling my lungs. I felt my chest expand and then drop; I imagined the exhaled air keeping the walls at bay. I breathed in again, slowly. I tried to focus on the end of the torch beam in front of me. The darkness around me was all-encompassing. It swept wildly through my spirit and body, forcing my energy and spirit to keep pushing on. Then, above my head, I thought I heard the whisper of a familiar woman's voice.

I pitched my head forward so that I could hear a little better. Lying still in the blackness, I was sure that I could hear my wife, Ellie, call out my name, her voice crystal clear in the pitch. I stopped wriggling about and listened, praying that she would call out to me again. But I heard nothing more.

I closed my eyes and squeezed my body a few inches further forward, pulling Truth with me. I could feel cold water from a puddle behind me. It soaked into the back of my jacket and began to slowly seep through my shirt, cooling my over-heated body. My warm breath formed a fog around my head. The tight spot in front of us was a large rock sticking out from the right wall; I started to push forward again. As I inched by the rock I could feel the sharp edges scraping the skin from my ribs. With each breath, my chest expanded, locking me between the walls.

My heart pounded uncontrollably as I slowly pushed forward, pulling Truth behind me with each move I made. I breathed out, moved, rested, breathed out again and moved a little further. I shuffled and pushed my body further upwards until the passageway slowly began to open out. The rock around us became a little easier to get a foothold on, and after about another fifteen feet the tunnel felt less closed in. In front of me was a damp new wall of bedrock. I shone the torch at it and realised that we were finally coming towards the mouth of the tunnel. I pulled myself up along the heavy gravelled floor of the hole until my hand finally reached a slimy rim, a thin skim of viscous mud covering it.

A few more inches up and the wall's pebbly surface showed through, and for the first time since we entered the cave I could feel fresh air blowing against my face. It took another twenty minutes to haul myself and Truth up along a tight ridge of limestone, which finally brought us back up on to solid ground. I turned off the torch and we crawled out of the mouth of the cave into a full-blown electrical storm. I sank to my knees in the dense undergrowth of the woods and reached for Truth and held her as tightly as I dared, then we both fell onto our backs in the wet grass.

The two of us lay there, exhausted, the wind blowing and rain pouring down on our faces like tiny pebbles, the starless night sky above our heads exploding with thunder and lightning.

CHAPTER
TWENTY-SIX

A violent bolt of lightning lit up the night sky in front of us, its incandescent skeletal fingers reaching down to stroke the earth as Truth and I ran from the open ground outside the mouth of the cave into the dense canopy of the woods. The night air was heavy with the scent of ozone and damp moss; rain hammered down, soaking our clothes; the sodden ground sucked at our feet as we stumbled through the thick brambles that formed a spiky boundary into the coppice. Although I couldn't see them, I had a feeling in my gut that Paxton, Jardine and the rest of their men were close by. I had no idea where we were going and didn't want to switch on the torch for fear of giving ourselves away.

Truth clung on limply to my hand; I could feel her pace beginning to slacken behind me, her little body becoming heavy with fatigue. I turned and gathered her up in my arms and held her against my chest. She folded her arms around my neck, her head buried under my chin, then clamped her legs around my waist. Her breathing was heavy, her tiny body icy cold. I quickened my pace a little as I tried to blindly navigate myself through the wooded terrain. Rain poured down my brow into my eyes, making it hard for me to see anything in front of me. My head was pounding and every bone in my body ached. Each step I took sent a new wave of muscular pain shooting right through me.

Another crack of lightning lit up the sky, and as the thunder rolled across the heavens I thought I saw something move in the undergrowth at the side of me. I peered out into the darkness, the rain still beating at my face, the tree branches above us violently rustling back and forth as they were battered by the heavy wind. I wiped away the rainwater from my eyes and face with the palm of my hand and tried to get a better look around me, but could see nothing. I pressed on into the pitch black, Truth weighing heavy in my arms.

They say that, just like birds, hunters know no borders, and that was certainly the case for our pursuers. They had silently preyed upon Truth and I with the tenacity and determination of a snake eagle. One of the stealthy night predators who had been carefully tracking the two of us through the woods only made his lethal presence known when it was too late for me to do anything about it. The body blow that knocked me off my feet and threw Truth out of my arms came out of the dark, fast and furiously. A huge set of shoulders connected with my legs just above my knees, sending all three of us sprawling in different directions across the wet ground. Disorientated and dazed, I rolled onto my side, my body shuddering. I pulled myself up onto my knees and elbows, quickly fighting to get my breath. My mouth hung open, gasping in air, my eyes couldn't focus, and a high-pitched sound roared through my ears. I could

288

feel warm blood running down the side of my face. I clenched my teeth and grasped the clods of earth in the palms of my hands as I pushed myself back up onto my feet.

As I rose, I felt a swift rush of air as the foot and leg of my attacker flew towards my face. My head snapped backwards, the tip of the man's shoe raking sharply against my chin. I dipped my body forward and threw a stray punch, catching the man under his ribs. He came back at me hard; I bobbed to my left, bent my knees and felt his knuckles graze the top of my scalp as he swung at me. I squared myself on my feet, dipped low and threw a dirty uppercut that caught him square in the mouth. His head sank forward and I lashed my fist down across his left ear and along his jawline; then, as he fell further towards the ground, I brought my leg up, smashing my knee into his face. The man shot back on his heels, both arms springing out at his side. I caught hold of the sleeve of his jacket and yanked him off his feet. As he fell, I drew my arm back and drove my fist into his face. His head flew back and his hands flew up to cover his nose. I grabbed at his shirt and I heard the rasp of material ripping as I heaved him closer towards me. A feral rage burnt in my chest as I raised my fist and hit him again. I kept raining blows down about his head and face until I felt his body become limp and heavy. I let go of the man's torn collar and watched as he dropped like a stone at my feet.

I spun round and began to frantically search the sodden ground around me for Truth. I found her a few feet from me, unconscious, lying on her stomach. I bent down next to her, turned her over and dropped my head onto her chest, my ear pushed against her wet clothing, listening for signs of breathing. As the rain fell down in huge droplets onto the back of my head, I felt her ribcage rise and fall, her tiny lungs ebbing and flowing, her heartbeat murmuring back at me.

I put my arms under Truth's knees and behind her neck then lifted her up close to me. I scrambled back up onto my feet and began to run, just as a gunshot blasted out in the pitch. The bullet cut through the night air and splintered into a tree in front of me. I heard the sound of someone working the bolt action of a rifle, the empty shell casing clinking as it was expelled, and another shot rang out, pinging into the vegetation around me. I was now sprinting for all I was worth, zigzagging through the wood, tree branches whipping back across my face and chest, my feet pounding through the soaked leaves and soil. The trees in front of me became tightly spaced.

I heard another shot ring out; the bullet burst past me only inches from my head. I sunk my chin to my chest and charged on, crashing through the undergrowth. I ran without any sense of direction, the muscles in my legs burning, my stomach knotted with fear and pain. Gunfire rang out again, this time much closer. I instinctively ducked and pushed myself to move faster, and as I did I felt the earth under my feet begin to sag and become loose. My legs suddenly gave way as the ground around me fell away and I started to violently fall forward. For the second time that night, I lost my grip on Truth's body, the two of us torn from each other as we were savagely thrown down into a darkly veiled abyss.

My body hit the ground with a nasty crack as I was pitched head over heels down a sharp, gravel-lined ravine. I felt myself gaining momentum as I rumbled blindly through branches, weeds and nettles, my arms flailing at my sides as I was violently thrown further downhill. In the darkness, I heard Truth suddenly scream out my name then felt the back of my hand slap against wet skin as I collided with her, our bodies tumbling wildly over one another as we fell headlong down through the thick, water-logged foliage into the unknown. I finally crashed backwards through a sharp-thorned bramble thicket, my head striking the pebble- and rock-strewn base of the steep incline hard. I rolled onto my back, my ears thundering with a high-pitched squeal, my breath coming out of me in a deep sigh. I squeezed my eyes shut tight then opened them quickly. Above me I could just pick out a dense canopy of tree branches.

Heavy fog began to drift out through the overhanging foliage in thick clumps and started to drift towards the ground. The white noise in my ears faded and I could hear the sound of running water in front of me and the voices of men calling out overhead. I pulled myself up onto my rump and rested my back against the side of a large tree stump for a moment, my eyes picking out the fast-moving stream that ran noisily only a stone's throw from where I was sat. I tried to roll the pain I felt out of my shoulders and pinched at the tightening muscles at the back of my neck before shakily raising myself back up on to my feet. Truth had rolled directly over me and fallen only a few feet away. I made my way over to where she was lying on her back. She was thankfully conscious but remained motionless, her body covered in leaves and mud, riddled in shock, her frightened eyes wide open, staring blankly up at me. I saw her blink a couple of times as I knelt down at her side. Neither of us was able to speak. My body was wracked with pain as I reached underneath her body and once more lifted her back up close to my chest. Then, with the last vestiges of any strength I possessed, I stood upright and walked out into the darkness and into the water.

A thin mist hung just above my knees as I waded across the stream then stumbled out onto the bank on the other side. I lay Truth on the grass in front of me then saw lightning roll out from behind over my head. The rain twisted out of the sky like spun glass, the heavy droplets bouncing off my head, the water burning my face. The air was now so heavy with ozone that I could taste it in my mouth, its electrical scent like scorched metal on my parched lips.

I fought to stay on my feet, and in the pitch I thought I saw something moving out in front of me. I felt myself trembling. I squeezed at my eyes with the tips of my fingers as a sharp, piercing pain ignited in my temples, and my insides knotted violently as a wave of nausea shot through my body. I dropped to my knees and desperately reached out and snatched up Truth's tiny fingers in my own as I helplessly watched as two wraithlike, faceless figures emerged out of the fog.

292

I fell to the ground and a blanket of heavy numbness covered my body. I briefly heard a faint voice speak to me but could not understand what it said. I felt myself being lifted from the wet grass then blackness taking me by the hand and walking me towards its dusky sanctuary. I remember being cold and the water soaking through my shoes. I remember the smell of burning tobacco lingering in the air and feeling Truth's fingers fall from my own. But most of all, I remember seeing the reflection of my dead wife Ellie's face staring back at me from the eternal and labyrinthine paradise that she now called her home.

CHAPTER
TWENTY-SEVEN

The warmth on the side of my face from the rays of the early morning sunshine woke me from a heavy and dream-filled sleep. I had no idea where I was. Feeling punch-drunk, I tried to raise myself up off a pillow that was bolstering my head. I was lying on my back on the soft sprung mattress of a high-slung single bed in a room that felt like it was no bigger than a garden shed. Varnished wooden walls boxed me in. There was no door that I could see, only an ornate panelled frame that ran around the top and sides of the sleeping area. A cut-glass mirror hung at the foot of the bed, making the little space that I had been sleeping in appear to be a little larger than it actually was. My naked body was draped in a series of heavy, knitted, brightly coloured bohemian blankets.

I lay still for a moment, staring up above me. A watery film covered my eyes, blurring my vision. I struggled to focus and squinted at the brightly decorated maroon and gold intertwined fabrics that covered the ceiling. A gentle, warm breeze wafted in from an open window above my head and the fresh air rolled over me, lovingly caressing my forehead, cheeks and neck, followed by the heady scent of wild flowers.

Still disorientated, I slowly raised myself up off the bed by my elbows; then out of the corner of my eye I caught sight of someone standing over me. In surprise, I shot backwards, my head and shoulders slamming into the cushioned headboard behind me. At the side of the bed stood a scruffy-looking young boy, no more than ten years of age, staring inquisitively back at me. The kid suddenly broke out into a grin, revealing two missing front teeth. He continued to eye me up and down for a while longer before sticking one of his fingers up into his nostril and beginning to leisurely pick at his nose.

I grabbed hold of the edge of the blanket and quickly drew it up around my neck, covering up my bare chest like a shocked damsel protecting her modesty from the untoward attentions of a frisky rogue. The kid stood his ground by the bedside and kept on staring back at me.

"Who the hell are you?"

"Fella, this here's Connell: he's my young 'un."

Startled, the boy jumped away from the bed as a woman's voice snapped at me from out of nowhere. She had a guttural, deep Irish accent. The child swung around nervously as I slowly arched my head around the panelled frame to see who was speaking. A large-set, pretty-looking, raven-haired woman stared back at me; her muscular arms were folded over each other and resting firmly on the lacquered edge of the bottom half of a caravan stable door. She stabbed at her breast with her thumb by way of an introduction to me. "I'm Drina. What they call ye, mister?"

"My name's Joseph."

The boy raised his arm and pointed in my direction then spoke to his mother in a strange foreign tongue, the like of which I'd never heard before.

Drina listened to her son and continued to watch me suspiciously before answering her child in the same mysterious language, her voice now calm and soft. The boy listened intently to his mother's words then backed away from me, never taking his eyes off my startled face for a moment.

"What was he saying to you?"

"Well, Joseph, my lad here wants to know who the pretty-looking dusky woman is . . . the one that's been watching over ye like a hawk while you bin dead to the world."

"Woman, what woman?"

"Connell here's talking about the poor soul that's bin hanging by your side till ye broke outta that hot sweat that's bin burning on ye. You've bin making an awful show a yerself for sure, calling out her name for half the night."

"Say what?"

"Ye heard me." Drina shook her head and laughed to herself then opened up the stable door, walked in and stood behind her son. She put her arm around the shoulder of her child, drawing him close to her. "My boy here, he sees mullos, like the one ye had watching over you."

"A mullo?" I could feel the pincer-like grasp of a headache pinching at my temples. I squeezed my eyes shut tight with my fingertips and shook my head in confusion, unable to make head or tail of what she was talking about. Bewildered, I looked back up at her. "What's a mullo?"

"A ghost . . . Jaysus, don't be telling me ye've never heard o' one o' those?"

Ghost . . . The unwelcome word rattled around in my fuddled head. My throat tightened a little, and I swallowed hard and coughed as I felt a series of thick perspiration droplets breaking out at the top of my forehead. Nervously, I rubbed the palm of my trembling hand over my brow and across my scalp, while Connell continued to burn his gaze into me.

"Oh, I've heard of 'em, all right." I shook the unwelcome images of unseen spectres from my mind and nodded towards the boy. "Why's he starin' at me like that?"

The woman shook her head and quickly jabbed a couple of fingers into her child's back by way of a reprimand for his bad manners then pushed him out of her way towards the caravan door.

"Ah, take no notice of the lad. Connell here, he ain't never seen no west phari before."

I may not have understood the language she was speaking, but I sure as hell knew what her words meant. The woman smiled then quickly turned away, calling back to me as she walked down the steps of the caravan.

"Truth is, ain't none of us have seen many of your kind, specially one that's bin keeping company with a pretty little white gorjer, like what my old fella found ye holding on to last night."

Her words suddenly jolted at my woolly memory. My head throbbed, then panic struck me from out of nowhere. I felt a heavy weight pull at my insides and my head sank down in shame and fear, the sharp, pin-like bristles on my chin striking against the bare skin of my naked chest. A bitter metallic taste coated the inside of my mouth and a wave of nausea rolled over me as I threw both legs out of the bed. I frantically pulled the blanket around my waist then hauled myself up onto my feet. I took a couple of unsteady steps, and as I did I felt the blood rush to my woozy head and fell back onto the edge of the bed. Staring down at the floor, I weakly called out after Drina to come back. I heard voices chattering outside and took a deep breath then looked back up towards the caravan door and unexpectedly came face to face with my young companion.

I watched as Truth slowly and silently walked up to me, a neatly folded blue shirt and a pair of men's pinstripe trousers in her outstretched arms. She carefully placed the clothes on top of a small chest of drawers at the foot of the bed then came and stood at my feet and looked at me, tilting her head inquisitively. I saw the corner of her mouth tremble a little as she bit nervously at her bottom lip before plucking up the courage to speak.

"Who's Ellie, Joseph?"

Truth's out-of-the-blue enquiry hit me harder and meaner than a prizefighter's uppercut. I felt my body straighten and my fingers ball into nervous fists. My head became woozy as it filled itself with cruel echoes

298

from my veiled past. I felt myself choking back the wall of tears that had begun to well in my eyes as I struggled to find the painful words that the little girl beside me patiently waited to hear me speak.

CHAPTER
TWENTY-EIGHT

The sky outside was blue and clear, the air still and humid. I stood unsteadily at the foot of the steep steps of the caravan, closed my eyes then rested my back against the porch entrance for a moment and let the heavy rays of the sun warm my face. I rubbed at the stubble on my cheeks and jowls and opened my eyes. It took them a moment to become accustomed to the brightness of the hazy June day. The caravan had been unhitched underneath the canopy of an oak tree, its heavy branches laden with the season's full bloom of leaves, hanging down towards the ground. The old tree offered a welcome umbrella of shade to two large piebald horses, which were securely tethered by long lengths of navy rope to a couple of metal pegs hammered into the parched earth. Around me was a dense wooded area that acted as a secluded perimeter to a meadow of rich green grass populated by shining buttercups and wilting dandelion heads.

By my side was an old ex-army two-man tent that had been pitched next to the remains of a dug-out campfire that still smouldered in a shallow pit. Above the glowing embers, tied to a metal tripod, an iron pot filled with hot water steamed. Its opaque vapours gently rose into the air and wafted towards a row of drying clothing that had been hung on a makeshift washing line that was hitched by a thin cord between the limbs of two trees. I caught sight of my own jacket, shirt and trousers hanging next to a woman's bra and lace underwear. I felt myself flush with embarrassment. Averting my gaze, I turned sheepishly and took a closer look at the place that had been my overnight refuge.

The brightly coloured paintwork of the bow-topped Gypsy caravan was as extravagant and ornate outside as it was indoors. A large weatherboard hung over the ornate wooden stained-glass door, and carved on each side of the entrance were two vicious-looking lion's head gargoyles that gave off the appearance that they were protecting the mobile domicile. Either side of the van above the waist boards were four small sash windows, the inside of the travellers' home masked by lengths of decorative lace curtain. I rubbed admiringly with the flat of my hand across the flamboyantly decorated fascia; the fancy painted wood panels felt warm and comforting to the touch.

"There he is then, an' about time too."

I turned on my heels and found the woman called Drina standing a few feet behind me. She smiled then rested both hands leisurely on her hips.

"So, you'll be liking the vardo then?"

"The what?"

"The vardo . . . our wagon."

"Oh, yes, it's beautiful."

Drina laughed to herself. "Beautiful, is it . . . Listen to ye. Ye wouldn't be saying that in the dead o' winter

301

when it leaks and feels like a fecking icebox inside there."

"Maybe so . . . I'm still tryin' to acclimatise myself to the winters over here. It's certainly very different from home." I chuckled thoughtfully to myself.

"And where'd home be then?"

"Barbados."

"Never heard of the place. Is that in Africa?"

"The Caribbean — a long way from here, that's for sure."

"A long way, ye say. Ye a travelling man then, Joseph?"

"More of a runnin' man at the minute."

"Running . . . from what?"

"Seems just 'bout damn near everyting."

Drina looked lovingly at her home and at the wooded area behind us. "None of my people have ever been great ones for running; besides, it ain't easy to get to the gallop when yer towing ye bloody home behind you."

I nodded my groggy head in agreement then took a couple of steps away from the caravan and felt my body teeter forward slightly. Drina reached out toward me and took hold of my arm just underneath my elbow and rested her body against my own.

"Ye look like a corpse, fella. Ye need to neck a brew."

"Neck a what?"

"A brew." Drina raised an arm up into the air in disbelief at my ignorance. "Tea, ye eejit . . . I'll go mash ye a cup. Ye sit yerself down, ye can wait here for my old

302

fella: he's the one that found ye and the child in the woods last night."

I sank down onto the edge of a large log that had clearly been left for future firewood. I stretched out my aching legs and watched as a bee, its familiar low drone echoing in my ears, flew from flower to flower, sipping nectar and collecting grains of pollen, which it held in huge yellow sacs at the backs of its legs. I looked out across the meadow. In the middle of the grassland I could see both Truth and the boy, Connell, sitting. She was happily chatting away to her new-found friend, something that took me back a little at first. Since we'd met she'd been reticent about opening up to me, choosing to speak to the other adults she had met. When she'd finally plucked up the courage to ask me the question about my deceased wife, Ellie, earlier, it was me that had been struck dumb. I'd shooed her out of the caravan door, telling her that I needed to get dressed and that I'd maybe answer her question later. Despite my own aloofness on the subject matter and my reticence to answer to her, it was good to see Truth relaxed and in the company of another child of her own age.

I felt drained and tense; my body twitched and jumped. The skin on the palms of my hands itched and was clammy to the touch. I took a deep breath and let the continuing warmth of the sun caress my head and neck. I tried to loosen myself up by rolling my shoulders back and forth; the muscles creaked and groaned inside as I tried to work out the tension. I closed my eyes and listened to the sound of birdsong.

My troubled mind began to unwillingly trawl back over the dark events that had occurred during the last few days, remembering the violent death of Doc Fowler and reflecting on the presumed demise of both Benny and Lazarus. Once again, not only had I brought trouble and bloodshed into my own life, I'd gone on to share a fair deal of that unwelcome misery with innocent folk who hadn't deserved to be touched by such cruel misfortunes. Under my breath, I cursed myself, berating my own stupidity and lack of good judgement. I'd let the desire to make a fast buck turn my head and, in doing so, had dragged myself up to my neck into a mire of trouble. With my eyes still shut, I quickly became lost in a world of my own bleak thoughts. Wallowing in self-pity and anger, I failed to hear the sound of someone moving towards me.

"Well, look at that . . . the phari's managed to raise himself outta his pit, has he?"

Startled, I shot to my feet, my fists clenched, my body stooped like a boxer about to bolt out of his corner after hearing the clang of a bell. Heading towards me was a short, muscular, big-set man, his barrel chest arched out in front of him. His determined gait was more of a swagger than a natural walking movement. He was dressed like an English country gent out on a morning's grouse shoot. A thick red polka-dot neckerchief was tied tightly around his throat and a faded black bowler hat tipped precariously across the front of his lined forehead completed the stranger's unusual look. In one hand he carried a heavy-looking hessian sack and in the other an antique shotgun. He

304

laid both down on the ground and moved a little closer towards me.

"Take it easy, fella. What's a matter wid ye, don't like to be called phari?"

"I've been called worse."

"I bet ye have. Sit yer arse back down on that tree stump, fella, before ye fall down."

I did as I was told and dropped back heavily onto the makeshift seat.

"So, what name did the Lord Almighty be giving ye then?"

"Joseph, my name's . . . Joseph."

"Is that right, Joseph? Well, don't ye have a truly biblical name, that's for sure." The big man suddenly smiled at me then stretched out a tanned, muscular, heavily tattooed arm and stuck a calloused, hard-looking hand in front of me. "I'm Milo Hughes."

I took hold of the man's hand and we shook, his grip firm, the stubby fingers and huge palm rough to the touch. "I'm pleased to meet you, Mr Hughes."

"Stop with the Mr Hughes malarkey: call me Milo."

I nodded back at him. "It would appear I owe you a debt of gratitude, Milo."

"Get ta bugger. Gratitude, for what?"

"Your wife told me that it was you that found the girl and me out in the woods last night."

"I did. Finding ye wasn't the bother. It was the carrying ye back." The big man grimaced then looked at me sternly for a moment before winking mischievously up at his wife, who had just arrived carrying two white enamel mugs filled with steaming-hot tea. Drina passed over one of the mugs to her husband before handing me the other. She put her hand on top of my shoulder then pointed behind her towards the caravan.

"I just put the pan on, will ye have a fry?"

I had no idea what she was talking about and didn't get the chance to answer her peculiar question. Milo snapped at his wife, "Course the fella will, from the look o' him he could do with a good plateful. Cook Joseph and me here up a pound o' rashers, there's a good girl."

Drina shot her husband a hard stare. "Less o' the 'good girl' from ye, and pass me up that sack by yer feet."

Milo did as he was told and handed over the bag to his wife. "There's four good-size rabbits in there. I'll gut an' skin 'em after me fry." Milo clapped his hands together and nudged me hard in the shoulder with the tip of this elbow before rubbing at his belly with the flat of his hand. "I do like a good fry, Joseph, and my Drina knows how ta cook a grand one. I tell ye now, yer in for a treat for sure, fella."

Milo looked out across the meadow and pointed at Truth. "The chavi there, she belongs to you then?"

"No . . . She's ain't my kin. You could say the child's in my safekeeping for a while."

"Safekeeping? I never heard it called that. From what or who are ye keeping her safe?

"I ain't exactly sure any more."

306

"Maybe it's from those gobshites that were on to the pair o' yous last night?"

I felt my guts sink and looked up gravely at Milo. "Did you see any of them?"

"No, I didn't need ta, they was making enough o' a din out there in dark for me to know they was up ta no good. Me and the boy were setting pike traps down by the stream. We found you up on the side o' the bank, that child was clutching on ta yer hand for dear life, God bless her."

"And they didn't see you?"

Milo looked down at me indignantly. "Fella, I work this land at night for a living, an' I bin doing it for as long as I can tink. I only get seen when I wants ta be seen."

Against my better judgement, I pushed another question at the big man. "And you don't think you were followed?"

"Followed? Out there, I don't tink so." Milo jabbed his thumb towards the woods. "The stream ye crawled outta is a mile an' a half from here. I know that cos I know my miles and I know I carried yer heavy phari hide over my shoulder ta get ye back here. Nobody followed me or my boy, get that inta yer t'ick skull."

Milo left me with his words ringing in my ears. He walked back to the caravan and went inside and then moments later returned and stood in front of me. In his hand he held the army holdall Lazarus had given to me. Milo dropped it at my feet. I reached down, undid the straps and opened it up. Inside, everything was the same as when I had packed it. On top of a heap of damp children's clothes sat my wristwatch, revolver and the envelope containing the wad of dirty money that the cop, Beaumont, had given to me in exchange for Truth. I looked back up at Milo, but he was already walking away from me back towards his wife and home. I was about to call out after him to offer my thanks when his gravelly voice bellowed back at me.

"We're tinkers, not thieves, Joseph."

I've heard it said, "I never wonder to see men wicked, but I often wonder to see them not ashamed." At that very moment I felt the evils of both wickedness and shame wrap themselves around my insides and begin to draw me into a bleak and tempered underworld reserved only for the wretched.

CHAPTER
TWENTY-NINE

We Barbadians have a word for the stupid or foolish. We call those blighted with the continual ill-fated ability to be unthinking or thick-headed as "dumpsy". To this day I can still hear my momma scolding my sister, Bernice, and me with the same old phrase whenever we'd been thoughtless or imprudent: "You, listen, you, de higher de monkey climb, de more he does show he tail." My assumption that Milo would have taken the opportunity to root through our belongings in the holdall or perhaps pilfered something said much about my own suspicious nature and my inability to see the inherent decency in my fellow man.

Drina had cooked a wonderful late breakfast of thick-cut bacon, fried duck eggs, tomatoes and field mushrooms, the hearty food piled mountain high and dished up on pristine-looking willow-pattern china plates. With the sun high in the sky, its warmth beating at our backs, we'd all eaten our meal outside at a large fold-out camping table complete with a fine linen tablecloth and an antique Georgian silver cutlery and cruet set. Milo and Drina Hughes were fine and generous hosts, and their hospitality and good grace was unexpected and very welcome. I had a lot to thank both of them for, more than they could have ever realised.

After we'd all finished eating, Drina, Milo and I sat in silence for a while and watched as Truth and Connell ran and played in the meadow in front of us. I nervously looked down at my wristwatch; it was just after one in the afternoon. I stared back over at Truth and down at the holdall sat at my feet.

Drina leant forward slightly in her chair and gently placed her hand on my arm. "Ye got somewhere important ye gotta be, Joseph?"

"No . . . I've lost track of the time, that's all."

I watched as Drina turned and looked knowingly at her husband. She took his hand in her own and squeezed it gently then looked back at me and pointed at my watch.

"Ah, time . . . It's easy ta lose when ye live the life o' a Romany, for sure it is. Ye probably noticed, we don't go much for man's time round here."

I nodded. "Tings do move kinda slowly, I'll give you that."

"Better to move slow and know where ye are than move fast and be lost, Joseph." Drina smiled at me. "Milo and me are tinking you might just be lost an' in need o' pointing in the right direction. All ye gotta do is ask, fella." Drina got up out of her seat and began collecting the plates from the table and carried them back into the caravan. Milo drank the last of his tea and set the mug down on the table then pulled out a brass lighter and a packet of Woodbine cigarettes from his jacket pocket, stuck one in his mouth then offered one to me.

"No thanks. I don't."

Milo shrugged his shoulders and lit his cigarette, taking a long draw on it and blowing the smoke out across the table towards me. I pointed to the packet of smokes.

"I used to work where they made those."

Milo looked at his Woodbines. "What, the fag factory? Geddaway wid ye, is that a fact?"

I nodded my head and laughed to myself. "I managed to stay in the job all of ten months befo' I was given the sack."

"Given the sack, ye say. Were ye on the fiddle?"

"No . . . But a man called Meeks wasn't too keen on the way I worked."

"Or on the colour o' yer skin, I'd wager?"

I raised my eyebrows and didn't reply.

Milo took another deep pull on his cigarette. "What kinda troubles you in, fella?"

I looked down at the ground and swallowed hard before returning to make eye contact with the big man. "The worst kind. The sort that strangers shouldn't be drawn into, Milo."

Milo slapped the table and laughed. "Fella, I was born in trouble, you let me be the judge if I wanna be drawn inta yours or not. Who was it on yer tail last night?"

I took a deep breath before replying. "Two men by the name of Paxton and Jardine, along with some of their buddies."

"They gavvers?"

"What the hell are gavvers?"

Milo blew out a sharp breath of air and shook his head at me in despair. "Is it the filth that is onta ye? Ye know . . . the police."

I nodded my head. "Yeah. American and English police."

"Yanks . . . What would Yankee gavvers want with a phari fella like yourself?"

I pointed across the meadow towards Truth.

"The chavi?" Milo sat back in his chair and took another deep drag on his cigarette then pointed one of his stubby fingers at my face. "Ye snatch that poor youngster?"

"No." I felt my shoulders sink as I spoke. My head ached, pain nagging again at my temples. I rubbed at my forehead with the tips of my fingers to try and work out the discomfort. I heard Milo drop his cigarette into the dregs of his tea mug.

"Joseph, why don't ye tell me just what the devil is going on?"

And that's exactly what I did. For the next ten minutes I sat and explained everything that had happened to Truth and me over the last few days. I felt like the sinner seeking the sacrament of penance, my soul and sins opening up inside a confessional of my own making. Milo sat and listened to me unburden my woes without uttering a solitary word. When I had finished talking, he pulled himself forward in his chair and tapped at the top of the table with his finger.

"And what is it I can do to help, fella?"

"I need to get to a phone."

"A telephone? Who ye need ta call?"

"A relative back in Bristol. My cousin, Victor."

"And this Victor, he can help get ye outta the mess yer in, can he?"

"We're family, Milo: we look out for each other." I smiled to myself. "And Vic knows his way round trouble better than any man I ever knew."

"This fella Vic likes a fight, does he, Joseph?"

"Always has, been throwin' punches ever since we was kids back home. Fight anyone or anyting. Vic's got the heart of a lion and the temper of a sea snake. The man always loved to box. He's just taken on a gymnasium for fighters."

"Ye talking 'bout the boxing there, young fella?"

"Yeah. Vic owns a gym back in St Pauls."

"Ah, he does now. Well, they say the phari like ta scrap, ain't no doubt about that."

"You like to box, Milo?"

"Like ta box, can ye hear yerself? Quit acting the bollocks, will ye. I was t'rowing a punch while you was still hanging off ye mother's teat. I've toed the line at horse fairs, racecourses, backs o' pubs an' knocking shops from here to Sligo. Anywhere travelling men meet, argue or brawl, that's where I make me brass, with this." Milo raised one of his sizable fists at me and shook it in front of my face. "Me daddy, he scrapped all his life. Killed he was, right before me very eyes, God rest his soul." Milo stretched out in his seat then stood up and rested his forearms on the table in front of me.

"Joseph, ye just had what we call the kris and ye didn't even know it, boy. Ye see my people use the kris to hold court with another fella, ye tell 'em yer troubles then afterward the kris fixes them troubles. Let's get ye fixed before it's too late for the pair o' ye. We'll break up camp before nightfall. Get ye to that telephone that ye need. Have the chavi and you ready to leave when the sun just touches the tops o' them there trees behind us. We'll have pray to the Lord Almighty that those gavvers ye just told me about are still lost in those woods back there." Milo clapped his hands and began laughing to himself.

I hadn't the heart to raise a smile. I stared bleakly back out towards the outcrop of dense woodland behind me and shuddered. I knew that Paxton and Jardine would soon pick up our scent and that the time for me to start praying had long since expired. For a man like me there'd be no God worth his salt that would want to break bread with any of my sorry business. In my experience, those kind of lost and tormented petitions could only beseeched unto the ear of the Devil himself.

CHAPTER
THIRTY

Drina laughed and called over to Truth, "Child, I wouldn't be standing too close to him if I were ye. That poultice he's smearing all over himself ain't fit for the smelling. It'd knock a fly off a bucket o' shite, it would."

Truth began to laugh, and it was a welcome sight. Somehow during the last few hours she had seemed different, less tense. Her face, which had previously held an unmasked sadness, now seemed a little brighter; her eyes had begun to slowly come to life, their original dull stillness replaced by a sparkle that you only ever see in the young. In just a few hours it appeared that the Hughes' young son, Connell, had successfully used a little of his traveller's charm to prise her away from the withdrawn, sombre world in which she had been held prisoner and had brought her out into the light. I could not have been more grateful to the little boy.

Truth was sitting on the steps of the caravan with Connell watching me apply the thick yellow liniment Milo had given to me to treat a series of small cuts and scratches on my ribs and lower back caused by the bramble thorns I had fallen through the night before.

315

Whatever the stuff was it stank to high heaven and was fiery hot on my skin as I rubbed it into the tiny lacerations. I stuck two fingers into the old jam jar, pulled out another lump of the foul-smelling lotion and began to apply it to one of the deeper abrasions.

"What the hell is this stuff, Milo?"

"What ye tink it is? It's mustard."

"Mustard? I'm smearing damn mustard on my skin?"

"Course ye are, ye damn eejit." Milo began to snigger at me. "Mixed wid a drop o' horse piss."

Truth, Connell and Drina burst out into fits of uncontrollable laughter. In disgust, I looked at the repellent contents inside the jar then slung it as far as I could across the meadow.

True to his word, Milo had the camp broke and cleared and the caravan laden to the brim with their belongings before nightfall. Drina had cleaned Truth up, tended to her knocks and grazes, and got her a change of clothing from the holdall. I'd washed and put on my freshly laundered clothing, and sat with Drina and the children among the pots and pans inside the caravan.

"I'm gonna take ye ta a fella, name o' Bodden. He lives in a village called Bradley Cross, about two miles as the crow flies. He has dat telephone you'll be needing. I'll tow us along de old miner's track through Mascall's Wood. It's quiet and we won't be bothered, wi' any luck. There's a gathering o' tinkers pitched up just outside o' the village. I'll take ye and the chavi from there ta Bodden's place. You make yer telephone and we can be gone. After that, I know of an old unused barn at the back of the White Hart pub in Cheddar, just down road from Bodden's place. It's safe and it's quiet. You can lay low there till yer man comes to get ye. Once yer there, mind, ye'll be on yer own. How's dat sound?"

"Sounds fine by me, thank you."

Milo nodded his head matter-of-factly at me and then swiftly closed the caravan door, sealing the four of us inside.

Our journey to Bradley Cross was a bumpy and slow one, and it was just after eleven o'clock in the evening by the time we reached the travellers' settlement. Milo unhitched the horses, and from inside the caravan we could hear the sounds of Romany men chattering amongst themselves.

A short while later Milo swung open the door. Behind him, bunched up in a semicircle, stood ten or fifteen travellers, all staring keenly at their friend's new-found cargo.

"Never mind dem eejits, dey won't bother ye. Come on, fella, time for us ta be on our way."

Milo smiled at Drina and then summoned Truth and I to get out of the van. I grabbed up the holdall from between my feet, thanked Drina, took Truth's hand in my own and went to get out. As I was rising to my feet I felt Truth squeeze on my fingers and tug on my arm. I turned and watched as she slowly raised her tiny right arm and hand out towards Connell. The boy leant forward and took Truth's slender hand in his own grubby mitt. The children sat like that for a moment, just looking at each other, holding on to each other's hands. No words were exchanged, just a series of simple smiles and unspoken gestures given and shared between two innocent youngsters, both of whom knew that they would probably never set eyes on each other again.

We walked into Bradley Cross in the shadows with the moon rising up behind our backs. Milo led us quickly through tiny cobble-stoned backstreets made up of small tenant farmers' houses and shabby-looking run-down estate cottages.

In the darkness the village sure didn't look like it amounted to much, and I'd no interest in hanging around to see what the damn place looked like by daylight. Milo turned to me and whispered, "I know old Wilf Bodden from my time working the land round here. He's a game warden for some swanky fella in the big house up the road. Bit of a gobshite, but the fella's keen on the horse races and likes the folding stuff. Hand him a coupla quid and we'll be fine with him, for sure."

At the furthest end of the village we approached a small cul-de-sac, and the sulphurous stink of farmyard animals hit me immediately as we tramped up a dirt track towards the only house on the blind alley. Even in the dark I could sense the open expanse of the moorlands either side of the road, stretched out around us. It was still a warm night, and as we approached the gate to the ramshackle property the whispering flutter of a calm night breeze blew across the fells and gently caressed our faces.

Milo opened up a large iron front gate, the ageing metal hinges creaking as it moved. I felt Truth squeeze hold of my hand a little tighter as we made our way up the path to the house. I pulled her in a little closer to me as Milo lifted the brass knocker and rapped it against the front door. Two dilapidated copper lanterns were flanked either side of the farmhouse entrance. Inside, wax candles burnt at the low end of their wicks, offering us the barest illumination. Milo gave the knocker another hammering against the wood panelling.

I looked at my wristwatch; it was a little after twelve thirty.

A few moments later, the sound of a series of locks being unbolted could be heard and the door swung open. A thin, grey-haired man in his late fifties, his trouser braces hanging around his scrawny waist, peered out from behind a poorly lit hallway. "Who the bloody hell is that banging about at this time of night?"

Milo stood in the dim candlelight and broke out into a huge smile then raised himself up onto the doorstep, leaving Truth and me looking like a couple of wayward strays behind him.

"There's the man. Evening ta ye there, Bodden. It's me, Milo Hughes. I'm sorry to be troubling ye at such an ungodly hour, but I'm looking for yer help so I am. I have a fella wid me here. He's in dire need o' the use o' yer telephone and willing ta pay handsomely for the call."

Bodden stuck his head out into the night and gawped down at both of us.

"What the bleeding hell are you doing wandering around the place in the dark with that coon and kid in tow? Have you lost your senses, man?"

"Ah, Bodden, that's no way ta talk about a man's friend. Be a good Christian now and let us in. Yer the only fella I know in these parts with a telephone. It's urgent. What says ye let me man here have a crack on it."

I stuck my hand into the inside pocket of my jacket, pulled out two five-pound notes and pushed them past Milo towards Bodden. "Like Milo says, I'm willing to pay you."

Bodden looked at the cash in my hand for a moment and rubbed greedily at his chin. I could feel his itching palm from where I was standing and took an instant dislike to the man. Milo stood to one side and Bodden moved towards us out of his doorway, stuck out a spiny-looking hand and with pinched fingers snatched up the money from me.

"You better come on in quick then." Bodden reluctantly stood away from his step and quickly ushered us into his hallway, shutting the door behind him. Inside, the house stank of a gagging mix of rotting vegetables and stale body odour. Milo sniffed the musty air, blew out a breath and grimaced to himself. "Jaysus, Bodden. I live in a damp seventy-year-old caravan and it still smells better that this fecking dump. What ye bin doing in here, painting the walls wid cow shit?"

Bodden, his face like thunder, stood with his back against his front door. "Mind your bloody cheek." He stabbed one of his bony fingers at Milo's face. "You

320

must be off your pissing rocker, man. What the hell are doing bringing a wanted man to my house?"

Milo's face went blank. He looked across at me gravely then back at Bodden.

"What ye talking about, a wanted man. Joseph here's no felon."

"No felon. Come off it, Hughes, do I look a bloody fool? The police have already been here, scoured right through every house in the village they have, looking for the wog and that child. Your Negro friend here's in big trouble with the law and that's the end of it. The coppers are saying he's dangerous too."

"Dangerous, me arse! Does the fella look dangerous to ye?"

"It don't matter what I think. He's on the run, wanted by every bobby from here to the English Channel."

I reached back into my jacket pocket, pulled out a handful of five-pound notes and shoved them towards Bodden's chest. "Here, how much do you want for the use of your telephone? Look, here's sixty pounds for your trouble. I'll make my call and be on my way." I wafted the money in Bodden's face a couple of times. "Sixty quid for one phone call. What do you have to lose?"

Bodden swallowed hard. I could see the beads of perspiration beginning to bubble up at the edges of his grey hairline. I watched as he covetously eyed up the notes. "My freedom, that's what I have to lose: just like you, nig nog."

Bodden stared down at my chest, his gaze directed towards my jacket pocket. I clicked on quick to what he was after. I reached into my coat, pulled out another wad of cash and counted out another thirty pounds in front of him. Milo, angered at his friend's avarice, reached out towards me and tried to stop me handing over any more of my money.

"Bodden, why are ye acting the bollocks? Let the fella use the damn telephone, won't ye?"

I moved Milo's arm out of the way and pushed the money into Bodden's grasping old hand. "Take it . . . that's a hundred pounds. Easiest money you'll ever make."

Bodden looked down at his new-found wealth, splaying it out like an oriental fan between his fingers. He looked up at me and nodded towards an open door further up the hallway.

"The telephone's back there in the parlour. Go use it and be damn sharp about it. These two can come in the kitchen and wait for you there." Bodden pushed past me and walked down to his parlour, flicked on the light switch and turned to face the three of us. "Come on, I'll put the kettle on, make us a brew while your friend there uses my telephone." He spat out the words and disappeared into the kitchen behind him.

Milo reached down and gently took Truth's other hand. The little girl's fingers instinctively stiffened and began to hold on to my palm tightly.

I looked down at her and smiled. "I'll be five minutes, that's all." I felt her nervously knead at my hand again with her fingers. "It's OK, Truth, you'll be safe with Milo, I promise. Just five minutes, OK?"

Truth looked up at me. "OK, just five minutes." She let go of my hand. Milo winked at me and the two of them left me to make my call.

I walked into Bodden's grubby little parlour and found the black Bakelite phone sitting on a green wicker plant stand. I picked up the handset and dialled the number to Vic's gym then pressed the earpiece close to my head and waited nervously. The dialling tone must have rung out a dozen times before somebody finally answered.

"Yeah, who is it?" barked the voice down the line.

"Vic, that you?"

"Yeah, course it is, JT. I came hauling my ass back here as soon as Redman got a hold of me. He tole me you in a heap o' trouble again. Where the hell are you?"

"I'm stuck in the middle o' nowhere at a place called Bradley Cross, 'bout half a mile away from the village of Cheddar."

"Cheddar, Cheddar in Somerset? You tellin' me you is down in the sticks again wid all those hay-chewing muthafuckas? What the fuck is wrong wid you, brother?"

"Never mind what the hell's wrong with me. I'm up to my neck in deep shit here."

"Oh yeah, deep shit you say, what's new? Ain't you ever gonna learn? Everton, he tells me since I bin gone we've had that nosey flat-footed pig Fletcher looking fo' you here an' all over St Pauls. There's talk o' you doin' all kinds o' crazy shit. He's bin yackin' 'bout how he's

323

gone an' lost one o' his men, that greasy-assed bastard Beaumont. You know anyting 'bout that?"

"Beaumont's dead."

"Beaumont's dead. How'd he end up a stiff?" Vic snapped.

"I shot him," I replied blankly.

"What, you shot him? Well, ain't that just fuckin' swell. JT just became the first nigger in Britain to start his own version o' the gunfight at the OK Corral. Tell me you didn't croak ole Flush-it Fowler too, did ya?"

"Course I didn't kill him. That poor bastard was just the start of all of this. He was probably murdered by Beaumont or one o' the sons o' bitches that he was workin' for." I took a deep breath on the other end of the phone. I could hear a vexed Vic sucking in air through the gap in his front teeth.

"That honky copper Fletcher said you got some young pickney girl wid you, said you stole her from some damn orphanage or someting."

"I didn't steal anybody. Doc Fowler had already taken the girl, kept her cooped up underneath the old swimming baths out at Speedwell."

"Speedwell baths, that rathole? Oh, this shit just keeps gettin' better all o' the time. Look, you is playin' at some dangerous shit down there, cousin."

I barked back down the phone. "Look, I ain't playin' at nuttin', Vic. I been set up and played by a bunch o' crooked white folk that saw me comin' like a fool from the off. I got blood on my hands an' a heap o' dead folk mountin' up behind me. There's at least four or more

324

fellas who've been tracking my tail since I left Bristol and who want me and the child dead."

"What damn fellas?

"Probably more bent law from Fletcher's station, plus there's a couple of American policemen, one by the name o' Paxton, the other Jardine."

"American? You talkin' Yankees?"

"Yeah. Sounds like one of 'em put the strong arm on Loretta. Busted her up real bad to get to me." The line went silent. "You still there, Vic?"

"Yeah, I'm still here. Why'd these Yankee pigs go after Loretta an' do her harm?"

"Loretta put the child up for the night at her place, let me use one of Carnell's motors to get us outta Bristol too." I heard Vic sigh heavily into the mouthpiece at the other end of the line.

"Oh, you is a damn fool, JT."

"I know what I am, Vic." The line went quiet again. My mouth was dry. I closed my eyes, swallowed hard then coughed to try to clear my throat. I heard Vic throw something across the room in temper. I stayed silent and waited for him to speak again.

"Just gimme the details o' where you gonna be hangin' out. I'm gonna get my stuff an' leave St Pauls for you as soon as I can."

"I'm gonna be holed up in some barn way out at the back of a place called the White Hart pub. It's in Cheddar village. Milo said it's the only pub they got, so it ain't gonna be hard to find."

"OK, got it. Who the fuck is Milo?"

"He's a traveller fella that's been helping me out."

"Traveller, you talkin' 'bout a pikey?"

"A Gypsy . . . he's a good man."

"Good man, shit. You sure you still got a damn shirt on your back?" Vic sighed for the third time and began to laugh. "JT, brother, you done some crazy-assed shit in your time, but knockin' 'bout wid pikeys, well, that's gotta be takin' the fuckin' biscuit fo' sure. Don't you know a pikey would thieve the goddamn eyeballs outta a corpse? You'll be lucky if you still have any hair on that stupid black head o' yours by the time I get down there to ya."

Vic kept on laughing to himself. Finally, I managed to interrupt my cousin's new-found sense of mirth.

"We ain't got much time here, Vic, I think tings are gonna start to turn real bad, real soon."

"You just do as I say, an' stay cool an' hang in there. I'll be with you fast as I can." Vic then repeated what I'd already told him. "You gonna be in Cheddar village, the White Hart pub. The two o' you'll be waitin' in a barn way out the back o' the place."

"That's it. Thanks, Vic, I appreciate it."

"Sure you do." I heard my cousin about to drop the receiver back into its cradle and I shouted out after him.

"What's the matter wid you now?"

"Best make sure you bring along that old Colt o' yours."

"No shit, JT. What, you tink I was gonna drive all that way down there to 'behind God's back' an' turn up just holdin' on to my dick? Brother, sometimes you can be a bigger damn fool than I took you for."

CHAPTER
THIRTY-ONE

I walked down the dingy passageway into the kitchen and found Truth, Milo and Bodden standing outside under a bright moon drinking steaming tea from large earthenware mugs. Bodden heard me approaching, swung his head around and looked at me with piercing, accusatory eyes that were filled with the kind of hatred normally reserved for the gaze of an overseer of a slave plantation. As I walked out to join them, the corner of his mouth turned down into a cruel sneer. I watched as he put the rim of the mug up to his lips and then gulped back the remainder of his tea. Bodden hung the empty mug in front of my face as I stood next to Milo. "You want some, boy?"

I shook my head slowly. "No thanks, I'm fine." Truth caught sight of me, pushed between the two men and grabbed hold of my hands, squeezing them tightly. Milo turned, took hold of my elbow and led me and Truth quickly back indoors. Bodden followed, locking the kitchen door behind him.

"Ah, Joseph, there ye are. Come on, best we stay outta sight, even at dis time o' night. Did ye find yer man on the blower?" I nodded and said nothing. Milo was on a roll and continued his patter. "Wilf here's just bin telling me how he tinks it's way too risky for the two of ye to be wandering out there with all these gavvers about looking for ye and the young chavi here. He's gone an' offered to put you up while I go and fetch me a van an' a couple o' hefty fellas who could come in handy if there's a bit o' a ruck. Whaddya say, fella?"

"Like hell are Truth and me stopping here" was what I wanted to say, but I guess fatigue and the need to keep both Truth and me out of sight and away from the grasping hands of the law prevented me from opening my mouth and speaking my mind.

Bodden looked me up and down and sniffed to himself. "Boy, you paid me enough of your readies. I don't see how it's going to do me any harm to have you pair here while Hughes fetches one of his wagons."

I looked at Milo then suspiciously across at Bodden. "Why the sudden change of heart, Mr Bodden? A few minutes ago you wanted the two of us outta here faster than a kid chasing an ice-cream truck."

Bodden smiled again, a scornful, deeply covert smile that only I appeared to witness. "Ain't a man allowed to change his mind?

I shrugged at Bodden's reply and kept my mouth shut. This got the man on his high horse.

"Look, sonny, I don't give a bugger if the two of you piss off now. I'm doing a favour for Hughes here." Bodden stabbed his thumb in Milo's direction then kept riding that high horse of his. "You don't want to be under my roof, that's fine by me, you can leave the same way you bloody well came in." Bodden shot his

328

arm out and pointed down the passageway to the front door.

Milo quickly stepped in to placate Bodden's fit of bad temper, his voice calm and slow. He walked in close to my chest and looked up at me, then winked and began to speak under his breath. "Joseph, fella, listen ta me. The two of ye have come dis far. It'd be a shame to let the gavvers get a hold of ye when ye're so close to having yer kin from Bristol come pick ye up and get ye outta here. I'll be back in two hours, no more. Have ye on yer way. You'll be back in da big city before ye know it."

I looked down at Truth, who had wearily sat herself down on one of the dining chairs at the kitchen table. She looked beat. Bodden was leant against his kitchen wall, staring down at the floor.

Milo squeezed at my arm. "So, what'll it be, fella?"

I looked uneasily at Milo. "You say you'll be back in two hours?"

"No more. What's that timepiece o' yours say it is now?"

I glanced down at my wristwatch. "It's one forty-five."

"I'll be back here just after three, give or take a few minutes. Sun comes up around five. Ye'll be outta that barn and well on yer way by then."

I nodded at Milo in agreement. "OK, but if you ain't here by t'ree fifteen, I'm gone."

Milo looked down at Truth then back up at me, and smiled. "Then I'd better get a wriggle on then, hadn't I?" Milo turned to Bodden. "I'll bring me wagon round

329

the back, take 'em down the poachers' track inta Cheddar village. Have yer gates open for me ta pull in."

Bodden nodded his head. Milo spat into his palm, stuck out his hand and the two men shook.

As a kid, my momma had a saying for those she mistrusted or felt to be dishonest. As Milo walked out to leave, I nervously shifted my gaze across to Bodden and her wise words echoed through my head: "You know what them say 'bout slugs, Joseph? They always leave slime in their tracks."

I got the feeling that Wilf Bodden could not believe his good fortune. They say luck favours the brave, but I didn't think that was true in the case of our grasping host. His new-found prosperity had little to do with personal courage and had simply been derived from my willingness to pay him handsomely. He had swiftly pocketed himself the tidy sum of a hundred quid's worth of hard cash all for a phone call and the prospect of a two-hour babysitting job. I watched as he followed Milo down the hall, heard him letting him back out into the night and then the dispiriting sound of the front door being closed and locked. As Bodden returned up the passageway to the kitchen, I stuck my hand into the holdall and pulled out my service revolver then quickly stuffed it out of sight inside my waistband.

When I was a policeman back home, after many years of witnessing so much crime and violence, I'd come to believe that ordinary folk could sometimes, if pushed in the wrong direction, do terrible things to each other on the flip of a coin. Something inside told me that Wilf Bodden was one of those kinds of people,

330

and that the time for him to spin that single bit of spare change into the air was close at hand.

I sat down next to Truth and waited for him to join us in the kitchen. He prowled back into the room like a bloodhound sniffing out its quarry and forced a twitchy smile.

"Milo tells me you'll be heading for the old barns down at the edge of Cheddar village, that right?"

I nodded in reply. Bodden wasn't satisfied with the answer and like any good hunting dog kept on snuffling for more tidbits of information.

"He told me you're being picked up by family, that right?"

I gave another nod.

His hackles rising, Bodden sucked in his cheeks in exasperation at my lack of interest in making conversation with him, then exhaled a heavy breath of air from his mouth, unhappy that he had been summarily dismissed by me in such an offhand manner. I could see his conniving little mind ticking away behind those ball-peen hammer eyes of his. When he spoke to me again, he chose a less probing form of the third degree than his previous quizzing.

"The two of you need anything?"

I looked at Truth. "I'd be grateful for a blanket for the child here, and we could both do with using your bathroom if that's all right with you?"

Bodden pointed a scrawny finger above his head. "Bathroom's at the top of the stairs. I'll get that blanket for you."

I picked up the holdall and took hold of Truth's hand, and we walked back down the passage and up the stairs. The place stank worse on the landing than it did in the kitchen. Bodden called after us as we reached the top step.

"Light for the bathroom's on a pull cord on your right-hand side."

"Got it, thanks." I tugged at the cord. The bulb flickered on and I shepherded Truth inside. "You go first, remember to wash your hands afterwards. I'll wait outside just here for you, OK?" Truth nodded at me and went in.

I rested against the wall and listened to Bodden walk back into his parlour and snap the door shut quietly behind him. He knew he was about to flip that coin. A man alone in a room, with a phone, cunning, with a pocket full of money and the chance to make a hell of a lot more by giving us up. What was that old bastard up to? The toilet flushing broke me out of my stark reverie. I heard Truth turning on the water tap and I knocked at the bathroom door.

"You can come in."

I turned the doorknob and went on in then reached over Truth's head and turned both sink taps on full.

Truth, confused, looked up at me. "What are you doing?"

"Giving us a bit of privacy, that's all." I dropped the holdall on to the floor and knelt down and fished out my pocketknife and the box of shells for my service revolver.

"Milo's right. This place smells like cow's poo. I don't like that man downstairs, Joseph."

I broke into a smile at Truth's apt remark, but it soon fell away when I thought of Bodden downstairs. I put my finger to my lips and whispered to Truth, "Me neither. But we ain't gonna be here for long, little one." I dropped the knife into my hip pocket along with a couple of handfuls of cartridges then took my gun from my waistband and broke it open. I took out the six cartridges from the swing-out cylinder and rotated it a couple of times to check the action was smooth then returned the bullets into their cradle, snapped it shut and returned it out of sight underneath my jacket.

"Is there going to be more shooting, Joseph?"

"I hope not. You never can tell with people like Mr Bodden downstairs. Let's say it's better to be safe than sorry."

I stood up and looked at my reflection in the bathroom mirror. I was a mess. I could have hung laundry in the bags that fell beneath my eyes, and the salt-and-pepper growth of stubble that had sprung around my cheeks and jowls reminded me that I really had begun to resemble my father. I reached behind me and felt at the heavy metal pistol nestled under my coat. My daddy had been a great shot with both rifle and handgun. What he aimed at, he always hit. I hoped that I'd have some of his sure hand and keen eye should the need arise later. I leant across to the toilet and flushed it again then turned off the taps, took Truth by the hand and gave it a warm squeeze.

"I'm scared, Joseph."

"I know you are. But it's gonna be fine. I promise." I smiled at her and opened up the bathroom door. "Come on . . . Let's go see what ole stinky's up to, shall we?"

We walked out to Bodden, who was waiting for us at the foot of the stairs, one hand on the banister, the other holding a tatty-looking dark-blue woollen blanket. "You want to come on through to the sitting room, wait for Milo there?"

"We'll be fine as we were in the kitchen, Mr Bodden, thanks all the same."

"Suit yourselves. I've gathered already you ain't the talking type; I don't see any point in forcing our company on each other unnecessarily if that's how you feel. I'll be back here if you need me." He handed me the blanket and wandered into his front room, closing the door behind him.

I walked Truth down to the kitchen then sat her down on one of the kitchen chairs and wrapped the old blanket around her shoulders. I walked across to the kitchen door and quietly turned the brass handle. It was locked and there was no key to be seen. I looked around for another way out. On the right-hand side was a pantry. I walked over, opened up the door and peered inside. It reeked of damp. Four shelves hung on the back wall with a few tins on them. There was clearly no exit out into the back yard. As I walked out of the pantry I could hear the sound of a woman's voice singing. There was music coming from Bodden's sitting room.

334

I knelt down in front of Truth. "I'm just gonna have a word with Mr Bodden. I want you to stay here and you are not to move till I return. You hear me?"

Truth nodded. "Are we leaving soon, Joseph?"

"You bet we are. We leave as soon as I've spoken with ole smelly drawers back there." Truth began to giggle. I put my finger to my lip again to hush her then tipped her a wink. "Be back real soon."

I trod softly along the passageway until I reached the sitting room door then took out my revolver and let it rest behind the back of my right leg before knocking. I gave the wood panel of the door a single hard tap. Inside I could hear Patsy Cline's "You Belong to Me" playing on the gramophone. There was no sign of Bodden coming to the door. I rapped at the panel again, only this time a hell of a lot louder. I put my ear to the wood and listened then heard Bodden grumbling to himself as he rose out of his chair. He called out over the music, "Yeah, what is it?"

I took a step back, waited, then saw the handle of the door beginning to drop towards the floor. As Bodden drew it open, I raised my leg and kicked out hard at the centre of the door, sending him flying backwards across his living room. I rushed in, slamming the door shut behind me. Bodden, clearly dazed, desperately tried to pull himself up onto his elbows, but I was on him like a mongoose on a cobra. I kicked at his chest with the heel of my shoe, knocking him back onto the floor, then dropped down on his torso, pinning down one of his arms with my right foot.

"What the fucking hell are you playing at, you dirty wog?"

I pushed my revolver into Bodden's cheek and reached across to the volume dial of the gramophone and turned it up. Patsy Cline's voice filled the room.

I cracked the back of my hand hard across Bodden's left cheek and dug the gun's barrel a little harder into his face.

"Who's coming for us?"

"I don't know what the hell you're talking about, man."

"Don't piss me 'bout. Who'd you call while we were upstairs?"

Bodden squirmed under my weight, his face flushed with anger and desperation. White spittle formed at the sides of his mouth. He bellowed at me over the din of the music. "I didn't call anybody, you fucking dolt. I'm trying to help you, for Christ's sake."

I jammed the gun barrel underneath Bodden's nose then pulled back the hammer and watched his petrified eyes follow the cylinder holding the bullets slowly revolve. I screamed down at him, "Bullshit, Bodden! Either you start talkin' or I'm gonna put what little brains you got all over the tiles of that nasty-lookin' fireplace you got on your back wall. Now, no more o' your crap. Tell me, how long is it befo' Paxton and his cronies get here?" I saw a scared man's eyes become even more fearful when I called out the name of the Yankee copper. I quickly swung my arm up and pistol-whipped it across the side of Bodden's head then immediately stuffed the gun barrel into his already bleeding ear.

The music stopped and a deafening silence enfolded inside the sitting room. I screwed the barrel a little deeper into Bodden's ear. "How long befo' he gets here?" I felt Bodden's body almost shrink under the weight of my own. His face went white and his lips turned a nasty tinge of blue as he resigned himself to the inevitable. He tried to pull his head away from the gun barrel, but I applied more pressure, pushing his face against the harsh fibres of the carpet.

He breathlessly rasped out the answer I'd been waiting for. "Not long, he's on his way now."

"And Milo, was he part of all this?"

Bodden shook his head weakly under the heavy pressure I was applying to his skull with the gun.

"No, damn it. He knew nothing about them coming here for you."

I rose up off Bodden's body and slammed the side of the revolver into his guts. His legs instantly drew up into a ball as he writhed in agony on the floor. He pulled himself up tight into the fetal position and started to cry.

"Where'd you put the back door key?"

Bodden, rocking back and forth, coughed. Flecks of light crimson-coloured saliva and blood flew from his mouth, spraying the beige tiles that ran along the foot of the hearth. He gasped and croaked out a faint reply. "It's in my back pocket, you black bastard." I reached down and yanked it from out from his trouser pocket then quickly backed myself out of the room without saying another word.

As I rushed along the grimy passage back to the kitchen and Truth, Bodden yawped pathetically after me. "You're fucking dead, nigger! Dead, that's what you are. You hear me?"

I didn't want to hear him; I never wanted to hear his ugly mouth utter another filthy word again. The only thing that I could discern coming out of Bodden's sitting room as I began to swiftly unlock the kitchen door was the loud, repetitive clicking noise of a stylus head as it bounced in and out of the final grooves of the record he'd been playing.

CHAPTER
THIRTY-TWO

With both arms stretched out in front of me I pointed my service revolver into the pitch black of the night. Across the yard I could just pick out a wire fence that separated Bodden's property from the inky void beyond. I turned to Truth and beckoned her over to me with a nudge of my head. The little girl stood up and let the blanket around her shoulders drop to the floor. She picked up the holdall at her feet, ran across to me and stood close at my back. I leant across to the light switch by the kitchen door and flicked it off, took the holdall from Truth and slung it over my shoulder, then grabbed the little girl's hand and made a run for it across the backyard. When we got to the fence I picked Truth up under her arms and lifted her across the wire then climbed over to join her. I immediately dropped on to one knee, dragging Truth down beside me. I could feel her body trembling against my arm and I pulled her close to me.

Moments later I heard Bodden's front door fly back against the wall as Paxton and his men steamrollered in. Then all hell broke loose inside the place. I could just make out Bodden's voice as he began to squirm and protest to his unwelcome house guests. The sound of glass splintering and Bodden letting out an ear-piercing scream made me sink as low as I could down in the grass. I listened as one of the Americans began yelling, "Bodden, you damn stupid son of a bitch. What the fucking hell happened in here?"

"He jumped me, pinned me to the floor. The black bastard threatened to kill me if I didn't tell him that it was you who was coming for the two of them. He pulled a gun on me, and then they both took off out the back."

One of the men ran down the hall and shone a flashlight out into the yard, strafing the air in front of him. I pulled Truth towards me and we sank down low on the ground. Another Yankee, his voice more high pitched, snapped at Bodden, "You asshole. All you had to do was hold 'em till we got here, you shit for brains."

Bodden continued to stutter out his excuses. "But, but he went wild. I didn't stand a chance. He's dangerous, just like you said, Mr Paxton."

The first Yank snapped at Bodden, silencing his whimpering. "How long they been gone?"

"Not long, about five, six minutes maybe." Bodden whined on at the American, continuing to dig his own grave. "Look, Mr Paxton . . . I told you where the coon was intending to go with the young 'un. You'll find him heading for the next village, the White Hart barns. He ain't gonna get far. That nigger's too bloody stupid not to get caught."

One of the men laughed. "He ain't as stupid as you, old man." Suddenly the house lights went out and the place fell into darkness. Moments later I heard the

340

familiar thud from a suppressor-fitted handgun and at the same time saw the briefest of muzzle flashes.

Although I didn't see it happen, I knew that Wilf Bodden was dead. It would be chalked up as another murder that I had committed while on the run. Paxton had once again found his very own patsy and another excuse to keep hunting me down to get to Truth. I sank the side of my face to the ground and then began to slowly back up on my belly across the grass. Truth, holding on to my hand, instinctively followed. We slithered away from the fence, inching further out into the open field, distancing ourselves from any further beams of torchlight that Paxton's men may have shone out across the open moorland. We back-pedalled like that for about twenty feet. I stopped, raised my head a few inches off the grass and caught sight of four men in the distance, walking slowly towards us, silhouetted by the moonlight. None of them had as yet spotted the two of us.

I quietly pulled the old army holdall through both my arms so that it hung from my back, slipped the safety catch off my revolver then slowly got to my feet. I pulled Truth up off the ground and we started to run.

All I could think about was putting as much distance between us and Paxton and his men as possible. In the blackness I began zigzagging across the open heath, with no idea of the terrain and unsure where we were running to.

The bright moonlight above us aided me in navigating the open expanse of the rough, divot-potted field. But just as the night light worked in our favour, it also hindered us.

With the adrenaline pounding through my body, I swear I thought I heard the heavy thud of Paxton and his men picking up their pace behind us. I slowed down ever so slightly, stuck my revolver into my jacket pocket and pulled Truth towards my right thigh, scooping her up in my arms, then pushed myself on. As soon as I spurted on I realised that carrying Truth while I ran was going to be a real problem. I gasped in mouthfuls of air as I picked up my pace again, still criss-crossing the ground in front of me. Then, out of the corner of my eye, I thought I saw the dark shadowing of a row of bushes to my right. I clutched tightly at Truth's legs and torso, drawing them up towards my chest, then put my head down and headed for the still, dark profile of the hedgerow. Gasping for breath and almost bent double with the creasing pain from the stitch in my belly, I pelted across the short grass, hoping that I could make the dense shrubs without either of us being seen. Every time my foot hit the turf I was expecting to hear the silenced thud of rifle or pistol fire, to feel a bullet tear into my flesh. I pushed myself to run faster, to cover the ground unseen. I felt blood pulsating madly through my veins with each new step, the sides of my temples pinched with razor-like pain. My lungs burned and clawed to burst out of my chest, then out of nowhere I felt the top of my head hit a heavy wall of leaves and branches, the sheer bulk of it knocking me backwards onto the grass. I lost my grip on Truth and she fell over the top of me, her body falling to the ground directly above my head.

Without catching my breath, I thrust out both arms and caught hold of one of her flailing arms and clawed the little girl back over my chest. I rolled onto my side, looped my left arm under Truth's belly and, without knowing where I was going, dragged the two of us underneath the hedgerow. I sank down as low as I could, my head scraping against the sharp tips that hung from the bottom of the hedge. My heels dug into the soft earth, helping me to haul both our bodies backwards while still clasping tight onto the lower half of Truth's chest. I pushed at the earth with my shoulder, twisting and turning like an earthworm caught in the sun, until I finally scrambled out onto the other side from the base of the heavy thicket.

I heaved the two of us back onto our feet and continued to run to my left along the length of the hedge. I could feel the ground below me starting to dip; the terrain started to become less easy to traverse and the grass underneath our feet quickly turned to smooth pebbles then bigger rocks. I slowed my pace, held on to Truth's hand a little tighter and after a few more feet stopped for a moment. I felt a sharp gust of wind blow out of nowhere and hit me square in the face. I carefully reached up and lifted one of the straps of the holdall away from my shoulder then wriggled it away from my back. I dropped the bag at my feet, bent down, then pushed my hand inside it and fished about until finally I felt the handle of my slim Eveready torch.

I pulled the flashlight out, switched it on and shone the tiny beam down in front of me. I swept the thin stream of light across the ground, its faint glow catching the rough edges of pieces of stone and disrupted mossy earth. I bent forward a little further and was again caught head on by another sudden flurry of cold air. I stretched out my arm a little further and let the remaining shallow ray of light from my torch extend as far as it was able. I scanned the blackness until I realised there was no more ground for my lamp to scour or touch. I let the flashlight arc down, back towards the ground, but its pencil-thick beam was immediately lost, extinguished by the dark abyss that lay at our feet.

CHAPTER
THIRTY-THREE

I felt my head spin and my heart sink as I stood at the sheer drop. Nausea crept through my body as I cautiously edged myself away from the craggy rock face. My legs became unsteady with fear, my feet heavy and clumsy. I forced myself to move and, without realising, nervously backed myself straight into Truth, catching her face with the pointed corner of the holdall. She gave a sudden, startled yelp; I turned on my heels, swiftly caught hold of her arm and covered her mouth with the palm of my hand then dropped the two of us down onto the ground. I pulled the little girl in close to me, switched off the dimming flashlight, and drew us back into the damp, shrouded undergrowth. Paxton, Jardine and their men didn't take long to head our way. I closed my eyes and listened as they began to scour the open terrain only a few feet from where we were hid. Realising I was holding her face way too tightly, I gently lifted my hand a few inches away from Truth's mouth and felt her warm breath leak through the gaps in my fingers. Her body shook and juddered against my chest. I rested my chin on her head, shuffled us further back into the vegetation and looked up into the darkness. Three piercing torch beams suddenly erupted through the dense hedgerow above us, their ghostly shafts of light cutting viciously through the still night air. The men had clearly adapted quickly to the nocturnal conditions, the result of good military training.

They moved stealthily like seasoned pack predators, their footsteps treading lightly across the turf as they stalked us, never uttering a sound as they continued to search across the moor and along the perimeter of the thicket we had crawled through, their silence made all the more eerie by their probing torches, which shone down into the blue blackness around us as they doggedly hunted. I let my right hand slowly drop from Truth's mouth, reached down and pulled my revolver from my jacket pocket, and raised it up against the side of my face, the back of my arm and hand cushioned by the thick shrubs. I felt the cold metal of the gun lightly graze the side of my cheek. I cocked the hammer full back with my thumb and then rested my perspiration-coated finger uneasily against the trigger, stared back up into the coal-black void and waited for them to pick up our scent.

As a youngster, my father would often scold me for the innocent, childlike ways I'd sometimes exhibit in his presence. Thomas Duffus Ellington could never have been described as a tolerant man, especially when he'd a jug of rum inside his belly. Drunk or sober, my father could be prone to bouts of violent temper and ill moods. Impatient by nature, he would often raise his huge hand to me and bark his disdain for my own lack of innocent adolescent restraint. "Pickney, any damn fool can hold on ta de helm when de sea is calm."

346

From an early age I'd learnt the hard way how to be patient, educated in such matters by an ill-tempered patriarch, a man more accustomed to making his point by striking me with his leather belt than by an edifying word.

I had not given a great deal of thought to my father's brutal rages and cruel behaviour towards me for a very long time. The man I'd grown to despise as a child had unwittingly crawled back into my memory and joined Truth and me as we sat huddled up in the dark, biding our time, hoping that Paxton and the others would finally move their search for us further afield.

Finally, after what seem like an eternity, the strafing beams from their torches overhead suddenly disappeared and the hedgerow and moorland above us became devoid of any human life. I lifted my left arm up close to my face and peered down at my wristwatch. I could just make out the faint luminous hands on the dial: it was 3.20a.m. I rested the revolver on the top of my thigh, released the hammer slowly back down behind the rear sight and slipped the gun into my jacket pocket then bent forward a little and whispered into Truth's ear.

"We're gonna wait here a while longer, make sure that those guys are well outta the way."

Truth turned her head towards me and whispered a reply. "And then what are we going to do, Joseph?"

I looked straight ahead of me, out into murky gloom, unable to answer her. I could offer no assurances to the poor child. No master plan for our escape, no magic I could conjure up to make things right.

Truth, sensing my fear and reticence, drew herself up as close as she could and let her head fall limply against my right shoulder. She reached down and took hold of my hand, her little fingers quickly wrapping themselves around my own, and squeezed them tightly. We sat in silence, motionless, enveloped by the thick, dank undergrowth around us. Two scared souls hiding in the dark.

I turned on the torch and ran the narrow beam along the ground until it reached the craggy rocks at the cliff face. I moved a little closer, and with my back close to the undergrowth, I leant out over the edge and shone the light down the left-hand side of the face. I began to pick out a series of thin stone outcrops that hung like steps down to what I thought could be the ground. I got to my knees and tried to pick out what was below, but the weak flashlight beam struggled to break through the inky pitch to the floor. I followed the steps down along the side rock wall with the light and could see that what I had first thought of as being a vertical drop into nowhere was in fact a man-made wall of dug out craggy limestone, which I believed could reach down into an old mine. I let the torch beam skirt along the middle of the stone wall and made out a series of large boreholes, probably made by miners who had at some time drilled then sunk gelignite into the rock to blast out the much-prized lime.

I looked up into the darkness above me and then back down into a black unwelcoming nothing. We had two unknown routes of possible escape: the moor and the limestone mine below. If we returned to the moor I felt sure it wouldn't take long for Paxton and Jardine to be back on our tails again. We'd stand little chance of staying one step ahead of them. I decided we'd take our chances by going down. I sat on my butt and made sure the holdall on my back was secure then shone the torch at the stone outcrop less than a foot below me. I swung my legs over the edge then turned to Truth and let the beam of the torch sit at the tip of her feet. "OK, little one, I need you to scoot down towards me on your bottom; can you do that for me?"

Without making a sound, Truth got on to her haunches then slowly pushed herself towards me. I leant backwards and reached out my arms, catching hold of her by the waist, then sat her down beside me. I shone the torch back onto the first limestone step that had been cut out of the rock face, found a solid piece of rock to use as a handhold for me to grip, and twisted myself round, then let myself slowly drop down onto the ridge. I steadied myself and shone the torch to my right, picking out the next outcrop, perhaps another foot and a half away. On the rock face in front of me and below I could now see dozens of deep boreholes that had been blown out of the alabaster rock face, each making a good foothold for our descent. I looked up at Truth and reached out my arms towards her.

"I want you to lean forward and put your arms around my neck, then you gotta spring down to me and hold on to me real tight."

Truth peered down warily at me. "Why, what are you going to do, Joseph?"

"No questions, child, you gotta just do as I ask, OK?" The little girl looked down into the blackness below her. I raised my hand up to Truth's face and caught the underside of her chin with the tips of my fingers.

"Don't look down there, little one. I need you to look at me. You gotta trust me again. Just like you did last time, back in the caves. Can you do that for me?" Truth nodded her head at me compliantly. "Good, now reach down and clasp your arms around my neck like I said."

Truth leant forward and let herself slowly drop, throwing her arms out as she fell forward. She wrapped her legs around my waist and grasped on for dear life around my neck and shoulders.

"OK, there you go. Good girl. That's the worst part over. Here's what you gotta do for me now. I want you to shut your eyes and I don't want you to open them till I tell you to, understand me?"

Truth stuck her face into the crook of my neck and nodded her head.

I stuck the torch into my mouth and held onto it with my teeth then reached across to my right and grasped hold of the inside of the borehole and stretched my leg out down onto the next limestone outcrop. Once standing on the thin crag, I again shone the torch back across the side of the wall.

Another two feet below us was a further overhang, this time cut a little deeper into the corner face of the limestone. To get to it meant reaching out across the face of the rock again, grabbing another blast hole and then climbing the short distance down to it. I chose the

350

nearest handhold and looked for somewhere in the limestone to stick my foot into. I gripped hold of the torch with my teeth again and felt Truth's body stiffen. She clenched both her arms and legs tightly around my neck and waist as I moved towards the edge of the crag.

"Here we go, keep those eyes shut." I reached out with my left hand and snatched hold of the hole in the wall then swung my foot towards the foothold below. The toe of my shoe jammed itself into the shallow recess and I pulled myself across, my right leg following after me, the sole of my shoe scraping the wall as I tried to find another secure footing. Truth tensed and became heavy around my torso. My leg flailed about in mid-air as I struggled to find something for my other foot to perch on. She instinctively tightened her grasp around my neck, almost choking me.

I felt the chalky limestone around my left foot begin to give way; my fingers cramped and spasmed and began scrabbling to keep hold of the edge of the borehole. I quickly looked down at the overhang less than a couple of feet to my right and felt a surge of panic run through my body. Without thinking, I flung myself across the rock face and fell down onto the flat lip of the overhang.

The impact shot the torch from my mouth, sending it flying across the smooth rock. My right leg twisted and I felt my knee give way as I rolled hard onto my back. A wave of pain ran up through my body as I lay on the ridge, gasping for breath. I looked down at Truth, her head still tucked away in my chest, her tiny arms still gripping the life out of me.

The two of us sat for a short while with our backs against the wall of the overhang. I'd retrieved the battered torch, which still had the faintest of battery life, and tried to rub the pain out of my knee. I felt Truth's body lean against my arm. I looked down at her and could just make out that her eyes were still tightly snapped shut. Without my prompting, she eventually opened her eyes then lifted her hand and rubbed at her throat.

"I'm thirsty, Joseph."

"Me too. I'm gonna find us someting to drink as soon as we're outta here. You got my word on it."

I could feel my own throat tightening and the inside of my mouth drying as I spoke the words. The thought of finding us both fresh water made me forget the pulsating waves of pain and fatigue that shot sporadically through my worn-out body. I edged across towards the ledge of limestone overhang and shone the torch down below me again.

As I stuck my head further out to look at the next outcrop below, I was suddenly hit by a sharp blast of cool air. Rather than the wind dying away above me, the breeze became more intense and free flowing, its touch caressing my cheeks and brow. I grasped the flashlight tightly and stretched my arm down as far as I could: two further limestone outcrops stood out from the rock face to the right of us, again no more than three feet apart. As I brought the torch beam back up, the pencil-thin dying light caught something that was large and black, different from the white rock that was around us. I slowly drew the beam back up and, after searching in the darkness for a moment, picked out a large iron girder that appeared to rise up in front of the rock face. I turned to Truth, catching her dirt-coated face out with the torch's beam, and stuck my arm out in front of her.

"Come on, let's go find that water."

The climb down to the next outcrop presented less of a challenge than the previous one. We took another short break then slowly descended to the third limestone plinth. The cool breeze became stronger and the iron girder work behind us had begun to reveal itself as part of an enormous conveyor belt. I could just make out rotting wooden tipping jetties hanging either side of two large decaying engine mountings that would originally have driven the stone along the length of the belt. My eyes, which were now growing more accustomed to the dark, looked down at the machinery. I followed the conveyor downwards towards the outline of a larger bank of stone that spread out in a long slope towards what looked to be the mine floor. Scaling down the limestone escarpment took another twenty minutes.

I carried Truth the rest of the way down the steep slope until my feet touched solid ground. I lifted her back onto her feet and shone the torch on the face of my watch. It was four thirty.

Our descent, although time-consuming, had not been as difficult as I had thought. The dark had given the impression that it was a greater drop to the bottom of the mine floor than it actually was. I took hold of Truth's hand then followed the edge of the old conveyor belt along a wide, long tunnel that seemed to go on forever. The path alongside the mining machinery sank down into a dip before gradually rising upwards. Truth called out to me.

"Where are we, Joseph?"

"In some kinda mineshaft, I think."

"I'm tired. Do you think we're ever going to find our way out?"

I stopped in my tracks and bent down in front of her so that our faces were only inches apart. "Well, I ain't plannin' on spendin' the rest of my days down here, child. How 'bout you?"

Truth unexpectedly giggled at me in the darkness. I reached down, picked the little girl up in my arms and began to slowly trudge further up the gradual incline of the mineshaft with no real idea where I was walking to.

I kept pushing on, unsure of how far I had actually walked. My head sunk low towards the ground and my feet ached inside my battered shoes, my gait unsteady as I strode forward. Truth became increasingly heavy in my arms. Each step started to become painful; splinters of muscular pain shot through my legs and thighs as I ploughed on into the unknown. I began to count each step I took, forcing myself to slog on along the path while I made a mental note of my footfall. My tongue felt like it was swelling in my mouth. Huge beads of sweat fell from my face, my clothing soaked in my own heavy perspiration. I became unsteady as I marched on, my elbow occasionally touching the side of the mine wall as I walked, and this contact my body made against the limestone rock became more frequent the further up the incline I walked. I lifted my head and

354

looked up and could see that the walls either side where closing in around the conveyor belt, slowly pushing me against the wall as I walked. The ceiling above me became lower and the path began to thin inwards the further I climbed. My head sank again and I took another forty hard steps. I lifted my head once more and out of the corner of my eye caught my first glimpse of what I thought to be light.

Whatever it was started to glisten back at me like the illusion of water in a desert mirage; the thin shards of weak light that now sprang out in front of me seemed at first to be nothing more than a cruel will-o'-the-wisp-like apparition. I felt my legs spasm and lock as I pushed myself towards the distant light source. It must have been another five minutes before I finally reached the entrance to the shaft and stumbled out into the mouth of the mine and fell to my knees. I let the cool dawn breeze blow around me as I looked up towards the brilliant orange-hued rays of the morning sunrise, only then truly believing that what I was seeing was real.

CHAPTER
THIRTY-FOUR

I'd found water, if that's what you could call it. Just outside the mine entrance stood the remains of an old weighbridge office and plumbed in next to the front door was a decaying brass standpipe. With what little strength I still possessed I'd managed to kick at the top of the rusted tap until it had loosened. I'd turned the tap full on until it reluctantly began to spurt out a slow dribble of sulphurous-smelling, sludge-coloured spring water. After a short while, the standpipe began to flow erratically, glugging and churning as the mucky liquid came up the pipe. As the water spilled onto the ground, the colour became a little less dark and it didn't stink as much. I'd sipped a handful; it didn't taste great but I doubted that drinking it would do the two of us any lasting harm. I'd let Truth take a drink, watching that she didn't wolf down too much and make herself ill. When she'd finished I'd taken my handkerchief from my hip pocket, wet the cotton cloth under the standpipe and cleaned the mud and dirt from her face.

Truth and I collapsed on a bank of grass opposite the weighbridge office; above the door was a small wooden plaque with the fading words "Black Rock Quarry". We sat facing each other with our backs resting against two

356

large boulders. I looked across at the mouth of the entrance of what I could now see to be a disused limekiln and mine.

Not a dozen words had passed between the two of us since I carried Truth out from the darkness. Exhaustion had suddenly taken a grip of my washed-out body and mind, and I struggled to keep my eyes open. It had been just six days since Ida Stephens had casually walked into my office and paid me to find Doc Fowler. Just over twenty-four hours later I'd witnessed the doc's death and found Truth hidden by him underneath Speedwell swimming baths. It wasn't long before the shady American police officers Paxton and Jardine, along with Detective Constable Beaumont and a sizable crew of his fellow corrupt Bristol and Avon police officers, were throwing their weight about and had tried to hunt down the two of us across half of Somerset and the West Country. In just over a hundred and forty-four hours, Truth and I had been shot at, tracked through underground caves and woodland, and run to ground like scared animals, and I was still struggling to understand why.

I stared thoughtfully across at Truth and wondered to myself how the two of us had managed to survive the last few days. The odds had been seriously stacked against us, but somehow, beyond all hope, we'd managed to find ourselves still alive and sitting peacefully in the early summer sunshine on a late June morning. Something told me that our new-found calm would not last: Paxton and his cronies wouldn't lose our trail for long and would soon be snapping at our heels.

Truth, realising that I had been watching her, shyly dropped her eyes to the ground. She sat forward, away from the boulder, and rested the palm of one of her hands on her knee then began to hum a tune to herself while making circular patterns in the soil with one of her fingers. She sat like that for a short while before plucking up the courage to raise her head and make eye contact with me. She gave a brief, timid smile before speaking.

"Who is Ellie, Joseph?"

I immediately felt a lump rise in my throat and quickly looked back towards the entrance of the old mine, my eyes darting anywhere rather than make eye contact with the child. Truth waited patiently for an answer. I rubbed the palms of my hands together nervously and fixed my gaze on the tree line that ran alongside where we were sat.

"Ellie was my wife."

Truth, taken aback a little by my reply, stared down at the ground before speaking again. "She was your wife. You mean you don't live together any more?"

I felt my throat tighten. I coughed a couple of times to try and clear it then looked at Truth. "No, we used to live together, but she died."

Truth kept her eyes fixed to the ground, her fingers digging deeper into the soil. "Died? How did she die?"

I swallowed hard. "It was in a fire."

I watched as the little girl slowly shook her head in disbelief. "That sounds so horrid."

358

I nodded. "Yeah . . . yeah, it sure was."

Truth, with all good intentions, innocently tried to lighten the mood. "You have any children, Joseph?"

"I did. Ellie and me, we had a little girl, her name was Amelia. She died with her momma."

Truth repeated my daughter's name to herself. "Amelia, that's a pretty name."

I nodded my head to myself, and kept nodding it, over and over again, trying to hold back a flood of tears. I tried to clear my throat again and finally croaked out a quiet reply. "A pretty name . . . Yeah, ain't it just."

Truth didn't say another word; she just kept staring down at the ground. A few moments later she turned her back to me, drew her legs up to her chest, linked both arms around the front of her calves then rested her chin on the tops of her knees. I sat watching her through tear-filled eyes, thinking to myself that even an inquisitive, well-meaning child knew better than to mess with a man's grief.

It was just after five forty-five. The sun had begun to lift itself higher into the sky, its early morning warmth washing down onto the glimmering dew that hung from the blades of grass and purple-flower-tipped moss that covered the tumbling moorland stretching out from the hill where Truth and I were now standing. I looked down across the valley and could clearly see the village of Cheddar just a mile or so away.

I knew that Vic would be waiting somewhere down there for the two of us. All that was stopping me from finding him was some pretty inhospitable, rambling heathland and five or six heavily armed coppers intent on taking me and the girl out at the neck. I knew it was too dangerous for Truth to walk down into the village with me. I turned and looked back blankly at the old limekiln entrance then down at Truth. I didn't have to say a word to the child; she already knew what I was going to ask.

We walked back down into the mine and Truth and I began to search about the place. About twenty feet inside the entrance, spurring off on the left-hand side, I found a thin passageway cut out of the limestone. We walked along the short stone corridor and found an old miner's lean-to. It had been carefully tucked away, a place of refuge for tough men who had once worked underground. The lean-to was situated far enough past the opening of the disused workings to remain concealed but not so remote that it made you feel you were returning to the foreboding bleakness of the dark tunnel. Inside the hut, the walls were covered in thick dust and old cobwebs. A bunch of old picks and shovels were stacked up next to the door along with three lengths of old tarpaulin. Two wicker and cane chairs sat either side of an old card table, its green baize top long rotted away. On the back wall stood a small carpenter's bench. Various rusting tools were strewn across the top of it along with a couple of brass miners' lamps.

I picked one up, put it to my ear and shook it. The paraffin oil inside sloshed about from side to side. I reached into the holdall and fished out the box of matches that Lazarus had given to me. Truth watched me as I took a match, opened up the little door on the side of the miner's lamp then struck the match against the box and let the flame rest against the wick until it ignited the oil. The lamp began to glow and quickly lit up the small lean-to. I placed the Davy lamp back on the bench and checked the other one. It had less oil in it but would come in handy if the first ran out. Truth turned around and looked about the hut.

"This is just like the place Theo left me, Joseph."

I nodded my head. "Yeah, kinda, I suppose."

"You're going to leave me here, aren't you?"

"It's gonna be the safest place for you to stay while I go find Vic."

Truth looked up at me and I saw her mouth begin to tremble. "Theo left me. He never came back."

I knelt down in front of Truth and brushed the side of her cheek with the back of my hand. "I know he didn't. But I will, you've got my solemn word on it."

I pulled out one of the wicker chairs and sat down then lifted Truth onto my knee. "I'll be gone a few hours. I'll find my cousin Vic and the two of us will come get you straight away, I promise."

Truth stared up at me, desperately trying to fight back a flood of tears. "You promise?"

I nodded my head. "Promise."

I sat with Truth on my lap for a while longer. She said nothing more about being left alone. She knew she didn't need to. She had witnessed with her own eyes what Paxton and his men were capable of, and those cruel deeds had been enough to persuade her that she would be safer lying low in the old cabin than by my side as I tried to find Vic.

Before leaving I showed Truth how to light the other Davy lamp then pulled the carpenter's bench away from the wall a little, dragged a length of the tarpaulin across and rolled it down the back of the bench.

"On the off chance you hear anybody out there that ain't me, you blow out that lamp light and get behind here under this canvas as quick as you can, understand?"

Truth nodded her head at me. I picked up the holdall, walked over to Truth and dropped it at her feet then pointed down at it with my finger.

"OK, in that old bag we've been haulin' 'bout with us, we got ourselves over a thousand pounds."

Truth looked up at me in disbelief. I bent down and took out the envelope containing the bank notes and gave it to Truth.

"When all this is over and we get back to Bristol, this is yours."

Truth looked at the wad of cash inside the envelope. "Mine?"

"You bet, so you best start countin' it, make sure it's all there, then put it back in that bag for safekeeping. Don't let it outta your sight, got it?"

Truth looked down at the money again and squeezed the envelope tightly. She looked back up at me and began to nod her head up and down excitedly. "Yeah, I got it!"

"Good, I'm gonna get going. Find that cousin of mine."

As I began to walk towards the cabin door, Truth rushed after me and grabbed hold of the tail of my jacket and pulled me back. I turned to face her and she flung her arms around me, squeezing me tightly.

"You will come back, won't you?" she whispered.

I reached down and brushed at her soft, downy hair with my hand. "Course, I will . . . I'll be back befo' you know it."

Truth slowly released me from her grip. I turned and walked out of the lean-to. As I made my way back down the passageway I could have sworn I heard Truth begin to cry. I stopped and looked back down the stone corridor but could hear nothing. I turned around, put my head down and kept on walking towards the mine entrance, telling myself it was just my imagination. My conscience, on the other hand, told me that the hushed weeping I'd heard was very real.

I headed out from the mine and quickly found a gravel road that led through the old Black Rock Quarry and on to the main road, which looked like it ran straight down into Cheddar village. Rather than follow the narrow gorge road and be an easy target, I stuck to the shaded wooded area that ran alongside it.

It took me a while longer to cover the distance, trudging over moss-covered crags and steep downhill footpaths. Every muscle in my body ached. I thought of Truth sitting back in the lean-to at the mine and pushed myself on all the harder. I finally walked into the outskirts of the village at just after 7.30 a.m. There had been no sign of Paxton or any of his men; I just hoped it would stay that way.

I had no idea where I was heading; all I knew was what Milo had told me, which was that the White Hart inn was tucked away at the far end of the village. I kept to as many back streets as possible. Few people were about at such an early hour. If I saw anybody heading my way I quickly dipped into a doorway or snuck over a garden gate to avoid any unwanted attention. I was hoping that Vic would be holed up in one of his motors as I neared the pub, but finding the public house was proving to be a real problem. I walked along a series of narrow side streets, lined either side by attractive thatched cottages, and eventually came to a crossroads. To my right was a track road leading up to what looked like a copse or wooded area. Parked up next to a row of trees, halfway along the track, was a red Commer postal van. I looked about for the postman but could see no one. I crossed the road and took the left-hand lane; a street sign nailed high up on the side of the wall of one of the cottages read "The Bays". I kept walking down the lane until I reached a small fork in the road.

On the right-hand side, next to an old, disused farmhouse, ran a low walled path, and on the left, nestled right at the back of the lane, sat the White Hart inn. I looked behind me. There was nobody about. The pub was understandably quiet so early in the morning. The curtains were still drawn at the front of the grey stone building and the few cottages behind me seemed equally subdued. I wanted to call out Vic's name but decided that would be a bad idea. I turned to my right and looked up along the long path next to the farmhouse. Was that where I'd find the disused barns Milo had spoken of, the place Truth and I were to hole up until Vic arrived? I felt my stomach knot and the

364

hairs on the backs of my arms and neck rise. I stuck my hand in my jacket pocket and pulled out my service-issue Smith & Wesson revolver, clicked off the safety then held it loosely at my side and began to slowly walk up the path. I peered over the left-hand side of the wall that separated the path from what appeared to be the entrance to an old allotment. I nervously held my revolver out at waist height and kept walking slowly towards the rear of the farmhouse.

At the edge of the building was a wooden yeoman farm gate. I opened it up and walked on in. I looked about the yard and could see nobody. The rear of the house was boarded up and the dilapidated outside toilet had seen better days. I looked up towards the open fields beyond the property in front of me. In the distance, I could see the barns Milo had told me about. Feeling a little less apprehensive, I slowly let the revolver drop to my side and rest against my leg.

Then I heard the gentle click of metal catching against metal and the sound of leaves rustling over the concrete floor of the yard, followed by the gagging odour of men's cheap cologne. Out of the corner of my eye I saw the polished edge of the butt of a pistol break through the air. I tried to raise my arm in defence and then instinctively snapped my eyes shut just as the weapon cracked against the side of my head. Then there was nothing.

CHAPTER
THIRTY-FIVE

I knew that I was alive because I could still smell the stink of cheap aftershave in the air. My head pounded with an intense pain that almost prevented me from opening my eyes. I was sat in a high-backed wooden chair, my wrists and ankles tied tightly to the arms and legs. I lifted my head and shook it, then forced open my eyelids and tried to focus. I was in what looked to be a fairly large pigsty, the brick whitewashed walls around me flaking and yellowed with age. The concrete floor seemed to be slightly sloping, giving the impression that I was about to topple forward onto my face at any moment. At the bottom of the wall in front of me, a deep gutter ran towards a drain at the foot of a rotting stable door. The room felt airless and was dimly lit. A low wattage bulb hung from a rope rose in the ceiling above my head. I could feel the sticky trickle of warm blood as it ran from the wound on the back of my scalp where I had been hit. It poured down my neck and along the side of my face and dripped slowly from my chin onto the floor, landing in red-dotted splashes by my foot. The fact I smelt the rank cologne again also told me I was not alone. I got the feeling that whoever it was that reeked so badly wasn't standing too far away from me. I tried to arch my back off the chair and turn my head to get a better look behind me. The palm of a man's hand suddenly struck me across the back of my head, sending a piercing wave of pain through my skull. My head whipped forwards and my ears rang with a high-pitched buzz.

A man's voice spoke, the thick accent coated in a lazy drawl. "Don't you go cricking your neck, nigger. There ain't nuthin' fo' you to gawp at back here."

I felt the room begin to spin around me. I squeezed my eyes shut and tried to retain some sense of balance. More blood ran down the side of my face, dribbling down my neck and soaking into the collar of my shirt. The droning noise in my head suddenly stopped and was immediately replaced by the sound of hob-nailed boots clicking across the concrete floor. I tensed my arms and legs against the ropes as a man's hand clenched hold of my cheeks and jaw and yanked my head backwards.

"This is what you need to be looking at, nigger."

I opened my eyes and stared up at the face of my mystery captor. The man squeezed my jaw a little tighter and lowered his face closer to mine. He ran the tip of his tongue across his discoloured front teeth and grinned at me.

"We ain't bin properly introduced yet."

I coughed weakly and breathed in deeply through my nose. "I ain't in no real rush to get acquainted."

The man pinched underneath my cheekbones with his powerful fingertips, sending a wave of pain up into my temples, then pushed his face in closer towards me, the tips of our noses almost touching.

"You ain't being very civil, boy."

I felt the spittle from his mouth hit the top of my lip and his warm, sour breath wafted up my nose. Now I had the man's halitosis as well as his rank scent to stomach.

The man increased the pressure on my jaw with his hand then snapped his fingers open and released his grip, pushing my head and neck backwards, then stood erect in front of me. He was all dense muscle and brawn, and I immediately recognised him as one of the American coppers I'd seen back at Lazarus' place.

"My compadres in the military police corps address me as Sergeant Jardine. My late, blessed momma on the other hand, she used my God-given name o' Nathan. An' I got a redbone floozy waiting back home in Macon, Mississippi, who just calls me Mr Nate . . . I think it's best you just call me sir, nigger."

I turned my face away from Jardine in disgust. "I ain't callin' you nuttin'."

Jardine swung the palm of his hand and backstroked me across the side of my head again. "You got yourself a lotta sass, Ellington."

I gritted my teeth in anger and glared back up at the muscle-bound lawman. Jardine stood back from me, and I watched as he raised his hand to his mouth and casually began to bite at a hangnail on the edge of his thumb. He nipped at the skin then spat out a wad of saliva onto the concrete.

368

"You sure been leading us on a right ole coon hunt, boy. Damn, I thought at one point we'd never sniff out your worthless black hide." Jardine put both hands on his hips and kicked at my foot with his polished army boot. "So, where's the girl?"

I looked down at the ground and whispered a reply. "She's dead."

"What's that . . . Dead, you say?"

"Yeah, she gone."

"Gone? Gone where, boy?"

"She fell, back when we were running on the moors last night."

Jardine slowly nodded his head. "Fell. Where she fall?"

"Out by the cliffs, as we neared the gorge. It was dark, we were running, her hand slipped outta mine an' she went over the edge."

"Just like that, hey?" Jardine began to slowly circle around me, stopping behind my back. I felt his hands touch either side of my shoulders and start to massage at the muscles just below my neck. "You know, you an' that other worthless old nigger, Fowler, gone an' caused us a dung pile o' trouble. Seems like me an' my pardner bin trawling cross half this worthless goddamn country looking for that child, and now you're tellin' me she's dead. Whadda I look like to you, coon, chopped liver?" Jardine pummelled my shoulder a little harder. "Now, I'm gonna ask you again. Where's the damn girl?"

I slowly shook my head and began to repeat what I had just said. Jardine slammed his fist deep into the side of my guts. I could feel the searing pain sink all the way into the bone. I gasped in air and watched as Jardine came around to face me again.

"You better start spilling something I wanna hear, boy, an' you best do it before my pardner, Mr Paxton, gets back. Where is the girl?" Jardine hammered another blow in my solar plexus then smashed his fist into my cheekbone and nose. My head and body flew sideways and I slumped at an angle in the chair. Jardine leant across me and pulled me upright. My head fell forward, my chin touching my chest. My breathing fell to a wheeze. Blood filled my mouth. I coughed a couple of times then spat out red-tinged saliva onto the floor. I raised my head a little but all I could see was the golden snake's head belt buckle hanging just below Jardine's flat stomach.

Jardine leant back towards me and stabbed at my forehead with the tip of his finger. "My pardner, he's pissed at you, an' he's a real son of a bitch when he's pissed. We lost three good men in that shoot-out with those friends of yours back at that old shack of a bar we ended up burning down. Beaumont, that limey asshole, he bought it too." Jardine smiled to himself after speaking the dead policeman's name. "Though I doubt anybody's gonna be grieving that prick's demise." Jardine reached around to my head and squeezed at my neck with his fingers. The pincer-like grip brought tears to my eyes.

"Mr Paxton, on the other hand, well, he's grieving. He don't like to lose any men. Don't like complications or loose ends. That nigger friend o' yours back at the

370

inn, he caused some loose ends and casualties in that firelight. Paxton took his bullshit kinda personal. He was still alive with his guts hanging outta his belly when we found him. Mr Paxton made him scream before he died. Made him tell us where you was heading. We ain't bin but a gnat's breath from your black butt all the time you bin running with the child. But when you went to ground last night, Paxton decided he'd hotfoot it back to the airbase an' round up a couple o' dudes that have a special knack o' tracking down uppity coloureds like you. Looks like he ain't gonna need 'em." Jardine squeezed at my neck again, only this time a lot harder.

I bellowed out in pain. "Look, man, I told you, the kid is dead. She took one heck of a fall, it was an accident."

"Accident, my ass. You're jiving me, boy!"

I spat out more blood down at my feet. "I ain't jiving you, man, I swear. The kid's dead. When she dropped over the edge o' that cliff there was nuttin' I could do. I searched 'bout in the dark a while, an' when I couldn't see her I came into the village to get myself picked up like I'd arranged."

Jardine pinched at my neck and frantically shook my head back and forth then bent down so that his face was staring at the side of my own. "Picked up by who?"

I gasped in pain as Jardine kept my neck in a vice-like grip. "Just a dude I work with; he's nobody."

"Well, zip-a-dee-doo-dah, he's nobody, is he? You know something, Ellington, you're starting to get so far up my nose I'm beginning to feel your prissy shoes on my chin." Jardine applied some more pressure to my neck. "Nigger, just take a look around you. I don't think you've quite grasped the severity of your situation. You're about two minutes away from being a corpse. It's time you started to wise up."

I felt Jardine's hand reach down and unclip something from his belt. I heard the slick gliding sound of a knife blade being smoothly drawn from its scabbard. Jardine let go of my neck and ran his fingers through my hair then knotted a clump of it in his fist and wrenched my head back.

He then let the side of his dagger drag along the side of my cheek before inserting the thin blade of the knife into my nostril. He held it there for a moment then ran the tip of the blade down across my lips and along the other side of my face and let it rest inside the edge of my ear.

"Why don't you start again an' tell me exactly where that fuckin' child really is. No more crazy talk 'bout her being a stiff, you hear me?"

The knife sank a little deeper into my ear. I tensed my arms and legs against the ropes as Jardine tightened his grip on my hair then slipped the knife blade further inside.

"Nigger, you got 'bout twenty seconds to start tellin' me what I wanna know or I'm gonna jam this knife so far into your head that you'll be able to feel the end of it scratching on the inside o' your worthless skull."

I closed my eyes as Jardine tightened his grip again on my scalp and inched the razor-sharp blade closer towards my eardrum. I felt a scream begin to release itself from deep inside of me and surge its way up from my burning lungs towards my mouth. I could taste my own fear and felt it rise up into my throat like vomit. Behind tightly shut lids, my eyes rolled in their sockets and my strength ebbed away from me as if my very life force was being yanked from my spirit. I felt my head fill with a dull, arcing light then heard the stable door being violently kicked open and the thunder-like blast of a single gunshot. I felt the blade of the knife rush out of my ear and Jardine's fingers suddenly release their tight grip on my hair. A warm, fast-flowing draught blew up around me as his muscular body flew backwards and was slammed against something hard.

My body sank in a heap and I gasped in the cordite-tasting air that filled the room. I slowly raised my head and saw Vic staring down at me, his hand steady, gripping a cold Colt .45 that was still aimed across my right shoulder. He took another step forward and looked down at the body of the man he'd just shot and killed, and spat at Jardine's feet.

"Shit, that sour-assed honky sure did love the sound o' his own muthafuckin' voice." Vic dropped the .45 a little. Still aiming it towards Jardine, he walked up to me. He picked up the knife from the concrete and began to cut the cords from my wrists and ankles. I felt the ropes drop to the floor then sank back in the chair and began to rub at the raw skin around my wrists.

I looked up at my cousin and the gun still poised firmly in his hand. "Vic, that damn knife o' his coulda shot clean straight t'ru my head!"

Vic glared at me. "Hell wid da knife. What you talkin' 'bout to dat fool, you callin' me a dude? You sayin' I'm a nobody? Do I look like nobody to you?" Vic stabbed indignantly at his chest with his thumb. "Who's dis that's just saved yo' ass a'gin. Fuckin' Santa Claus?"

I turned and looked at Jardine's bloodied corpse, his arms flung out at either side of him, a gaping mush of bone, split teeth and charred, disfigured flesh where his face had once been.

My body sank low in the chair, my head throbbed and exhaustion started to take hold of every fibre of my being. I bit at my bottom lip and felt a tear fall from my eye and run down my cheek. Vic gently rested his hand on top of my shoulder and gave it a gentle squeeze. I yelped like a child. He moved in closer then looked down at me and shook his head wearily.

"JT, evah since you was a pickney, I bin keepin' your sorry butt outta trouble. I guess some tings never change." He grinned at me and winked.

My head fell to the side and my bloodied cheek rested against the back of my cousin's hand. I closed my eyes and listened to my heart as it pounded away in my chest. I was about to thank Vic when I felt him lash out and kick savagely at Jardine's limp foot with his shoe. "Man, that cracker sure had a bucket full o' brains to spray 'cross this wall. That damn drain back there's gonna come in real handy."

Vic was right in his solemn reminiscence: some tings never do change.

CHAPTER
THIRTY-SIX

Vic had been busy before he'd kicked in the gate door of the sty and saved my butt. My cousin wasn't the kind of man to waste any time if he thought that trouble was on his tail. I listened to Vic cuss and moan as he dragged in the limp, lifeless body of one of Jardine's compadres from the yard outside and dropped him unceremoniously up against the wall in front of me. "This muthafucka weighs a ton! You know whadda piss'ole of a joint this place was ta find? What is it wid you an' hangin' round old dosshouses like dis?"

I held my tongue and nodded down at the man Vic had just dumped on the floor. "He dead too?"

Vic looked at me in disgust. "Course he ain't dead. You tink all I do all day is waste honkies? I clubbed the bastard wid this." Vic lifted the pistol he'd shot Jardine with up in the air and waved it at me. "US army-issue Colt .45." Vic kicked the man in the leg and pointed at him with the gun. "This bucked-tooth cracker here gone an' wasted that other cracker layin' on his ass over there." Vic looked about him and sucked air in between the gap in his front teeth. "Way I sees it, it's a simple open-an'-shut case. Just two honkies fallin' out over who gets to live in this run-down pile o'shit!" Vic slapped the top of his thigh and began to howl with laughter.

He looked at me and saw that I wasn't sharing the joke. I was in no mood for laughter. The only thing on my mind was Truth and if she was OK. I got up out of the chair and looked down at my wristwatch. It was just after 9.30a.m.

Vic walked across to Jardine's body, stuck his hand underneath his back and pulled my Smith & Wesson revolver from out of the dead man's belt, then handed it to me. "He ain't got no need for this." Vic shoved past me and headed for the door. "Come on, let's git the fuck outta here."

As Vic and I walked across the yard at the back of the run-down old farm I found a stone cattle trough filled with rainwater. I quickly sank my head into the trough and threw some of the grimy water over my face. Vic sat on the edge of the granite crib, looked at the cut at the back of my head and sniggered.

"Shit! You had worse when we was foolin' 'bout as pickneys. Don't sweat it. We'll soon git you cleaned up."

I pulled up the front of my shirt and used the tail to wipe my face dry then stared at Vic. He looked real sharp and made me feel just like I looked, which was a damn mess. He was wearing his favourite black leather jacket, a black polo shirt buttoned up to his neck, and slim-fitting black denims. The only concession to his dour look were the short grey turn-ups at the end of the legs of his strides. I tucked my damp shirt back into my trousers and attempted to tidy myself up a little. Vic sniggered at me again then pulled himself away from the trough and walked off across the yard. He called back as he reached the alleyway at the side of the farmhouse. "Quit foolin' wid that tatty shirt; you wastin' time, cuz. Where'd you put that damn pickney at?"

Truth had been left for over three hours, sat in that old miner's lean-to, alone.

I'd promised her that I wouldn't leave her for long. I'd broken my word to the child and that hurt more than the cut on the back of my head. I followed behind Vic as he moved quickly down the alley away from the farmhouse and out of the cul-de-sac. Everywhere was thankfully quiet. At the end of the lane, Vic grabbed hold of my jacket lapel and pulled me to the right, into the old track road, and began heading towards the red Commer post van that I'd seen parked up earlier. I leant my hand against the bonnet and stared at Vic.

"What the hell's this?"

Vic shook his head and swore under his breath. He walked around to the driver's side door, stuck a key into the lock and opened up.

"Stop with the damn bitching: it's a shitbox, I know. But this shitbox gonna git you and that pickney back to St Pauls without drawing too much attention." Vic got into the cab and pointed at me. "An' you know how I hate unwanted attention. Now, will you just git yo' sorry black ass inside the damn ting!"

Vic didn't waste any time following my directions back up to Black Rock Quarry. I knew we didn't have long before Paxton and his mob got back, and I didn't want us to be around when the Yankee copper returned to the farmhouse and was greeted with the carnage that Vic had left for him to clean up. We drove at speed along the gravel road back towards the old limekiln. Vic pulled the van as near to the entrance of the mine as possible.

We got out and he followed me as I ran up the green grass bank, down into the mouth of the mine and along the stone passageway towards the lean-to. I called out Truth's name as I pushed open the hut door and bolted in. I found her sitting on the floor, cross-legged with the holdall at her feet. On top of it was the battered envelope containing the money. By her side, offering meagre illumination, was one of the Davy lamps, its flame now all but a low flicker. I walked across the hut and knelt down in front of her. She stared at my swollen cheekbone and pointed at it with her finger.

"What happened to your face?"

I reached across and pulled Truth in my arms, tucking her head underneath my chin, and began to hug her. "It ain't nuttin', child, just a bump, that's all. I'm real sorry I took me so long to get back to you," I whispered. I felt the little girl begin to tap slowly at my back with the palm of her hand.

"It's OK, Joseph. I knew you'd be back . . . You promised you would, and you said you never broke a promise."

Truth lifted her head from under my chin, looked down at the money and tapped the envelope with the tips of two of her fingers.

"I counted it. There's over a thousand pounds, just like you said."

378

"A thousand pounds! Damn, JT, ya rasclat. What you doin' leavin' that pickney wid a thousand pounds?" Vic was leant against the door jamb, shaking his head like a madman, staring down at the wad of cash on the floor.

The little girl looked up at Vic suspiciously. I smiled up at him then looked back at Truth.

"Truth, I'd like you to say hello to my cousin. This is Victor." Vic's top lip curled when he heard me call him by his Sunday name. Vexed, he scowled back at me and angrily tapped at the door jamb with his fingernails.

"Hello, Victor," Truth said softly.

Vic flinched at the sound of his own Christian name being repeated again, then, under his breath, grumbled back a petulant greeting to the child. I bit my bottom lip and tried not to laugh. My head throbbed and my body ached as I crouched on my haunches next to Truth. Even feeling at my worst, Vic had still managed to lift my mood with his familiar grouchiness and avarice.

I groaned in pain as I gathered up Truth and the holdall into my arms. As we left the lean-to and walked down the passageway and out of the mine, I could feel Vic close at my side, like some terrier protecting a bone. He muscled in next to me, his broad shoulders pulled back, his stride confident and strong. He put his arm around my shoulder as we headed back to the van. He never took his beady eyes off the money in Truth's hand for a single moment.

I got into the back of the van with Truth. I laid her down on a pile of old mail sacks and covered her with my jacket. She lay with her head on my lap and shut her eyes. I whispered for her to try and get some rest while we were on the move. Within ten minutes of leaving the mine, she was fast asleep.

Vic drove carefully but quickly. He chose as many quiet back roads as possible to get us safely back to Bristol. It may have taken us a while longer, but it meant, just as my cousin had assured me earlier, that we remained out of the sight and away from any unwanted police attention. I felt like I had been dragged through a hedge backwards. My body and clothes stank of sweat and dried blood. Every muscle ached and my head felt as if it was being held between the plates of a farrier's vice. My eyes stung with fatigue and became heavy. I fought to keep myself awake, but the rocking motion of the van as it travelled around the twisting bends and turns of the country roads meant that I quickly relinquished my grip on the conscious world and was very soon welcomed into the land of Morpheus.

Vic had pulled over in a lay-by just as we were approaching Bristol. The sound of my cousin pulling on the handbrake of the van immediately woke me. I rubbed at my face in an attempt to knock some feeling of life back into me. I looked down at Truth, who was still fast asleep. I rooted around at my side for another mail sack. I eventually found one, folded it in four and carefully put it underneath the little girl's head. I climbed over into the cab and sank down in the passenger seat next to Vic. He looked at me and jabbed towards the back of the van a couple of times with his thumb.

"That pickney, she still pawing that damn money?"

"Yep, she sure is."

"Shit! She gotta tighter grip on a wad o' cash than Loretta Harris does."

I snapped my head back towards Vic when I heard him mention our friend's name. "How's she doin'?"

"Better than she was. I rang the hospital to check on her befo' I came lookin' fo' you. I've got Redman Innes hangin' 'bout outside o' the ward in case she need anyting. I'll go and see her later, send yo' regards. She gonna kick five bags o' shit outta you when she gits out, you know that?"

I nodded at Vic. "Oh yeah, don't I know it."

Vic laughed then turned the key in the ignition, pulled the van back out onto the road and put his foot down. It was just before one in the afternoon by the time we drove into St Pauls. Still sitting low down in the passenger seat, I'd closed my eyes again and let the rays of the sun filter through the windscreen and warm my face. I didn't open my eyes until I felt the van stop about twenty minutes later. Vic jammed on the handbrake and turned off the ignition of the Commer van then sat back in his seat while the old banger juddered for a moment. I raised myself up in my seat and looked out of the passenger window.

"What we doing on York Road?"

Vic smiled at me and pointed out of the window up at the house he'd parked outside. "These are yo' new digs till the heat's off."

"New digs?"

I stared out at a two-storey run-down tenement building and couldn't believe what I was seeing. I glared at Vic. "You gotta be kiddin' me, right?"

Vic shrugged his shoulders at me. "Kiddin' 'bout what?"

I turned back to face the house and watched in disbelief as a scantily clad young white woman, no more than nineteen or twenty years old, stood leaning against the door jamb kissing the cheek of a middle-aged white guy. I slowly shook my head from side to side, tutting to myself in disgust, then turned and looked disbelievingly at my cousin.

"It's a whorehouse."

Vic grinned at me. "Yeah, I know. It's my ho'house."

I closed my eyes, feeling despair wash over me. "I don't believe this . . ."

"Believe what? Don't tell me you gotta problem wid ho'houses now?"

"Damn right I gotta problem with 'em. I ain't stopping in no bordello with the child."

Truth had woken; she grabbed hold of the backs of our seats, pulled herself up off the floor and stuck her head in between Vic and me. "What's a ho'house, Joseph?"

"Never you mind what it is. All you need to know is we ain't stopping in one! Sit back down."

Truth mumbled under her breath and dropped back onto the floor of the van. I scowled back at Vic.

"What you gittin' so sniffy 'bout? It's a bed fo' the night, ain't it?"

382

"Bed fo' the night . . . You just don't get it, do you? I ain't takin' Truth into one of your knockin' shops!"

"Why the hell not? Do the pickney good to see a different side o' life."

I looked back at Truth then gave Vic a hard stare. "I think the child's seen enough degradation and immorality these past few days. She don't need to see any more, spendin' a night in one of your nasty creep joints."

"Nasty! Our grandaddy was born in a ho'house. Shit, he practically lived in one all his life . . . The muthafucka died in one, that's fo' sure." Vic leant forward and stuck his finger in my face. "JT, ho'houses is in the Ellington blood."

I grabbed hold of the dashboard and shifted in my chair. "They ain't in my blood." I sighed heavily, at my wits' end. I frantically rubbed at the top of my scalp then looked back out of the van window and up the sandstone steps at my cousin's dilapidated shack of ill repute. I stared back at Vic. "How long you had this place?"

"None o' yo' goddamn bidness how long I had the place. You wanna stop in the muthafucka or not?"

I looked back up the steps of the house and then down at Truth, and realised that I had little choice. Both the police and Paxton would know where I lived and have somebody watching the place. I breathed another heavy sigh then resigned myself to the inevitable.

"OK, but you keep those women away from me and the child. You hear me?"

Vic began to laugh. I held out my hand in front of him and he clammed up.

"And one other ting."

Vic huffed at me loudly then shook his head. "What the hell now?"

"I want you to send out one of your friends in there over to my place on Gwyn Street. Get 'em to knock for old Mrs Pearce. Tell her that I need her here."

"What! Why you want dat hard-mout' cow?"

"Just do as I damn say, Vic! Either you get me Mrs Pearce, or the child and I are sleeping on the streets. Believe me, we slept in worse places these last few days."

Vic hit the steering wheel with the palm of his hand and got out of the van, slamming the door behind him. He stood in the street, swearing and stamping his feet on the tarmac before turning around and pushing his nose against the glass of the driver's door window. He pointed down with his finger to where Truth was sat in the back of the van.

"Ax that damn pickney what she intend to do with that thousand notes! Ain't right a child walkin' 'bout with all those readies on her!"

I watched as Vic ranted to himself. He walked around the front of the van and headed towards the front door of the house, cussing obscenities at me. I sat back in my seat and listened with hidden delight as Truth giggled at Vic's blustering rage from behind the passenger seat.

CHAPTER
THIRTY-SEVEN

We were greeted at the front door by the same cheapjack harlot that had been plying her trade on the doorstep when we pulled up outside of the house. Vic brazenly waltzed into the hallway with Truth and me in tow, took us through into the kitchen at the back of the property and plonked down a couple of decrepit deckchairs on either side of a large wooden dining table. I watched as Vic walked back out into the hall, took hold of the girl's elbow and drew her close to him. He began to whisper into her ear then the two of them shot off upstairs to no doubt try and scrub up one of the fleapit rooms for the two of us to stay in. The place was a mess. The walls were lined with ageing chipwood paper, which had greyed and was hanging away from the plaster architrave and the battered skirting. It looked like there wasn't a single carpet laid on any of the downstairs floors and I doubted whether the upstairs boards would have fared any better. The house stank of lingering damp, stale reefer smoke and male sweat. Mouse droppings lay scattered across the Formica work surfaces and on the kitchen floor, and the waste bin next to me was piled high with foul-smelling rubbish. I'd been in cleaner prison cells.

Truth looked around the threadbare, filthy scullery and turned her nose up when she saw the heap of dirty dishes piled up high in the sink and on the draining board.

Truth stood up, leant across the kitchen table and whispered. "Do we have to stay here, Joseph?"

I nodded my head. "We ain't got a lot o' choice, little one."

Truth sank back down on to her chair and stared up blankly at the ceiling. "I'd like to see where you live."

"Me too . . . But we're in a jam at the minute. This place is gonna have to do."

Truth huffed to herself and continued to gaze up into the air.

I heard Vic clambering back down the stairs. He stuck his head round the kitchen door and looked at Truth. "What da hell she starin' at?"

I got to my feet and pointed my finger at the ropy-looking kitchen ceiling. "The child's mesmerised, Vic. She ain't ever seen such a palace."

Vic raised an eyebrow, affronted by my comment. "Damn pickney's an orphan. What kinda joint she bin stoppin' in, to be so choosey?"

"The orphanage was always clean," Truth snapped.

"Less wid her backchat," Vic snarled back. He glared at me then disappeared. I heard him stomping back up the stairs, chuntering to himself. Moments later he shouted down to me, "You wanna come see dis room or not?"

Truth ran out in front of me and bolted up the stairs. As I reached the top step I heard her complaining. "It smells in here, Victor."

I stood on the landing and watched as Vic stuck his head into the bedroom and sniffed the air. "Yeah, the place is kinda frowsy, ain't it?" Vic stood back from the door and let me into the tiny box room. "JT open a damn window for dat pickney. She makin' my ass itch wid all her bullshit!"

It was just after four thirty in the afternoon by the time the immersion heater had warmed up enough water for Truth to take a bath. I made Vic scrub out the tub and sink before either of us stepped foot into the place. Once it was reasonably clean, I ran the hot and cold taps and let the bath fill.

While Truth bathed, I sat on the end of the bed and wrote a note for my elderly neighbour, Mrs Pearce. In it I explained where I was staying and asked if she could kindly collect a spare change of clothes for me and then come over to the house on York Road as soon as she could. Earlier in the year I'd given her a spare key in the event that I ever lost my own. Mrs Pearce liked being a keyholder to my place. During the daytime, while I worked over at the gym, she'd often let herself in and clean around then leave me one of her special home-cooked meals. While she tidied she also snooped through my drawers and personal belongings. She was nosey by nature, judgemental and had a fiery temper. But she was also kind-hearted and generous and someone I genuinely thought of as a friend.

Vic sent one of the girls out to deliver the note and then pick up a fish and chip supper for the three of us. He also made it known that the place was out of bounds to any punters until me and Truth had vacated the building. Thinking about my cousin's sneaky, unscrupulous and illegal involvement in running the cathouse made me feel sick to the pit of my stomach. Vic was kin and I loved him, but sometimes I hated the way he chose to live his life and the unorthodox, illicit ways in which he made his living.

While Truth ate her fish and chips downstairs in the kitchen with Vic, I took a bath. I lay in the steaming hot water for over half an hour, letting my tired muscles and limbs benefit from a long soaking. When I finally hauled myself out and pulled the plug out of the tub I was shocked at the filthy colour of the water, a murky mixture of dirt and blood. It felt good to see it swirl away down the plughole. My skin felt clean, purified of the muck and squalor that had clung to me these past days. It was a shame that I didn't feel as wholesome inside.

I leant against the sink and wiped the condensation from the bathroom mirror with the palm of my hand. My face didn't look too pretty. The swelling around my right cheek where Jardine had laid into me had come up a treat. I felt at the cut at the back of my head from where I'd been hit by the butt of the gun. It didn't feel as bad as I'd first expected. There was a sizable lump, but it was no longer bleeding and a scab had started to form over the wound. I dried myself, wrapped the towel around my waist, walked out onto the landing and came face to face with Mrs Pearce standing at the top of the stairs.

"Dear God, man, just look at the state of you!"

I stared down at the floorboards like a scolded child as the old woman walked along the landing, stood in front of me and stuck her tiny head underneath my chin to get a better a look at my face.

"So, that's why you asked for the iodine, is it? What have you been doing, fighting?"

I nodded and kept my lips buttoned.

"Do you know you have the police looking for you again, Mr Ellington? What in the name of sanity have you got yourself mixed up in this time?"

"A spot o' bother, that's fo' sure."

"Bother, you say. Pull the other one, it's got bells on it. You're up to your silly black neck again, aren't you? That crooked cousin of yours downstairs no doubt has something to do with it all, yes?"

I shook my head. "No, not this time, he hasn't."

"Well, that makes a change. So, are you going to stand there in the altogether or are you going to change into these clothes of yours that I've brought for you?" Mrs Pearce lifted up a large beige leather shopping bag and pushed it at my chest. I took the bag and thanked her then walked back into the bedroom. The old woman walked in behind me and looked around the box room in disgust.

"Just look at the state of this place. Tell me that you're not thinking of sleeping in that bed. That mattress is alive with God knows what. It looks like it could crawl out of here on its own."

I turned around to face my neighbour. "We haven't got a lot of choice, Mrs Pearce."

"We? What do mean we? Are you talking about that no-good relation of yours?"

I shook my head. "No, this is not 'bout Vic. I have a child here with me."

"A child . . . Here with you, in this awful place?"

I nervously shuffled from one foot to the other and nodded.

"But this is a house of ill repute, Mr Ellington."

I looked at the old woman in shock "How did you know what this place was?"

Mrs Pearce put both hands on her hips and glared at me. "I might look green, but I'm not a bloody cabbage, man. This dive has been a disorderly house for more years than I care to remember. You ought to be ashamed of yourself, bringing a child here."

"I don't have a lot of choice. If I'd have gone back to my digs on Gwyn Street, the police would have lifted the two of us within a couple of hours."

"What are doing with a child anyway?"

"She's an orphan. A little girl. I found her here in Bristol and she's somehow connected to a heap o' trouble that I'm stuck bang in the middle of now."

Mrs Pearce rested her arms back down by her side. When she spoke again, the tone of her voice was softer. "Tell me, what kind of trouble are you in, Mr Ellington?"

I stared back down at the ground and laughed to myself then looked back up at Mrs Pearce. "The kind where folk start off tellin' me lies then keep on lyin' and

I'm plain stupid enough to keep on believin' 'em . . . I need to find out why I've been lied to, Mrs P, then make tings right."

Mrs Pearce sighed deeply and smiled at me. "And what do you want me to do for you, apart from fetching you a fresh change of underwear and your razor?"

"I need you to take care of Truth while I find out what all this madness is 'bout."

Mrs Pearce looked at me disbelievingly. "Truth . . . What kind of name is Truth for a young child?"

"Dat's just what I was tinkin', woman. Trute! Crazy, dottish ting to call a pickney, ain't it."

Mrs Pearce almost jumped out of her skin when she heard Vic bellowing behind her. She turned on her heels to viciously chastise my loud-mouthed cousin but suddenly fell silent when she saw Truth quietly standing at his side, smiling at her.

I let Mrs Pearce treat the cut on my head with iodine then picked up the leather shopping bag and left Truth and my neighbour to get acquainted while I went back into the bathroom and shaved. When I'd finished, I changed into a pair of fresh grey flannel trousers and a blue cotton short-sleeved shirt, splashed on a little aftershave and gave my shoes a polish with the end of the towel. I put on my grey herringbone tweed jacket then snuck past the bedroom door, leaving the ladies to talk, and went downstairs to find Vic.

He was sat on the settee in the front room, with his feet resting up on the corner of a battered wooden coffee table. He was smoking a huge joint, listening to Stevie Wonder's "Uptight" on the radio, his fingers busily drumming away to the beat on the arm of the sofa. A bottle of Mount Gay rum was perched on the edge of the table along with two tumblers.

Vic looked up and me and grinned. "Well, you is lookin' sharper. Take a pew, cuz." He pulled himself up from the sofa, reached over for the bottle of rum, unscrewed the cap and poured three fingers of the pale gold liquid into each glass.

I sat down in an armchair next to him and he reached over and handed me one of the glasses. We chinked our glasses together and I took a long swig of the warm spirit. Vic knocked his hooch straight back, refilled his tumbler then stuck the mouth of the bottle over the edge of my glass and sloshed in another two fingers. I took another draught of my rum and watched as my cousin leisurely sank back into his seat. Vic eyed me up knowingly. "What you want, cuz?"

I relaxed back in the armchair and sipped slowly at my liquor before answering him.

"I need you to break the law for me."

Vic breathed in deeply then sank down the rest of his booze and sat staring at me, thinking about what I'd just said. He neither moved an inch nor uttered a solitary word.

I nervously shifted in my chair. "You got a problem with that?"

Finally he spoke. "When you evah know me worry 'bout anyting?" Vic winked at me mischievously then reached for the rum bottle, filled his tumbler to the brim and took a swig. The cold look in his eyes as he drank sent a shiver down my spine.

CHAPTER
THIRTY-EIGHT

I found Mrs Pearce standing in the hall making a telephone call from the wall-mounted payphone near the front door. I waited in the kitchen until she had finished talking and walked out to meet her just as she was about to climb the stairs and return to Truth. My neighbour pinched her face into a brief smile then quickly looked up towards the top of the stairs. She tapped anxiously with her fingers at the the banister, her nails clicking against the chipped magnolia paintwork, then turned to face me. When she spoke, it was in a grave tone that instantly reminded me of my old school governess back home on Barbados.

"She is a sweet child, Mr Ellington."

I nodded in agreement. "Yes . . . yes, she is."

"And she's clearly been through a great deal."

"Damn . . . You can say that again."

The old woman looked stony-faced at me. "I don't need to hear you curse, or to repeat myself, Mr Ellington.

I felt my cheeks heat with embarrassment and had to clear the frog from my throat before speaking again. "No, you're right, I'm sorry."

My venerable neighbour suddenly lost her dour look and the intonation in her voice became less stern. "Right, I'm going to do what you've asked of me. I'll look after the child until you have sorted out all this madness, as you call it." Mrs Pearce quickly raised her hand in front of my face, halting the words I was about to speak firmly in their tracks. "But I'll not care for her here, not in this hovel. I'll be taking the girl to my sister's in Portishead." Mrs Pearce turned away from me and began to climb the stairs. "And we'll hear no more of it . . . I'll write down the address we'll be staying at and you can come and get her when this is all over."

I remained silent and watched as the old woman quietly disappeared along the landing. No words of thanks could have truly expressed my gratitude to her, and as I stood motionless alone at the bottom of the stairs I realised how blessed I was to have such a loyal champion and thought myself truly undeserving of her friendship.

Truth had fallen asleep when I returned back up to the bedroom. It was just after eight thirty in the evening. Mrs Pearce had left to collect an overnight bag for herself, and Vic was downstairs on the telephone arranging for his friend Redman Innes to drive my neighbour and Truth the short twenty-mile journey over to Portishead, on the Somerset coast. I collected the holdall containing the little girl's remaining clothing and took it downstairs, letting the child sleep a little longer.

394

Vic put the receiver of the phone back into its cradle and leant his shoulder against the wall. "Redman be here fo' the old goat an' dat damn pickney at nine. I'm gonna git dat kit we're gonna need from one o' my lock-ups then go git us some wheels. OK?"

"OK." I watched as Vic walked back to the kitchen and picked up his leather jacket from off one of the deckchairs and put it on, then pick up a huge bunch of keys from the draining board. He walked back past me and slapped my arm hard. "What you lookin' so damn miserable fo'? You 'bout ta git rid o' two heaps o' trouble, bossman. Good riddance to 'em!" Vic chortled to himself and walked down the hall, slamming the front door behind him.

I turned and began to climb the stairs to go and break the news to Truth that she would be leaving shortly and that I would not be joining her on the next part of her journey.

I walked quietly back into the bedroom, sat down on the side of the bed next to Truth and gently ran my hands along the side of her face and hair to wake her. She grumbled and rolled over onto her back then slowly opened her eyes and looked up at me. Her face was filled with sleep and puzzlement. I smiled down at her. She looked up at me and could clearly see that I was ill at ease.

"What's the matter, Joseph?"

"We need to talk, little one."

The girl suddenly came to life and drew herself up off the bed on her elbows. Truth looked at me nervously. "Talk about what?"

"I've asked my neighbour, Mrs Pearce, to keep an eye on you for a little while."

Truth looked confused. "Why does she have to look after me? Why can't you?"

I shuffled uneasily on the edge of the bed. "Because I need to settle this bidness with the orphanage and find out why those men have been causin' so much trouble for the two of us."

Truth sat bolt upright. Her face became sullen and the corners of her mouth suddenly turned down and began to tremble. "I don't want to go with her." I could see her fighting off the tears that were welling at the edges of her eyes.

"This ain't no time to be kickin' up a fuss, child. You gotta do as I say. Where I'm goin' and what I'm gonna be doin' ain't no place for a child to be. Mrs Pearce is a good woman, Truth. You're gonna be safe with her an' I ain't gonna have to worry 'bout you while you're with her. You understand?"

I watched as a single tear ran down Truth's left cheek. I caught it with the tips of my fingers and brushed it from her face. Truth put her arms around my waist and clasped hold of me for all she was worth. I rested my chin against the top of her head and spoke softly through her blonde hair. "And she's gonna be takin' you to stay by the sea too."

Truth drew herself away and looked up at me. "And you'll come and get me as soon as you're done?"

I gave a firm nod. "Soon as I'm done."

Truth sank back towards me and latched her tiny arms around my back. I squeezed her tightly against my chest and prayed that the little girl would not feel the sad and fearful beating of my heart.

CHAPTER
THIRTY-NINE

I'd got the impression from my two fairly brief meetings with Ida Stephens that she thought of herself as a cautious and keen-eyed woman. She'd given me the impression of being a creature of habit, the sort of person who took great delight in strict routines. I felt sure she would be at her happiest living with set patterns, doing the same thing during a certain time period of the day, night and week. Her journey to work at the Walter Wilkins orphanage was one she undertook each day, whether on foot or by car, bus or bicycle, but her pilgrimage today was going to be a very different one from what the administrator was accustomed to.

Vic and I were sat in the cab of the postal delivery van parked up in a side street directly overlooking the gates of the orphanage on Cotham Road. We'd been waiting for Stephens to arrive at her workplace since just before dawn broke. I looked at my wristwatch. It was just after eight. Vic rested his elbows against the steering wheel of the van while he played about with a battery-operated cassette recorder. I nodded down at the contraption sat in his hands.

"You sure you know how to use that ting?"

Vic gawped at me and angrily sucked air through the gap in his two front teeth. "Do me look like a goat head? Course I know how to use the damn ting!"

I looked at the tape recorder in Vic's hands then back up at my cousin. "Just make sure that you record every word that woman utters when we get her inside here. Got it?"

Vic grumbled a churlish reply and laid the recorder in the footwell of the van by his feet then stared out of the window into the street and tutted to himself. "When dis ole hag gonna turn up fo' wuck?"

He looked up and down the street impatiently then stuck his hand into the left pocket of his jacket and brought out a pair of leather gloves. He pulled the gloves over his huge hands, slipped his fingers between each other to push the soft kid fabric further down towards his knuckles and then glowered indignantly at me.

"Git dem mitts o' yours on!"

I reached down next to the handbrake and picked up a pair of identical leather gloves along with two lengths of rope that Vic had already prepared into loops with slipknots. I yanked the gloves over my hands, put the ropes into my jacket pocket then looked at the face of my watch. It was just after ten past eight.

For the next twenty minutes, Vic and me sat in silence. The time passed slowly. Outside the sun began to rise high up in the blue, cloudless sky, and despite it being still quite early in the morning, I could feel the day was beginning to heat up. There appeared to be little traffic about and few pedestrians walking past. I looked out of the passenger window and saw a red and white Bristol Omnibus Company coach turning out of St Michael's Hill and then pull up at a stop about twenty yards away from where we were parked.

I peered out of the window nervously and watched as the doors opened. Ida Stephens got out, alone, and began to stride along the pavement towards the orphanage. I let the bus drive off a short way along Cotham Road and slapped Vic on his arm.

"OK, we're on."

"'Bout damn time too!" Vic turned the key in the ignition and gently licked the accelerator with his toe. The engine revved itself into life as I clambered into the back of the van and knelt down by the back doors. I turned to look back out of the windscreen just as Vic stepped on the gas and pulled the van sharply out into the street. He sped across the road and up on to the pavement, boxing Ida Stephens between a low brick wall and the van's wing and bonnet. I kicked open both doors, jumped out into the road and ran around the side of the vehicle. Stephens froze when she saw me rushing towards her then panicked. She dropped her handbag and quickly turned to try and crawl across the bonnet of the van. I lunged forward, grabbing her by the back of both shoulders, pulling her backwards. As she was about to swing around and throw a punch at me, the passenger door flew open and Vic's huge hand and arm reached out and snatched her by her hair, dragging her towards him. She screamed and threw her arms out either side of the door to try and stop herself being hauled inside. I bulldozed straight

400

into her back with the side of my shoulder, and Vic pulled her further into the cab. He savagely gripped at the back of her neck, yanking her head and face down onto the seat beside him, then jammed a rag into her mouth.

I grabbed hold of her flailing legs, pushed them with my thigh against the side of the door and quickly looped one of the ropes around her feet.

I tugged on the cord, drawing it tightly around her ankles, then grabbed at her thrashing arms and pinned them behind her, fastening the second cord around her wrists. Vic grasped hold of the back of her jacket and manhandled her inside. I slammed the passenger door shut, snatched up Ida's handbag from off the pavement, ran to the back of the van and dived inside. I got to my knees and reached for the handles of the back doors and heaved them together just as Vic reversed, swung the van back into the road and drove off.

Vic quickly navigated the postal van along various back streets, buffeting me backwards and forwards until suddenly coming to a halt. I reached over the passenger seat and took hold of Ida Stephens underneath her arms and heaved her into the back of the van. She dropped onto the floor at my feet like a lead weight and started to lash out at me with her bound legs. I stepped back and let her thrash about a bit to let her wear herself out then reached down and grabbed hold of the back of her collar and slung her against the side of the van, tearing the fabric of her jacket as I did. I snatched up one of the hessian postal sacks by my feet and threw it over the top of her head, pulling it down across her shoulders and back while Stephens continued to struggle and mumble behind the gag in her mouth.

I climbed back into the passenger seat, drenched in sweat, beads of perspiration pouring down my brow. I wiped at my face and head with the sleeve of my jacket and sank back against the leather-upholstered seat, breathless and tired. Vic grinned at me and looked over his shoulder at Ida Stephens. He watched in amusement as she continued to frenziedly throw herself about in the back of the van.

"Woman's got spirit fo' sure. All dat crazy flounderin' 'bout make her look like an alligator caught in a trip snare." He sniggered to himself then pulled the postal van out into the street and tore off down the road.

We drove north, down into the Hotwells district of Bristol, travelling close to the banks of the River Avon and the busy docks. Vic kept his speed down, confidently guiding the van along narrow roads lined with rows of run-down tenement houses. He pulled up at a junction, took a sharp left turn and swung into an avenue that ran down towards the wharf at Cumberland Basin. At the end of the avenue, opposite a timber yard and set well back from the road, was a large red-bricked garage. Two separate steel shutter doors stood either side of a dividing wall that had a large, fading Esso sign painted on it.

Vic reversed the van across the forecourt up to one of the doors then got out. I watched in the wing mirror as he quickly unlocked and raised the shutter then yelled at me to get behind the wheel. I climbed into the driver's seat and backed the van inside. Vic dropped the roller door down onto the concrete floor then flicked at a bank of switches on the wall. I turned off the ignition and got out of the van just as the fluorescent light strips hanging above me began to spark into life.

Next to the van stood a pristine-looking saloon car, its polished two-tone baby-blue and grey paintwork gleaming under the lights. I looked around in amazement. The place was a treasure trove of stolen goods and black-market gear stacked from floor to ceiling. Hundreds of crates of booze and cigarettes stood side by side next to cardboard boxes filled with perfume, nylons and ladies' silk lingerie. On the back wall next to a long wooden workbench stood two olive-green ex-army steel gun cabinets, both chained and padlocked.

Vic walked around the van and opened up the back doors then took a Bakelite mechanic's inspection lamp from the top of the bench behind him and plugged it into a socket in the wall at his feet. He pulled the long cable across the garage floor and climbed into the back of the van then hung the lamp head by its cage from a hook directly above Ida Stephens' head. Vic then leaned over the driver's seat, reached down into the footwell of the cab and retrieved the cassette recorder he'd been messing around with earlier.

Vic switched on the lamp, filling the interior of the van with a brilliant white light, and I climbed inside to join him. I stood close to Ida Stephens and held on to the top of the hessian sack for a moment. I watched as her body jumped in fright as she sensed the close proximity of my body to her own. I waited for a moment before snatching the sack off. The bright, dazzling light above her made Ida turn her head immediately to the side, her eyes squinting and watering under the intense beam. Vic crouched down and grabbed at Ida's jaw, pulling her head back underneath the stark glare of the lamp. She tried to look away, wrestling her head back and forth feebly against Vic's strong grip.

He drew himself closer towards her face and spoke in a deep, thick Bajan accent. "It don't mek no difference ta me if ya wanna look at me or not, woman." He squeezed the tip of her chin tightly between a couple of his fingers and thumb then pushed his face even closer towards her own. "Ya headed fo' da dead house anyways." Vic reached into his jacket and pulled out a thin-bladed bush machete. "Ya like me Collins?" He lifted the huge knife up in front of Ida Stephens' face and ran his gloved thumb down its length. Ida pushed her feet against the metal floor of the van, her heels sliding along the ridges as she unsuccessfully tried to push herself away from Vic and the hefty blade.

I bent down and spoke quietly against Stephens' ear. "Just so you know, a Collins is the name we Barbadians give to any big knife." I smiled at the already petrified administrator then reached across and pulled the old rag from out of her mouth. I watched as Vic pressed the red record button on the cassette machine.

Vic stared up at me. "You got questions?"

404

"Yeah, I do. An' I'm expectin' some straight answers outta Mrs Stephens too." I knelt down next to Vic and stared at Ida.

Vic squeezed Ida's jaw a little tighter and she yelped in pain. "Then git ta askin' the woman what you wanna know befo' I mush her face to a pulp."

I leant my hand against the wall next to Ida's face. "Let's start with Dr Theo Fowler."

"What about him?" snapped Stephens.

"How long had he been workin' for you at the orphanage?"

"Three, four years . . . He was our house GP."

"It was Fowler's name signing off on those children's death certificates I got back from him, wasn't it?"

"Yes, you know it was!"

"And he falsified those certificates for you, didn't he?

Ida dropped her head and looked down at the floor of the van. "Yes."

"Only those kids weren't dead, were they, Ida?"

Stephens nodded without lifting her eyes.

"Speak up, Ida, that microphone needs to hear every word that comes outta your mout'."

"Yes, they were all alive." Ida bit at her bottom lip in a desperate attempt to stop herself giving away any more incriminating evidence. Vic stuck his hand underneath Ida's chin, squeezed at her throat and lifted her head up towards my face.

"What happened to those children?"

Ida baulked at answering the question. Vic squeezed a little tighter and her face became scarlet, her neck stretching upwards.

"They . . . they were sold."

"Sold? Who to?" I barked.

"To Jack Paxton."

"You're talkin' 'bout the American who shot Doc Fowler? The one that's been on my tail all this time, yeah?"

"Yes. He's a military policeman."

"What's a Yankee lawman doing buying orphan kids from a place like the Walter Wilkins?"

Vic locked his other hand at the back of Ida's neck and smashed the back of her head against the van wall.

"He's selling them on in the US."

"Selling them on? What the hell you talking 'bout?" I nodded to Vic to apply a little more pressure. Vic kindly obliged and began to steadily knead at Ida's throat with his huge fingers. Stephens' face became redder as she choked out her reply to my question.

"He's running a business. He pays the orphanage money for each child he takes off us. He's trading the children back in the States."

"Trading, who with?"

"I don't know . . . Couples, I think."

"Couples? What do you mean?"

Vic shook Ida's head like a rag doll in his hand.

"Couples . . . Men and women who can't conceive a child of their own."

"Jesus . . ." I rubbed at my chin, not believing quite what the woman was telling me. "How'd Paxton get involved with the orphanage?"

"Through my boss, Edward Matherson. Matherson has a fuel business that supplies the airbase Paxton is stationed at. They met there a few years ago."

"Which airbase?"

"I'm not sure . . . Somewhere in Gloucestershire, RAF Fairford, I think."

"Who else at Wilkins is involved in all of this?"

"There's another of my colleagues, a social worker called Andrew Balfour, and a few police officers from Bridewell station in the city."

"Bridewell . . . What are the police officers' names?"

"I don't know!"

Vic suddenly released Ida's neck and replaced his hand with the edge of the machete blade. He slid the knife slowly along her skin from the tip of her right earlobe down to her left breast. Ida began to sob. Spittle rose at each corner of her mouth and sweat poured from her brow, the perspiration falling down her face and neck, soaking into her silk blouse. I watched as her secretive, repellent world began to slowly unravel in front of her. Vic returned the blade to Stephens' throat, bringing Ida back to my question.

"There . . . There's one policeman whose name's Martin, David Martin, and another called Beaumont."

"Beaumont's dead."

Stephens swallowed hard when she heard me say the word "dead".

I leant closer in towards her sweating face. "How's all this work?"

"I don't understand . . . What do you mean?"

"I mean, does Paxton come and collect the children from the orphanage or are they delivered to him?"

"It all depends. If he's coming for just one of the orphans he'll come to the home on his own. If we have to deliver more than one child, we take them to Burwalls for him to collect."

"Burwalls? What's Burwalls?"

"It's a house out by Leigh Woods. We exchange the children for the money there."

Vic forced the blade of the machete up against Ida Stephens' jugular. "Tell de man why dis Paxton bozo is wantin' de trute so badly."

Ida Stephens' face went ashen. Vic let the edge of the razor-sharp blade nick at her woman's skin; a trickle of blood ran down the length of the machete and began to drip down onto her chest.

"Truth . . . She belongs to him."

"Say what?"

Ida began to sob uncontrollably. "Paxton bought and paid for her, weeks ago. When Fowler found out that Paxton was going to keep her for himself, he took off with the child. He disappeared with the girl overnight and the two of them went to ground. Paxton and the police searched, but they couldn't find them. That's when I came to you for help in tracking him down."

I shook my head, sickened by what I was hearing. "Well, wasn't I the lucky one?"

"Listen to me! You don't understand. When Paxton found out Truth was gone and it was Fowler that had taken her, he went berserk, he started threatening all kinds of things. Matherson and Balfour panicked. They came up with your name after Beaumont gave it to them. It was the police at Bridewell station that gave us your name."

"Did they now? That don't come as any surprise, Ida. Me and the boys in blue at Bridewell, we don't see eye to eye."

Vic moved the blade up and down Ida's neck.

I pushed her to keep talking. "When did you last hear from Paxton?"

"Last night. He told me that you'd been causing him a lot of trouble. He said that if you got in touch, I should call him straight away. He told me to tell you that if you called that he was prepared to pay you for the girl's safe return to him."

I laughed. "Safe return? You gotta be kiddin' me. I give up Truth to Paxton fo' a pocketful o' cash, that's what he expects me to do?"

Ida nodded her head, the tears streaming down her face. "Paxton doesn't care about how much it costs. He just wants the child. I saw the way he used to look at Truth when he came to the home. He offered Matherson thousands of pounds for her, month in month out. Matherson always refused his offers."

"Why'd he refuse?"

"Because it's harder to hide the death of an older child than it is a toddler. Most of the orphans that have been sold to Paxton have either been babies or very young children: six, seven years of age at most. Matherson only caved in and sold Truth when the price on the table became so great that he couldn't resist."

"How much did he pay this Matherson?"

"I . . . I don't know."

Vic made another paper-thin nick underneath Ida's neck with the machete blade.

"How much?" I screamed.

Ida bellowed back at me, spraying snot and tears at my face. "It was six thousand! He paid Matherson six thousand pounds for her."

I fell back against the wall of the van. My stomach began to churn over and I felt like I wanted to be sick. I cupped my hand over my mouth as I started to retch. I cleared my throat and spat a wad of saliva out of the van door. Vic slowly lifted the edge of the machete from Ida Stephens' neck and rested the blade on his shoulder then looked at me, his eyes filled with disgust and bewilderment.

Ida slumped down onto the metal floor and looked up at me. "Paxton's a monster, Mr Ellington. A real monster."

I glared back at Stephens, unable to contain my disdain. "And even though you knew what kinda animal the man was, you still went ahead and allowed those bastards you work for to sell Truth to him."

Ida turned her head away from me and screamed through another wall of tears.

I got up and stood over her. "How do I get in contact with this . . . monster?"

Ida Stephens lifted her head and stared up at me. "I have his telephone number . . . It's in an address book, in my handbag."

Vic got up off his haunches, reached cross into the cab of the van and retrieved the bag then tossed it over to me. I rifled through the contents until I found a small blue pocket address book. I dropped the handbag at my feet and leafed through the pages.

I heard Ida Stephens whisper to me. "You'll find the number listed under the letter H. Paxton's number's next to the entry that's called 'Holiday Fund'."

I turned to the page headed with a capital H and scrolled down the handwritten names and numbers until I found the words "Holiday Fund". Next to it was the number GLO 4567. I couldn't bring myself to quiz Ida any further. Why had she chosen to name Paxton's number with such a strange coding? It all seemed like madness.

I kept reading the two code words and the number over and over in my head until they became indelibly lodged into my brain. I felt hot and dizzy, my mouth dry, my stomach knotting and griping as a wave of nausea came over me. I climbed out of the van, retching and coughing. I stumbled over to the workbench and felt my head become lighter as my knees start to give way. I rested my arm against the edge of bench, bent my head towards the ground and vomited. I stood, puking my guts up, unable to catch my breath, until there was nothing left inside me to expel. I fell onto the garage floor clutching onto Ida Stephens' little blue address book. I stared blankly at the plain, unassuming card cover and shook my head, unable to comprehend the horror inside. It had sickened me to my very core.

CHAPTER
FORTY

I sat at an old teak desk in a small office at the back of
the garage and watched out of the window as Vic wiped
down every inch of the interior of the postal van with a
chamois leather and polishing rag. My guts ached and
my throat burnt after being sick earlier; my body felt
tense and weak, like every ounce of strength had been
wrenched out of me after listening to Ida Stephens
come clean. I stared down at the phone and the open
address book in front of me and swallowed hard. I
cleared my throat then picked up the receiver, dialled
the four-digit Gloucestershire number and put the
telephone to my ear. I listened nervously as the dialling
tone rang a half-dozen times or so before being
answered. When the man's voice on the other end of
the line spoke, it was with a lyrical, homespun Yankee
accent.

"MPC Duty Office."

I waited a moment before talking. "I need to speak to
a man, name o' Paxton."

When I mentioned Paxton's name, the man on the
other end of the phone went silent for a moment. When
he finally spoke again his tone was more refined, more
matter of fact. Suspicious.

"Sergeant Paxton isn't on duty at the moment, sir. Can I help?"

"Yeah . . . I need you to get a message to the man, real quick."

"A message . . . Is this a base police matter, sir?"

"Oh, you bet it's a police matter, mister."

Ruffled by my blunt remark, the man on the other end of the line hesitated before replying.

"OK. What's your message, sir?"

"Tell him that Mr Ellington called. Tell him that I'm in possession of the missing cargo he's gone an mislaid an' I wanna get it back to him befo' the end o' the day." I listened as the man on the other end of the line busily scribbled down what I was saying. "Tell Paxton he can reach me on . . ." I looked down at the printed disc in the centre of the telephone and read out the number. "Bristol 6847."

The man repeated the number I'd just given him, thanked me for my call then cut me off without saying another word. I gave a deep sigh, sank back in my chair and waited for the phone to ring.

I was lost in my own thoughts and didn't hear Vic walk into the office. He quietly crept up behind me and spoke, nearly making me jump out of my seat in shock.

"Be a good idea to put this ting under lock an' key?"

I spun round in my seat just as my cousin was lifting the cassette recorder up in his hand. He shook it at me then casually reached across the desk and opened up a drawer next to me. He pulled out a large Manila envelope then ejected the tape from the player, dropped the cassette into the envelope and sealed it. Then he took both the recorder and envelope over to a small, floor-standing Chubb safe behind me and took out a bunch of keys from his hip pocket. I watched as he selected two keys: a long iron key and a smaller brass one. He unclipped both from the ring then knelt down and unlocked the safe. I watched as he moved a sizable wad of bank notes to the back of the safe then placed the envelope and recorder inside. Vic locked the safe, stood up and handed me the two keys.

"One to git you in the place, one to unlock the safe. Gimme 'em back when you finished." Vic sat on the edge of the desk, looked out of the office window and nodded at Ida Stephens sitting in the back of the van. "So, what we gonna do with that crazy bitch now?"

"The police are gonna be havin' a long chat with her. I need to get 'em to put the heat on her and those fellas Matherson and Balfour she was talkin' 'bout."

Vic raised both hands in the air, the palms in front of his disgruntled face. "Forgit it, JT . . . I ain't goin' near no Babylon."

I shook my head. "Don't worry, you ain't gotta go nowhere near the police." I gritted my teeth and pointed out of the window. "That van out there, has it been stolen?"

Vic gave me an insulted scowl. "Not everyting I own has to be pinched, ya know. I picked that ole heap up for fifty quid at an auction in Redland last month."

"It registered to you?"

My cousin smirked. "Not yet."

"Good, cos I want to leave it as close to Bridewell police station as we can."

Vic raised an eyebrow. "Well, yo' can drive the damn ting round to the cop shop. Me, I've got me own wheels. I'll follow ya an' pick ya up when you drop that rustbox and the ole hag off."

Vic rose from the edge of the desk, stuck his hand in his jacket pocket and pulled out a silver Ronson lighter and a Wills Traveller brand tobacco tin. He opened the tin, picked out a hand-rolled cigarette, put it between his lips and lit it. He stood next to the door and took a long pull on the reefer then picked up an old leather and canvas stovepipe golf bag that was resting against the wall. He put the bag under his arm, exhaled a mouthful of pungent marijuana smoke then walked out of the office, leaving me alone with the thin, grey whispers of piquant vapour floating gracefully above my head.

It was just after one in the afternoon when the phone in the office finally rang. I sat back down at the desk, rested my hand on the phone, took a deep breath and let it ring out a couple more times before picking up the receiver and answering. When I spoke, I kept cool and calm.

"Yeah?"

On the other end of the line I could hear the shallow breathing of the caller. When Paxton eventually began to speak to me it was in the same guttural southern drawl that his deceased partner, Jardine, had spoken in.

"How 'bout giving me a name?"

"You talkin' to Ellington."

"Ah, that right . . . the runaway Negro? It's 'bout time too, I was gittin a little sick o' hound-dogging you, boy."

"I didn't much like being treated like I was part of some ram hunt either."

Paxton grunted. "You bin tearing a helluva shitstorm fo' me and my boys. I've gone an' lost myself some good men tryin' to bring your black hide in."

"My heart's bleeding fo' your loss, Mr Paxton."

I could feel Paxton's agitation seeping up the phone line towards me.

"Ain't no need to go speakin' ill o' the dead like that. Show some respect."

"I'm getting a little over the hill for being nice, Paxton. You wanna hear what I gotta say or not?"

"I think you already talked yourself out, boy. I got your message saying you know the whereabouts of some missing cargo I'm in need o' retrieving. All you gotta do is stop blabbering and give it to me."

"And what's in it for me?"

Paxton's breathing became heavier as he considered my question. When he finally answered me, there was a vitriolic timbre in his voice. "You already had all the fuckin' money you gonna git outta me, nigger."

"Then we got nuttin' else to talk 'bout." I went to put the phone back in its cradle then heard the American bark after me.

"How much you want?"

I plucked out a random amount from my head. "Two thousand."

Paxton laughed. "Say what?"

416

"You hard of hearin' or just plain shit stupid?"

"Who the hell you think you talkin' to, boy?"

"I'm talkin' to a man who's got enough cash burning a hole in his pocket to pay me what I just asked him fo'. Now you want your damn cargo. You bring me what I just asked for tonight, I'll be in Leigh Woods opposite Burwalls house, 8p.m."

"How you know 'bout Leigh Woods?"

"Let's just say that your previous supplier had a real big mout'."

Paxton's voice became ill at ease. "You say 'had'?"

"Yeah . . . but you ain't gotta worry 'bout your ole friend Ida comin' after you fo' her cut o' the deal. She's gone an' found herself outta the picture, permanently." I looked out of the office window at my bedraggled hostage sat in the back of Vic's van and smiled to myself. "Bring me the money at eight and I'll bring you your cargo. We keep it nice and simple, you never see my black face again."

I waited while Paxton considered my final words.

"OK, you'll git ya cash. But you can meet me further inside the woods. I don't want to be eyeballed by any ole son of a bitch while I'm doin' business. Bring what you got fo' me to the back o' the Swiss chalet that they got erected up inside that woodland, got it?"

"I got it."

"Good. Just don't you go thinkin' you can git wise an' fuck me over, nigger. You don't wanna be pushin' me any more than you already have done. We do the deal tonight an' we both walk away happy men."

Paxton slammed down the phone, leaving me with the burring tone singing in my ear. I put the receiver down then rested my chin in the palm of my hand, closed my eyes and began to mull over in my head the deceitful utterances of a man who I knew was already preparing to erase me from this mortal earth with the brutal swiftness of Cain.

I found Vic loading the stovepipe golf bag and a large metal toolbox into the trunk of his latest set of wheels. He dropped the boot lid and stood back from the immaculate vehicle and admired it lovingly.

"Well, whaddya tink? Beauty, ain't she?" Vic walked around to the driver's side door and lovingly caressed the paintwork with the palm of his hand. "Nineteen fifty-nine Mark Two Ford Zodiac. Goes like shit t'ru a goose . . . Naught ta sixty in seventeen seconds. Man owed me a few quid. Couldn't pay up, so he signed the log book over ta me." Vic jumped in, started up the motor and pumped the accelerator a couple of times, sending the engine into a noisy frenzy. He bounded back out of the car and smiled at me. "Right, I'll open back up . . . let's git that nasty piece o' work outta my garage."

He pointed to the side of the van then headed for the roller doors. He shouted back at me as he was about to unlock one of them. "That damn woman, she gimme the creeps. She bad t'ru and t'ru, brother. I don't want no part o' her, no more."

I'd never heard my cousin speak with such foreboding in his voice or with so much moral outrage.

418

I walked around to the back of the postal van and looked inside. Vic had sat Ida Stephens upright against the wall. He had straightened her clothing and cleaned the thick streaks of mascara that had run down her teary face. I leant against the back door and watched as she stared poker-faced at the floor.

"The child gotta have a surname."

Ida Stephens looked up me. "I'm sorry, what did you say?"

"I was asking 'bout Truth. What is her surname?"

"It's Mayer. The child was born in Clifton Court Maternity Hospital, I believe. The woman that gave birth to her, as far as I can remember, was a Jew. Her surname was Mayer."

"Woman . . . Don't you mean 'mother'?"

Ida Stephens stared back at me. Her cruel, piercing eyes bored deep into my own. "Mothers have their babies at home, Mr Ellington. Whores have theirs in hospital."

I pulled on my leather gloves, climbed into the van and walked over to the orphanage administrator. Ida quickly started to panic again and was about to begin screaming. I quickly reached for the old rag at her side, grabbed hold of her face with my hand, pinched her cheeks with my fingers and rammed the saliva-soaked gag back into her mouth. I walked away, leaving Ida to curse and plead unintelligibly behind the dirty cloth. I jumped back out, swung the doors and locked them, then with leaden steps and a desolate spirit made my way back to the cab of the van, feeling as if I had just closed the fiery gates of hell upon Satan himself.

I drove the Commer postal van the short distance back into Bristol city with Vic following close behind in the Ford. All I could think about during the brief drive was how Truth was and how I now knew her surname, Mayer. I parked the van up in a quiet side street close to Bridewell police station and turned off the engine. I headed over to a phone box and put the keys underneath the phone book until I found the number listing for Bridewell police station. I rang my finger underneath the small print on the page then put a coin in the pay slot and dialled. The line rang a couple of times then a cheerful young woman's voice answered but was cut off by the pips. I quickly fed four one-penny coins into the slot and the young woman repeated her introduction to me.

"Good afternoon, Bristol and Avon Police. How may I direct your call?"

I held the phone close to my ear and spoke. "Could you put me through to Detective Inspector William Fletcher please?"

The young woman initially hesitated after hearing my request and I readied myself for a barrage of questions as to why I wanted to speak to a high-ranking police officer, but then I heard her start to patch my call through the reception exchange. "Certainly, sir, just one moment, please."

Fletcher's phone seemed to ring out forever. When he eventually picked up the receiver he sounded breathless, as if he'd had to run up a couple of flights of stairs to answer the damn thing.

"DI Fletcher here."

"How you doin', Detective Inspector? It's Joseph Ellington here." I waited for the penny to drop and for the policeman to unleash his vocal wrath upon me. I didn't have to wait long.

"What the bloody hell do you think you're playing at, Ellington? I've got coppers from 'ere to the south coast combing the streets looking for your black arse."

"That ain't no surprise, but it ain't me you need to be lookin' fo'."

"Oh, that right? I suppose you're innocent of all the charges again. Let me guess, who you got holding out an alibi for you this time. Rosa Parks? You're in deep shit, old son, you need to hand yourself in pronto."

"Oh, I don't think so, Mr Fletcher. I've already had my fill of British police hospitality. One night in one o' your cells was enough fo' me, thank you."

"Look, I ain't got the time to be pissing about making small talk with you. Either you hand yourself into the nearest nick or you're gonna end up as part of a major manhunt, do you hear me?"

I held the phone away from my head for a moment, took a deep breath then put the receiver back to my ear.

"Fletcher, do me a favour . . . I want you to shut your fat mout' and pin those big ears o' yours back, cos what I'm 'bout to say, I'm gonna say just once. Git yo'self a pencil and write down what I'm 'bout to tell you."

Fletcher went to interrupt me, but I didn't give him the chance to speak and kept rattling out the facts.

"You got more dirty coppers in that station of yours. I got the names of two of 'em. An officer by the name of Martin, David Martin. Him and your ole buddy, Beaumont. Both are up to their filthy necks in some real bad bidness. I found out that the pair of 'em are involved with a bunch of Yanks who are workin' out o' an airbase in Gloucestershire. One of the Americans is a military police officer, a real nasty piece o' work by the name o' Paxton. He was the guy who murdered Doc Fowler. There's also two civilians you need to be putting the heat under, a couple o' fellas who are involved in the kidnap and sale of young children from the Walter Wilkins orphanage."

"Involved in what?" snapped Fletcher.

"Did you hear what I said 'bout shuttin' that mout' o' yours? I ain't got time fo' your priss-assed questions now. The names o' the men you lookin' fo' are Andrew Balfour and Edward Matherson. One's a social worker here in Bristol; the other's some big name in the oil and petrol game. You need to sniff 'em out and haul 'em into your interview room pretty sharpish." I took a breath and continued. "OK, now git your ass outside and down to Nelson Street. You'll find a Royal Mail postal van parked up by the side o' the road. Inside the back o' the van you're gonna find a woman by the name o' Ida Stephens. She's an administrator at the orphanage and part o' all of this madness. She hired me to find Fowler and she was involved with the others in settin' me up to take the fall fo' his death. Tell her you spoke to me and put the thumbscrews on her. She's a cunning piece o' work so you gonna have to come down hard on her. She's gonna come screamin' at you 'bout how I gone an' abducted her. I had to do what I had to do and I got a recorded confession outta her earlier today where she spills the beans on the whole sorry affair. I've got a few other tings to finish sortin' out, then you can question me. I'll give you the tape and the woman's address book sometime tomorrow. For now, you an' one of your monkeys can sweat the rest o' the information outta Ida Stephens yourselves. Now git down to that van befo' that bitch starts cookin' to death in the back of it."

I could hear Detective Inspector Fletcher swallow hard on the other end of the line. He was about to hit me with a question. I held the receiver out in front of me then put my finger on the black button in the cradle and cut him off.

I looked out of the phone box window into the street just as Vic pulled up on the other side of the road. I walked across the street and got into the passenger seat of the car, then my cousin and me drove off and quickly blended into the rest of the city's bustling afternoon traffic.

Vic wound down his window, rested his arm on the sill and looked across at me. "You doin' all right?"

I nodded. "Sure." I stared down at my feet, desperate to avoid my cousin's enquiring stare, all too aware that my heavy-hearted reply was fooling nobody.

CHAPTER
FORTY-ONE

Vic drove us along the Portway Road to a place called Sea Mills, a peaceful, leafy suburb about three miles outside of Bristol. The village was hushed and anonymous and was the perfect place for the two of us to lay low for the rest of the day. We turned into a small side street and made our way down a thinly gravelled road that ran parallel to a stretch of disused railway track. On the right-hand side of the road, nestled in next to the sidings of the railway tracks and the tail end of a large, twin-arched red-brick bridge, was a small workman's lock-up.

Vic drove underneath the bridge then pulled up close to the side of the old rail worker's storeroom and got out. I followed and watched as Vic went to the boot of the car, opened it up and took out the golf bag and toolbox. My cousin stood at the door of the lock-up and looked suspiciously up and down the desolate gravel road before fishing out a large bunch of keys from a drawer in the top of the large metal toolbox. He stuck a small Chubb key into a brass padlock and opened up the place up.

I walked in and shut the door behind me just as two light bulbs flickered into action. Inside was yet another

Aladdin's cave of knocked-off goods, illicit booze and antique *objets d'art*. I turned and looked at Vic.

"How many o' these places have you got?"

"Look, mister detective, I needs places to store my goods and somewhere to git my head down if tings git a little heated with the law. Man got a right to some privacy, ain't he?"

"Privacy? You must have some sort o' shed, garage or lock-up in every part o' this city. How'd you do it?"

"None o' your damn bidness how I do it. Just be grateful I got 'em!"

Vic walked over to a small bench and dropped the bags. He opened up the smaller of the two and pulled out a couple of heavy-looking cloth-wrapped parcels. He laid them out in front of him then carefully peeled back each of the cloths to reveal two pristine Colt .45 automatic pistols.

"You carryin' that ole police pea-shooter revolver o' yours?"

I reached around into the waistband of my trousers and pulled out the Smith & Wesson .38.

Vic reached out to give me one of the automatics. I took a step back and waved away the pistol with the palm of my hand. I looked down at my old .38, squeezed its wood grip and weighed it in the palm of my hand then looked at my cousin and smiled. "No thanks . . . I'll stick with what I got."

Vic shook his head "What you got there ain't good enough . . . This ain't no game, JT. We do this my way or we're both gonna end up dead. You git me?" Vic rubbed his mouth, never blinking once. He let the .45

hang by his leg for a moment before lifting it up in front of his face. He chambered a round, clicked on the safety then pushed the pistol firmly at my chest and held it there. "Now, take the fuckin' gun!"

I hesitated for a moment then reluctantly took the blue-steel Colt from him and stuffed both of the guns into the back of my waistband. Rather than get into a huge argument with my volatile cousin about my preference of firearm, I took the path of least resistance and decided to keep my mouth firmly shut.

In matters concerning violence and the application of it to others, Vic was a master and it was no use trying to argue against any decision he'd made when he had bloodlust coursing through his veins. I casually leant against the wall of the lock-up and watched as Vic undid the canvas golfing bag and drew out a sawn-off shotgun. He cranked open the breech and loaded two twelve-gauge shells into the twin chambers. He snapped the shotgun to and laid it on the top of the bench next to his own automatic then turned and walked over to where I was stood and rested his back against the wall next to me.

I reached into the inside pocket of my jacket and handed Vic a small slip of folded, lined paper. "I need you to do something for me."

He took the note from me and stuck it into the back pocket of his trousers without even looking at what was written on it then stared down at the ground.

"If anyting should happen to me, I want you to go get Truth from Mrs Pearce and take her down to the address I've written down on that paper. It's in Porlock,

426

in Devon. The woman you'll be takin' the child to is Loretta's kin. Her name's Estelle Goodman. She'll sort everyting from there. You just need to drop Truth off and leave."

Vic shrugged his shoulders and tapped at the paper in his pocket with the palm of his hand. "Got it."

"I've made a note of where Truth is stayin' in Portishead on there for you too."

We stood in silence for a moment until Vic looked at me and spoke.

"Don't sweat it, I got it covered." Vic made a nervous coughing sound and cleared his throat then put his hand on my arm. "JT?"

I looked at Vic, surprised by his sudden tactile gesture. "Yeah, what is it?"

"Just so you know . . . Ain't nuttin' gonna happen to you out there in those woods. You got my word on it, cuz. Just be cool."

Vic stared back down at the ground then sauntered back over to the bench and picked up the shotgun. He raised it up in front of his face then looked at me with his delinquent, impish brown eyes and grinned.

"So, come on, tell me . . . How we gonna play it wid these Yankee fuckers out in the woods?"

Just after seven, we bundled ourselves into the Ford Zodiac and Vic followed the same route back to Bristol, travelling south-west towards the city and over the Clifton Suspension Bridge. Grey clouds hung heavily high in the evening sky, which was quickly turning to dusk. A dense mist that had been low lying, just above

427

the fast-running water of the River Avon, had slowly begun to rise up behind us out of the gorge and filter through the trees as we approached Leigh Woods. At the western end of the suspension bridge we drove past red-bricked walls to the grounds of Burwalls house and then turned right down into a long avenue of young copper birch trees, which eventually led into the mouth of the woods.

Vic continued to drive down a dirt track until we reached a slight incline, which led down to a circle of hazel trees and thick coppice growth. Vic turned off the car's engine then let the motor slowly freewheel itself to the bottom of the coppice and bring itself to a halt near the dense thicket. We got out, and Vic opened up the trunk and took out the sawn-off from inside the canvas golf bag then filled the pockets of his long leather jacket with handfuls of shotgun cartridges and brass .45 shells from the toolbox. He grabbed the tarpaulin from the back of the car then quietly shut the boot lid and handed me the keys. Vic unfolded the large green waterproof sheet and the two of us quickly draped it over the body of the Zodiac. We then pulled up as much undergrowth and loose foliage as we could find and threw it over the tarp, camouflaging the motor. Vic pulled the slide back on his Colt and chambered a round then stuck the gun through his trouser belt. He looked at me and winked.

"OK, this is where I gotta leave ya. I'll have me eye on ya. Stay sharp, ya hear me?"

My mouth was as dry as a bone. Unable to speak, I nodded to my cousin that I understood him. I cautiously began to walk into the thick undergrowth of Leigh Woods. A few steps in, I turned to give a silent thumbs up of reassurance to my cousin, but as I returned my gaze to where he had just been standing, Vic was nowhere to be seen.

I reached into my jacket and took out my .38, slipped the safety off and tucked it back into my waistband then dipped my hand into my back pocket and pulled out the Puma knife that Mrs Pearce had given to me. I opened up the blade then bent down, pulled up my trouser leg a little and put the knife inside my sock. I pushed down onto the top of the knife butt so that the tip of the blade went through the fabric of the sock into the sole of my shoe. I straightened my jacket then continued to walk further into the centre of the woods until I caught the dimming light that was seeping through the top of the thin tree canopy at the furthest edges of the wood. I finally reached a path that took me along the grassy slopes above the river and led to a bluff overlooking the bridge and the rear of the grounds of the mock Swiss chalet that Paxton had told me to meet him at. I walked to my left and looked up at the suspension bridge looming out in front of me, then peered down through the thick bracken at my side into the gorge below.

"Quite some view, ain't it?"

Paxton walked out from shadows created by the high fencing that separated the chalet from the woods. He walked onto the path then stopped abruptly. He was stood about fifteen feet from me. He was wearing blue jeans, tan leather gloves and a beat-up brown leather military bomber jacket. The jacket was unzipped and I could see the butt of a pearl-handled revolver sticking out of the top of his trousers. Behind him followed four white men, all dressed casually, all carrying guns of varying size and model. The men drew into a loose semicircle behind Paxton and began to scrutinise me like buzzards eyeing up rotting carrion lying in the road.

I watched as Paxton's jaw set, his right eye twitching slightly. He pointed his finger out in front of him directly towards my face then spat on the ground before speaking.

"You carryin' a piece?"

I remained silent but nodded my head.

"OK, reach in real careful and toss it at my feet."

I lifted the front of my jacket, lifted the .38 from my trouser band and did as I was told. Paxton picked up my gun and put it into his jacket pocket.

"Good . . . Never saw the use of a nigger owning a gun. Now, where's my cargo?"

I took a step backwards. "In my car. I got it parked back on the other side of the woods. What I've brought you is safe in the trunk."

"The trunk? Boy, you better not have damaged any part of my belongings."

"Oh, she's perfectly safe." I saw Paxton's eyes charge with adrenaline when I said the word "she". I didn't give the American time to react further and pushed on with the deal. "Where's my money?"

Paxton smiled, tapped the side of his pocket and then slowly reached inside, drew out a wad of bound bank notes and shook them at me.

430

"Throw those car keys on the ground. We're gonna take ourselves a little walk, make sure you're on the level."

I did as he said, reached slowly into my jacket pocket then slung the keys at my feet. Paxton gestured to one of his men to pick them up.

"Which way we heading, boy?"

I turned around and pointed my hand out straight ahead of me, towards the thick undergrowth of Leigh Woods.

Paxton turned to one of his men. "Get down there, spread out an' make sure we ain't gonna have any surprises. I wanna make sure the coon here ain't 'bout to pull the rug from under our feet. You see anything suspicious out there, put a fuckin' bullet in it."

I watched as the four men walked out in front of Paxton and me and spread themselves out as they headed into the woods. Paxton came up behind me and jabbed a finger into the centre of my back. "Get walkin'."

I began to move forwards, aware that Paxton was no more than a foot behind me.

"How long's my cargo been in that goddamn car trunk, Ellington?"

"No more than ten minutes, I didn't want her to be bawlin' the place down while we talked bidness. She's gonna be fine."

"Oh, it better be more than fine by the time we reach that motor o' yours."

Paxton's men had continued to spread themselves out further into the undergrowth. In the low evening light, I was struggling to get a fix on them. I kept walking through the bracken and after a few hundred yards looked back up again. The four men were now out of sight. Paxton pushed at my back with the flat of his hand. "Let's pick up the pace, boy."

I began to speed up my pace through the wood. I saw a clear pathway to my left and crossed over onto it. Paxton followed close on my back, and our bodies were suddenly through the waist-high vegetation. I kept moving forward and looked out across the thick undergrowth and the trees to the front and either side of me. The light was fading now, the air thick with river mist and the smell of rotting moss and leaves. A warm breeze blew up in front of us, and that was when the first gunshot rang out.

I heard Paxton pull his gun from his belt. He kicked me behind the back of the knee, dropping me swiftly to the floor. "Don't you move, nigger."

Paxton came around to my side and looked down at me, his gun held firmly at my temple. I lifted my eyes up towards him and could just make out his face, which was slick with sweat. I could smell the rancid stench of body odour coming off his sweaty hide. A second gunshot ran out, its report cracking out in front of us. Paxton raised his gun in front of him, both his hands gripped around the pearl handle of the revolver. He darted his head to the left and right then bellowed out to his men. "What the fuckin' hell is going on out there?"

When the American got no reply, he took a step forward and I dropped my right hand down towards the bottom of my trouser leg. Paxton released one of his hands from the butt of his pistol and grabbed at the top of my hair with his long fingers. He yanked me closer towards him, and as he did, I grasped for the knife in my sock. I gripped at the tiny handle and held on to it as tight as I could then let my arm quickly drop to my side. In front of us the woods had begun to light up in a barrage of heavy gunfire.

Paxton looked down at me and yelled over the shooting. "Nigger, when this shit is all over I'm gonna make you beg for me to kill you quick, you hear me, boy?" The American yanked me another few inches closer towards him until I could feel the fabric of his jeans touching the side of my cheek. I heard the roar of both barrels of a shotgun being fired, the bursts' screaming like cannon fire.

Paxton pulled on my hair and lifted my head up hard. He bent down in front of me and shoved the barrel of the gun into my face. "Who the fuck you got out there with you in the dark, nigger?" He pulled back the hammer on his revolver and went to push it underneath my nose. Two further shots of pistol fire pinged over our heads. Paxton swung himself round just as one of his men came running out of the trees. Another gunshot rang out behind the runner; the bullet tore through the middle of the man's throat. He dropped to the ground in front of us. Thick streams of blood burst out of the corners of his mouth and he fell face down into the dirt.

Another burst of gunfire whizzed out over our heads. Paxton yanked at my hair, pulling me like a dog being brought to heel on a short lead right up close to his body. As he struggled to keep a grip on me I brought my left knee up and found my balance on my foot. Paxton raised his gun out in front of him and began to fire. I counted the shots: when he triggered the fifth I swung myself around, lifted my arm and sank the blade of the knife into the inside of his thigh.

Paxton screamed and immediately let go of my hair, and instinctively reached down towards the knife buried to the hilt just underneath his groin. I bounced up off the ground and sank my fist into the American's face. He flew backwards and rolled back into the undergrowth. I heard him scream again just as another gunshot sounded out. I ran head first into the scrub but was knocked backwards and slammed to the ground as Paxton stormed out at me like a rampaging bull. He stomped his boot down on my chest then grabbed hold of my jacket and pulled me up towards him and began to rain down a series of heavy blows to my head. I tried to raise my arm and sideswipe him in the guts with my fist, but he was moving way too quickly for me to hit my mark. The American twisted my jacket in his huge fingers and shook me about like a cloth doll. He pulled his arm back and drove his fist into my face then went to repeat the savage blow. I heard further gunshot buzz across our heads and Vic yell after me. Paxton let go of my lapel. I fell backwards and watched the military policeman limp away, back towards the grounds of the Swiss chalet.

Blood ran in a torrent from my nose and mouth. I felt woozy and fought to keep myself conscious. I rolled over onto my belly and hauled myself up onto my ass. My trembling hand reached around to the grip of the .45 at the back of my waistband. I got onto one knee, lifted the Colt up in front of my face and watched through watering eyes as Paxton began to disappear into the night.

I squeezed off a shot through the trees. The .45 recoiled hard against the palm of my hand and a flash sprang off the muzzle like a miniature lightning bolt. Behind me in the distance I heard another series of automatic pistol shots ring out and Vic calling my name again. I got back up on to my feet, briefly stumbling to stay upright as I felt the blood rush to my head. I squeezed my eyes open and shut then raised the Colt out in front of me in both hands and set off after Paxton.

I reached the fence that separated the chalet grounds from the woods and followed it back towards the grassy slopes above Avon Gorge. When I reached the edge of the fence I stepped back a couple of paces and swung myself round onto the path that ran directly along the side of the property. As I began to move forward I saw a flash of bright light out of the corner of my eye and heard the boom of a single shot being fired from a gun. I felt a sharp burning sensation cut into the top of my left arm. My body arched downwards and my gun was kicked from my hand, sending it arcing through the air and into the hedgerow. I raised my head and saw Paxton right in front of me. I watched as, almost in slow motion, he lifted his arm then brought it down towards my brow. He pistol-whipped me across the temple with the barrel of his gun. I felt a burning spike of pain run through my skull then fell backwards onto the ground. I saw the American moving towards me and began to raise myself up onto my elbows. Dazed and overwhelmed with pain, I kicked out my legs and tried to draw myself away from him with my heels digging into the dirt.

Paxton moved in quickly and stood in front of me, blood streaming from the knife wound in his leg, my own .38 pointing directly at my head. He inched forward, spat blood onto the path and bellowed down at me.

"Where's that fuckin' girl o' mine?"

I tried to catch my breath, coughing and spluttering red-tinged saliva onto myself as I started to speak. "Like I told you, she's back in the trunk o' my motor."

Paxton kicked at my leg with the toe of his boot. "Bullshit, I want the Truth!"

I felt another wave of pain burn through my arm; my chest tightened and a bitter taste rose up into my mouth. I looked up past Paxton's cruel, bloodied face and stared up at one of the enormous suspension bridge buttresses that rose up over the tree line. Its shadow hung over my body like Azrael waiting to claim my soul for the afterlife.

I heard Paxton curse under his breath then aim the gun at my legs. He fired a shot into the soil close to my feet and took a step closer towards me. "Did you hear me, you dumb nigger? I said I want the Truth."

I looked up at Paxton through my clouded vision and rasped out a reply to his embittered enquiry with as

436

much venom as I could muster. "Well, you ain't never gonna have her."

I saw him draw the hammer nose back and close one eye. I watched as his finger curled around the trigger. I swallowed hard and tried to wet my dry lips with my tongue. I flailed my legs out in front of me and cursed their inability to distance me from my assailant. I felt my hand buckle at my wrist and I slumped further backwards. I looked down at the ground and I felt a rush of air hit my face.

As I lifted my head I heard the sound of metal hitting stone and saw a .45 pistol skirt past Paxton's feet. I watched the American hesitate for a moment then saw panic drop across his face as he swung to his left. I watched him fire my service revolver at the same time as the blurred image of Vic's body collided with tremendous force into Paxton's side. I saw both men fly up into the air in front over me and then followed their brutal trajectory as they hit the waist-high stone wall that separated the cliff path from the vertical drop into the gorge below. I heard Jack Paxton let out a piercing scream and watched as the two men fell headlong into the endless chasm below.

I crawled to the wall, lifted myself up and looked down into the black abyss, and bawled out my cousin's name over and over again. I kept calling out in the darkness, hoping that at any moment Vic would pull himself over the rampart and he would again be at my side, but that moment never came.

I felt another wave of intense pain charge through my body. I collapsed onto my back in the dirt, my battered body cold and shivering. I felt the iron-like taste of blood catch on the back of my throat and I looked up at a darkening sky that seemed to be littered with a million cascading stars.

I felt the tears stream down my face and run down my neck, and then felt the wind blow around my dormant frame. My fingers grasped at a loose clump of grass by my side and I closed my eyes. I began to drift out of consciousness, and in my head I heard the whispering, gentle voices of a swathe of lost children as they quietly began to sing me a lullaby to what I believed would be an eternal sleep.

Epilogue

I woke twelve hours later and found myself lying in a bed on a ward in the Bristol Royal Infirmary with a concussion, three broken ribs and a sizable laceration to my left arm where Paxton had shot me. Another eight inches across and he would have blown a hole through my heart the size of an apple. I was escorted from hospital twenty-four hours later, shackled in handcuffs by Detective Inspector William Fletcher and two other police officers. Before finding myself in a cell at Bridewell Police Station, I was taken back to Vic's garage in Hotwells to retrieve the envelope containing the cassette tape with Ida Stephens' confession on it. When I unlocked the safe and took out both the recorder and envelope, I noticed that the stash of bank notes I'd seen inside previously had mysteriously disappeared.

I spent four sleepless days and nights at Bridewell being questioned by Fletcher and a whole load of his constable lackeys. Despite being leaned on by Fletcher, I never changed my story once. At one point during my interrogation I was placed in a line-up parade with six other black men. I later found out that Ida Stephens had been stood behind a two-way mirror staring at the seven of us. For reasons known only to herself, Stephens never picked me out of the line-up.

Soon after that, Ida Stephens' secret little world started to crumble. The social worker Andrew Balfour and the orphanage's chief administrator Edward Matherson were brought in for questioning and the pieces slowly started to come together, aided by the confession Stephens had given to me, recorded on the cassette tape.

Arrests were later made at RAF Fairford and at least ten other men were finally charged with offences ranging from perverting the course of justice to kidnap of a minor. The bad apples within the Bristol and Avon Constabulary slowly started to unwillingly float to the top of the barrel as Matherson, Balfour and Stephens started to lose their cool and confess their full involvement in a cruel and very sordid affair. Later investigations uncovered that more than sixty children, their ages ranging from six months to nine years, had been abducted from Walter Wilkins orphanage between the year 1964 and the summer of 1967. Most of the children had been transported out in US Air Force planes, across the Atlantic to new lives in a country over four thousand miles away, their fates not fully known. I believed that the fresh beginnings the children were no doubt promised by Paxton would have quickly degenerated into physical suffering, emotional starvation and perhaps much worse. The thought of the cold absence of love, of the lack of tenderness and care that each of those stolen children would perhaps have to

440

endure was a horrific contemplation that would haunt me to my grave.

I continued to maintain that the orphan I had found myself on the run with, the girl I had later found to be called Truth Mayer, had fallen to her death while we were trying to escape from Paxton and his men on the moors close to Cheddar Gorge. The police searched the area, but no body was ever found. I maintained that Paxton had gone to retrieve Truth's body and disposed of it, and that the events at Leigh Woods were a cleaning-up exercise to silence me and the knowledge I had of Paxton and his men's involvement in the kidnapping of minors from a Bristol orphanage.

The charred remains of two American servicemen, along with those of Detective Constable Beaumont and Laszlo Dolan, were found in what was left of the burnt-out Hunters Lodge inn at Priddy. A fifth man, who I knew to be my friend Benjamin Goodman, was never identified by the police. When asked if I had any idea who the fifth man may have been, I told the police that the only two men I knew by name were DC Beaumont and my good friend Lazarus Dolan: the friend I had turned to when I found myself on the run from Paxton and his men. Although it broke my heart to deny the fifth man's existence, I knew that I needed to keep Benny's name out of the picture.

Jack Paxton's battered body was found floating in the tidal harbour at Cumberland Basin. His corpse was collected by the United States Air Force and he was shipped back to his home country. When his coffin arrived stateside, it was not draped with the American flag.

The body of Detective Constable David Martin and three other deceased American servicemen were found lying in various parts of Leigh Woods. All had died after receiving multiple gunshot wounds.

After a week of police searches along the Avon Gorge and Leigh Woods, and the extensive dredging of large sections of the River Avon, my cousin Vic's body was still not found. It was presumed that the tidal river had either washed his corpse further downstream or that the muddy waters of the Avon had taken him down into the deep silt and that his remains would perhaps never be found.

The police made much of my cousin's disappearance and presumed death. Here was a black man with a history of consorting with the city's nefarious villains and crooks. A man who had connections to racketeering, theft and the handling of stolen goods, of trading on the black market and establishing properties for illicit behaviour, was an easy target for a police force who desperately wanted to pin a face to the crimes committed. Detective Inspector William Fletcher needed a suspect for the deaths of two of his police officers and four other American servicemen. It didn't take him long to weigh all the evidence towards an obvious culprit: a man with a motive and criminal intent — my cousin, Victor Ellington.

Five days after being arrested I was released pending further police inquiries. Inquiries that subsequently saw me fail to be charged with any offence. To this very day,

442

I don't know how the hell I got away with it. I'd walked out of Bridewell police station with a nagging sensation deep in my gut, a suspicion inside of me that sensed that DI Fletcher knew I had been lying about the death of Truth. I never got to know why the wily old goat didn't pursue a further line of inquiry into the matter. Perhaps he'd read between the lines of my partially fabricated story, and after uncovering all the misery caused at the Walter Wilkins orphanage he simply thought better of bringing down a little more heartache on another poor parentless child. At least that's what I hoped he was thinking.

I returned to St Pauls, picked up some fresh clothes from my digs and spent the next two days at the home of my aunt Pearl and uncle Gabe, Vic's mother and father. We consoled each other at the loss of our kin, we sobbed, we held each other and we reminisced. I drank rum to ease the physical pain I felt and to mask the torment that I had been responsible for my cousin's death.

Without a body to mourn and bury, Gabe and Pearl refused to believe that their son was dead. I wished that I possessed their conviction, but my heart told me otherwise.

It had been nearly a week since my neighbour, Marjorie Pearce, had taken Truth to her sister's in Portishead. I needed to go and pick the little girl up then take a drive to Porlock. I left Gabe and Pearl's home without saying goodbye just as dawn broke and returned to my digs on Gwyn Street. I bathed, shaved and cleaned my teeth, changed into my grey herringbone suit then walked the short distance to Loretta Harris' home. I stood outside the door of her ground-floor flat on Brunswick Street and waited for an age before plucking up the courage to knock. She opened the door to me, her face cut and bruised, and wearing a sling supporting her right arm. She greeted me warmly on the doorstep then, once I had come in off the street, proceeded to slap me repeatedly across the face.

For her, the grief upon hearing the news of Vic's disappearance and death was almost as painful as that of her deceased and much loved husband, Carnell, who had been tragically taken from her so many long months ago. She bellowed and bawled at me in the hallway of her home for another ten minutes. Then we cried and held each other until there were no more tears to sob. We sat at her kitchen table and drank tea and I explained the events of the last two weeks in their entirety. When I'd finished talking, Loretta got up out of her chair, walked across to kitchen drawer and returned with my car keys. She placed them on the table then looked at me and smiled.

"Come on, honey, let's go take a drive."

Loretta joined me on the short journey to collect Truth from Mrs Pearce in Portishead. We left Bristol on a beautiful sunny July morning, me driving Carnell's old Cortina again, and headed out of Bristol. Twenty minutes later we were driving along a remote coastal road and arrived at the address my neighbour had given me. Loretta waited in the car and I walked up a stone path across a well-maintained lawn and garden to the

444

door of a small bungalow. An elderly lady who looked as if she was the twin of my neighbour opened the door, greeted me and welcomed me into her home.

Marjorie Pearce was stood behind her sister in the hallway. She smiled and embraced me in her frail arms then took me by the hand and walked me through the kitchen and out of the back door into the garden. Sitting on a tartan blanket in the middle of the lawn, with the sun caressing the back of her long blonde hair, was Truth. Mrs Pearce let go of my hand and patted me gently on the back, then returned to the house. I stepped on to the lawn then slowly walked across the grass and cautiously sat down next to the little girl.

When Truth realised it was me, she flung her arms around me and didn't let go for the next half an hour. I let her keep hugging me. I think I needed to be held more than she did. Heck, the kid had proved to be tougher than I ever could be.

Two hours later, after a lunch of ham and cucumber sandwiches and a bucketload of tea, Truth, Loretta and I left Mrs Pearce and her sister and started on the long journey down to Porlock in north Devon. Truth and Loretta sat on the back seat of the Cortina. We listened to music on the radio, we sang, we laughed, and I tried to hold it all together.

We arrived at Benny's garage just after six thirty that evening. I pulled the Cortina into the forecourt and we all got out and walked down to the garden at the back of the garage. At the garden gates we were greeted by Claude, the Irish wolfhound. It was his barking that alerted Estelle and Cecile to our arrival. After the briefest of greetings, Estelle and I sat in private in her sitting room and I broke the news of Benny's death. We sat in that room until well after dark, and I held my good friend's widow in my arms while she sobbed inconsolably. It was just after eleven when I finally spoke of the promise I'd made to Benny back at the Hunters Lodge inn, regarding Truth and bringing her to Estelle for safekeeping. Estelle remained silent as I explained. When I had finished speaking, she got up out of her seat and rested her hand on the back of mine. The only words she said to me before leaving me alone in the room were simply, "Thank you."

After breakfast the next morning, Loretta and I prepared for the journey back to St Pauls. Before leaving, Estelle, Cecile and Loretta sat in the kitchen while I took a moment to be with Truth. With the sun high on our backs, we left the house and walked back across the buttercup-lined meadows we had walked on with Benny less than two weeks previously. Truth held on to my hand the whole time. It was in those fields that I explained to the little girl that the men who had caused her so much pain and fear were no longer around. That Paxton and his cronies were gone and would never return. Truth listened to every word I spoke without asking a question or uttering a sound. I then told her that I was going to leave her with Estelle and Cecile and that she would not be returning to any kind of orphanage again.

The news hit Truth hard. She held on to me and cried and pleaded for me to take her back with me to Bristol. I explained to the child that it simply wasn't possible and that if I did the authorities would soon find out where she was and take her away from me. Truth, unwilling to accept what I had told her, ran back to the house in floods of tears. I followed after her, my eyes welling up with so much water that I could barely see.

Loretta had thrown off her sling and chosen to drive back in the Mini she had loaned me to get down to Porlock. She said her farewells to her relations and to Truth, then walked down to Benny's garage and drove the little car up to the forecourt and waited for me there. Estelle and Cecile hugged me and Estelle told me that she would be in touch with good news very soon. I looked at Truth, who was standing close to Cecile. I leant forward towards her and reached out my hand, but Truth backed away behind Cecile. I straightened myself, and Estelle touched me on the arm and smiled at me.

I kissed Estelle on the cheek then bid my farewells to my friends and walked out of the kitchen, through the garden and back up to forecourt to where Loretta was waiting for me. As I was about to get into the Cortina, Truth came rushing up behind me and threw her arms around my waist. I bent down on one knee and took the little girl in my arms and embraced her while she cried and squeezed at my back with her tiny arms. Finally, she drew herself away from me, reached down for my hand and pushed something into my palm then closed my fingers around the object. She wiped at her face with her hands then smiled at me. Before I had a chance to thank her she had turned and run back down the forecourt and into the garden, back to Estelle and Cecile.

I got into my car, looked down at my hand and opened my fingers. Sitting in the middle of my palm was the sixpence-coin ankle bracelet Cecile had given to her. A gift to keep away the juju was what the old woman had told me it was for. Something to keep the dark spirits at bay. I turned the key in the ignition and drove off. The talisman burned in my palm and never left my hand while I made the long journey home.

Six weeks passed without word from Estelle. I returned back to the gym each day. I cleaned my office and the changing rooms, I swept and scrubbed the gymnasium floors and the ring, then I sat at my desk drinking Mount Gay rum and got slowly more drunk day by day. Nobody came looking for my services to undertake any enquiry business and I sure as hell didn't go looking for work. My wounds healed, I paid my rent and I took one shopping trip into Bristol to buy myself some new shoes, shirts, a couple of pairs of trousers and a new raincoat, courtesy of Ida Stephens. I'd stashed away a little of her money at home before I left with Truth, just for emergencies. To offer up some sense of normality I put on a brave face and spent a little time each day in the company of my uncle Gabe, aunt Pearl and Loretta. My family knew that I was hurting but went along with the façade. When I'd had my fill of them all I'd return to my digs on Gwyn Street to hide away from the world and thought of nothing but my cousin Vic and the little girl, Truth. At night I slept very little, and when I did drop off in a drunken haze I was visited in my dreams by the ghosts of my past.

Then, on a rainy Thursday afternoon in mid-September, while I was bumming about at the gym on Grosvenor Road, I received a phone call from Estelle Goodman. Her call to me was brief. Estelle could hear the sadness in my voice as we spoke. She offered me some consolation by explaining that Truth had quickly settled and that she was doing fine. Then, in no roundabout fashion, she told me to smarten myself up, get a good night's sleep and meet her at Southampton docks the next day at 1.30p.m.

My drive down to the south coast and the port town of Southampton was made in good time. It was just after twelve thirty in the afternoon by the time I parked my car in a side street across the road from the docks. I got out and headed towards to the giant moored vessels on the dockside. After searching about for a while I eventually found Estelle, Cecile and Truth standing at one of the furthest edges of the docks. A huge passenger-carrying Fyffes banana boat, the TSS *Camito,* overshadowed the three of them as they stood by its side with a crowd of other people. I cut through the mingling array of passengers that were just starting to board the ship.

When Truth saw me heading towards them, she bellowed out my name and ran hell for leather down the concrete dock and flung herself at me. I could barely recognise her. She was dressed in a beautiful yellow-flower-petal cotton dress, white ankle socks and white patent shoes. Gone was the tired, sullen face of a frightened little girl. It had been replaced with happiness and love. Truth smiled up at me then continued to hug me for all she was worth.

I looked up and watched as Cecile and Estelle spoke. Cecile lifted her arm and waved at me, then she turned to the gangplank and slowly began to walk onto the ship. Estelle made her way along the dock towards Truth and I. Benny's widow smiled at me then thanked me for coming. She took my hand in hers then kissed me on the cheek and assured me that everything was going to be all right.

She reached into her handbag and showed me the tickets she had purchased for the three of them to sail out to Barbados. I felt a lump rise in my throat as Estelle stood away from me and looked down at her wristwatch.

She took Truth by the hand and the three of us walked towards the gangplank. We stood and talked while other passengers started to berth. Truth told me about all the wonderful things she was going to do when she arrived in her new island home. She spoke of how Cecile had told her that the sun always shone and that the sea was so blue and clear that you could stare down into it and see your face beaming back up at you. She laughed and skipped at my feet with excitement. Then Estelle explained to her that it was time for them to leave. That's when I felt my hand tighten around the little girl's fingers. Truth looked up at me and saw the tears in my eyes. She pulled me down towards her and whispered into my ear.

450

"Thank you, Joseph, thank you for being my friend and for keeping your promise. You came back for me, just like you said."

Then she kissed me on my cheek and I felt her tiny fingers slip from my loosening grasp. I watched as Estelle and Truth walked up the gangplank and boarded the ship. Before they were lost in a crowd of passengers, Truth turned to me and pointed with her finger above her head then shouted. "You needn't worry about the money, Joseph. I know a man who says he's going to look after it for me." She smiled at me again then walked along the deck and began to climb a staircase with Estelle. I watched as they disappeared in a throng of fellow passengers then stood back on the dock and looked up above me.

There, staring down at me from the upper deck, was Vic, his left hand resting on the top of a long, thin cane. His face now sported a thick salt-and-pepper beard and his right eye was covered with an elegant black silk eyepatch. He leant against the iron railing and raised his right arm and waved at me. I looked up at him, the tears streaming down my face. He shook his head at me as if to say, "Stop with those tears, cuz." Then I saw the familiar mischievous smile break across his face and I watched as he put his hand to his mouth and kissed the tips of his fingers with his lips. He threw his arm out in front of him in a final farewell, then my cousin backed away from the rail of the ship and disappeared from my sight like a shadow swallowed by a cloud.

Acknowledgements

"When's the next book out?" It's a question that I was first asked during the swanky London launch of my debut novel *Heartman* back in the summer of 2014 and I've continued to be asked on a very regular basis ever since.

Heartman's sequel *All Through the Night* had, in fact, been written as a first draft long before *Heartman* had even hit the bookshelves. The road to getting into shape the book you now hold in your hands has been a lengthy one: one I dearly hope will have been worth the wait.

It was always my intention to write a trilogy, three standalone novels that would feature my Barbadian "Enquiry Agent", Joseph Tremaine Ellington, "JT", each set roughly two years apart, starting in the winter of 1965 and coming to an end in the summer of 1969. However, as they say, "the best-laid plans of mice and men oft go astray . . ." Let me explain.

I'm the kind of writer that likes to plan ahead. However, no amount of advance planning could have prepared me for what was to come. The original trilogy's story arc was meticulously preplanned over a decade ago. Moleskine journals containing the minutiae of Ellington's world were carefully mapped out, character development refined and locations spotted. Now, none of that commitment to detail actually prepares you for the process of writing the books, and it has to be said that *All Through the Night* wasn't an easy book to get down on paper despite all my bravado planning.

I believe many writers would agree with me when I say that no matter how much groundwork you put in, it is ultimately the characters who dictate where the final story takes the earnest scribe, and I was no exception to that rule. The journey I originally set out to undertake was dramatically altered as JT, Vic and the cast began to weave their magic from chapter to chapter — strangely, this allowed the characters that I have created the opportunity to take me, the writer, into places I'd not before considered and, at times, into even darker places, each mysterious, scary and unexpected. I believe this approach to the writing left me with a stronger, tighter story and one I hoped readers would approve of. *All Through the Night* expands both on *Heartman*'s original story and delves deeper into JT Ellington's back story, offering a greater insight into both the man and his motives, and developing characters from the first book in more concise detail.

The wonderful response to the publication of *Heartman* has been overwhelming, and since July 2014 I have been inundated with emails and social media messages from readers of the book who are both eager to know more about Ellington's '60s Bristol, details on characters, where I write, my creative influences, when JT will hit the TV screens and, of course, to ask, "When will book two be out?"

That final question, I'm pleased to say, has now been successfully answered.

All Through the Night has hit the shelves and I nervously await the response from you, dear reader, as to whether I have succeeded in pleasing you with the next instalment of Joseph Tremaine Ellington's "Child" trilogy. Ultimately, it has to be said that I write the kind of books I'd like to settle back with and, preferably for me, read along with a pint of best bitter at my side. The final book in the trilogy, *The Restless Coffins,* is well underway, and despite those best-laid plans I previously mentioned, and after a great deal of thought and soul-searching, a fourth Ellington novel, *The Rivers of Blood,* is in the pipeline. It will see my wily Bajan detective return, entering a bright new decade and back in Bristol, circa 1970.

All Through the Night would not have been possible without the generous assistance and support of a raft of brilliant folk. I'd like to offer my sincerest thanks to each and every one of the readers who have been in touch to say how much they enjoyed dipping into *Heartman.* Writers are nothing without readers and I have been graced with a legion of readers to be proud of.

Thanks must go out to a vast list of book bloggers, especially Abby Jayne Slater-Fairbrother, Richard

Latham, Liz Barnsley, Mark Hill, Mike Stott, Ayoola Onatade and Sandra Robinson. Special thanks also to the teams of amazing booksellers at Waterstones here in Leicestershire, in Loughborough and across the UK, and to Debbie James at Kibworth Books and to Robb Norton at Foyles Books in Cabot Circus, Bristol.

I tip my battered trilby to fellow crime writer and dear friend Richard Cox, who kindly undertook a first read-through of *All Through the Night*'s manuscript, offering both an author's no-nonsense opinion and some sound advice. Thanks also must go out to another dear friend, former CWA judge and author of the wonderful *Crime Scene Britain and Ireland*, John Martin. Your continuing support has been invaluable.

Gratitude by the bucket loads to fellow crime writers Ken Bruen, Susi Holliday, Nick Quantrill, Steven Dunne, Luca Veste, Anne Zouroudi and Howard Linskey, and to Steve Plews at the Gas Dog Brewery for the great ales.

Thanks to Simon Heath and Jake Lushington at World Productions for seeing something special in both *Heartman* and *All Through the Night* and for taking a punt on a manuscript that at the time had not even found a publishing home.

I am indebted once again to the miracle worker that is my editor, Karyn Millar, and to the very special team at Black & White Publishing: Alison McBride, Campbell Brown, Janne Moller, Thomas Ross, and my publicist, Laura Nicol. As with *Heartman*, they have done a sterling job in bringing the book out in such great shape. Cheers guys.

All Through the Night is in part dedicated to my literary agent, Phil Patterson, at Marjacq Scripts. If it wasn't for Mr P there'd be no JT Ellington. I owe you more than I can say. Thanks mate. My sincerest thanks to the rest of the Marjacq team, Guy Herbert and Sandra Sawicka, and also to my brilliant film and TV agent, Luke Speed at Curtis Brown.

The second recipients of this book's dedication are my parents, Ann and Pat. You've been on this long old journey since day one. My writing is my way of saying thank you for everything. Thanks also to a great mate, Alex Kettle, for the kind words, the hard graft and continuing support. I'd also be lost without the friendship of my dearest and oldest friend, Ken Hooper. A mixologist, astrophysicist and by far the most learned man I have ever known. You're a diamond.

Lastly, thanks and love to my amazing wife, Jen, and to my beautiful daughters, Enya and Neve. You make it all worthwhile. I'd be lost without you.